Staccato Publishing
Zimmerman, MN

First US Edition: December 2010

The characters and events in this book are fictitious. Any similarity to real persons, living or dead, is coincidental and not intended by the author.

ISBN:978-0-9835742-9-3

Printed in the USA

for my mom

Life Blood

by HK Savage

Ch. 1

The cold place was frightening. Ava couldn't see the contents of the dark room past the blinding glow of the single light shining overhead. She sensed someone else in the room and heard the clanging of metal on metal nearby. She tried to roll off the table to go find her mom, terrified when she couldn't move. Her body wasn't listening and something hot burned in her arm. She shivered.

There was a sound when he came, a loud bang as a door was thrown open. Muffled arguments and then warm hands under her scooped her up and she felt the crisp cotton of his shirt so warm against her cheek. Ava burrowed against him, feeling safe. He told her everything would be okay, he would take her home to her mother and Ava raised her heavy head. She wanted to see, but the lights were behind him blurring anything more than his profile. When he looked down at her, she could see his dark eyes as holes in the pale skin. The glow of the lights disappeared into temporary darkness, metal squeaked, the door boomed shut behind them and the sound of buzzing insects was all around her.

Ava Brandt woke to the buzzing of her alarm at five thirty. She'd had the dream again. She still carried the memory of the way his smell combined with those of summer in her mind, although it was already dancing out of reach, soon to fade completely as only dreams can.

She assumed the man was her father. She had seen brown eyes like his in pictures, though the photographs never elicited the same warm safe feeling within her. Where memories brought comfort, pictures only left her wanting. There was a different sort of feeling when she stared at the man in those two dimensional images.

Her dream was the only memory she had of her father, she had been only five when he had died in the accident she'd walked away from. The few things she knew about him came from her mother. According to Katherine, he had been a kind and gentle man, both a great father and wonderful husband. They had met in high school, married shortly afterward and along came Ava. A small town fairy tale come true. Joel Brandt had to have been a great man, her mother had never gotten over him. Life had frozen for his widow the day he died. Katherine had lost the house on only one income, but kept the same job in the same town. The only thing that changed in her life was Ava, who had insisted upon growing up.

It was no surprise Ava had dreamt of her father that morning, the same dream always came to her when she was anxious, and today she had good cause. Her Master's thesis was due this morning and though her confidence at its inception had started out strong, she was no longer confident that her findings were conclusive enough to back her hypothesis. Her analysis of how American factories were underutilizing the efficiency and safety procedures exemplified by Italian factories such as Natuzzi and Ferrari was not as convincing as time wore on.

She could only trust that the academics reviewing it would not be as critical of her own work as she was. Given the blanket of self-doubt that colored everything she did, that was actually a very real possibility. Ava pushed herself in an effort to please her mother, grateful to have a motivator, because she feared if left to her own devices she would stagnate.

Groaning her displeasure, she threw back her fluffy down comforter, one of her only extravagances, and stretched her feet toward the floor. The plush rug gave her feet a luxurious landing pad before she had to strike off across the well trampled builder's beige carpet that ran throughout her small apartment. The few things she allowed herself to splurge on were mostly in her room, making it a much needed safe haven.

Rugs were quite unnecessary in the third floor apartment given the constant roasting temperature of seventy-five degrees, completely uncontrollable by thermostat, despite her endless tweaking. Refusing to give up the weight of the down comforter she found so, well, comforting, Ava instead ran a fan in her room and slept in a tank top and shorts even on the iciest days in February.

She stood, smoothing her tousled auburn hair from her face, and felt around for the switch of her bedside light. Fingers curving around the pen she kept on the notepad at her bedside, Ava jotted some final, final edits before pushing herself toward the bathroom to shower and prepare for the day ahead. If she skipped breakfast, she could still make the few changes she wanted and have time to reprint the whole thing before she had to drop it off with her advisor before eight.

As is always the case with last minute changes, the computer was uncooperative and took a long time to come up and even longer to open her now large and incredibly unwieldy document complete with graphs, charts and lengthy statistical analysis. When Ava made her changes, she checked in print preview to confirm nothing had moved dramatically which of course, it had. After yet another fifteen minutes of shifting figures and footnotes, Ava saved the document to her jump drive and rushed to FedEx to have it printed and bound and as would be her luck, was promptly caught in a small traffic jam just outside her Hopkins apartment, adding another half an hour to her now rushed morning. This stuff never happened when she had time to spare, she said a silent prayer to the powers that be to give her a break.

The academic gods heard her and smiled upon the remainder of her morning. Traffic loosened up and she moved efficiently through the network of freeways that led her to the FedEx off campus, where they knew her all too well, and she grabbed a coffee from the Dunn Bros next door while they bound her freshly printed thesis. Miraculously, Ava even found a parking spot within a block of campus, and with a sprint to the finish, she jogged up the short set of stairs and handed her paper to her advisor. With a firm handshake and a wish for good luck from her guide of the past two years, it was done. Now all that was left to do was wait, but for what she couldn't help but ask herself.

Ch. 2

Ava had to work most of the day at Elle's, a higher end clothing and furniture consignment store near her apartment. It wasn't her dream job, however the owner was a childhood friend of her mother's and had let Ava shift her schedule around to suit her needs through six years of schooling.

It would be a few more weeks before she knew for sure if she could put that behind her now, but already she wasn't sure how she was going to use an advanced degree in business. Ava didn't care for the confinement of the classic corporate structure, and she was too fearful to strike out on her own. Her mother had assured her business was the right way to go and she had followed the direction, eager to please. So here she was again, her future opening up before her with no idea where to go from here.

"Ava honey, what's wrong? You've been straightening that rack for the last ten minutes and I think it looks worse now than it did before you started." Elle DiMarco chided from close behind her.

Jumping at the unexpected voice breaking in on her thoughts, Ava spun and had to catch herself on the aforementioned, and yes horribly molested rack, to keep her feet. She stood face to face with the owner of the store. Elle was smiling affectionately, reaching out to touch Ava's shoulder and steady her.

A gracefully aging woman in her late forties, Elle looked like she'd just stepped off the pages of Vogue. Her well tailored clothing, usually suits, accentuated her shapely figure and her makeup drew people's attention to her most striking feature, bright green eyes. Elle's dark, mahogany hair was always carefully coifed in a clip to call attention to her long, graceful neck and shoulders.

"Sorry Elle." Ava smiled, automatically shrugging off her flash of embarrassment. Easily startled, it was pretty commonplace for her. Her mother excused it away, saying she'd been doing it since she was a kid. "You're high strung Ava and there's nothing you can do about it." Katherine seemed to forever be trying to ease Ava's worries.

Elle stroked Ava's shoulder. "Are you nervous about your thesis?"

Ava simply nodded, not wanting to discuss it.

"There is nothing you can do about it now. It's turned in and you did a great job, I'm sure they'll like it. *I* was impressed." Elle had looked at it for Ava last week. Sensing Ava's discomfort, Elle changed the subject. "Say, they're sweeping the street out front later today. Do you think you could move your car out back?" She offered a conciliatory smile. "The city only let me know a few days ago, they didn't even put signs out yet." Then, her face lit with a genuine grin, knowing she had something that would please Ava. "I have a truck load of unusual and antique pieces that came in this morning from an estate in Edina. The owners died and the kids don't want to sell it all on Craig's List to people who won't appreciate it. They were hoping we could find good homes for everything. Do you think you could help me price it all?"
Heaving a relieved sigh, Ava bobbed her head excitedly. "Antiques?"

Elle smiled knowing she had Ava's full attention now.

"You grab the laptop, I'll move my car and be right back."

Eagerly Ava jogged out and hopped in her car, meeting Elle in the back when she was done.

Seeing Elle standing amidst the pieces scattered about the loading dock, Ava began mentally digging through the store, searching the inventory for like pieces. Her mind's eye wandered around various displays she had helped to build and had taken pride in. She wished she could continue working here for Elle full time. Ava hadn't brought the subject up with her boss or mother, fearing they would see her education as a waste of time and money. Both of the women were hugely important to Ava in their own ways and she didn't want to disappoint either one.

Ava grabbed the laptop from Elle's offering hands and started searching the internet. The bell over the front door would alert them to any customers but it was doubtful there would be much traffic before ten on a weekday.

Looking for their new items' values online had taken Ava's mind completely off of her worries. It wasn't until Elle straightened from digging through the partially staged items and put her hands behind her hips to stretch her back that Ava saw how much time had passed.

"I think we've earned ourselves some lunch, don't you think?"

Ava agreed, realizing she hadn't had anything since her cup of coffee this morning. Her head spun as she stood from her chair and she quickly set the computer on her seat to keep from dropping it.

The bell out front chimed announcing customers and Ava followed Elle back through the curtained doorway to the front of the store to help.

On their way up front they agreed they would get delivery from their favorite sandwich shop so they could keep working.

Elle did the honors while Ava handled the three women now noisily perusing the merchandise. They were friendly and talkative, enjoying the elation that accompanied springtime in the Midwest. Northerners especially cherished the re-appearance of nature's greenery after months of nothing but white snow and brown slush. Rain last week had brought a hint of green to the brown branches and still dormant lawns.

Ava sold one of the shoppers a scarf and handbag, another a sundress in hopes of warmer weather while the third declared she was merely there as an opinion for her friends. Not a believer in the hard sell, Ava didn't push and gave them a warm farewell when it was time.

After the trio was gone, Ava made her way to the rear corner of the store and cleared out the rejected sundresses from the fitting room. While she wrestled the strappy dresses back onto their hangers she heard the bell chime again, leaving it to Elle, assuming it would be their lunch.

Ava's mind wandered. The task at hand wasn't exactly mentally taxing, and the busywork afforded her a rare moment of peace from her constantly whirring thoughts. A fuzzy cocoon of quiet wrapped around her as she stood inside the small wood paneled room. The familiar sound of Elle's voice hummed at the periphery of her hearing as she spoke to their visitor. The low indistinguishable answering rumble identified their delivery person as male.

His voice stirred something in Ava's mind. It was something distant and foggy, but it nagged at her nonetheless. Interested, Ava laid the dresses on the bench in the fitting room, and followed the sound.

Elle's was a small shop, it wasn't more than a half a dozen paces from the fitting room to the front of the store where Elle and the delivery guy were talking. Ava walked out the open door and stared at him curiously. The man was not their delivery guy. The visitor wore a black sport coat, not a t-shirt professing freaky fast service. He was facing Ava, and looked up curiously at her sudden appearance.

Ava's world stopped as she stared at the pair of eyes she had seen so many times in her dreams. It had been sixteen years since she had seen them while awake, but she could feel a surreal mixing of reality with fantasy as her dreams intruded upon her waking state. The man stared, blinking back at her. Memory had not given her a recollection of the features of her dream man, but when he turned away, his profile was exactly as she remembered it.

Elle turned to follow the man's gaze and her eyes widened just as Ava's knees buckled and her world blackened around her. Her dreams came rushing up to meet her.

The room was dark but for the lights at the table nearby. Illuminated by the glow was the silhouette of a man hunched over a metal table. Light cast the liquids in the bottles in front of him as dancing shadows projected onto the ceiling above. The sounds coming from the hunkering figure were mumbled in a language unintelligible to the young Ava lying on the table behind him. His hands shifting something around on the table making a clinking and clanking sound that echoed in the cavernous room.

She was afraid, but the woman who had brought her here told her he was a doctor. She'd given Ava candy while she chalked on the sidewalk in front of her apartment. The neighbor was supposed to be watching her until her mother got home.

Ava had eaten the candy. It tasted bitter, but she didn't want to say anything or spit it out and hurt the lady's feelings. She was so pretty she looked like a movie star. Ava remembered her thick, blonde hair, bright blue eyes and smooth, pale skin were only accented by her one flaw. Her bottom teeth were slightly crooked and pushed out her lower lip when she talked. Ava watched her mouth, mesmerized.

Now, lying on the cool, hard table, she worried her mother would be upset with her for talking to a stranger and for wandering off. She couldn't remember having done it, but she must have. Here she was.

The mumbling grew louder as the man moved toward her. The lights above him worked to keep his features in shadow and the light he had attached to his head blinded Ava as she tried to focus on him through the fog of the drugs muddling her mind. All that she could see was the very outer edge of his dark hair lending him a dark crown against the light.

She saw a sparkle of light on metal as he held something shiny in one hand and used the other to pull her arm toward him within her restraints. Helpless to struggle, Ava watched. Her limbs felt heavy and slow within the confines of the straps holding her down. She knew she shouldn't be letting him touch her. Her instincts told her he was not a good doctor there to help her. Her mother would be very upset with her and Ava worried about telling her. A prick of something sharp stung the inside of her forearm and the man's breathing sped up in excitement. She could hear a fever behind his muttering that frightened her.

Ava's eyes were growing heavy again as she watched the doctor hook the tube coming from her arm to a clear plastic bag and lay it on a little table below her. The tube filled with a dark liquid and she couldn't tell if it was coming or going. Her body got colder and her teeth began to chatter in the icy chamber. Sleep begged to pull her down into total darkness and Ava's lids slid closed.

A sudden bang brought Ava back to consciousness and she heard the doctor yelling over her. The light from his head was aimed past her and she craned her neck to see.

A thin beam of light shone through a door she hadn't realized was there, and another form was advancing toward them rapidly, holding a flashlight.

"Give me the girl." The newcomer shouted furiously, the threat of violence from him clear. Ava was scared all over again and her tired heart tried to beat faster making her dizzy. She watched entranced as the angry man approached her.

The doctor's headlamp lit upon the face of the angry man. His eyes were dark and his strong features set in anger, but they were fixed on the doctor, not Ava. She felt relieved, hoping he would ignore her. She wondered where the lady had gone, and if she would come back to take her home. She *had not been mean or angry.*

The doctor was shouting heatedly back at the angry man only Ava didn't understand what he was saying. His accent made his words incomprehensible, but she tried really hard to concentrate. It started to make some sense as she realized they were speaking English.

"Don't take her, she is special. Leave me this one, you can have the others if I can have this one."

"No! I saw what you did in Amsterdam. It isn't going to happen here. You're lucky I don't have a gun or you wouldn't walk out of here."

By now the doctor had backed away and the angry man was beside Ava. She felt her stomach tighten anxiously, but when he looked down at her she saw his brown eyes soften and the light above cast a halo around his head. "Don't be scared little one. You're going home now."

Another pinch in her arm and Ava heard fabric tearing before something was tied tightly around her arm. The doctor did not interfere when the man scooped her up off the table to hold her cradled gently but securely to his chest. He felt strong and warm and Ava snuggled in against him hoping to warm herself. Ava's consciousness was fading in and out and her weakness was overcoming her will to remain awake.

One thing she heard before she faded was the doctor shouting clearly, his accent sharper in his fury. "We are the same, you and I. At least I am honest about the cost."

And the warm man holding her so carefully spoke clearly, his words rumbling his chest against her side. "We are nothing alike. Your greed destroys innocents like this one and I am trying to protect them." He paused long enough to push open a door with his foot and a cool evening breeze made her shiver, snuggling up into the body heat radiating through his clothing. The electric hum from the single outdoor light shining down from a tall pole brought her head around to see her savior.

"Relax, you'll be home soon." He assured her and she believed him.

Ava smiled as she faded out.

Ch. 3

"Ava, Ava. Wake up honey." Elle's voice was shaky and when Ava's tawny eyes opened she saw the worry plainly written on her face.

Weakly, she smiled. "Sorry. I guess I should have eaten breakfast, huh?" She reached up and brushed a clump of hair back from her forehead, taking stock of herself. How embarrassing to have fainted. Ava felt her cheeks warm and she closed her eyes for a moment. Aside from a headache and mild nausea she felt fine. The hand that had pushed back her long bangs continued to the back of her head, stopping at a sizable knot there, explaining the headache. Ava pushed herself up off the hard floor into a sitting position, wanting to get off the sales floor before anyone else saw her. She put her hand on a sweater table and started to stand.

"Here could you help me with her?" Elle spoke to someone behind Ava in a nervous rush.

Ava's gaze followed Elle's and she twisted to see, afraid she already knew what she would find. When she saw him again her periphery went dark, as if seeing him through a tunnel. Nothing else registered but his face, just as she had just seen him in her memory. His arms were around her at Elle's request, and he caught her before her knees buckled again.

When his arms closed around her, Ava felt her world spin. Impossible. Those eyes and the faint woodsy, soapy smell she had remembered in her dreams had always belonged to her father, not this stranger holding her now. Mind swirling as her illusion of "what was" was called into question, she was struck dumb with shock.

Elle stood up with her, a hand on Ava's back. Ava could feel her friend and employer staring at her, but couldn't break her visual with the apparition from her past now before her, touching her. Scattered memories that had always come to her in pieces fell into place, Ava remembered what her mind had so carefully blocked off. Worse yet, tears pricked her eyes as she fought to keep her last "memories" of her father intact, worrying it had never been him at all.

Ava brought her hands up between them and pushed off. Hesitant, he let her go and Elle's arm went around her back, afraid she was going to faint again. Ava let herself be held, welcoming the smaller and weaker embrace Elle offered. It was nothing like his, and that was good. Sensing her apprehension, he backed away, the look on his face unreadable. Finally, he wheeled and briskly strode out without a word. The bell chimed and they were alone.

No outward evidence that she was crying but her watering eyes, Ava let herself be gentled and stroked by Elle for a few minutes more before wiggling to let her know she was done. Elle understood and let her go.

“I’m going to go wash my face before anyone sees me like this.” Ava laughed dismissively at herself, wiping at her eyes, thankful she didn’t wear mascara.

“Are you sure you’re okay?” Elle was reluctant to let Ava go anywhere alone fearing she might go down again.

“Yeah, I just need something in my stomach. Lunch’ll be here soon and I’ll be fine.” She headed into the back to use the restroom. After the door was locked, Ava stared at her own pale reflection in the mirror. Normally her skin tone was toward the olive, but the face staring back at her was pasty and damp with sweat. She looked like she had seen a ghost. Maybe she had. She splashed water on her face and tried to reason with herself and somehow explain away what she had just seen.

This man had saved her from what she had only vaguely remembered until today. The thought that he had been real and someone other than her dead father was devastating. Yet, once she let her mind reach beyond that detail, so many questions rose to the surface she found herself gasping for air, glad her stomach was empty. Ava’s self-restricted little world was shaken to its very foundation. She was still reeling when Elle’s gentle knock sounded on the door.

Ava opened it. Elle’s eyes searched her face. “Ava, I want you to go home.” She put her hand on Ava’s arm, steering her as she stepped out of the restroom. “But first, I want you to eat something.”

Ava felt her stomach knot in protest at the mere suggestion of food except Elle wouldn’t let her out of her sight until she at least got something into her system. Obedient but cautious, Ava tore off a piece of bread from her sandwich and put it in her mouth. Her stomach responded almost instantly, and not with nausea. The growl it sent out was enough to make Elle ease up enough to laugh.

"I guess that settles it." The older woman looked relieved and pointed at the sandwich. "Eat."

Ava began to feel better after she had a few bites and sipped at her water. The food had gone down well enough, still she could only force herself to eat less than half of her sandwich. After six years of working together, Elle was well aware Ava wasn't a big eater and, satisfied she'd had enough, released her to go straight home. Without any thoughts to the contrary, Ava got into her aging Jetta and did just that.

Once home though, she couldn't just lie in bed. That had never been one of her strengths, lying around. Instead, she picked up the phone and tried to call her mother. Katherine didn't answer and Ava had to settle for a message, asking her to call as soon as she could, reassuring her it wasn't an emergency. It was indeed necessary to give that caveat as Katherine Brandt tended to be more than a little overprotective when it came to her daughter. Now that her mind was attempting to put the pieces of her childhood back together, she was starting to understand that her mother's protectiveness might have been for good reason. Unless she was going crazy, she chided herself.

Ava had always considered Katherine's overbearing nature a side effect of the car accident that had taken her father, now she wasn't so sure. Her mother might have been hiding something from her all these years. The thought gained momentum the longer Ava chewed on it.

For the first time in her life, Ava didn't have any school work to occupy her mind while she waited for her mother. She tried to pick up a few books she had been waiting eagerly to read after the drudgery of her thesis was completed, except when she flipped through the pages of one, she found her mind scattered in a million different directions. Who was the brown eyed stranger and had he really been the one who saved her so long ago? From the way he had reacted to the sight of her, she thought there might be something to it. Only it didn't make sense that he had remained unchanged over time, or was that her mind playing tricks on her? It was uncanny how much he looked like the man in her dream. He couldn't have been more than a few years older than she was *now,* which should put him in his early thirties, not the forties he would have to be if he really was the man from her dreams.

The phone rang less than an hour later. Ava fought the urge to jump on it at the first ring, knowing it would only fan her mother's fears that something bad had happened.

"What is it baby?" Katherine's voice was strained and husky from years of smoking. She had quit last year after much prodding from her daughter, but Ava feared the damage had already been done.

Struggling with how to begin, Ava just blurted it out. "Mom, what happened to me when I was little?"

Silence.

"Mom?"

During a *very* long pause, Ava's only clue her mother was still on the line was the sound of her labored breathing from the other end. "Why?"

Ava sighed heavily, hating to bring it up, knowing it would stress her mother but she needed to know. "I remembered something today. It was weird. I remembered a lady coming to the apartment. She took me to a place and there was a man there. Maybe a doctor?" She let her adult knowledge make sense of her child's memory, being careful not to say anything about the mystery man she'd seen today. "I think he took some blood or something. I remember a needle."

Katherine's harsh voice cracked and she gushed, in a hurry to rid herself of the secret that had caused so much concern for her through the years. "Baby, I never knew exactly what happened. You were so little and you were in shock, you really couldn't explain it to us. All I ever knew for sure was what *we* could put together." A hint of a wheeze drew out Katherine's words. "You were playing outside and Mrs. Jorgensen was watching you. She said she went inside for a minute to answer the phone, you were right outside her window so she could still see you. She was out of sight for just a few minutes and when she looked out you were gone. The police came and looked all over but no one could find you."

Ava could hear that her mother was getting close to tears, and could picture her twirling her earring like she did when she was upset. Her heart went out to Katherine, knowing she had been alone, fearing the worst. It must have been horrible.

"We looked for you all night. I couldn't sleep and had stepped out for just a minute." She didn't say but Ava knew she would have been outside smoking. She never did it in the house. "Then a police car pulled up and an officer said he would take me to the hospital. He said they had found you at a rest stop. You were okay, but you were weak." Her voice broke and Katherine had to stop.

Ava waited patiently for her to continue, both of them finding comfort in hearing the other one's familiar breathing on the other end of the line.

Composure if not breath regained, Katherine continued. "I didn't know what to expect when I got there. They said you weren't hurt except you were missing a lot of blood. There was only one needle mark on the inside of your left elbow. The doctors ran every test they could think of trying to find any sort of drug, but nothing turned up, only tiny amounts of laudanum. You needed a transfusion for all the blood you lost, nearly two pints. In a few days they cleared you to go home and I took you. They never caught who did it."

Ava had more questions, trying to fill in the blanks. "Didn't you ask me what happened? Did I ever say anything?"

"The police asked and I did too, but you just sort of blanked out whenever anyone mentioned it so we stopped. You started remembering your father rescuing you, having dreams about him, it seemed to make you feel safe. The doctors said sometimes shock will do that to a person and it was natural. I didn't know what to do so I didn't bring it up anymore. You seemed happy enough most of the time, but different. I thought you forgot." Her rough voice softened and grew quiet. "You father was gone, I tried to do what I thought was right."

Guilt needled Ava at the mention of what she worried had been a false memory of her father. "You did Mom. I'm fine. I don't know what I would have done differently if I were you." Her own voice broke thinking of her mother going through that alone. Their family was scattered to the winds, her mother's parents having both drank themselves into early graves when Ava was just a child. Katherine's brother and sister had both moved far away and they didn't really talk much. It had just been the two of them for the most part while Ava grew up, apart from occasional visits from Elle.

Katherine begged off the call first, fatigue evident in her voice. The retelling of the incident had been difficult, and her break was over. Katherine had to go back to her job in the bindery department at the small printing plant in Mora, the same one she'd been at since high school.

Ava returned the phone gently to its cradle, her mind trying desperately to put together all the pieces. Children were often abducted, though the circumstances of hers were strange. The blonde woman had drugged her and taken her to some sort of private lab. The man she had thought was a doctor had taken her blood, but why? Who would want a child's blood, and would he have taken all of it if the other man hadn't come for her? It was all too strange to believe. There had to be something else, some huge component had to be missing.

She had far more questions than answers and plucked at her subconscious for any additional details she might still have buried in there. Sleep finally came late that night and when it did, it was awash with strange visions. Ava had no way of knowing the difference between fact and fantasy as her mind twisted itself in confused knots.

Ch. 4

The next day Ava was awake, once again, before her alarm. Thinking it might clear her mind, she thew on sweats and strapped on her runners. Stepping outside, she breathed in the brisk spring air and felt a tingle in her nose from the mild chill. Other than some thin gloves and a stocking cap, she didn't have to wear any additional layers and better yet there was no ice to worry about. In a few more weeks, even the gloves would be superfluous.

Ava wasn't a runner, preferring to jog and walk her combined four miles. The path behind her apartment led to a network of trails heavily used by non-motorized traffic, but out of sight of roads and cars. It was almost enough to make her think she was in the country, the serenity soothed her easily frazzled nerves.

Arriving home just before six with a clear head, Ava went straight into the shower and emerged to the sound of her ringing phone. She slipped on the tile floor as she hurriedly hopped and toweled off her feet, barely avoiding a fall but not before she hit her shoulder on the doorframe. She was still rubbing it when she caught the phone on the last ring just before it was sent to voicemail.

"Hello Elle." Ava wasn't surprised when she heard the familiar voice on the other end. No one else would call her this early in the morning unless it was an emergency and no one else worried about her as much as her mother, except her boss. Her lips curved into a smile.

Elle sounded relieved to hear Ava's lighter mood. "I was just checking to see how you were feeling and to let you know if you don't want to come in you don't have to."

Ava fought down the annoyance rising within her. She didn't like being treated like a fragile china doll even though now she finally understood why. Elle had to have known about the abduction, being Katherine's best friend since childhood. Reminding herself that both women had only been trying to protect her, Ava took a breath through her nose and forced a smile to keep her tone light.

"Have you finished pricing *and* moving all of those new antiques by yourself then?" She teased.

It was clear from the moment's hesitation before she answered that Elle had not been able to do either task, yet she still tried to give Ava the option of staying home. "It isn't like they need to be placed today. A few days isn't going to make a bit of difference."

"We're going to have more foot traffic with the break in the weather, and the fact that they aren't going to get snow on their new goodies when they move them means more people are going to be looking at furniture."

With a pleased sniff at her associate's understanding, Elle conceded the point. "If you're feeling up to it, I would sure appreciate the help."

"I'll be in at eight so we can make some headway before we open."

"Take your time."

Ava had no intention of sitting around her house all day. That was probably the worst thing for her to do when her mind was all knotted up. Not for the first time in the past twelve hours, Ava kicked herself for her stupidity. She had been so upset when she saw the strange man yesterday, she had failed to get his name or find out anything about him. Other than a flashback and her mother's limited report, Ava had no idea what had happened when she was taken.

Her mind continued working on itself as does a starving body with no food, it's lack of new fodder twisting it up into ropes. Absently she chewed her bowl of Cocoa Crispies while she pretended to read her news online before she had to go in. Anything to keep her mind busy and give it something to work on other than the obvious.

It was with a much lighter heart that Ava turned her key in the locked front door of Elle's at quarter to eight. Not seeing the Mercedes on the street, Ava went around back again to see Elle had beaten her there.

As with many small business owners, the woman virtually slept there. Ava had teased her that she liked it when they had sofas or chairs to sell saying she did just that, never mind Elle had a husband and comfortable bed waiting at home.

"Back here Ava." Her employer's pleasant singsong greeting floated through the curtained doorway to the back.

A quick glance at the counter, revealed by its absence, that the computer was already in use in back. Ava sipped on her bright red coffee traveller and followed the sound of Elle's summons.

Ch. 5

Between the two of them, they had the new items priced and staged by noon. The shop was reorganized to accommodate some of the larger items, and Elle finally gave her nod of approval just before they closed their doors at six.

Elle's phone rang while they were counting out the register and prepping the night's deposit. Ava hummed to herself and Elle walked away to speak quietly into the phone. Ava guessed it was home calling. Elle and her husband had never had children, which was why she'd been so happy to have Ava come stay in the city with her. While she'd stayed with them for her first few years, Ava had seen some profound cracks in their marriage. She'd wondered privately if the lack of children had been a choice, versus the medical reason she'd always assumed. As much as Ava tried not to pay attention to their personal business, there were signs that she couldn't ignore.

Her husband, Bill, was allegedly an insurance agent. Yet he came in sporadically during business hours, dressed in sweat pants, to have heated conversations with Elle, much to her mortification. To avoid drawing the attentions of the customers, or Ava, Elle always took him into the back office. Even with it being all the way out on the dock, Ava had still heard him yelling at times.

On the phone, Elle was trying to hide her irritation by speaking lower and lower, but the heat behind her words was tangible. Ava moved farther away to avoid learning any more than she wanted. Hanging up minutes later, Elle came back shaking her head in frustration. Ava didn't miss the tears in her eyes, although she didn't comment out of courtesy.

Elle continued to the register and grabbed her purse off the back counter, leaving the pleather zipper deposit bag beside it. "Honey, could you finish up here and lock up? There's something I need to take care of for Bill."

She would have done it anyway, then, hearing the strain in Elle's voice, there was no way for Ava to refuse in good conscience. "Sure. I'll take care of it. Did you want to do the deposit on the way out or should I when I leave?" She flicked her eyes to the bag.

The deposit had to be to the bank by seven to be counted for the next business day. If Ava was going to do it, she would have to come back to clean up the shop.

Elle glanced down at her watch and Ava saw her jaw tighten.

Ava forced a smile and waved a hand. "I can do it. It'll let me do my deposit too. I can come back and do the cleanup, no problem."

Ava tried to ignore the gratitude she saw threatening to produce more tears and spill over onto Elle's cheeks. Ava had a soft heart, but was not good with handling people's deeper emotions head on. She didn't like the intensity. It made her squirm, she didn't know why.

Knowing all too well Ava's discomfort, Elle limited her gratitude to a nod and a thank you, sniffing to keep the tears at bay. She tucked her purse under her arm and rushed out the back door. A few minutes later, Ava had the register counted and the deposit ready. Keys in hand, she hustled out the back door in plenty of time to make it if she got lucky with the lights.

On the short drive back, Ava passed her favorite coffee shop and treated herself to a vanilla Nirvana, a vanilla latte with a twist of Hazelnut. Quietly, Ava slipped in the front door and locked it again behind her. She set her coffee and cranberry orange scone, also known as "dinner tonight," down on the counter and went to the back to grab the mop. There had been a lot of customers, and the mall had blown out the sprinklers for the year leaving puddles on the sidewalk. The dried gray blobs on the light tan tile needed scrubbing. While she was back there Ava would check the dock door for the night, Elle had been more than a little upset when she left and might not have locked it.

Just as she crossed through the curtained doorframe, movement off to her right caught her eye. With a surprised gasp, Ava twisted and threw her back against the short expanse of wall beside her granting her some minor cover. The short hallway was about two feet of sheetrock that transitioned the large square room where they received shipments and the front of the store. The source of movement had darted into the office around the corner on the right wall in the dock area. The sound of the door latch reached her ears, now on hyper alert.

She struggled to put on a collected front. "I've called the police. They'll be here soon." She eased her phone out of her pocket and slid it open. It took three tries to steady her hands enough to coordinate her dialing. She had pressed 9-1-1, her finger hovering over the send button, when her phone was snatched out of her hand.

Terrified, Ava screamed. Her recently recalled memories of childhood trauma giving new insight to her fear of being helpless. She was determined not to be there again, and in a surge of desperate strength, her clenched fist shot out, connecting with the tall figure in front of her.

The figure cried out in pain and she heard her phone hit the concrete floor with a plastic clatter. His large hands covered his features before she could see anything and he bent down reflexively.

Operating out of fear, Ava stepped forward swinging her foot and striking his leg twice before aiming for more sensitive places. When she missed, his hand caught her ankle and held it. Struggling to retrieve her limb, Ava lost her balance and landed on her back, taking her wind from her lungs in a rush. The hand she'd put out to catch herself was pinned awkwardly under her body in the process. Ava's screech was soundless with no air behind it. She lay on the ground, clutching her now numb hand and rolled into a defensive ball, trying desperately to suck air into her empty lungs.

The intruder's hand had released her ankle when she fell and she heard a sickening choking noise coming from somewhere nearby. Panic shot through her as she realized it was her attempts to find air she was hearing, and so could the intruder. He would know she was defenseless.

Rolling to her knees, Ava crawled, gasping to find her phone. She'd heard it land only a few feet from there. Spots sprouted, obscuring her vision, as her body threatened to pass out from lack of oxygen and overexertion.

Just as Ava's hand closed over her phone, a shadow fell over her. The skin on the back of her neck prickled in anticipation of blows, a sharp stab or some other painful attack. Instead of hurting her, she felt hands slide under her arms and pull her to her feet, her phone clutched tightly to her chest. She could not stop the fearful whimper that escaped her lips as he lifted her up.

Realizing she wasn't being assaulted, slowly, she raised her eyes to his face and saw warm chocolate eyes staring back at her. Ava's mouth fell open and she stared, dumbstruck.

When he spoke, it was with the same voice her memory told her to expect. "I don't believe we have ever been properly introduced. I'm Ben Pearson."

Ch. 6

Ava continued to stare at Ben, unable to speak, wondering if she'd hit her head in either fall he'd caused her today. She studied his face in wonder, seeing none of the telling lines or wrinkles that should be there to mark the passage of the years since she'd seen him last. Ben continued, his deep voice vibrating his chest where their bodies touched, déjà vu interposing past perception upon present.

"I'm a private investigator working on a case involving some estate items you received in your store yesterday. My visit obviously upset you, so I thought I would come tonight after you left." His tone remained even, as if breaking and entering was the most normal thing in the world. Ben's arms loosened and Ava was supporting her own weight.

"Were you watching the shop?" Her air had finally returned to her leaving her panting.

Her need to ask him what she wanted to know jumped to her tongue and stopped. Now that he was in front of her again, she couldn't bring herself to ask him the questions that burned in her mind. Ava was afraid of what he might tell her. Certainly he would tell her it was a case of mistaken identity. Brown was a common eye color and it was possible his features were similar enough to trigger her memory. That made far more sense than her thinking this was her hero from sixteen years ago. He couldn't be older than his late twenties. This wasn't her savior. It was impossible. It had to have been her father, as she had always believed. This was a matter of stress induced hallucinations, she'd read about them.

Ava took a big step back and smoothed her shirt, willing her heart rate to steady. Standing outside of his reach so she could look up at him without hurting her neck. Ava was only 5'5," Ben had to be six feet easy.

"Yes, I was." His tone was soothing, yet he was ill at ease, shifting his weight and glancing past her to the doorway beyond. "I need to get into the desk they gave you. My client says there's something in there that belongs to her." Ben looked down at Ava, his messy, short black hair falling forward. Interestingly, his skin was pale. With his coloring, he should have been darker like Ava, instead he looked like he avoided the sun on a regular basis.

"So you figured breaking into the store and assaulting me would be less upsetting than showing up here during the day?" Ava snorted derisively insinuating the idea was preposterous. "You needn't have risked the felony. *You* didn't upset me. I hadn't eaten all day and then... I mistook you for someone else, that's all." She downplayed her reaction, not wanting him to think she was crazier than he probably already did. The phone slid into her front pocket, hand resting on it just in case.

Ben smiled mildly. He had a nice smile, probably nicer when he didn't have blood on his teeth and wasn't wincing. "I don't agree to your version of who did the assaulting."

Ava assessed the damage she had done and flushed. "I'm sorry. Can I get you some ice?" She started toward the office a few paces away. There was usually an ice pack or two for lunches in the mini fridge and paper towels, definitely need paper towels.

His hand went up to tentatively trace the cut in his upper lip. "You're stronger than you look." He smiled again and winced, putting the hand to his mouth. Instead of accepting her offer of ice, Ben glanced down and reached forward, pointing to Ava's injured hand. He stopped and glanced back up. "May I?"

"It's fine." She pulled her hand up to her own eyes and rolled it over examining it. The palm was red and some ginger palpations indicated she too should be using some ice. Carefully, Ava clenched and loosened her hand. "It's not broken, but I'm definitely going to have a bruise."

"I apologize. It wasn't my intention to scare you, but my client would prefer not to involve the police." He did look apologetic yet his mention of avoiding the police interested Ava more.

"Why not? Who's your client?" She couldn't remember the name of the sellers. Once an item came in, the seller was logged and assigned a number. Ava had written their number, 7715 about ten times today and that was how she knew them. Initially she'd thought it was kind of cool that the kids of the deceased parents didn't want the antiques sold to people who didn't know what they were getting. Maybe they didn't deserve so much credit.

"My client prefers to remain anonymous although she said there is a folder hidden in the desk. Would it be possible to look?"

He was asking but Ava had no doubt he was going to look regardless of what she said. Normally they would call the customer if they found something in an item that was personal and ask if the sellers wanted it or if it should be discarded, no such item had been found in their inventorying. Ava nodded. "Let's see what's in there."

Ben watched her step aside to give him a wide berth, waiting for him to pass her and go first. She kept an eye on him, keeping a respectable distance as they walked into the retail space of the store. They halted at the desk in question where Ben moved in and Ava scuttled back, waiting to keep their distance.

"Excuse me." He glanced up and she saw his mouth tighten minutely before he relaxed his features.

"I have to tell you, we go through each item when we receive it and check all the drawers. We didn't find anything in this one." Ava didn't see the harm in him checking for himself, maybe then he'd go. For some reason, the idea gave her a pang.

Ben wasn't interested in the drawers, instead dropping straight down on his knees and leaning into the space where the chair would go. Ava heard the sound of wood sliding in a groove followed by papers rustling. The wood slid again and Ben's back end eased out toward her as he removed himself from the space that looked suddenly small framing his wide shoulders. Ava caught herself watching his maneuverings with a marked interest.

When he sat up on his knees and turned to face her, Ava was blushing. A shadow crossed Ben's face for a second before he pointed at the manila envelope now in his hand.

"I think it's safe to say the seller's kids didn't know this was here. They won't mind my client taking what rightfully belongs to her."

His logic made an odd sort of sense and Ava was too flustered to argue. "Fine with me."

Ben stood and brushed off his knees as he reached to tuck the envelope into the back of his dark jeans under his black sport coat. He knew how to dress his long athletic frame, the black shirt and coat offset his coloring very well, and he moved with the confidence of someone who knew how to handle himself.

Ava stopped herself there. She was acting like someone off her nut. This was a stranger. So what if he reminded her of someone who had been kind to her? That didn't make it okay for him to break into the store and physically assault her. She shook herself trying to feel a backbone in her body somewhere.

Ben noticed her discomfort. "Look, I know this is strange. If you would like to check my credentials," he fished in his jacket pocket and pulled out a card holder containing several business cards. He handed her two.

Ava reached for them and when she did, their fingers touched. The tingle she felt took her by surprise. Inhaling sharply, her eyes flashed up. Ben had felt something too. Shock colored his face for just a few seconds before he smoothed out his features to again appear calm and collected.

She brought the cards up to her eyes and focused on them, glad to have a distraction. His name was indeed Benjamin A. Pearson and he was a licensed Private Investigator. The card below his was for a detective in the Minneapolis Police Department by the name of Albert Sharpe.

"Al is one of the detectives that I work with at the Department. He can vouch for me if it makes you more comfortable."

"Thank you. I'll do that." She retrieved her phone, sliding it open and dialing the cell number. Ava let the phone ring three times before it was answered.

A deep baritone answered sounding annoyed. "Detective Sharpe."

Thrown by his rough greeting, Ava stammered. "Um, hi. This is Ava Brandt and I'm standing here with a man named Ben Pearson. He says he's a Private Investigator and you can confirm that? Is that true?" She glanced up at Ben, watching his face to see if he was bluffing. If he was, he was good. He appeared completely relaxed.

Detective Sharpe guffawed loudly. "Yeah, Ben's a P.I., a damn good one too. Has he done something I'm going to get a call about?"

Ava looked down at the card in her hand, hiding her relief. "Does that happen a lot?"

"No, not a lot. Just guessing that's why you're calling." He lowered his voice. "Ben's a good guy, unconventional maybe, but you can trust him." Detective Sharpe cleared his throat and prompted impatiently. "That all you need?"

"Oh, yeah. Sorry. Thanks."

"No problem." As the phone came away from her face, he added, "Hey let Ben know I need to talk to him. Have him give me a call tomorrow."

Bobbing her head as though he could see. Ava said that she would and hung up.

"He said you should call him." She said to Ben, looking up to meet his gaze.

He was watching her calmly. "Are you satisfied?"

She ignored the tightening in her stomach. "Yes, I guess I am."

With that, Ben moved past her toward the back door.

"I can let you out the front." Ava offered.

"I parked out back." He turned only partially, giving her a view of his profile.

Ava tried without success to find a difference between his and the one in her memory. "Oh."

Ben continued moving and Ava, not knowing what to do, walked behind him. They stopped at the smaller, people door kitty corner to the large dock door taking up almost the entire back wall beside it. He turned to face her and Ava was unsure if she should say good bye or lock the door and call the police.

For a moment Ava thought Ben looked equally uncertain how to handle the end to their strange meeting. He watched her for a long moment before he finally reached out to take her sore hand where it hung beside her. Ava let him draw it up to his lips and held her breath as he kissed it gently on the darkening palm. She could feel the heat in his swelling upper lip.

"I am very sorry to have caused you any pain. It was not my intention." He told her formally, regret ringing in his words. "You should put some ice on that."

Ava held her breath while she tried to remain outwardly calm while her pulse raced and she worried he could hear her heart thudding in her chest. "It's fine." She breathed. "I'm fine."

With a strange smile, Ben released her hand and patted his back where he'd tucked the envelope before opening the door. "Thank you." He walked down the metal steps into the parking lot. Ava watched his shoulders move as he strode easily toward a dark car parked just outside the ring of light cast by the halogen atop the big dock door.

The sound of his engine gave her a start. She hadn't realized she'd been staring. She watched his car pass through the halo of light, an old Mustang in pristine condition. She imagined for a brief moment riding in the black car with the top down on a summer afternoon.

She remained in the doorway for a long time after the lot was empty before finally going back inside, making sure to lock up. She still had to straighten up and mop before she could leave. Glancing at her watch she swore under her breath. It was going to be nine o'clock before she got home. It was a good thing she'd gotten something to eat from the coffee shop.

Ch. 7

The next morning was Thursday. Ava was off work and sometime between her toast and shower she had come up with an idea of how to spend her day.

Her laptop sat on the small bar joining the kitchen and "great room" of her tiny six hundred square foot apartment warming up while she made herself a cup of herbal tea. Mint sounded good, she even had honey to add a little sweet to it.

Computer on, tea in hand, Ava shuffled over to the couch and eased herself down. It was a delicate balancing act to avoid dropping the computer or dumping her steaming tea in her lap. It was also a well rehearsed maneuver she performed without incident, even with a tender hand. She'd assumed right, it had bruised nicely.

First Ava tried the obvious sites, starting with the usual search engines, looking for anything and everything on all combinations of Ben's name. Ben Pearson, Benjamin Pearson, B. Pearson, with and without the middle initial, etc. She wondered what the "A" stood for. That might help her search. She had to find some sort of proof that she wasn't imagining the whole thing. Try as she might to disparage it, she felt that somehow Ben Pearson had something to do with her disappearance.

At some point in her digging Ava made the discovery that it wasn't just the curiosity of Ben's past she was interested in, it was also his present. Where could she find him if she were to go looking, for example? Sure he was attractive, she couldn't deny the physical draw and flushed again when she remembered the feel of his body against hers. More than that was the way he affected her.

When they were in the dock Ava had made an effort to protect herself. *She* had struck first and she hadn't given up, not until her body did. Then, in the store, she'd found the nerve to call Detective Sharpe right in front of him. She had been brave and strong. Whatever it was about Ben she found attractive at least some of it was what he inspired in her, even if it was just reactionary. It was the most decisive she'd been in her whole life.

Ava spent a significant amount of time searching. There were no hits until she limited it to just Pearson. That was a jackpot, but unfortunately, it was too much and too general. All she found was other Pearsons. There were a number of references to an A. Pearson in some county records from a small town outside of Philadelphia in the sixties. It was too old to be him, but she took down the information on the news story anyway thinking it was somewhere to start. It could be a relation. There were several other stories she found, all of them too old to be *her* Ben. *This* Ben, she corrected herself.

She went on to find Michael Pearson from Saratoga, Florida in the forties, Jim Pearson in Billings, Montana around 1910 and the most recent was a Brad Pearson operating out of Santa Barbara, California in the nineties. Whatever the connection, Ava was sure it was familial. Two of the stories had pictures and although they were grainy scans of news clippings, the men in the photographs seemed to bear some resemblance to Ben. Their hair and clothing were different yet the features were uncannily similar. In Santa Barbara, Brad Pearson had a stubbly beard made popular by Don Johnson and Miami Vice. She smiled thinking how that beard had come back, though thankfully, not the pastel tank tops.

The commonality among the stories did not end at a family resemblance. There was also a family trend toward law enforcement. Each one was either on the force or affiliated in some way; two were Private Investigators like Ben.

Wanting what the internet couldn't give, Ava shut down the computer and grabbed her bag. One of the best things about being a student and writing a thesis is learning about the resources at both the local public and campus libraries. The internet had some great information, but there was no comparison for in depth exploring or certain credibility. Ava couldn't bring herself to fully trust an encyclopedia *anyone* could post to.

Traffic was light and the drive was short. Ava had her sunroof open and heated seat on. It was her favorite luxury, she even did it sometimes in the winter on a sunny day for the fresh air. Today the sun was out and she cranked up the latest Kings of Leon song on the radio to drown out her off key accompaniment. Smiling when she stepped out of her car, she strode through the doors of the Hamline University library. It was one she had spent the better part of six years in and felt like a second home.

Ava was more than familiar with the microfiche section, going straight to a desk and laying out her things. She started by hunting down the articles she had found reference to online. The picture accompanying the Florida article hadn't been scanned for the internet, though it was included in the actual clipping.

Ava stopped dead. Her hands froze and she sat staring at the screen in front of her. This Pearson and the one she'd met in the store could have been twins, they looked exactly the same. The photo was of a Michael Pearson leaving a courthouse in Saratoga after testifying in a case. Apparently he disappeared shortly afterward according to the article, foul play was suspected. The physical resemblance was unbelievable, and there was something in the way he was poised in the photograph. The angle of his shoulders and length of his stride brought to mind Ben's gait as he had walked away from her the night before.

From there Ava moved on to finding *Ben* Pearson, starting in the local phone records. There were about fifteen Pearson listings and one was for a B. Pearson. Bingo.

She copied down the number and address. Before packing up she made photocopies of the pages from each of the other cities' phone books that had similar listings. Her stack of notes was building. Ava told herself it wasn't weird, there were plenty of perfectly good explanations as to why she was researching a total stranger. She listed them for her own benefit to appease her concerns that she was stalking.

Gathering her things, Ava heard someone move beside her. Jumping, she dropped her notes and phone books on the table with a loud bang.

Spinning around, Ava saw the classmate who had been in every study group she'd joined, as well as being the bane of her existence over the course of the last two years. "Hey Martin." Her tone was flat.

Martin was the only person she'd ever met who was as jumpy as her. She'd found their combined energy made her skin itch whenever he was around and, as a result, she'd declined his every request to go out. Her consistent lack of interest had yet to deter him. Perched on the balls of his feet, he was nervously bouncing up and down. Ava could feel her shoulders pinching already.

Several inches taller than Ava, her would-be suitor was slight of build and wore frameless glasses in keeping with his obsessively neat appearance. One look at him and it was easy to think, "Future cover of Forbes Magazine." Going out with someone for money and not for love didn't sit right with Ava and she'd declined his frequent requests for dates. Some of their fellow study mates had jokingly suggested they would make a perfect couple, if properly medicated. Ava hadn't laughed.

Martin flashed a cocky smile at Ava before looking down at the stack she had dropped on the table. "What are you doing with all of this? Aren't you done with your thesis yet?"

Ava felt her face freeze as if she'd been caught red handed. "Just doing some family research." She wasn't technically lying, she hadn't said it was *her* family. There was no way she could admit what she was doing without sounding like a stalker or a total nut. She couldn't explain it to anyone, least of all Martin.

"Need some help?" He made a move to grab the book on top.

Swiping them into the crook of her arm Ava removed the books from his reach. "No." She said too quickly. Ava smiled uneasily, softening her refusal. "No, thank you, I'm just heading out."

Martin tipped his head, a curious expression on his face. "Are you okay? You seem wound up, more than usual."

Two years of now unnecessary tolerance for his hypocritical cracks and jabs boiled over, Ava glared at him. "As a matter of fact, I *am* wound up Martin. *You* make me nervous, twitching and fidgeting all the time. Next time you're going to make jokes about someone's nerves, maybe you should start a little closer to home." Without waiting to see the fallout from her tongue lashing, she slung her bag over her shoulder and angrily slammed the phonebooks and microfiche into the rack to be refiled before marching out the front doors. Two undergrad students skittered out of her way as she stormed past.

Out in her car, Ava threw her bag down in the passenger seat and turned the key. Before she put it into first gear, she stopped. Raising her hands in front of her face, she saw they were shaking as badly as the rest of her.

Why had she done that? Martin was irritating and she wouldn't miss him if she never saw him again, but what she had said was intentionally hurtful and cruel. Ashamed of herself, she considered going back in and apologizing then worried he would try for a sympathy date and she just might feel guilty enough to relent. Deciding she didn't want the remorse should she have to turn him down after hurting his feelings already, she did nothing.

Disappointed in herself and frustrated, Ava put her hands on her steering wheel, hid her face on her arms and closed her eyes against the wet heat behind them. This stirring up of things with her memories and Ben, or whoever it was he reminded her of, had Ava on edge. She couldn't remember the last time she'd cried yet recognized the signs well enough, a big one was on the way.

Maybe it was the relief from finally being done with school, or it was the fact that she was directionless, but she was falling apart and it scared her. Whatever it was, she had to get herself under control before someone decided to medicate her for a breakdown, which she might very well be having.

After a good cry Ava sniffled and wiped her eyes, pulling out the sheet with Ben's address and studied it. Without thinking through what might happen next, she typed it into her GPS. She was in luck, Ben's address was a few minutes' drive from campus on the Minneapolis side of the river, just over the bridge. Dutifully, she followed the directions until she was parked, facing a building advertising itself as a newly built complex of condominiums. There were four buildings, all on opposing corners in an area known for unique restaurants and great wine. The most well known of its neighbors was Surdyk's wine and cheese shop.

Ben's building was kitty corner to Surdyk's and faced the street. Each unit had a separate entrance and small black rod iron fence with gates forming a comically small yard. Through her open sunroof Ava heard a gate click shut and glanced over at another unit a few doors down where a woman was leaving her "yard" with her fawn Boxer on a rhinestone embellished leash.

Ava stared at Ben's door, uncertain again what to do. Should she go up and knock? And say what, "I'm stalking you because you make me what?" Feel comfortable in her own skin? She needed to know if it was him or her father she'd been dreaming about all these years? Nothing was going to make her fascination sound sane because it wasn't. Still, the best way to deal with her obsession was to meet it head on. She made her decision.

Consciously forcing her reluctant feet to follow her temporary nerve, Ava got out of her car and pushed the button to lock it. Feeling strangely disconnected from her body and scared as hell, Ava walked straight to Ben's front door. She opened the gate and saw his tiny 10 foot square yard was exactly as well tended as his neighbors,' with not a hint of individual taste.

His front door was not marked with his name or personalized in any way. Ava worried she had the wrong place. Hesitating only for a few seconds in which she took a deep breath and exhaled, Ava rang the bell.

Ch. 8

Nothing happened. Again she rang the bell with the same lack of response. Telling herself she was better off for not having to come up with a lame excuse, Ava rang one final time and turned without waiting.

Behind her she heard the tightly fitted metal door releasing itself from the nest of rubber weather stripping with a squelch. She stopped but didn't turn around. Now that the moment she had goaded herself into was upon her, she didn't know quite where to take it and was afraid to see his reaction.

"Ava?" Ben's voice raised goose bumps on her arms.

Holding her breath, Ava made herself face him. Her mouth automatically formed a stiff smile. "Hi Ben."

Recovering quickly from his surprise and what looked like a hint of something akin to fear, Ben stepped backward into his home. "Would you care to come in?"

Ava couldn't say no. The mysterious siren song that was him called to her and she answered. "Um, sure."

He stepped aside and Ava followed him in. The walls were a soft shade of mustard in the entryway opening on the right into a large great room with rust colored walls. The floors were dark hardwood, the curtains cream. The kitchen had dark stone countertops, stainless appliances, and a light colored stone floor she could see at the end of the hallway across from her. Ava walked past the staircase at the left of the hall that led from the circular foyer and curved upward out of sight, leading to what Ava imagined was at least one bedroom and an office, if the size of the unit was any indication.

"Wow, you could get my apartment in here twice." Ava marveled. She thought about removing her light spring coat, then decided against it. There was a definite chill in the unit and she wasn't sure she was staying. She wasn't sure what she was *doing.* "My apartment is really hot. Do you have trouble heating this place since it's so big?" She'd only had the one apartment and wasn't sure how anyone else's heat worked but his didn't even feel like it was on.

Ben rubbed the back of his neck, watching her. "I have the thermostat set to sixty-five when I'm not home. It should warm up soon."

Ava looked at his face and saw no swelling. "What happened to your lip? I mean, it's healed." She took a step forward without thinking until she saw him take a step back, keeping the distance between them exactly the same. Ava tried hard not to let her hurt show. It was ridiculous for her to think there was more to this than there was.

"I'm a quick healer." His explanation was abrupt, defensive. Ben's voice softened and he pointed to her hand. "How are *you* doing?"

Ava held it up for him to see. There was some purple starting to show on the palm extending down to the wrist. The swelling was significant and her ring finger was ballooned out around the band that never left her right hand.

Ben's face changed, he was immediately concerned. "You need to get that ring off. I think I have something that might be able to cut it off." He moved toward the kitchen.

Hiding her hand behind her, she shouted without thinking. "No!"

Ben whirled and Ava saw the confusion on his face. Hearing the sharpness in her tone still ringing in her ears, she tried to explain. "This was my mother's wedding ring. She gave it to me when I was fourteen and I haven't taken it off since." Pulling her hand out from behind her, she held it up so she could look at it.

He stepped forward, holding his hand out just as he had the night before. "May I?" He didn't move until she nodded. More tenderly than his strong hands appeared capable, almost reverently, Ben took her hand and first appraised the bruising. His brow furrowed and his lips were tight. Ava saw his jaw working and guessed he was angry, she worried she'd overstepped her bounds by coming or that he was angry at her for being stupid.

His probing fingers lightly moved up to Ava's finger where they touched the ring her father had given Katherine over twenty-five years ago, sending pleasant sensations up her arm the whole time. She winced as he touched the band ever so lightly and it pushed into her bruised skin.

His response to her reaction was instant. "That needs to come off. Do you see how the skin around the band is getting dark? Your circulation is being cut off. You could lose the finger or damage the nerves if it stays on."

Again Ava moved to hide her hand behind her back except his grip shifted to her wrist and he tightened his hold, his hand becoming hard in an instant. She was unable to move the captured hand without hurting herself or outright fighting with him, something she was starting to consider as panic at being trapped tightened her throat and made it hard to breathe.

"Ava, you need to let me get this ring off of you." He insisted, anger sparking behind his eyes.

Stubbornly she shook her head. "No. It was my mom's, Dad gave it to her." Her chest was constricting and she fought for breath.

"It needs to. We can put it back on when the swelling comes down."

How did she explain to him what it meant? That her mom had given her the ring at an awkward stage when she'd struggled with being without a father. Katherine had told her that as long as she was wearing his ring, her father would be with her. It hadn't left her finger since. Call her superstitious but she feared removing it, even for an instant, would break any connection she'd been granted to her lost parent with its receipt.

Ben's tone softened. "Do you want to tell me about your father?"

Ava answered, keeping her eyes on her swollen hand still in his grip though it had loosened. She could have gotten loose if she'd tried, the knowledge allowed her to relax. "He died when I was five."

"I'm sorry. How did it happen?" He sounded genuinely interested. It struck her as strange that she was discussing her father with the very man whom had possibly supplanted him in her memory. *Impossible.* She told herself yet again.

"Car accident. We lived rural and we were on our way home from the store. The snow was falling hard and the roads were icy. He slid off the road and hit a phone pole. I was in the back. They said I slept through the whole thing." Talking about it had never been hard since she had no first hand knowledge, her memory of the incident was gone. She was regurgitating someone else's story.

Ben had been watching Ava very closely during her telling. He was either a good listener or he was trying to figure something out. It was probably the investigator in him, she surmised. Letting go of her wrist he held up his hand. "Stay here. I have an idea."

"I'm not letting you cut it off."

He shook his head. "I don't intend to. I have another idea."

Dubious, Ava watched him walk out of the room and heard his footsteps hurrying up the steps. While he was gone, she thought to start reducing the swelling by putting some ice on it.

The fridge of a bachelor's apartment is often an adventure in bacteriology. Ava didn't imagine Ben's would be by what she'd seen already. He was older than the bachelors she was used to both by dating and attending the traveling study sessions she'd taken part in. His house was incredibly tidy and he obviously either cleaned it regularly, or had the money to have someone do it for him.

So as much as she was not surprised by his refrigerator's contents, Ava was shocked by its sparseness. It wasn't so much empty as devoid of anything packaged, significantly reducing the clutter most people had. There was a curious bag of what must have been tomato juice, the only thing on the shelves and two very full drawers of fruits and vegetables. There was not a single condiment in sight, not even ketchup. She closed the door and took a towel off the stove door, laying it on the counter to put the ice from the dispenser in. The towel was nearly full of ice cubes when Ben returned to the kitchen.

"What are you doing?" He rushed to where she stood and insinuated himself in front of the fridge, Ava was flattered he was worried about her filling her own towel with ice.

"Don't worry, I'm almost done and if anything touching the ice has been helping. I haven't had any on it since this morning." She didn't want to admit she'd been too busy researching him to think about the hand.

He relaxed and got one more handful of cubes before wrapping them up. He was holding the towel and motioned for her to move toward one of the stools on the opposite side of the island. Ava climbed onto and leaned against the cushioned back, glad for the support. The stool was leather and well padded, she relaxed.

Ben motioned for her to put her hand on the counter and she obeyed. The towel of ice was laid on top. The pressure only hurt for a minute. It was hard to tell if the hand had been this sore this morning, or if typing and surfing microfiche all day had exacerbated the swelling. It hadn't really hurt before, but it sure did now.

In a few minutes Ava's hand started to go numb. Ben pulled the towel away and reached to touch the band again. This time it didn't hurt so badly and she saw that the swelling was coming down, the color returning to a more normal pink. The towel was put back in place and Ava tried to start a casual conversation.

"So how long have you been a Private Investigator?"

"I was licensed in Minneapolis about six years ago." He adjusted the towel to cover most of her hand.

"What made you decide to become one? Was anyone in your family in law enforcement? Your dad or your mom?"

Ben's hand had stilled in its ministrations. "My parents are gone, I don't have anyone else." He said decidedly.

"I'm sorry. What happened?" She hadn't read that in her findings. His family must not have published an obituary.

"My mother died when I was a child, my father passed more recently. They were both from small families." Ben's eyes were downcast, studying her hand. She didn't want to push, yet it didn't make sense if her findings were accurate. At the same time, Ava couldn't say anything or he would know she had spent the better part of the day cyber stalking him. Her mind was busily trying to figure out scenarios in which Ben was not lying to hide something or that there was a parallel Pearson family, much larger and with a penchant for cranking out investigators who looked just like Ben.

"Hold this." Ben pushed the top of the towel toward her where he held the corners and sides together, keeping the ice in.

Ava did as she was told and watched him, enjoying the comfort she felt being here with him. Ben stood on the lower rails of his chair and reached across the counter to grab the dish soap. Carefully, he took the delicately folded towel from her hand, lifting it so that he could see the finger in question.

The swelling was down and he pumped the dish soap directly into his fingertips. He looked up, making sure he caught Ava's eyes and held them. "Let's get this off while we can. It isn't going to come down much more until we get the ring off and let the blood circulate more freely."

Nodding her head was the only answer she could muster. She really couldn't logically argue keeping it on, as much as she worried about what she might lose. He had a point about her finger being in danger and besides, Ben wasn't going to argue in favor of cutting it. He only wanted to pull it over the swollen knuckle. Then again, it was really going to hurt and she didn't look forward to that.

Ben massaged the soap onto the finger, all the while staring at her, his eyes warm and entrancing. Ava felt her heart slamming in her chest and was having trouble catching her breath, painfully aware of his proximity. Her head spun and she was very aware of his hands. One was softly encircling her wrist, the other gently massaged soap on her finger. Ava was staring at his features.

In a rush she nervously blurted. "I Googled you."

His hand tightened on her wrist, the other jerked the ring and off it slid. He set the gold band down with a clatter.

"Ow!" Ava howled, bringing her hand up to hold it protectively against her chest.

Quietly, Ben asked her to repeat herself. His eyes were at once hard and dark.

In that instant, Ava justified to herself that it didn't seem so weird what she'd done. He *had* been in her store and she could argue that one phone call to someone he suggested wasn't necessarily a thorough reference check, nor did it excuse his trespassing. He didn't have a warrant or anything. Ava hurried to clarify. "I was checking your references."

He rose from his seat and moved around the counter to wash his hands. Ben did not look up and had neatly tucked away any outward signs of irritation. "And what did you find?"

She wasn't sure if he knew his similarities to his extended family but did not see any harm in sharing what she had learned. "There are quite a few old Pearson listings going back to 1910. None were local but several were in law enforcement or investigation work like you. Do you think you're related?"

Ben was drying his hands on a dishtowel he retrieved from a drawer beside the sink. He shook his head, "I doubt it. Like you said, it's a common name."

"Yeah, but they looked just like you."

His hands stopped moving. "You saw pictures? I thought you said they were old articles."

Something in his behavior was off, though Ava wasn't sure why he would be upset to learn about his extended family, especially if he thought he was alone. He was probably just surprised, that was all. "Yes, some newspapers have posted their old editions online. It makes it far more convenient to start a search. From there you can dig further at the library. The pictures are always better on microfiche." She stopped, realizing she was too close to letting him know the extent of her obsession.

He seemed too distracted to notice. "Do you have copies?"

"Yeah, they're out in my car. Would you like to see them?"

"I would."

"Okay. I'll be right back." Ava retraced her steps to the front door and put her shoes on. She was aware of something at the periphery of her conscience, warning her that she was treading on dangerous ground. She pushed it aside, wanting to believe what her heart was telling her.

He wouldn't hurt her. This information was new to him and he didn't know how to take it. Ava tried to think of how she would feel if out of the blue she learned she possibly had family somewhere she hadn't known about. He was probably deciding whether he should track them down. He certainly had the skill set to do it.

When Ava stepped back inside, Ben was not at the door. She retraced her path back to the kitchen and found him sitting at the long dark wood table. He was sitting on the far end and a matching cream chair closest to him had been pulled out.

Ben smiled thinly at her. He was trying to appear calm yet Ava could see the tension in his jaw and shoulders. She sat in the seat he offered and laid down her blue plaid messenger bag on the table, painfully aware of how abused it was. Her mother had given it to her when she had first headed off to college over six years ago now. There was nothing overly special about it, except she couldn't bring herself to part with it.

She unpacked the folder she had put all of her day's findings in and slid it over to him. Trying to downplay the time she had spent on it, she commented with a nervous laugh. "It was really easy to find this stuff. It didn't take long at all."

Ben was silent as he leafed through the articles, skimming through the copy but studying the pictures closely. Finally he set them back down on the table and looked up. "Can I keep these for a while?"

"Of course." Ava was pleased with herself for finding something that had obviously peaked his curiosity. "Isn't that interesting that your family has been drawn to the same field as you for a century, maybe longer? Justice must be in the blood."

"Yes, that is interesting." Ben twisted his wrist to check his watch. "I'm pleased you stopped by, but I have an appointment this afternoon."

"Oh, sure." Ava was again the nervous, bumbling girl. She snapped the flap down and slid the bag off the table, standing up.

Ben walked her to the door and reached around her to twist the knob. He reached out to take her good hand.

Ava let him. He turned her hand palm upward and reached into his pocket, bringing his closed hand up to lay something in her hand. He released her and she glanced down. "For your ring until your hand is better."

He had given her a delicate gold chain. Before she could object, he told her quietly. "Thank you for the information, I intend to look into it."

Saddened by her clear dismissal, Ava smiled nervously and raised her hand now closed around the chain. "Thank you. I sure hope it helps. Sometimes it's nice to know you're not alone."

Ben hesitated, a queer look on his face before he smiled, nodding a last good bye to her.

When the door shut behind her she fought down the feeling that their parting was final.

Ch. 9

The next day Ava was scheduled to work a full day. She was glad she had something to distract her from where her mind really lay, miles away with a dark eyed man. She found her hand going to the ring around her neck often, telling herself she wasn't dishonoring her father by believing Ben was connected to that day.

Days passed, nothing changed. Ava found herself watching the door, waiting for it to open and for him to walk through. She entertained the fantasy that he would want to come by and share with her what he'd learned about his family and thank her for her help. He didn't. Twice she offered to close the store. Elle agreed, happily thanking Ava for giving her the opportunity to spend some extra time at home. Still, Ben didn't come.

After the fourth day of nothing Ava called him after work. She held her breath, listening to his voice on his outgoing message.

"Hi Ben, it's Ava. From Elle's? I was just checking in to see if you were having any luck on those articles I gave you. I could help if you needed it, research is kind of my thing." Stopping herself before she sounded too needy, Ava ended with a quick, "My hand is looking much better, I wanted to give back your chain. I, um, I don't think I need it anymore." She hung up feeling more than a little foolish.

Ava was infatuated with someone she barely knew and, as cliche as it sounded, there was something about him that made her feel she had known him for years. Whether it had been him that night so long ago she didn't know, but she wasn't willing to give up the idea just yet. Regardless the why's of it, she couldn't deny how he affected her. More even than the confidence she had with him and the familiarity she felt, there was the feeling from her dream that he resurrected, it had not been since her childhood that she had felt that safe and comforted.

After a full week had passed Ava came to the conclusion that Ben didn't want to have any further dealings with her and, though disappointing, she couldn't blame him. Even if he *had* been her hero, a fact she waffled on daily, that didn't mean he wanted to have any sort of relationship with her. If he'd wanted to know her he would have contacted her by now, right? Sadly, she thought of the chain he'd lent her. She had been raised right and didn't want to keep something that wasn't hers. It didn't seem safe to mail such delicate jewelry so she wrapped it in a tissue and put it in an envelope, taping it shut.

When she was done with work that evening, Ava drove over to Ben's condo, intending to leave her package shoved in the door. The storm door would hide it from any passers by until he could find it. Then, she pulled up in front of his building and Ava's mouth fell. Shocked, she sat staring at the "For Sale" sign hanging on his front gate.

When she recovered herself, Ava ran through everything Ben had said to her. There had been no indication he meant to uproot. He had said he would "look into" his family and he was working on something with the local police even. What could change his mind and make him sell his home in a week she wondered?

Making a panicked leap, Ava tried to ignore the thought that ran through her head, it was too awful. Maybe one of his clients wasn't happy with something he had discovered. He had been so secretive about the woman he was working for that had brought him to Elle's, it could be a possibility. He'd said he had an appointment that day when he'd ushered Ava out. Maybe the client had been upset by what he had found, or one of the other kids he'd mentioned found out he was digging around and they did something. Would his unit be up for sale so quickly if he had been harmed? The thought made her stomach lurch.

Whipped into a state, Ava dialed the number for the realtor listed. She was in the office wrapping some things up before she went home. She confirmed that the unit had been listed three days ago. It had been arranged via phone by an attorney on behalf of the owner. She didn't know anything about the owner himself, never having met him. She'd dealt with the attorney before, saying she was with a very reputable firm, Johnson & Bradley. Ava asked if the realtor could meet her for a showing.

The realtor, Dana Larson, was hesitant at first but with Ava assuring her she was very motivated she agreed. Dana could be there in an hour. Although that was very generous it still felt like forever. Killing time, Ava wandered through Surdyk's and bought a bottle of wine and a small Chinese chicken salad from the deli for later. She was tempted to have a glass while she waited. She had never been much more than an occasional drinker. Tonight seemed like a great time to dull her faculties. Sober, the last fifteen minutes she had to wait in the car dragged by.

Finally, when Ava was deciding if it would be to pushy to call the realtor again, she saw a tan LeSabre pull up and a woman step out. Dressed very casually in jeans and wheat colored sweater, she didn't look like a realtor prepared to show a house. Ava fought down her disappointment, glancing down to fiddle with her CD collection though nothing fit her mood. She was debating between Joe Cocker and Muse when there was a knock on her window.

Startled, Ava virtually threw the disk in her hand, hearing it clatter off the dashboard as she wheeled to face the sound. Standing there was the woman she had just seen pull up. She beckoned for Ava to exit the vehicle and stepped back. Doing precisely that, Ava opened her door.

"Are you Ava Brandt?" She stuck out her hand. "I'm Dana Larson, ReMax Realty."

Shaking it firmly, Ava didn't want to delay. She couldn't wait to get inside and look around for any hints of what might have happened there, and to pump Dana for information. It was possible she knew more than she realized.

"Thank you for meeting me so last minute but I just love the area and saw the place. I have to travel tomorrow and was hoping to see it before I leave."

Smiling broadly, Dana nodded her head. "That's what I'm here for. Actually, tonight worked out. My daughter is with her Dad and I was just going to work late anyway. This is close enough to the office it's no trouble at all."

Ava smiled back. It was forced and they shared that awkward moment between customer and seller when casual pleasantries have been satisfied and it's time to move on to business.

Dana had been in the trade long enough, she easily took charge. "Shall we?" She motioned with a hand toward the gate Ava wanted so badly to throw herself over bodily and rush into the house.

Not wanting to seem too eager, Ava merely nodded.

"Oh, what's this?" Dana pulled the tissue wrapped bundle Ava had left and clutched it while she leaned in to open the lockbox.

Ava angled herself so that she could see the code. She committed it to memory, saying it three times in her head. As they walked in Ava fought the urge to charge in and start hunting for something. What, she didn't know, but she knew there had to be a hint here somewhere.

The condo felt warmer than it had been, the agency must have turned it up for showings. It made her think of Ben's comment that he turned it down during the day when he was gone. It pained her that he wouldn't be coming back here.

Dana went into realtor mode. First she talked about the stone entry floor, the quality of the windows and the benefits of having a tiny yard for a pet or a small garden. Ava was tuning her out, looking instead for any signs of a rapid or hasty departure. A tiny voice in her head said to look for signs of a struggle, she ignored that. She wanted to believe he had walked out, not been carried out.

They entered the kitchen and great room. Fortunately it was expected that a prospective buyer open drawers and cabinets. Ava used it for an excuse to look in everything. All the dishes were neatly stacked and the drawers were all well organized.

"It's a great kitchen." Dana was beside her, the rustling from the counter alerted Ava to the tissue wrapped necklace's final landing place.

"Yes, it is. Has the unit been staged or is this all the seller's stuff?"

"It's amazing isn't it? This is the seller's furniture and he left the unit very clean. We didn't have to do anything. He must not have spent much time here, it's barely lived in."

Ava continued hunting through cabinets and wandering through the rooms downstairs, finding nothing in the living room or kitchen. They came back into the entry and ascended the staircase, new territory to Ava.

At the top of the wooden stairs there was a small open loft with a desk and wooden built-in bookcase. Being a book lover, Ava took a moment to peruse the titles. Ben was a lover of the classic writers and a health nut to boot, as if she couldn't tell from his kitchen contents. There was an odd blend of biology, horticulture and nutrition books on the shelves intermixed with classic fiction. She leaned in to look at a framed picture on the top shelf of the bookcase just above Ava's eye level.

Taking it down from the shelf, Ava lowered it to take a closer look. In the black and white picture was a carbon copy of Ben in a work shirt and dungarees, his sleeves rolled up pitching a bale of hay into the bed of an old Ford farm truck. A large black man in overalls held another bale on the ground, ready to pitch it up. The Ben lookalike had pushed his straw hat back on his head and appeared unaware his picture was being taken. There was a sign visible in the background and Ava moved the picture closer to her face to see it.

There it was, staring her right in the face, Ava saw the words and felt her reality tilt. Ben had said he didn't know any relatives in Saratoga, yet here was a picture blatantly showing someone who was obviously a family member, circa 1940 working on a farm under a sign for Saratoga Fruit & Vegetables.

He had known about his family. Why would he lie to her, a virtual stranger? It wasn't like she was something to him. What difference did it make if she knew where he came from or not?

"There are two bedrooms up here as well." Dana was calling her attention back to the condo showing.

Slightly less worried about Ben being stuffed in a freezer somewhere, Ava followed Dana into the first of the two bedrooms. She puzzled through why he would lie and what he was hiding. His mystery grew.

"This is the smaller of the two. As you can see they've chosen to carpet the bedrooms, which is of course, a blessing on a winter morning although you could re-floor them with wood should you choose to. It's very common."

The room was basic and staged for company, there was no sense that anyone had spent time there. The carpet looked brand new with no traffic patterns showing wear from regular usage.

Ava nodded her head silently at the realtor's prattling and pulled her head back out, following Dana to the bathroom. It was well decorated like the rest of the condo yet nothing special. Merely to satisfy her own curiosity, Ava peeked in a few drawers and cabinets. Nothing unusual, just the usual medley of hair gels, toothpaste and soaps that most people have in their bathrooms. The medicine cabinet held no medications though there was a very barely visible ring on the edge of the sink, about the size of a prescription bottle.

Dana indicated they were moving to the master bedroom next. Walking in Ava saw that this room had a separate thermostat, something she thought would be a boon especially in her sauna of an apartment.

The room was masculine, painted in a soft gray with charcoal bedding and a dark wooden headboard. Ava finally saw evidence that someone had lived within these walls and ran a hand along the soft, smooth duvet.

The dish on top of the dresser held cuff links, a watch chain like they wore with old pocket watches and a bottle of cologne. Ava walked over to look more closely, picking up the bottle and inhaling deeply. The smell of him brought to mind the feel of his body when she had been pressed against it and she felt the tension in her shoulders easing.

"The walk in closet is a large space with tons of potential." Dana continued from behind Ava.

Turning, she saw that Dana was standing in the doorway just inside the bedroom. In the age of massively fancy and expensive closet organizing and outfitting, this was a strange setup.

On one side was a long wooden bar still weighed down with men's clothing including a tie and belt organizer and a line up of shoes below. The closet was easily over ten feet deep and full on one side, yet completely empty on the opposite side from the clothes. Ava walked in all the way to look at the clothes, touching the fabric of one suit in particular that caught her eye. It felt incredible, and expensive. She looked at the floor and saw marks in the carpet where something heavy had been. Odd considering nothing else had been taken.

"What was in here, did they take out some racking?" Ava couldn't imagine why. Closet organizers were popular, surely a buyer would want that left in.

Dana didn't answer right away, her silence brought Ava's head around to gauge her reaction. She was a professional and recovered quickly, although her explanation was unconvincing.

"The owner had some free standing units he's taken with him."

There was not much else to see after that. Ava asked to see the garage. Dana begged off saying she had to get back to the office, assuring her it was sizeable enough for a larger car and a bike rack as well as some storage in the front. They agreed to be in touch, Ava thanked Dana, and they shook hands parting ways at the front door.

As soon as she was back in the Jetta Ava put it in gear and drove away. She waited around the block for a full ten minutes to allow Dana time to leave. Ava no longer worried that Ben had been harmed. The evidence inside the house *did* point to a rapid departure and he had taken only the barest of essentials. Ava was now thoroughly intrigued though the tiny voice in her head was telling her she was crossing the line from curious to pathological. It was possible Ben had a checkered past. Maybe he was running and now that Ava had found some connection to his family, he was afraid she would tell someone what she had found.

What did she really know about him? He happened to be polite when he wasn't breaking into her store, insisting it was for noble reasons? She had been naïve enough, and infatuated enough, to believe it. Now she was angry with herself and the mysterious details of his disappearance were drawing her in, as puzzles often did.

It was the detective in her. Ava wished she would have pursued a career in police work, if she could limit her cases to those that didn't involve field work. The idea of her with a gun and *her* nerves was laughable.

Ironically, her inner bloodhound had her contemplating committing her first crime. She drove back and parked in front of the condo. Confirming Dana was gone and the lights were out, Ava walked steadily up to the front door in the near darkness, wishing she had the outside light to see the lock box by.

A few turns later and Ava had the key in her hand. She didn't hesitate to put it in the lock. Securing the key back in the box, Ava slipped inside and shut the door behind her.

Her destination was Ben's bedroom, it was the only room that looked like it had been lived in. Any clues to where he'd gone would have to be there. She strode up the stairs, thanking the architect in her head for putting in so many windows, and allowing her to make the most of the outside streetlights in the failing light of day.

Closing the drapes, she flicked on the light in the bedroom, and stood alone in Ben's room. She went to his dresser and after reviewing the contents of the dish and tray saw that nothing glaringly obvious was missing, there were no holes where anything would have been. Feeling only slightly guilty, Ava opened the dresser drawers. They were packed relatively tight, leading her to assume she was correct that he had not brought much with him. There were similarly few gaps in the closet on the side with both the clothing and the shoes. To the best of her knowledge, Ava could only see that Ben had taken a pill bottle and the realtor had removed some sort of racking from the closet. And whatever that had been had made Dana distinctly uncomfortable.

Going on instinct, Ava shut off the light and went back down to the kitchen. There had been a loose key in one of the drawers and Ava thought she might know what it went to. Ben was living alone and the condo would have come with both sets of keys. He would only have used one. She recalled from conversations with her friends and her own landlord, that spare keys were often forgotten or left behind. Gambling on that Ava flicked on the light, found what she was looking for, and walked out.

She easily found the garage by its corresponding number to the unit. She didn't have a flashlight and night had fully fallen by now. The gods were smiling on her, a streetlight overhead shone on the garage door, it's flat black numbers reflecting the glow from above.

After a car passed, Ava unlocked the garage and lifted the roll up door to look inside. Unable to lose the feeling she was going to be caught and that everyone who drove or walked by knew she didn't belong there, Ava found herself hunching and startling at the sound of a slight breeze rattling tree branches nearby. Upon entering, at first she was confused. The garage was different from any other she'd been in before. It held no lawn machinery, no sporting equipment apart from a mountain bike and helmet, no boxed Christmas decorations or any clutter of any kind.

However, there were three-two foot wide by five foot high metal racks set up as greenhouses. They had grow lights still affixed and the plant trays appeared to be occupied though she was going strictly by feel and couldn't be sure. Ben was growing pot? She found that very hard to believe. As little as she knew about him, Ava had to say she could not believe that he was messing around with drugs. She wished she could have some more light to see what was in those trays. In answer to her hopes, a car approached. This time instead of ducking, Ava focused on the racks so that for the few seconds they would be illuminated, she could see everything necessary.

The car rumbled past and Ava saw that the trays had indeed been occupied but it wasn't drugs as far as she could tell. It appeared to be vegetables. Ava recognized the leaves of a tomato plant, green beans and bell peppers. On one of the lower racks she saw romaine lettuce protruding, nearly ready to be picked. Once the car was passed, she rubbed the leaves of the tomato plant and the smell filled the small space. He was growing vegetables? That was the thing the realtor was hiding? That was odd. Maybe it was odd that he was growing them in his closet, but given their short growing seasons it wasn't unusual for someone to have a greenhouse in the spring to get a jump start on their gardens.

Ava herself had seen her mother start her spring crop of peas in the living room every year she could remember. Dana must have worried not everyone would understand. She laughed at herself for even entertaining the thought that Ben would be involved in drugs. Although, with as little as she knew about him and his sudden disappearance, it was less outlandish than she would like to believe. Her laughter died.

Without delay and hoping not to get caught, Ava closed and locked the garage. Trotting quickly back she did the same at the house being careful to return the spare key to the drawer where it belonged and finish up the front door with the lock box key. Quickly and quietly she returned to her car and was barely able to concentrate on the way home for the pounding of her heart.

Once home and chicken salad partially consumed, Ava drank an entire glass of wine before she was able to calm down enough to analyze what she had learned. Ben left in a hurry after something that happened. He didn't bring his basic toiletries such as cologne and hair fixatives, but did take the time to take a prescription he was on. The need to flee was so great, that he himself did not even contact the realtor but had an attorney do so for him.

Ava drank the second glass before finding the contact information for Johnson & Bradley in Minneapolis. They would be open tomorrow, it was Friday. With the next stage of her plan of action forming Ava finished her glass. Feeling quite tipsy she ambled into her bedroom without brushing her teeth, crawling into the sheets to promptly fall into a heavy sleep.

Ch. 10

Ava dreamt again. Only this time was different. Her rescuer unmistakably had Ben's face and she had flashes of seeing him everywhere she looked in her youth. His face, partially hidden, as he sat in a black Mustang keeping watch her. She saw his likeness while she played in the park and driving past her as she walked to school. The feeling Ava had of someone watching over her as a child was something she'd always believed in her heart was her father's spirit, a fantasy her mother had encouraged saying he was watching them both from Heaven. But Ben's appearance in her life, or reappearance, was tearing at the fabric of her reality. The one she'd sculpted for herself long ago and clung to when she was lonely or scared or feeling like there was someone just around the next corner who might be waiting to hurt her. As it all began to make sense, her world felt even more like it was being shaken apart at its very foundation. And it was Ben at the epicenter of that earthquake. Ava had no choice in the matter anymore, she had to find out what he had to do with her. She had to see him again.

Ava was lost in her thoughts when she got ready to go for a run. So much so that she didn't notice it was raining until she stepped outside and big fat drops of cold rain hit her in the head. She ran back upstairs to her apartment and grabbed a jacket. Instead of clearing her head, her exercise only succeeded in making her cold, crabby and soaked through to her underwear. She returned home in a foul mood.

Ava peeled off her soggy clothes and hopped into the hottest shower she could manage, taking sick pleasure in the painful sting as the water burned her back. She idled in the water for nearly half an hour before lifting a finger to wash her hair or do any of her necessaries.

Emerging freshly scrubbed and pink skinned, Ava wrapped herself in a towel and sat down heavily on the edge of her bed. All of her doings had only resulted in calorie burning and cleanliness, her mind was still busily working over the details of Ben's disappearance and the oddities she'd found at his home.

In a moment of inspiration, Ava grabbed her phone off the nightstand and hunted up her purse to dig for the business card she knew was in there. She sat down at her table, listening to the phone ring.

“Detective Sharpe.” Again he sounded annoyed.

Unable to make herself calm due to a racing pulse and thick tongue Ava stammered. “Uh, hi Detective. I don’t know if you remember but I spoke to you about a week ago about Ben Pearson.”

“Yeah.” The one word response was drawn out, expectant.

“I was wondering if you’ve heard from him.” She tried to make it sound like an ordinary request and not the strangely desperate search it was becoming. “He loaned something to me and I wanted to return it, only I haven’t been able to reach him. I thought maybe he was out of town, working for you?”

The detective was silent for several seconds. “He was supposed to meet me last week to discuss a case. He never showed. I figured he was working on something, it happens.” Concern crept into his tone. “When was the last time you heard from him?”

Ava ticked through the days mentally. “It was last Thursday.”

“Hmm. I’ll send someone by his house to check on him.”

Ava held her tongue. The detective didn’t need to know she had already gone there. Instead she made a request that might yield some results and insight into how much the police would be able to discover. “Could you call me after you do? I would just like to know he’s okay.”

“Sure.”

Ava dressed and tried to comb through her hair which had mostly dried while up in a towel. The usually straight, smooth locks had dried a frizzy, tangled mess. She settled on throwing it up in a pony tail, grateful her bangs were long enough to brush back and not have to wrangle into shape.

When she arrived at the store, Elle was already there and looking tired. Her eyes were red and her appearance uncharacteristically sloppy.

"Elle, are you all right?" Ava asked the obvious, inside cringing at the potential for an emotional outburst.

Nodding with a sniffle, Elle smiled falsely. "Bill left."

"Oh Elle, I'm so sorry." Ava reached out and touched the woman's shoulder. She wished she could reach out to hug her. She wished she could. Except she had never been that person; the one who hugged friends, put her arms around someone in need. Ava couldn't do it. Maybe that was why she was so drawn to Ben. She had never had any doubt or discomfort with him. When he'd picked her up, put his arms around her, it hadn't felt like she was choking as was the usual physical response she had to closeness. It was comfortable and easy to touch him, like she'd known him forever and had gotten past that awkwardness she could never seem to get past with people other than her mother. She couldn't let that go unquestioned. Her mind needed answers. Whatever he was running from, he had to have good reason. She had to let him know she wouldn't tell anyone whatever it was she'd stumbled upon. He didn't have to leave his life here. Not because of her.

"It's for the best. We've been heading toward this for a while now." Elle was wiping her eyes and took a deep breath, calming herself.

Her phone rang, saving Ava from the awkward feeling she should be doing more to comfort her mother's best friend. She thought about silencing it but Elle waved her away, turning to face a rack that needed straightening. Gratefully Ava slid her phone open.

"Hello?"

"Ava? This is Detective Albert Sharpe." His tone was crisp. He was troubled.

She held her breath, knowing what was coming. "Hi Detective. Were you able to find out anything?"

She imagined he was shaking his head. "I don't know how to tell you this, but he's gone. He's put his house on the market and the realtor said a local charity was coming to get everything. Miss, did he give you any indication he was leaving? Did he seem strange to you the last time you saw him?"

"No, I don't know where he could have gone. I was hoping you had."

"So you knew he'd left?"

Ava realized her mistake too late. "Uh…"

"Miss Brandt, you need to tell me what you know. Mr. Pearson was a friend to this department and we take great interest in his well-being. If he's in some sort of trouble…"

She didn't know what to do. Ava had always been taught to be respectful of the police and do as she was told. However, her instinct at the moment was to hide what she knew. "I drove by his house and saw the sign. I wanted to know if you could find out what happened." Partial truths weren't really lies, she told herself. Meanwhile, an idea as to what he had done was forming in her mind. Though it assumed a level of manipulation on Ben's part she wasn't sure she was willing to accept.

He sighed, exasperated. "Miss, you cannot withhold information from us. It wastes man power and loses time, allowing the trail to get cold. Suspects could have gotten away."

True, but Ava no longer thought someone else was involved. This was an intentional disappearance if she wasn't mistaken. Only she still wanted to know why. The guilt that she was responsible drove her decision. She knew her next step and hoped she could beat the police to it. "I'm sorry Detective. I didn't mean anything by it, I just didn't know what to do."

"Let us know if you hear from him or think of anything else Miss." Detective Sharpe was back to sounding annoyed.

"Yes Sir. I'll do that." She promised falsely and hung up.

Without pause Ava spun through her recent calls and redialed ReMax Realty. She didn't want Dana. The less involved and aware the person was, the better her chances of getting what she needed.

"Hi, this is Heidi with the Sisters for the Poor." She picked a charity at random and tried her best to sound frazzled. "We arranged a pickup at a site being handled by your firm and our scheduler is out unexpectedly. It's all a mess and I wonder if you could help me to confirm the pickup time."

"Certainly. Could you give me the address?" The young sounding receptionist was more than happy to comply.

Ava regurgitated the address, waiting to be caught at any minute in her deception. All she heard was the sound of typing as her request was granted.

"Oh," the young woman sounded distressed. "I have here that you aren't the charity the seller has listed for pickup. He has the Paralyzed Veterans coming tomorrow morning at eight a.m. Are you working with them to coordinate the pickup?"

She hid her victory and sounded put off. "That must be. Well, we'll have to sort it out on our end. Thank you."

"I'm sorry Ma'am."

Click.

Her next stop was Johnson & Bradley, GPS showed it was downtown in the Foshay Tower. Ava parked in a nearby ramp and walked up to the building. The directory said it was suite 1012, Ava took the elevator up and walked through the double high gloss wooden doors.

The receptionist was an attractive blonde, perfectly coiffed and looking like she'd come with the modern office space and its light, angular furniture. Glancing up she smiled pleasantly at Ava's approach.

"May I help you?" She showed perfectly straight, freshly whitened teeth.

"Yes, I'm trying to find out who represents Ben Pearson." Ava wondered if hers was an unusual request. "I have some questions about a property."

By the hardening of the blonde's features, Ava was guessing it was. "I'm sorry, we do not give out that kind of information." Her demeanor had gone cold.

Worried she would think Ava was looking to sue Ben for some wrong he committed, Ava's rehearsed speech faltered. "Um, ah, I just wanted to find out about his condo. I guess it's for sale and I was ah, interested in it."

"Is there not a real estate agent you could contact?" The receptionist was not as naïve as her age would imply. She would give nothing up, the firm had chosen their watchdog well.

"Right, but I was hoping to leave the realtor out, you know, save on fees." She saw a shadow move behind the frosted glass of what was probably a conference room judging from the silhouettes of chairs visible behind the reception desk.

Fearful she was drawing attention to herself, Ava began to back away.

"You're right, I'll just call the listing agent. Um thanks, good bye."

Feeling like a complete ass and worried someone might have heard her inquiry and gotten suspicious, Ava moved quickly out of the double doors and was hitting the elevator call button obsessively when she heard the doors behind her.

A woman's voice called out just as the doors opened and she dashed inside. The doors closed before the hurried footfalls reached her.

Ch. 11

The next morning Ava called Elle to let her know she would be late. So distracted with her own personal issues, Elle didn't ask many questions. By seven thirty, Ava was inside Ben's condo folding his clothes from the closet in preparation for their shipping. One item was already in her car. She would keep that for herself. She prayed she was right as she waited for the crew to arrive.

Promptly at eight there was a rattle of the knob as the newcomers unlocked the already open door.

"Hello?" Came the echoing call from the entryway. Even with his things still there it sounded empty.

Ava stepped out of his bedroom to stand at the railing overlooking the entry. "I was told to come early and start getting everything ready for you guys." She waited, watching the crew standing there.

There were four of them, each in a dark blue pair of coveralls with a matched ball cap. The uniform gave them anonymity. Ava wasn't sure she could pick one out of a lineup. The front gentleman spoke for them.

"I wasn't told anyone would be helping on this end." He eyed her suspiciously. She saw his hand go toward his pocket, she assumed for a phone, still her throat went dry fearing it was worse.

"He told me he wanted to be sure his equipment in the garage didn't get left behind." Ava felt her heart hammering painfully against her ribs. It would amaze her if they couldn't hear it all the way down there, it was roaring in her ears.

He didn't sound convinced she belonged there. "Why are you in here then?"

"I thought it better to leave the equipment in the garage out of sight as long as possible, so I started in here."

The leader was thoughtful for a moment and his hand slipped away from his pocket. He nodded slowly, accepting her story. "Okay. We'll take over up here. Why don't you go start getting outside ready and we'll open up the truck?"

Nodding briefly, Ava went downstairs to get the garage key and go to her assigned task. Her ears were pricked for any hint her cover was blown, yet it didn't come. Instead she really did pack up the growing equipment in the garage, tossing the plants and plastic trays into a nearby dumpster and wheeled it out to the large moving truck parked on the curb. It was a short push and all paved so it wasn't very difficult. When she was done, she went inside the unit to offer her assistance.

It was amazing what she saw. In the hour it had taken her to pack up the garage, this crew had packed up and carried out Ben's furniture, books, clothes and were now wrapping up in the kitchen. Truth be told there were relatively few dishes in there. Still, she had never seen anyone's existence be wiped away so quickly. These guys were professionals, they weren't from a charity. Ben knew what he was doing when he hired them.

"Need any help in here?" She asked innocently.

One of the movers stacking a dish between bubble wrap replied without looking at her. "We've about got it. Thanks."

Fearful she was going to lose him, Ava pushed herself to do what she came there for. "So is this stuff going to him at his new place?"

The packer was busy emptying a cabinet of a short stack of bowls. "Yeah, we have a request to send some of it up to Billings."

He was going back to Billings. She considered what that meant. She had found family in Billings and now he was going there, even though he'd denied knowing about them when she'd asked. She couldn't figure out what Ben could be doing and how his family was involved. None of it made any sense.

She hung around for the next half hour while they finished up the kitchen. When the crew left she told them she would stay behind, clean and lock up. Tired and hungry for lunch, they didn't put up a fuss.

After the crew had left, Ava removed the notepaper on which she had jotted down the license plate number from the truck and the company name, Physick Enterprises. Not just because she didn't recognize the name as a moving company, Ava doubted these were normal movers. She had moved and helped friends move. It took longer to pack a bedroom than the two hours it had taken to pack and move this entire condo, sparse or not.

Upon her return home, Ava hopped on the internet. The most she could find out about the company was that it dealt with medical devices and shipped equipment for blood donations and transfusions worldwide.

Ava wondered if Ben could be working with a medical device company. He was a Private Investigator. Then again, nothing about his story made sense the further Ava dug. She was driven to find out who this man really was. The search was making her act in ways no one who knew her would have believed. Even *she* didn't understand what she was doing. She had broken into a private home, impersonated someone else on at least two occasions, she wasn't sure if misrepresenting a buyer constituted a crime or not, and now she was thinking it was up to her to bring him back. It might be foolish, but she couldn't help feel her bringing up his past had spooked him and sent him packing.

The swiftness of his departure and tying up of his loose ends was well rehearsed. Ava *knew* he was running from something, the question was what? She needed to undo any damage she'd done. It was still safe here for him and she promised she wouldn't tell a soul if he would just tell her what it all meant. He somehow held the lynchpin to her sanity and she clung to that desperately.

She had some vacation time saved up, but it was a terrible time to leave Elle. Ava was conflicted and spent her evening busily cleaning her house. It was an old habit. When she was stressed, she cleaned. Vacuuming, dusting, mopping, the whole shebang. Apartment thoroughly spotless and mentally exhausted, Ava climbed into the shower to wash off the grime and remnants of stress still clinging to her. Hair drying, she finally sat down to a dinner of tomato soup and grilled cheese. It was a childhood favorite that usually brought peace.

Her mother's meals were always a comfort. Her favorite was pot roast with red potatoes and carrots but she didn't have the energy or supplies so she settled for a Campbell's dinner and a chick flick she had gotten from her movie club through the mail.

Just as she was thinking it was getting late enough to try to sleep her phone rang. It was her mother.

"Hi baby. How are you?"

She was exactly who Ava needed right then. She smiled, "Hi Mom. I'm fine." Looking at the clock, Ava was able to guess exactly what her very predictable mother was doing. "Are you getting off work? Getting ready for bowling league right?"

Katherine's voice was shaky. "I don't know if you know, but Bill left Elle yesterday."

"She told me. That's awful." It didn't surprise her that her mother had already talked to Elle. The school friends had stayed in touch all these years. Elle, the adventurous one moved away, choosing a life in the "cities" and Katherine had stayed home to marry her high school sweetheart and raise her family. Fate had intervened and Katherine's family grew smaller by tragedy, still she stayed. It had been a given that when Ava said she wanted to go to school and live in the city that Katherine would have Elle look out for her.

"I think she needs someone right now."

Ava's stomach knotted, thinking her mother meant for Ava to provide her with a shoulder to cry on. She of all people knew that was a bad idea. "Mom…"

Katherine continued, cutting her daughter off. "I'm coming down for a few days. I wanted to let you know that I might be busy with her, but I'd like to get together with you while I'm there."

Here was the opportunity she had been looking for and it had just landed in her lap. Thinking quickly, Ava leapt at it.

"Actually Mom, I had an offer for a job interview with a company in Madison. Maybe you could help Elle in the store for a few days and I could go out there. I hadn't talked to Elle about it yet because I wasn't sure if she could handle the store alone. Especially now."

Katherine was quiet. Ava could picture her tapping her chin with her fingernail as she thought the scenario through. Finally she spoke slowly, still working through the details. "I think that will work. Call Elle and make sure she trusts me in the store first." She snorted. Elle was a terrible control freak and had taken a long time to allow Ava to handle anything other than straightening up.

"I will. When are you coming down?" She wondered when she could get a flight out. Driving would take too long. Ava knew she had enough in savings. She never spent much, it was hard to when she didn't really go out, and her time was spent working and studying. Her only friends were her study group partners and she doubted those relationships would continue now that school was over. Martin was most likely a dead end, she'd made sure of that. Guilt itched at her briefly and she pushed it away.

"My supervisor said I don't need to be back until Wednesday."

Tomorrow was Sunday. That gave Ava three days to follow her leads wherever they took her. "Great. I shouldn't be gone too long. We can get together before you go."

They talked about work and Katherine asked about the company in Madison, to which Ava replied with the vaguest of details. Yes, it was fast to get an interview. Her degree wasn't even finished for sure yet. Katherine was sure it was because of her baby's hard work and good grades. Ava let her mother go on, afraid the more she said, the higher the likelihood she would be caught in her lies. Until this week, she'd almost never bent the truth and now she couldn't stop.

Ending the call a few minutes later, Ava immediately dialed Elle. She was in a place that precluded her from asking too many questions. Ava felt bad for leaving, but knew her mother could handle crisis. She specialized in it. God knows she'd had enough practice at it. Not even putting the phone down after disconnecting with Elle, Ava dialed the airline.

They had a flight leaving first thing the next morning. She wondered how they could charge that amount in good conscience and gave them her card number anyway. After hanging up, Ava put her head in her hands. She barely recognized herself. She was about to fly to another state to find a man she hardly knew because of a sense of guilt and curiosity. Was that all, she asked herself? Not allowing herself the time to think through the answer, Ava logged on to the internet.

Ben had taken her notes so she had to backtrack. Searching for Pearson in Billings, she came up with seven. None for Ben, she searched for Jim the relative she had found previously and got nothing. She continued to search for the other names she had found associated with Ben's family and finally got a hit on Michael. As soon as she saw it, she knew it was the right one.

She spent the night tossing and turning, alternating between excitement and fear for the journey she was about to embark on. She didn't know how he would take her finding him again, though she hoped he would be relieved to hear he didn't have to leave his life out of fear of discovery. It wasn't too late to come back.

The next morning Ava boarded Delta flight 1272 to Billings carrying only a small bag with the barest of essentials. She had a rental car reserved and a room at a local hotel for the night. If she needed to, she could always extend it but for now she wasn't booked to fly home until Tuesday and a change fee was only $100 should she need it.

Strange and new though this was, Ava felt free. She was temporarily liberated from the fear and hesitation that had kept her from doing anything spontaneous or poorly planned her whole life. When the other kids were going to South Padre Island or Cancun for spring break, Ava went home. When other kids studied abroad, Ava stayed home. This was her first adventure of her adult life. The first flight she had booked for a purpose other than a family vacation with her mother. Despite the insanity behind it, she was excited. A bubble of anticipation stuck in her chest as she buckled into her seat and watched the flight attendant go through the emergency procedures.

A few hours later Ava was in a car programming the GPS to find directions to the home of Michael Pearson. As she drove, reality set in. What the hell was she going to tell Michael she needed Ben for? What possible reason could she have for following him from Minnesota to Montana? What would she say if she saw Ben? Why should he believe her that she wouldn't share whatever secret she had found?

She ran through different scenarios as she drove to the town of Yegen off Highway 212. She stopped at a convenience store to buy a bottle of water. As she paid, she noticed several flyers for missing children. Not all of them would be as lucky as her, she thought sadly. Her mind wandered while she followed the computer's voice to her destination. Ava parked the blue Focus along the curb half a block back across the street.

It was a normal enough looking tan rambler, nothing special about it. A short chain link fence surrounded the large yard. Michael Pearson did not have the same landscaping crew as Ben. The bushes were overgrown and the lawn appeared to have been neglected before the snow, it was patchy and brown, not yet awake from its winter rest. A rake leaned against a tree and clippers sat on the front stoop. Someone was making an effort to reverse the damage.

There was no activity visible from the street, but it being Sunday and with the lawn tools laying about, Ava assumed someone was home. With a renewed bravery she had felt only since meeting Ben, Ava stepped out of the car and walked up the street to Michael's front door. She swallowed her hesitation, feeling less than confident as she watched her hand reach for the doorbell.

It's chiming echoed through the house. Ava thought Michael must be as sparse a decorator as his relative. She wondered how they were related. It must be close to have such a resemblance as she had seen in those old photographs. She wondered if Michael was a descendant of Jim Pearson. He would be the right age to be a son or nephew according to the records she'd found.

Footsteps were moving toward the door and Ava held her breath as the moment of truth finally arrived. When the door opened, Ava's smile froze on her face. She hadn't been expecting to find him so soon. Standing in front of her was Ben.

Ch. 12

Ben was equally surprised to see her. His friendly smile slowly slid from his face. His eyes hardened. "Ava, what are you doing here?"

Ava struggled to find the bravery and adventurous spirit that had gotten her this far. "Uh, um, I was looking for you. I mean I wanted to tell you that you don't have to leave Minneapolis. I won't tell anyone what I found out about your family, I don't even know what I found out. Whatever it is you're running from, I wanted to let you know your secret is safe."

Ben remained silent and stepped back, waving her inside. Ava followed him in and looked around. The living room was empty except for a small loveseat. Obviously she'd beaten the movers.

The door clicked shut. His voice was hard and low behind her. "How did you find me?"

Not daring to turn, too uncomfortable to sit in the solitary furnishing, Ava stood awkwardly with her hands hanging at her sides at the threshold of the living room. "I remembered you had a relative here in Billings and he had a current listing under Michael. I figured you would come here since this was one of the names I'd found and gave to you."

She had started out well enough, but finished weakly as her story fell apart. There was no way she should have known he had gone to Billings instead of any of the other cities where she had found a relation. She was mortified, feeling her cheeks flush, she wished she could snap her fingers and be gone.

Ben remained calm. "You are very resourceful. I'll give you that."

Ava didn't answer.

Ben invited her to sit down. Obediently, Ava shuffled over the tile to take a seat on the small couch. Ben perched on the opposite arm not two feet from her.

He watched her calmly for some time. She grew increasingly uncomfortable under his scrutiny, feeling his eyes burning into her. Finally she was unable to handle the silence. She blurted out something she had been considering since finding out what had happened to her. "I want to hire you to find the man that abducted me as a child."

Her request was met with silence. She forced herself to look up at him, to see his reaction. She wasn't sure how he would react or if he would let on that he'd known something about it. When her eyes came to rest on his face, she saw shock.

Ben's normally pale skin had gone white and his mouth hung open. He looked like he'd seen a ghost.

Ava went on to explain herself like any normal client would. "You couldn't know this, but I was abducted when I was little. The details have only recently begun to come back to me. I must have blocked them out before. I remember enough to know that I want to find out the rest of what happened. As far as I know, the guy who took me hasn't been caught, but I would like to know for sure. Maybe there were others. Other kids." She found herself being convinced as well as she went on. "He had a place setup that would have taken some work and it didn't seem like it was his first time." In her mind's eye she saw the lab. It wasn't somewhere he would have just chanced upon, the doctor with the headlight had to have planned it out.

His face remained pale though he hid the rest of his emotions behind a professional mask. "What do you remember?"

Closing her eyes made it easier both recalling the details, and not seeing Ben staring at her. Ava's forehead wrinkled as she tried to remember everything. "A woman came to my apartment building where I was playing outside. She gave me candy. She was a stranger, but she was so pretty. I liked the attention. Dad was already gone and Mom worked a lot. It was lonely." She was glad her eyes were closed. Ava hadn't realized how personal this story was. Ignoring her discomfort she went on. "There must have been a drug in the candy because it knocked me out I guess. I woke up in some sort of weird lab. I was on a metal table and there was nobody else there except for the doctor. I think he was a doctor anyway. He was talking to himself, but I didn't know what he was saying. It was in another language. Maybe it was German or something, I don't know it's hard to say since I didn't recognize it back then. The weird thing is, the only thing he did was take my blood. It must have been a lot because I remember feeling faint." Her eyes remained downcast when she finally opened them.

He waited to make sure Ava was finished before speaking. When he did, his response was toneless. "He let you go." It was a statement.

Ava shook her head. "No, there was a man." She squirmed uncomfortably in her seat, ready to buckle in the face of such directness. "He argued with the doctor and he took me." Her memory of the incident had not felt like her own, more like something she'd envisioned after being told someone else's story. Here, telling it to Ben, she could see him judging her. His face was blank, he was trying to hide his anger at her. She felt tears prick her eyes. She questioned the truth of her memories, feeling doubt creep in and wished she could forget the whole thing. Being self-conscious and timid wasn't the worst thing in the world. Her flirtation with boldness was coming to a close. Ava was beginning to think Ben's involvement in the whole thing was merely wishful thinking and another way of distracting herself from having to actually make a real decision about her life.

Ben prodded. "What do you remember of the man who saved you?"

By now tears were starting to run down her cheeks, her humiliation settling in. She couldn't bring herself to look at him yet she had to say this last piece, she made herself. After all, when she left here she was going to return to her timid existence, never to speak of this again. "His eyes. He had brown eyes and he smelled good. He had a kind voice." Those few memories from her child's mind felt real.

Without a word Ben got up and left the room. Ava wiped her face and tried to bring herself under control. Her emotions were all messed up since she'd started digging in her past. Normally she operated on a rather superficial level. She didn't get too deeply attached to people and didn't think too hard about how she felt about things. This recent recollection of trauma had sent her spinning. She didn't have the ability to cope with the emotional maelstrom now throwing her off course. Ava tried to remember what she had learned of post traumatic stress disorder in her Psychology classes. Maybe that was what was making her behave so strangely. Maybe that was what was making her concoct this whole delusion and latch onto a complete stranger.

Ben's feet made a sound on the tile as he returned. His voice was close when he spoke. "Here, this will help."

She looked up as far as the hand he held outstretched and saw a glass of something brown. It was alcoholic, that she knew even before she smelled it. She took it from him and saw that he had a glass of the same in his other hand.

Taking a sip, Ava choked. She wasn't prepared for the burning sensation. It got stuck in her throat and took near Herculean effort to make her throat open up to swallow it. When she did, she gasped for air. Immediately she gulped again. It was no easier but she desperately wanted the result. She took a third.

"Easy with that stuff." He put a finger on the top of her glass to stay her from a fourth large gulp to finish. "It can hit you hard if you don't drink much."

"Do you drink much?" She wanted to talk about something real, not a figment of her imagination.

He chuckled. "I barely touch the stuff. You?"

"Oh. Uh, no. Not really." She felt the warmth spreading through her stomach, trying to recollect what she had eaten today. She didn't remember anything after the peanuts on her flight. This was possibly going to be a very bad idea very soon. As if it could get worse, she thought and tossed back the last of her glass.

Ben reached out and she let him take her glass, setting it down on the ground beside them. "Are you sure you want to go down this road?" His voice was gentle.

Dumbly she nodded. In fact she was not sure at all, but the thought of walking out of there right then and never knowing what really happened to her scared her more than anything she might find out. The doctor no longer had the ability to hurt her, yet Ben did. She had given him that power when she had unknowingly let him into her limited world. Something in him had called out to her. It still did. Only now she knew that after she left here, she would never see him again and it pained her to think it. Delusion or no, she'd developed an attachment to him.

"I feel I have to warn you. In my experience, digging for the truth after so many years can bring up a lot of unexpected pain. It might not end the way you're hoping it will."

Feeling a little dizzy as the alcohol's effects spread, Ava raised her eyes to his. "I don't have anything to be afraid of now. I just hope I can get all the pieces and then put it away."

Ben regarded her thoughtfully before he nodded. "You're young, you might not understand how this will affect you."

Ava stubbornly stuck out her chin and felt the stirrings of anger. "I'm not that much younger than you."

"I'm older than you think." He replied seriously.

The alcohol was hitting harder. Ava didn't feel well. "Can I use your restroom?"

Ben rose from his perch and turned to point her toward her destination. Ava stumbled and his hands shot out to steady her before she fell against him. Again she felt that comfort wash over her when he touched her.

She smiled a little lopsided as she stared up at his face. "Seems like you're always doing that."

His eyes were fixed on hers. "What, catching you?"

“No,” her tongue was thick. “Saving me.” She got her feet back under her and pushed off of his chest to amble off.

By the time she’d splashed her face and decided her drink would stay down, Ben was pacing the length of the room. Ava sauntered past him and slid down on the couch. Her eyes were tired and she leaned against the arm of the couch, laying her chin on it to watch the way Ben moved. Long legs gave him a big stride and he glided smoothly, setting down his feet softly unlike most people who tended to hit the ground with their steps in a jarring gait. His body was impressive to look at as well and she followed it attentively, catching him shooting her curious glances at intervals. Her lids were getting too heavy to keep up.

As they closed, she was aware he had stopped pacing and she could sense his nearness through the alcohol induced haze. His arms wrapped around her shoulders and she leaned into him as he scooped her up. She put her arms around his neck and inhaled his scent deeply. It must have been the combination of the alcohol and discussion of her abduction, but she again drew the parallel between him and the man who had saved her so long ago.

Ava felt Ben lay her down on a soft bed. Reluctantly she let him disengage her hands from his neck and put a blanket over her. Before he straightened she opened her eyes and looked into his, mere inches from hers. As the dark chocolate color filled her vision, she whispered, “I want to find him.”

Misunderstanding, Ben answered her quietly. “We’ll find the doctor if we can.”

Still not blinking, she shook her head. “No, I want to find *him*, I want to find the man who saved me.” Her eyes closed and she faded from consciousness.

Ch. 13

Waking to a pounding head, furry mouth, and stomach that didn't know if it should empty or fill, Ava opened her eyes. The room she found herself in was not too different from the one she'd been in back in Minneapolis.

The bedding was dark brown yet similarly styled, the headboard was leather. She looked around and saw a book on the nightstand by Oscar Wilde she'd read last year. Distractedly she ran a hand over it fondly as she scanned the room. There were no personal touches on the walls until she stopped at the dresser.

On it was a bottle of the same cologne she had seen at Ben's house and a picture of a man looking like Ben standing in front of a courthouse with a woman. Both were smiling, he wore a light suit. Her suit and hat were dark and she clutched a briefcase in her hand. A car parked alongside the curb looked like it was maybe from the 20's. The man must have been a relative of Ben's, again their family resemblance was uncanny. Only the clothing and hair had changed. Apart from a thin moustache, this man was Ben's twin.

Her mind was struggling in its sodden state. Ben and his family all in the same field through nearly a century, they all looked exactly alike and they had the same taste in decorating. It didn't make sense.

Ava carefully moved her feet over the edge of the mattress and eased herself up to a sitting position. The room shifted around her but she felt confident she wouldn't fall if she stood. Testing her theory and pleased to find she was right, Ava went into the attached bathroom. With a nervous flutter, she smiled that he had put her in *his* room. Of course, she reminded herself, it was the only one with anything in it.

She rinsed her mouth, taking a few drinks from her cupped hand and finger combed her hair while she was in the bathroom. Ava opened the drawer beside the sink and found toothpaste. Putting some on her finger she did her best to de-fuzz her tongue.

Setting it back down, she saw bottles of vitamins. Curiously, she looked at them. There were three: Vitamin A, C and Coenzyme 10. She wasn't familiar with the third and read the back, seeing it was a sulfur containing amino acid. Opening the bottle, she sniffed. It was awful. It was unbelievable anyone would put that in their mouth.

With her mind starting to clear, Ava became aware of voices coming from somewhere in the house and the sound of a large engine idling nearby. She moved quietly over to the window and peeked out past the curtain. A truck sat out front with its back doors swung open. It was the same moving van from Ben's condo.

One of the men in the same overalls as before was carrying a box and another behind him was doing the same. Ava tried to figure out the important piece of the puzzle that continued to elude her. She felt it at the edge of her awareness but when she reached for it, it moved farther away. The pills, her discovery of his family connections, and their strong presence in law enforcement all had to mean something. But what did it mean and why did it make him have to run?

Ava waited a few minutes for the truck to finish its delivery and go away, they would surely recognize her if she were to be seen. They delivered their cargo of boxes and garment bags as well as his other pieces of furniture. She watched them remove the growing apparatuses she herself had loaded from the garage.

Once the truck was gone, Ava heard her stomach growl. The smell of coffee combined with her hunger and she could stay hidden no longer. She padded down the hall in her socks and clothes from the night before looking like she had just rolled out of a hamper. Self-conscious, she pulled at and smoothed her shirt, wishing she had worn something stiffer, like cardboard.

Her attention was on a very stubborn wrinkle right above her left breast and she was staring down at it when she walked into the kitchen. Ava heard the snap of rubber and looked up just as Ben secured a tourniquet above his elbow and prepared to inject something into his arm with a huge old fashioned metal syringe. A plastic bag, the kind they used in hospitals, lay on the counter. Ava couldn't tell what had been in it before it was empty.

She had never seen anyone using drugs other than the occasional smoking of a joint at a party. That he would inject his body with poison acted like a cold shower for her. Suddenly she was wide awake and fully aware of what she was doing.

He had seemed so interested in his health, it was abhorrent to believe he would do that to himself. Ava felt that missing piece of the puzzle slide into place. Headlines of drug related crimes ran through her mind and Ava knew what he was running from.

Sickened, Ava felt her stomach heave and she covered her mouth, glad she was empty. She turned and fled back to the entry to find her shoes. She had them on in an instant. Out of habit, she patted her pocket and didn't feel her phone. In her mind's eye she saw it on the nightstand. It had her mother's numbers on it, she couldn't leave it here for him to find.

She rushed back down the hall, this time with no consideration of any sound she might be making. Ben was into drugs. She couldn't believe she had been so stupid. She'd been so blinded by fantasy she hadn't been able to see what was right in front of her face.

A falling out with someone dangerous and he had to leave town. His family must be hiding him. Maybe they kept him safe through their police connections or he had sold out someone important to buy his safety. Detective Sharpe was covering for him because he was under his protection. That had to be it. The very details that had painted him a wronged man yesterday now held a very different taint to them.

She had reached the bedroom and grabbed her phone off the nightstand, dropping it in her eagerness. With a curse, she fell to her knee to grab it. As she did so, she saw his feet in the doorway and her heart stopped.

Fighting to control her voice, she stood clutching her phone tightly in her hand. In her head she ran through his street address to make sure she could recite it if she had to call the police. She almost laughed, thinking this was the second time she was considering calling the authorities on him. She should have done it the last time. "Ben, please let me go." She hated the quake she heard in her voice.

He was upset. She could see him struggling with some dark emotion as he ran his hand through his already mussed hair. The other was braced against the doorjamb, his knuckles white with tension. She thought she heard the wood crack and caught her breath. "Ava, it isn't what you think."

"I didn't see anything." She took a step toward him, watching his body closely for any signs of aggression. "Let me go." She tried to sound more confident than she felt.

He stood in the center of the doorway lowering his hands to his sides. "No."

Ava felt the ball of fear settle in her stomach. Her chin quivered. "Please Ben. I won't tell anyone. I just want to go home."

Taking a step toward her Ben reached out a hand, his expression pained. "Let me explain."

She took a step back, trying to remember what she had learned in that series of self-defense classes her mother had made her take in junior high. Aim for the nose. It had worked at the store, although that was before she knew who he was and she hadn't been facing him like this. Ava corrected herself, she still didn't know who he was. He was the same stranger she'd faced on the dock. Steeling herself, she prepared to move.

Ben interpreted her silence as acceptance and took another step, then another, putting him within an arm's length. Ava's hand streaked upward toward his face. He moved at the last second and her palm glanced off of his ear. He growled and grabbed her wrist forcefully enough she feared he would break her arm.

Panicked, Ava's other hand shot out. Ben was ready and easily grabbed that one as well. He held her hands to her sides and she thought of the other defense available to a woman against a man. Unfortunately, Ben had the same thought. Just before she brought her knee up, he pressed her against his body so tight she couldn't move her legs, wrapping her hands behind her back.

Ava was furious she had been so blind and stupid, and now she was helpless. She could handle almost anything, but not helpless. They had played cowboys and Indians in grade school once and her friend had tied her hands and feet. Ava's terrified screams had brought her mother in a hurry and it was that same terror that gripped her now.

She felt her face crumple and tears wet her cheeks. She wished she could hide them so he wouldn't know how scared she was of him, but he was so close. The only place for her face to go was in his chest and she couldn't bring herself to touch him more than she had to. Twisting her face to the side, Ava closed her eyes.

"Ava." His voice was gentle.

She was shutting him out as best she could.

"Ava, please." He persisted, relaxing his grip on her wrists. "It's not what you think."

"I know what I saw."

"No, you don't. It wasn't drugs, it's medicinal. I have a condition and I have to take injections every day."

She wanted to believe him only she couldn't. Having a condition wouldn't make him walk away from his life as soon as someone recognized him. Emboldened by fear and angered that she could feel her body reacting to his nearness, she lashed out. "I don't believe you." She turned her face toward his and inclined her head in the direction of the street behind him. "I suppose they supply you with your drugs? Handy to get them to move your stuff too."

It gave her a thrill to see his face blanch at her mention of the movers. "I know what Physick Enterprises deals in. What are you to them that they are at your beck and call?"

Ben's brow furrowed and his lips set in a grimace. Without realizing what he was doing, his grip was relaxing even more as he pondered her words.

Ava noticed and took a deep breath. She gathered herself and spun her arms at the same time she dropped her weight into her knees, breaking his hold. Once freed, she put her hands against his chest and pushed. It caught him off guard and he stumbled back a step, reaching out to catch himself on the edge of the dresser. Taking advantage of the opening, Ava skittered sideways to stay out of reach and ran. She was nearly out of the room when she heard his voice and stopped.

He didn't yell, he didn't order. Quietly, Ben uttered the words from Ava's past. "Don't be scared little one."

She caught herself in the doorway with her back to him, hands braced against the wood to hold her steady as the world spun around her. "What did you say?"

“The same thing I said when you were seven years old. Do you remember?”

Ava gaped at him. He was asking her to believe the impossible, but how else could he know? She hadn’t told anyone he’d said that, she’d only remembered it in dreams how could she have repeated it? Only she and her rescuer knew he had said that exact phrase.

She heard the rustle as he regained his feet and walked up behind her. He was close enough though he did not touch her. “I said, ‘Don’t be scared little one. You’re going home now.’”

“How can you know that, did he tell you?” Ava whispered. “Why did he save me?”

He hesitated, trying to decide something. “I’m not sure. I saw her take you. I knew what they were going to do. They had done it so many times before, to so many children. I’d been always too late. With you I thought I would be there to catch them in the act, I knew they would be coming for you. I almost missed it that time as well, only I recognized her.” He took a breath and she felt him exhale, warm on her neck. “I followed her to find out where it was they took the kids.”

“How old are you Ben?”

“I’m twenty-seven.”

Ava shook her head, he was making no sense. “Who told you he said that? Was it your father? Did *he* tell you?” She thought of the men in the photographs.

His voice was certain. “No, it was me.”

Ava had had enough of his lies. He was being cruel, manipulating her using the information she’d given him. She spun around and was nearly nose to nose with him. Surprised he took a step back. Ava’s emotions exploded and hurt turned to anger. “I don’t know how you know that or what you’re trying to do, but it’s horrible. Whatever your game is, I don’t want to be a part of it anymore. Deal drugs, run away, I don’t care. I came here to tell you I wouldn’t say anything about what you’re doing and I won’t. I’ve said what I came to say. If you come back to Minnesota, leave me alone. I never want to see you again.”

She rushed out, half expecting him to follow her but he didn’t. It wasn’t until she had driven a few blocks that her rage gave way to hurt and humiliation, and she had to pull over until she could see through the tears.

Monday travel was heavy and there was no way Ava could fly standby. She paid the change fee and booked her seat on the early afternoon flight. That gave her over two hours to kill. First she went to the restroom and changed her clothes, brushed her teeth and, tired of the whole wispy mess, put her hair back in a bun.

Convincing herself that she was doing fine was going well until halfway home when the flight attendant served her a Pepsi and pointed out the fact that her book was upside down. Ava forced a smile and spun it around, failing to make sense of a single word the remainder of her journey.

Ch. 14

When she got home, all Ava wanted to do was watch dumb tv and zone out but her phone rang the second her keys hit the counter. Exasperated she answered it, unable to keep the annoyance from her voice.

“Am I calling at a bad time baby?” Her mother sounded offended.

She was instantly repentant. “I’m sorry Mom. I just got in and traffic was bad. How has your visit been?”

Mollified, Katherine was happy to unload. She sighed heavily. "Elle's hurting but I think she's going to be okay. She's always been a strong person. Are you thinking of coming in to the store tomorrow?"

"Yeah," Ava answered without hesitation. She hadn't thought about it until then but she wanted to get right back to keeping her brain busy.

They visited and had some much needed laughs by both, hanging up in time for Ava to have a bowl of cereal and watch stupid tv for an hour before bed.

The next day was uneventful at the store. Ava had to make up a story about her job interview, which she alone knew wasn't going anywhere. She felt guilty accepting both her mother's and Elle's well wishes. They did inventory, rearranged the store to rotate the merchandise, and did a top to bottom cleaning of the store. It was the way Elle dealt with stress. She purged her life of excess stuff and cleaned everything in sight. It was no wonder the two of them worked so well together.

That night, Ava begged out of dinner saying she was tired. The next, she tried to say she was under the weather but it was Katherine's last night in town and the older women put their collective foot down.

Elle would not take no for an answer and Katherine played the hurt card. Ava caved. Elle cooked, a talent she loved to show off. Dinner was spring lamb with baby vegetables and a berry cobbler for dessert. It was incredible, as expected.

After dinner the conversation turned to men. Ava was not paying much attention until something Elle said to Katherine caught her ear.

"What?"

"I was just asking your mother what she's going to do when she gets home." Elle winked at Katherine.

Katherine, however, looked distinctly uncomfortable. "Ava, I was waiting to talk to you about it. There's someone I've been seeing."

Ava's jaw dropped. "Mom, who? When were you going to tell me? Tell me about it, um, him."

"Well," Katherine started, uncertain. "His name is Robert and he sells insurance in town. He's got two grown children of his own. He's divorced." She fiddled with the spoon in her cobbler dish pushing the remains around to leave a purple trail on the white china.

Reaching over to touch her mother's forearm, Ava smiled genuinely when she looked up. "Mom, it's been a long time. It's okay."

Her mother looked relieved. "You know I still love your father. I'll always love your father. Robert doesn't want to be anything but your friend. You know, when you're ready to meet him."

"I would love to meet him, he sounds like a decent guy. You deserve to be happy Mom." She meant it too. She raised her glass to take a sip of wine.

Elle spoke up, "Well, now that we've established the fact that Katherine is doing well, how about you Ava? Anyone special?"

"Pardon?" She choked around a mouthful of wine.

"You know, any special man or whatever." Elle was giggly from the wine.

At least Ava could answer truthfully. "No, no there isn't anyone I'm interested in."

"What about that man that stopped by the store yesterday?" Katherine asked, shooting Elle a meaningful look across the table.

Ava's heart fluttered. "What man?" She wondered if Ben had followed her. Part of her hoped he had, then she chastised herself, remembering how things had ended. It was better not to get mixed up in whatever it was he was involved in she reminded herself.

"Oh I forgot about that. He *was* handsome." Elle said coyly.

Ava hated it when the two of them got together and drank. Sometimes they reverted to nothing better than a couple of teenagers and were twice as annoying.

Then her mother chimed in. "He was. Ava has always liked them tall and blonde. Back home there was one in high school. His name was what, Eric?" She looked askance at Ava.

Ava was dumbstruck. "A blonde?"

"Yes," Elle was definitely tipsy. She hid a small belch behind her hand. "He came in when you were at lunch. He wanted to know when you would be back and when you got off. I assumed he was your boyfriend. You didn't tell *me* you were dating anyone." She frowned, pretending to pout.

"Not that I'm aware of. Did he say he was coming back?" Mentally Ava ran through all the guys she knew from school. Martin was sort of blonde and tall and he was all right looking though to call him handsome was a stretch.

Katherine wiggled her eyebrows at her, caught up in the mood. "Want us to call you when he does?"

"No, I don't think I do." A tingling of fear ran through her. She didn't know what it meant, she worried it was related to Ben's dark dealings in some way.

"Well, all right. We will." Ella sniggered, ignoring Ava's wishes. Katherine tittered irritatingly.

Ava's mood soured. Standing up she faked a yawn. "All right party girls. I have to go home and get some sleep."

Amidst their arguments Ava begged out. Kissing them both at the door, she promised to bring lunch with her when she came in the next afternoon. She wasn't due at the store until one. That left her an entire morning to sleep in and, given the fact that it was already nearly midnight, she was going to try to do just that.

Ava got in her car. A buckle on her purse caught on the well worn upholstery tearing a small hole in the passenger seat. She had wanted to replace it after grad school, sighing she reaffirmed that plan in her head.

Elle lived in a respectable part of older Edina. Her house was a white walkout onto a prestigious golf course. There were very few cars in driveways or on the street, most were tucked away in their garages. Maybe it was a rule there. When her headlights came on, they illuminated a red car parked on the street with a tall blonde man inside it. Ava might have noticed the unusual detail if her mind wasn't already somewhere else.

Driving home, she ran through the evening's conversation. Her mother had a boyfriend and someone came in to the shop looking for her. She racked her brain thinking of any tall, *handsome* blondes she knew. It was Minnesota, they were a dime a dozen. She could think of at least three she had studied with in grad school and all of them knew where she worked. However, none of them had ever expressed any romantic interest in her. Thoughts of handsome strangers again brought her mind around to Ben.

Angry with herself for being so stupid, she shoved those musings away. The Ben she'd imagined had been very different from the real thing she'd seen in Billings. And the fact that he'd used such personal information to manipulate her was unconscionable. The things he'd known, he had to have found out through his family. Whoever in his family had helped her had been far more kind hearted than he. Whatever warmth she had felt for him had been for his relative. Anything she had felt for him had been false. It wouldn't happen again.

Mind in knots, Ava drove home and parked in a space outside instead of in the underground ramp. It was great to have in the winter but now that it was spring she kind of missed the walk outside to the door when she could smell the earth and greenery just waking up.

Walking in she would have noticed the same red car from Elle's pull up in front of building if she would have looked behind her, except she didn't. The driver remained in his vehicle, watching her.

The next day Ava slept in and read the paper, taking a brisk five mile excursion through the woods and even brewed a pot of coffee just for herself. Normally she would only go to the trouble if she had a lot of studying to do, but she felt like she needed to treat herself today.

When it was time to go to work, Ava dutifully got lunch on the way. She stopped at a Mediterranean place off 394 and got salad, pasta and something sweet for afterward. She again failed to notice the car following her.

Katherine stopped in at the shop to have lunch and visit before heading home. Elle had opened so it was only fair that Ava closed that night. She was mentally miles away when she finally finished with the cleaning and was checking lights and doors before leaving to take the deposit to the bank on the way home.

It was dusk and some cars had their lights on in the gloom. It felt soggy with the mist rising and ground still wet from the snow's final goodbye. Ava walked to her car, keys in her hand and noticed the light in the lot was already casting its halo. The timer on it needed to be adjusted for the earlier sunrise and later sunset but wouldn't be until after daylight savings. As a result, Ava's car was cast in an artificial glow and she saw the dew on it from the evening's short cloudburst. Her key stopped short of the lock when she saw the disruption in the water beads on the door. The car had been wiped dry around the handle area. Eyes wide, Ava examined the vehicle closely. There was more dry area around the top of the door.

Not understanding what it meant, Ava's hands trembled as she struggled to unlock her door and get inside where she felt safe. So shaken was she, she drove straight home without making the night's deposit. Only when she was inside her apartment with the door locked and all closets checked did Ava start to relax.

Every time a door banged, each sound from the furnace and water pipes jolted her out of her light sleep. By morning Ava's nerves were frazzled. Her shower didn't help the bags under her eyes.

Walking in the next morning, Ava was greeted by Elle's anxious questions though a steady stream of customers kept her from having to give more than a few brief responses.

Closer to evening when the sky was starting to grow dark Elle resumed her questioning. "Ava are you okay? Really, you look like you're sick." She came over to press her hand on Ava's forehead despite Ava's typical aversion to being touched. Elle got special dispensation since she had known Ava since birth. At least *she* thought she did.

Ava shrugged her off. "Elle, it's okay. I'm fine, I just didn't sleep well." Elle's brow furrowed. "My noisy neighbors were up all night." She told her knowing it was an open complaint and one that usually led to Elle ranting about apartment dwelling.

Elle nodded her head and began predictably. "You need to move to a different building. My friend..."

She went on and Ava zoned her out. Her complete focus was on the blonde gentleman who had just walked in the front door. He was indeed tall, definitely handsome and dressed like he was going to a meeting downtown. His blue pinstripe suit breathed money and although he was slightly out of place in this consignment shop, one look at him begged forgiveness.

The gentleman walked straight in and made a bee line for Ava where she folded scarves and arranged brooches and such. "May I help you?" She asked when he got close enough.

He stared at her without speaking.

Ava shifted uncomfortably. "Is there anything I can do for you Sir?"

He continued to watch her. Elle joined them, walking up from behind him. "Sir, may I be of assistance?"

"I believe this young lady has what I need."

Ch. 15

Elle stepped aside to get a better look at him and from her wink Ava could surmise this was her visitor from the other day. She could tell by a quick assessment he did not want to shop. That left only one option. He wanted to speak to her. Although the only thing Ava could know outside of this store and school, both of which she divined did not interest him, scared Ava senseless.

As Elle walked away, Ava ran her hands over a folded scarf. "What is it I can help you find today?"

His blue eyes were icy and cold when the locked on to her tawny gold ones, his accent held the faint remnants of German origins. "You are familiar with a Mr. Pearson?" He watched her pale and gave a tiny nod of understanding. "The balance has shifted and now you have become my responsibility. If you will come with me quietly no one else has to know." He tipped his head toward Elle. "Or I can make accommodations for one more."

Ava's body went numb. Her tongue was dry and thick when she tried to answer. Giving up, she just nodded.

He smiled politely at her acquiescence. "Good. Shall we then?" He indicated the back door with one hand, the other sliding up the inside of her arm to latch on.

She couldn't hide her shiver when he touched her. "Elle, I'm going to step out for a minute, do you mind?" Sadly she knew Elle would neither mind nor would she look for her for some time, hoping this was a good thing.

The blonde chuckled over her head and guided her out with one hand tightly grasping her upper arm. She knew she was in trouble. Her instincts told her not to even try to break away, it wouldn't end well for her. This man was dangerous.

Ava was directed to a red car parked on the street. Faced with it in front of her she remembered seeing it several times in the past few days, lurking. The blonde ordered her to drive. She thought about disobeying when he walked around to the other side of the car until he opened his jacket to reveal a gun. Ava tossed all thoughts of escape out the window.

At his command she drove to an office building, parking around their back entrance doors. She looked around for video cameras and saw none.

A chuckle from the seat beside her confirmed her opinion he was way ahead of her. "They have laid off most of the employees and their security systems are on the fritz." He made a motion for scissors cutting wire.

He had taken the time to find a place with limited security and a possibility that no one would find her for several days. With a limited workforce and being at the end of the week, a body could remain undiscovered for a while. This man would be long gone by then. She struggled to keep her wits about her.

Ava had read and heard about hostages and captives getting away by inciting sympathy in their captors. She tried her hand at it with him.

"I have a mother." She blurted out. "She needs me, she's alone." She stopped, realizing she had just mentioned a living relative. Ava had no idea if his man's "responsibility" extended to anyone beyond herself.

"Dear girl." He started with a smile. His lips were thin and his smile tight revealing a strong resemblance to a lizard. "You are not going to distract me from what I've come here to do. I know better than you do who suffers when you die. That is the point."

Her heart stopped. He had said, "when" not "if" referring to her demise. Her poor mother, it would break her heart. Ava tried to think of ways to escape. Her cell phone was in her pocket and she couldn't get to it without some digging. There was no way she could do that without him catching her. What else did she have?

The sudden glare of headlights flashed across both their faces. Ava turned and saw the killer do the same, equally surprised. The lights of a tan four door that had seen better days pointed directly at them as the car parked and turned off its lights. God bless horny teenagers, thought Ava. Two witnesses had just shown up and she was not going to lose the opportunity it granted. If he killed her, he had to kill them too. Although she didn't think that would give him pause for moral reasons, she didn't think it was practical for him to be able to keep all three contained long enough to do it.

While he assessed the threat of the car, Ava lunged. She threw her hands at him and managed to push a few fingers into one of his eyes. Partially blinded and fully angry, the killer swore and threw his hands up to protect his face. She took the keys from the ignition and threw them out the window into the lot. Running toward the parked teenagers, Ava waved her hands and shouted for help.

Startled there was someone in the other car not doing what they were, they started their car and drove away, tires screeching. Ava was at a loss but couldn't waste time with moping or shock. She was relatively familiar with this area; it was only a few miles from her store. She ran through yards and commercial lots trying to stay off the main road, assuming he would be chasing her in the car.

Ava knew there was a gas station less than half a mile down the road. It would be a dark road, and if she was fast she might be able to lose him. Thanking her lucky stars she hadn't worn the heels and skirt she'd eyeballed before settling on pants and more runner friendly footwear that morning, Ava bolted. She ran as fast as she could and, as much as she wanted to look behind her, she kept her eyes forward running with everything she had.

Out of breath and sweating, Ava slowed only when she crossed over the grassy hill into the well lit parking lot. Relief weakened her knees when she saw the crowded parking lot of the station.

Standing at the edge of the lot, deciding on her best defense, Ava felt her phone vibrate in her pocket. Puzzled, she watched the number pop up on the screen. Furious at him for his part in all this, she answered.

"I don't know what you're doing, but it's not going to work. Your guy came into the shop. Tons of people saw him and could describe him to the police." She left out that she was nearly pushed out by her overeager employer, the only witness that she'd left with the killer. "Call him off. I know you can. I'm going to go to the police and your detective friend is going to be very interested to hear that you're trying to kill an innocent girl. There's no way the police will let you get away with that, even if you *are* under their protection, I don't care who you've got dirt on." Ava was near exhaustion physically and mentally, silently she cursed Ben for his part in that. Her eyes threatened to leak and she cursed them too for their betrayal, pushing them back with a healthy dose of anger.

Ben's response was slow and deliberate. "Ava, I was calling to warn you they're coming after you. That is a very bad man. You have to run."

"Don't try to play the good guy. This guy showed up in the store right after I get back from finding you? I'm supposed to believe you want to *warn* me? I think it's far more likely you *sent* him. He said because of you, I'm his responsibility now."

His tone changed. He worked to hide the frustration building behind his words. "Ava, I know you don't want to, and I have no right to ask you to, but you have to believe me. I would never hurt you."

"Hah." Near breaking, her voice cracked.

Continuing, Ben started to sound desperate. "You can't go home tonight Ava. It's not safe."

"Duh. I know that. I saw him at my building the other night. You should be more careful who you hire in the future. Only an idiot tells someone their plan to kill them before they do it." She hated him for how little he thought of her intelligence.

He exhaled loudly, clearly frustrated. "You don't understand. I didn't send him. Someone else did. When I…" He faded away. "Can you go somewhere until I can get there?"

Ava guffawed, dumbfounded. "Are you kidding me? Call off your hit man. If you or he get anywhere near me, I'm calling the police. You and all of your crazy friends can go to hell. Leave me and my family alone." She slid her phone shut.

Walking into the station, Ava asked to see their phone book. She stood at the counter while she waited for a cab, hoping he would be quick. She had offered the dispatcher double if he could get a car here fast. Not often disappointed by the motivational factor of greed, Ava cracked a smile when she saw the white and blue cab pull up less than five minutes later.

Looking around she didn't see any sign of the blonde. To be safe, she offered to pay the cabbie an additional handsome tip if he could get her to the Radisson two towns over, fast. To prove her point, she flashed the card she always kept in her pocket. Mom didn't raise a fool. Always have money on you at all times, she had said. You never know when a date is going to go badly or a friend is going to make a bad choice, and purses are easily lost. The engine growled as the cabbie's greed overtook his fear of the police and speed limits. Ava nervously watched out the back window for signs of pursuit.

Ch. 16

Ava checked into the hotel and had to use her card, telling the desk clerk she was fleeing a domestic situation and would like them not to tell anyone if someone came looking for her. His eyes widened at the mention of her violent boyfriend and she could tell from his youthful indignation that he would consider this a personal mission.

She walked away from the desk, unable to stop looking over her shoulder and rode the elevator to the eighth floor. Ava made sure all of her doors and windows were locked and curtains drawn before she sat down on the corner of the bed. Her bones were screaming for her to lie down and rest but her mind was wired.

Ava called down to the front desk and asked to have a toothbrush sent up. The same desk clerk answered and said that he would have one sent up right away from the store. She wanted to shower although she didn't know if she could relax enough to get undressed. Paralyzed by paranoia, Ava stayed right where she was on the bed and turned on the television for background noise.

She was staring at a show about a guy who lived with lions on National Geographic when the knock at the door scared her two feet into the air. She got up and snuck barefoot to the door to peer out the peephole. There stood the young desk clerk glancing anxiously up and down the hall. Opening the door, she saw him smiling and holding a basket. In it was a cornucopia of goods from the store below. She nearly lost it thanking him for his thoughtfulness. He blushed uncomfortably, told her it was nothing, and excused himself.

Ava locked the door behind him with the deadbolt and sliding lock. She sat back down on the bed to assess her booty. The kind clerk had gifted her mouthwash, a razor, toothbrush and toothpaste, coffee singles, cream and sugar and, bless him, a split of Cabernet.

Determined to give him a shining review of her stay, Ava sat down and twisted the cap off her bottle. She watched a repeat of Friends and then turned it to HBO. It was showing a marathon of a series about vampires and other supernatural creatures. Too tired to get up, she watched it, scaring herself even more.

The effects of the wine and her exertions wore on her, and by the end of the second vampire show, Ava was unable to keep her eyes open. She slept in her clothes in case she had to run in the night. Her shoes lay beside the bed for quick retrieval and she propped a chair under the doorknob as a backup security measure and alarm system. When she finally slept, it was to the sound of the inane music on the information channel provided by the hotel and she dreamt strange dreams of Ben fighting with the doctor in the head light over who would get to kill her and drink her blood.

Soft knocking on the door woke Ava from a dead sleep. She was groggy from the wine and disoriented being in a strange place. Glancing around she tried to get her bearings. A second round of knocking hurried her to her feet and she got up to answer the door.

Cautiously, she looked through the peep hole and saw a uniformed hotel employee standing at the door holding a tray. Her stomach growled and told her to answer it. Saying a silent thank you to the night clerk who must have arranged it, she opened the door and accepted the tray with a grateful smile.

Ava was setting the tray on the little table by the door when she heard another knock. Wondering what the employee had forgotten, she opened the door without looking. The moment she turned the knob, a strong hand pushed it open the rest of the way and a blur of motion rushed in. She felt a hand against her chest driving her backward and she screamed, stumbling into the side of the table. The tray of food was knocked aside and the door swung shut behind them.

Ava was terrified but she was not going down easily. She flailed at her assailant, sure these were her last moments. Experienced and stronger than her by far, he quickly had her under control. In seconds, Ava was pinned under a pair of strong legs as he straddled her thighs, his hands pinning her arms up over her head on the floor. She was nose to nose with Ben, the single most despicable person in her world. And she was once again trapped.

"How did you find me?" She spat, furious at him, and at herself for being careless. "People know I'm here, you know. I called my mom last night and Elle is on her way. I don't know who you really are or what you've told the police to earn their protection but they'll send you to jail for this. You can't hurt me." She was babbling just to hear noise and cover the sound of her pounding heart and distract her from her fear.

Ben waited for her to run herself out, his face impassive. When she had, his voice was soothing, like he was calming a frightened animal. "Ava, I am not going to hurt you. Why would I save you if I wanted to harm you?"

"How dare you bring that up! You're nothing like the man that saved me. He was kind and gentle. You stick to cases of cheating husbands and hidden files for bastard children. I'll see you in jail before you lay another hand on me." It was a claim she had no way to back up, made even more ridiculous by the fact that he was doing exactly that while she threatened him.

His hands shifted so he held both wrists in one large hand and used the other to cover her mouth and muffle her shouts. His tone was tighter, tense when he spoke again, this time much louder. "Ava please! I am trying to tell you that I wasn't the one who turned you in to Peter. He works for people you don't want to know. They think you know something you shouldn't and they want to kill you for it."

Heart pounding, her eyes narrowed and her mouth moved against his palm as she disagreed with his assertion that he had nothing to do with this whole situation.

Ben kept his hand firmly in place and lowered his voice. "I'll tell you everything but you have to agree to come with me. I can keep you safe." His eyes burned with an undeniable intensity that frightened her.

Ava stared into them, unsure what to do. He either was telling the truth or was a very good liar. Either way, she liked her odds better with Ben than Peter. At least for now. The blonde had been a cool customer, not one to be swayed or put off by distraction like she had proven Ben could be.

In a show of good faith Ava stopped fighting and calmed her expression by sheer force of will. Ben slowly removed his hand from her mouth. She licked her lips to wet them. Calmly, she asked him. "What do we do now?"

He didn't appear completely convinced yet he swung his leg back over her body so that he was kneeling beside her, her hands still controlled easily by one of his. "We need to get out of here." He lowered his face closer to her and winked. "And you need to brush your teeth."

Cursing, she flipped away from him and he let her. She slipped into the bathroom to dress again and make good use of her courtesy basket. Ben took a seat on the chair she had left beside the front door. Less than ten minutes later she emerged, relatively decent looking, she thought. Her hair was pulled back, face and teeth clean and her clothes were pulled into somewhat passable order.

Ben stood when she entered the room. "Are you ready?"

She tried not to show her disgust with him, forcing a smile instead as she strode toward him wearing everything she had brought with her. She didn't even have room in her pockets for any of the amenities the hotel had given her.

He opened the door for her and stepped out, glancing in all different directions before motioning for her to follow. She did so and looked around them as well as she emerged snorting at her foolishness for buying into his bodyguard charade.

Ava recognized the black car in the lot when she stepped outside. It was a beautiful morning and quite a few people were out on the streets already, this being in a heavily pedestrian part of downtown. That was part of why Ava had picked it. It was easier to hide in a crowd and there were an infinite number of witnesses if she needed them.

He pushed her toward the passenger side. Ava considered breaking free for a moment, like last night. Then realized she would fare no better if she did run. He had found her here, Ben could find her anywhere.

The car quickly left the city, merging onto I-94 and heading south. Ben did not apparently believe in radios, his was the only car she'd ever been in without one and regrettably, Ava was left with no distractions other than the passing scenery.

"So, where are we going?" She asked, not able to completely hide her irritation. "Do you have *another* life you can just step in to? Maybe somewhere warm? What are you going to do with me? Detective Sharpe knows you know me." Ava hid how scared she was behind general nastiness.

He laughed bitterly and shook his head. "You're too smart for your own good." He shot her a look. "Do you know that?"

She took his question for a warning and clamped her mouth shut, crossing her arms tightly across her chest for comfort.

Ben glanced over at her sulking silently and his mouth went wide, incredulous. "You're mad at me? I save you from a killer, and *you* are mad at *me*?" He laughed acerbically and shook his head. "That is just perfect."

Ava barely considered what he was saying. That had been a hit man *not* hired by Ben? She found that hard to believe. Her life had been relatively mundane before she had met him. “No one wanted to hurt me *before* I met you. You get full credit for this one.”

Ben’s jaw tightened, the cording stood out in his neck and his eyes narrowed. He glanced over at her, furious. “Well, that’s not entirely true now is it?”

Ava blanched. She had seen how strong he was and at the hotel he was impossibly fast. She was being foolish to poke him like this. Temporarily cowed, Ava pushed herself into the far corner of her seat, away from Ben and remained quiet to wait and see what his plans for them were. He said not another word as the miles rolled by.

Ch. 17

In the late afternoon Ben exited the freeway just past Des Moines. He maneuvered the car through a series of turns, going past a Radisson to a stop at a small mom and pop motel. She looked questioningly at him.

He faced forward, refusing to look her way. “I’ve been traveling for nearly twenty-four hours. My eyes need rest. No one will look for us here.”

Ben got out, stretching as he shut his door. Ava stepped out as well and watched him closely over the roof opposite him. There were very few cars in the lot and no town to speak of around her. She didn’t want to raise his suspicions by making an escape attempt that wasn’t going to work. So for the time being she went along, patiently waiting for the right moment.

Ben went around to the trunk, pulling out a small cooler and overnight bag. He offered no explanation and Ava didn't want to admit she was curious about anything he did.

Together they entered the motel's small lobby. Ava studied the television behind the desk clerk while Ben checked them in under a false name. She watched the newscaster, an offensively friendly man, reasonably attractive if it weren't for his plastic looking hair. Ava hated the news. It was filled with close ups of people suffering, as well as stories of children being hurt. On some level, Ava supposed she'd always known what had happened to her, she was only beginning to connect it all now.

The newscaster was interviewing a woman from Social Services, declared the caption at the bottom of the screen. She was saying that the "median age of teen runaways has dropped significantly over the last several decades. Before 1980 the median age was fifteen, but after 2000 it had dropped to thirteen with some children leaving home for the first time by the age of ten."

The camera flashed back to the newscaster and his contrived sobriety. "The FBI reports that the number of runaways who return home has also declined to less than twenty-five percent. The vast majority simply disappear."

Ava was too old to be considered a teen runaway, yet she wondered if anyone would look for her when she didn't come home.

Ben's hand on her elbow made her jump. She glanced up to see he was also watching the news report, face set in hard lines making him appear older than his twenty-seven years. "Let's go." He turned to guide her to their room.

It was a small motel, only two floors. Their room was on the upper floor at the end. Ava walked in and went about the room doing her usual door, window and closet check. In a heightened level of paranoia, she even looked in the shower and under the bed. When she finished, she pulled the drapes and the light turned on behind her. Whirling, she saw Ben had his hand on the light switch, a curious expression on his face.

She looked past him and saw the door was locked, a chair under the knob. He had pulled the drapes in the front of the room as well. This was an older motel and had only a bed and bathroom with a counter along one wall containing a minifridge and a coffee maker. There was no sitting area, and no chair or couch. Ava refused to think about the sleeping arrangements just yet.

Ben set his cooler down on the counter, his overnight bag on the bed. "I don't suppose you have a change of clothes, do you." It wasn't a question.

"No, your charming friend didn't think I needed a change of clothes since he planned on killing me." She couldn't stop herself from pushing him.

Ben sighed and ran his hand through his hair doing a good job of looking remorseful. "You still don't trust me. I'm sorry, but I have to do this." He opened his bag and she heard the clanking of metal before she saw the handcuffs.

Her eyes went wide and Ava felt the terror beginning to ice her mind. "No, you can't do that. I'll scream!" She was backing away, shaking her head. Panic rose in her chest, her voice rising shrilly. "What if he finds me? I won't be able to run. You can't do this to me. You can't." She heard herself begging, it didn't matter. Anything to keep from being tied up.

Ben paused at the change in her. Gone was the sarcastic, angry woman he'd been facing. Ava was a frightened, wide eyed girl pleading with him for her very life. Out of necessity he approached her with the cuffs anyway. "Ava," he tried to soothe her as he reached for her. "I can't take you with me before dark, people are looking for you. If you're seen, I can't guarantee your safety and we both know that as soon as that door shuts behind me, you'll leave. Please, this is for your own good."

She was beyond reasoning, she felt herself cracking. Eyes wild, she backed herself up against the wall. Breaking into hysterical tears, Ava slid down, holding her hands behind her back, burying her face in her knees as she shook her head. "No, no, no."

He pulled her hands forward and fixed one end on her wrist before picking her up. Her body was limp, all fight gone from her, as he carried her. Even her sobs had gone silent. Ben laid her on the bed and attached the other cuff to the metal frame holding the headboard to the wall. Given her state, Ben didn't gag her. She stared blankly up at him.

Ben straightened, his expression unreadable. "The store is less than a mile away, I'll be right back. I promise."

Ava didn't move the entire time he was gone. Her body was still curled up on the bed when Ben returned after the fastest shop of his life fifteen minutes later.

He dropped the bag beside the door taking only long enough to secure it before he hurried to unlock her. She didn't move, eyes fixed on the ceiling with a blank expression on her face. She didn't try to pull away when Ben put his hand on her back, stroking her softly. "I know you didn't like that, but you dying is worse. You can't understand that I broke the rules, and now I have put you in danger. This is my fault and it's up to me to find a way out of this for you."

She didn't move. Ben's stroking became more insistent, searching for a response from her. "Ava, you need to get up. I have clothes for you. You've been seen in those, you should change. If you're hungry we can get room service."

He was babbling, his voice came to her from a million miles away and the words meant nothing. Ava heard Ben's voice on the phone when he called for food. Choices were limited in such a small hotel and he ordered everything on the menu.

When he heard the knock on the door, Ben hopped up and afforded a quick look out the peep hole to confirm it was only the food. He took the trays, not allowing the woman entrance. Again he secured the door before returning to her. He tried to interest her in food with no response.

Ava barely noticed when he picked her up and carried her into the bathroom. Then, in a rush, snapped back to full awareness when the shock of the freezing cold water hit her. She choked and braced her hands against him, trying to push off Ben's chest, not wanting to be touching him. After a brief struggle, her strength failed her, leaving her lying limply on his body. His eyes were troubled, staring down at her when she looked up. She saw the worry etched on his face. He hadn't known about the extent of her fear, torture had not been his intention in locking her up.

Her voice was hoarse when she spoke. "Don't tie me up again."

"I won't."

Her teeth started to chatter and Ben reached forward to turn up the hot water. His arms wrapped around her, holding her close for a long time. Finally, her strength returned to her and she struggled against him. This time he loosened his hold, letting her pull away.

Reaching behind herself she turned off the water and opened the curtain. Being closest, she grabbed a towel off the rack over the toilet for each of them. Ben nodded, still staring at her as though she were going to break at any moment.

Ava was ashamed he had seen her deepest fear, its origins only recently having become clear. She had been incapable of controlling her panic when restrained. Ben had seemed so genuinely worried, angry as she was at him for restraining her, she wondered if she should give him a chance to explain himself. Though the last time she'd given him something, he'd used it to manipulate her. Ava held her tongue.

She watched him closely as she dried off over her clothes before stepping out of the shower onto the tile, being careful not to slip. Ben was doing the same until he chuckled. It was a warm, pleasant sound.

"This isn't working." Setting down his towel on the sink, he began to unbutton his shirt. Seeing Ava's nervous reaction, he put a hand out. "Just my shirt, don't worry."

She let out a tense breath and turned to give him some privacy, still too dripping wet to walk out onto the carpet. Ben's shirt flopped to the bottom of the tub with a wet smack and the movement of his arm reaching for his towel caught her eye.

When she had turned her back to him, she had unwittingly come to face the mirror running the full width of the wall. Glancing up at the flash of motion, she caught sight of his chest and arms and froze, catching her breath.

Ben's body was well put together, she'd seen that through his clothing and couldn't help feeling it when they'd been close. Yet that was not what made her gasp. Her reaction was due to the large patchwork of angry scars marring his pale flesh. They were over his heart, on his upper arms and inside his elbows, as well as a long jagged silver scar running down one hip to disappear into his pants.

He stopped at the sound, staring at her in the mirror.

She told his reflection, "I'm going out to get changed. Give me a few minutes, okay?"

His image nodded, never breaking eye contact. She couldn't read his expression, it's boldness made her nervous.

She was dressed in the black running suit and shirt he had bought her, only mildly uncomfortable to put on a pair of underwear she found in the bag, grateful for once she wasn't well endowed and didn't have to have a bra to function.

"Ava?" Ben called from the bathroom.

"Yes?"

"Could you bring my bag to me?" He hesitated. "And the cooler? Please?"

She brought him both despite her discomfort with what she guessed was in the cooler. The door had been swung mostly shut and she reached inside, setting both on the counter. The mirror positioned how it was, Ava couldn't help seeing Ben's image. He had removed his pants and was bent at the waist, drying the leg propped up on the edge of the toilet affording her a view of his side.

She stared a little too long. He sensed her attention and again met her gaze in the mirror. Blushing hotly, she stepped back and pulled the door all the way shut behind her.

It wasn't until she heard the bathroom doorknob turn that she realized she could have left. A mostly naked man chasing a woman down the road certainly would draw attention. It hadn't been a conscious decision, and yet now that she thought about it, she wanted to know what was going on and he had promised to tell her everything. Even if she could eventually get away from Ben, she would need to know what she was up against for the future. Ava was willing to gamble that Ben was telling her the truth, at least about the man following her being bad. What remained less clear was *his* role in all of this.

When he emerged, clad in jeans and a gray Henley, Ben was running his hands through his still damp hair reminding Ava hers hadn't been touched.

"Do you have a hairbrush in that bag?" She imagined she looked like birds had been living on her head.

He raised his eyebrows at her ordinary request, taking it for a good sign. "Yes, there are a few essentials in there. I left them on the counter for you."

Happy to look somewhat normal on the outside, even if the inside didn't match, Ava emerged from the bathroom a few minutes later. She knelt on the edge of the bed opposite where Ben was sitting.

"Okay. I'm listening."

Looking past her at the food on the counter, Ben pointed to the trays behind her. "Best to hear this on a full stomach."

They picked through and each settled on something palatable in its now cool form, Ben gave Ava first choice. She took the chicken sandwich, Ben the cheeseburger.

He took a bite, chewed it carefully and sighed. "What I'm telling you is a closely guarded secret. You cannot share it with anyone. Ever."

Ava nodded somberly, munching on a cold French fry. She would have thought him melodramatic if it weren't for the appearance of the man intent upon killing her yesterday.

Ben was uncertain how to begin. Finally, he scratched his head roughly and began. "Throughout history people of every culture have had a fascination with blood. Each culture has its own lore concerning humans and gods who gain power or different attributes by taking blood from others. Then, five hundred years ago, doctors trying to save the life of Pope Innocent VIII made the first recorded effort at a blood transfusion. It worked temporarily, although the Pope eventually died. Doctors continued to develop the science using animals for human transfusions but the process was flawed. There were a number of unfortunate complications and in 1678 they were outlawed in Paris."

Ava curled her upper lip in disgust. "Animal blood?"

He raised an eyebrow. "How is that hard to believe? We grow ears on mice and harvest pig ligaments for human transplants. It all started with blood."

"I guess." It was still gross to think about pig blood circulating in a human's body.

"Philadelphia, 1795, an American physician credited with being the father of modern medicine, Philip Physick performed the first successful human to human blood transfusion in America."

Ava sat up. "The movers. That was the name on the truck."

He nodded. "Physick tried to publish his findings, only his methods were being criticized and politics prevented him from receiving the recognition he deserved. Frustrated with the medical community, he took his research to private donors. The company who owns that truck is just a small part of a larger corporation started long ago by Doctor Physick to continue his research. Since then, they have branched out into myriad different areas doing a lot of good things." Ben roughed his knuckles against his jaw. "At the time of his work, Physick wasn't satisfied with merely achieving a successful transfusion. He became obsessed with the idea that the recipient would take on the health and properties of the donor." Ben took another bite of his burger and chewed methodically.

"Do you mean blood diseases?" Ava tried to clarify.

Ben shrugged his shoulders. "Sort of. Only Physick went beyond that. He thought things like strength and intelligence would transfer. His experiments took a strange turn. He tried some different things, experimenting with male to female transfusions, he brought back animal to human transfusions hoping for hybridization, all sorts of things. Eventually even the private donors distanced themselves from him in his madness."

He picked a piece of strawberry off his plate and threw it up to catch it in his mouth. Ava raised an eyebrow and he winked at her. His playful side was unexpected.

"Somehow or another, right around 1810 a German doctor, Gerhard Bruder joined Physick after he hit on something quite genius. Youth was the key. If a donor was young, the blood was more potent. The recipient recovered faster and was rejuvenated for some time after a treatment. They tried with younger and younger donors, discovering that transfusions given on a regular basis from young donors fought free radicals in the body. Have you heard of the free radical theories on aging?"

Ava had some biology classes in her undergraduate work and recalled hearing of the theory. "Isn't it that the body creates free radicals that cause cellular degeneration?"

Ben's eyebrows went up and he smiled approvingly. "Right. The theory is that just by functioning the body creates free radicals. A free radical is an atom with an extra electron. They are created by our eating, exercising, by our very existence. It's the free radicals in the mitochondria that serve as our biological clocks. What Physick and Bruder found was that the infusions of young blood fought the free radicals and acted as antioxidants in the mitochondria themselves. They discovered the fountain of youth."

He finished and took another bite before pushing away his plate. Ava was done too and took their plates back to the counter, filling two glasses with water in the bathroom while she was up. When she returned, she handed him one and tilted her head curiously.

"That's fascinating, but I don't see how that has any effect on us here and now. It would be pretty valuable to a lot of people if they could find that technology. Still, it doesn't explain Peter and I'm not young anymore so they can't want my blood." Her last words faded out. "Was that what happened to me?"

"Yes," he was watching her, his expression guarded. "Physick made a practice of siphoning off a small amount of blood and using laudanum to confuse the kids' memories. They were left somewhere they would be discovered, and after a few days they were completely recovered."

"The man I remember was taking a lot from me. I remember being so weak."

Ben's face clouded over. His voice was tight. "After they figured out that youth was the key, Physick and Bruder had a falling out. Bruder got it in his head that some children were more potent than others, that their blood somehow deflected damage to their cells. Children that survived accidents often caught his eye." Ava's mouth dropped open. Ben nodded, continuing. "When you survived the accident that killed your father and the paper did a story on it, they targeted you. The 'special' kids, Bruder drained completely, not wanting to let any of the blood go. Physick tried to control Bruder, to stop him. He wasn't successful and Bruder eventually had him killed."

Ava was nodding along, following the lesson as completely plausible from what she knew of science until she hit a roadblock. "Wait, if Physick and Bruder were doctors two hundred years ago, Bruder would be dead by now. Are these people his followers or something?"

Ben shook his head slowly. He met her eyes steadily. "Bruder's still alive."

Ava covered her mouth with her hand, whispering the impossible. "Oh my God, he's immortal. Is he a vampire?"

"No, not immortal but the modern vampire stories have a lot in common with those like him. He's still human and can be killed, although if he can get a transfusion of young blood in time, he can actually heal from most life threatening injuries. The problem is, once he started doing the transfusions, he had to continue them or his true age would catch up with him. It goes faster as the blood leaves his system."

"How often does he need transfusions? How much does he need?" The impossible wove its way into her reality.

"A syringe every couple of days is enough to maintain his body, an injury takes more. Usually, however much blood is lost, and then the maintenance dose on top of that."

Ava felt something else click in her head and backed away, pointing at Ben. Shock paled her features. "Your condition, the needles. You do it too!"

He remained perfectly still. "Yes, I do."

"Why? Who's the blonde guy, Peter? What does he have to do with it?"

"Sometimes the kids who are taken remember, in spite of the drugs. If they put enough of it together, Bruder sends someone to 'clean up.' He figured out that you remembered something, and now you're in danger."

"How does he know I remember? You're the only person I told." Her tone turned accusatory, her eyes narrowed. "Did you tell him?"

Ben denied it vehemently. "No, I would never do that. But his people are never far from me. When I saw you in the store it was an unfortunate accident, a lapse on my part. You weren't supposed to be there. That's why I came back that night after I saw you leave. I didn't want to give them any reason to doubt your memory loss. Then, when you came to my home, I knew I had to disappear before they came after you." He smiled unhappily. "I told you you were too smart for your own good. You and that damned internet. Then, you showed up when the movers came." Ben's nod confirmed that he'd known. "They reported a strange woman in the house when they got there and I wasn't the only one who figured it out. The information got to Bruder's people somehow and when you found me in Billings, your fate was sealed. Now they won't quit until they kill you."

Ava stared at him, again questioning her sanity. "It *was* you who saved me." She watched his features soften at her acceptance of the inconceivable. "Why?"

His expression turned troubled. "After Bruder developed this 'special child' theory he went from taking *some* blood to all of it and killing the children. Murder drew a lot of attention and he and his people had to move around. It began happening only a few years before you were taken and when it did, I started to follow them through the news reports of accident survivors. I was too late, every time. Their man inside gets them the news before it goes out on the wire. Bruder and his people always beat me there, leaving me to clean up after them. I've buried more children than I care to count." Frustrated, he ran his hands through his hair. "I almost had them in Holland and then he came back to the states and I lost them again."

"When the report on *your* accident came, I happened to be closer and got there first. I watched you, knowing it was a matter of time before they came for you." Ben's lips drew up tight in frustration. "When they did come, they did on a day I'd left my gun behind and had to choose. Save you and give them up, or lose you and go back for the gun and try to track them." He waved a hand at her. "You know what I chose and I'm glad that I did." The smile he offered was a tired one. "I checked back with you a lot, making sure you were safe. When you were fourteen, that's when they consider a child's blood too old to be beneficial, you were truly safe from them. Until now."

"If you're working against them, why do they let you live?"

Ben tugged at his sleeve, unable to look at her. "Because I'm Physick's son."

Ch. 18

"What?"

"Philip Physick was my father." He repeated flatly. "Bruder is mad but he's not a fool. My father had enough sense left to see that Bruder wanted to push him out. Father kept vital information on the conversion process and maintenance from him. Bruder's formula is flawed and he and his staff are fading. It's slow, but their age is progressing. To fix it, he needs my father's research notes and only I know where those are. That is why I'm alive today."

"Your *father* did this to you?" Ava could see wanting to keep your child with you through eternity but to subject him to daily blood injections, making him live like he had a life threatening disease, all while taking blood from innocent kids. It was wrong, unthinkable. "Why, because he didn't want to see his kid die?"

Ben wasn't offended by Ava's accusations of his father. He patted the mattress, inviting her to come back. Ava accepted and eased herself back down across from him.

"When I was twenty-seven, I was on my way from my family's home in Philadelphia to visit a friend in New York. The carriage overturned and I was the sole survivor. By the time my father was summoned a priest was reading my last rites. Father was beside himself. I was his only son and he had already lost my mother in childbirth as well as most of his reason, quite honestly. He let the doctors think he was bringing me home to die, that was not unusual back then. Except he brought me to the lab and gave me a transfusion so large that it took the life of a young child. He traded someone else's child for his own."

Ava could see the trouble that caused him and couldn't fathom the guilt that would bring with it. "I never wanted to be a part of my father's experiments, but to have let myself die would have meant the child who died for me had died in vain. I've devoted my life to helping others and saving the children Bruder would have destroyed. After he began killing children, I made it my personal mission to keep Bruder and his people from killing more innocents." Ben's face hardened. "I've taken on others to help me search and we have met with success on numerous occasions. My goal remains the same; I will catch him and I will kill him. Until then I must remain as I am."

"You take blood, I've seen it. How are you any better than him?"

"Yes, I need transfusions." Raising his hand to stop her protest, he added, "But I have a phlebotomist friend. Whenever she draws blood from a healthy candidate, she takes a small amount extra. No one is harmed by my living, and she gets extra money to take care of her children." He smoothed his shirt and sat up straighter. "Physick Enterprises continues my father's research today. After he saw the ongoing need for transfusions and Bruder went off the rails, my father began to search for an alternative to blood. A research facility in Oregon has been working on a synthetic blood alternative for nearly thirty years. We are very close. It will let those of us who want to continue this way do so causing no harm to anyone."

"Well, why not kill Bruder? You've probably had another chance in the past sixteen years."

"No, I haven't. After that night when I saved you, Bruder went underground. There have been rumors that he's been conducting his own research, attempting to discover what he's missing, although it's nothing concrete. I haven't been able to find him since. I continue to follow stories of children who are abducted, run away under mysterious circumstances, or survive accidents figuring our paths will cross eventually and the next time, I will be ready."

Ava was quietly mulling it all over, her fingers tracing the outlines of pastel flowers on the aged bedspread beneath them. "So you'll never get any older or die as long as you have 'young blood'?"

Ben tipped his head one way, then the other in a pseudo nod. "Sort of. You see, the blood fights the effects of the radiation our bodies produce, but if I were to treat my body badly the blood would have a limited effect and the transfusion results would not be as long lasting. I would need more blood." He nodded when she wrinkled her nose. "Exactly, so to limit our needs, we eat healthy natural foods and virtually never drink alcohol. I grow most of my own vegetables and am experimenting with hybrids that will be more potent than those on the market. And, as you noticed, I keep my home at sixty-five degrees. The combination of all of those factors slows our bodies' natural production of free radicals. The regular infusions take care of the rest."

"So that's why you had the greenhouses in your closet." His eyes flicked up in surprise.

Ava shrugged, no longer embarrassed that he knew she'd been at the house. "I saw the marks on the carpet and the realtor was funny about showing me the garage. So, I found the key and checked it out on my own. I saw them in your garage."

Unexpectedly, Ben threw back his head and laughed. "You are something, Ava. Maybe *you* should be the private eye."

She laughed too, "Yeah, I *am* something all right. A fool."

He sobered. "Except for a time when I was called away, I have watched over you since that night. You have always been special to me, and it means a great deal to have you fighting *with* me and not against me." He stood an arms length from her and reached out to run a hand down her hair, he watched his fingers slide through it.

Ava was dumbstruck. All that time she'd felt safe, it had been him. The mysterious stranger who had saved her, the feeling that a spirit had been watching over her she'd assumed had been her long dead father; all of it had been Ben. Sadly, she let go of the last vestige of belief that her father had been her hero all that time.

While it made her sad, she did not feel lost. Instead, she chose to see her father's hand in it after all. Her father had sent Ben to do what he couldn't. The very accident that had taken him from her had brought Ben.

Feeling peace at the revelation and gratitude for his years spent keeping her from Bruder, Ava leaned forward and put her arms around him feeling the welcome return of the comfort she had felt only from him. There was no question that, in her heart, she believed him. It all made sense to her. Even the lost feeling she'd had when she was fourteen and her mother had given her the ring; it had been at the same time as he'd left.

Ben stiffened in surprise at the gesture only for the briefest moment before wrapping his arms around her as well. His hand came up to stroke the back of her head and he twisted his neck to put her face under his chin. She nuzzled more securely against his chest.

Ava wiggled closer on her knees, unable to get enough of the security he offered and she needed. Her body grew warm against his and she was very aware of everywhere they were touching. She saw him in her mind's eye, toweling off.

Suddenly, Ben's hand froze on her head and he stopped breathing. "We have to go." He pushed Ava gently, albeit firmly away. "Grab your things. We need to move now."

Confused, Ava watched him rush around the room gathering their clothing and pulling a gun out of his bag to tuck in the back of his waistband. His black sport coat hid the bulge when he slid it on giving Ava insight into why he always wore one. "What's going on Ben? I thought we were safe here."

He zipped his bag, his back to her and mumbled. "I see things sometimes."

"Pardon?" Ava sat back down on the bed.

Frustrated, Ben turned to face her and frowned when he saw her sitting. "Ava, we have to go. He's coming."

Ava's brow furrowed, "How do you know he's coming? What do you mean, you see things?"

Feigning patience he didn't feel, he knelt down in front of her and put his hands on the either side of where she sat. "Didn't you wonder how I found you at the hotel?"

She nodded.

"Sometimes, after we have been alive for a while, we develop certain awarenesses. Kind of like ESP."

"Ben, I am about at my limit for the day. If you throw another crazy thing at me, I think my head will explode." She was only half joking.

He took her hands. "After I touch someone, I can find them anywhere. That's how I knew he'd gotten you. I could see you together and it scared me. After I called you and you accused me of trying to kill you..."

Ava tried to interrupt, to apologize for her accusations, but Ben pressed on.

"I knew he'd found you and they wouldn't believe me that our meeting was coincidence. I knew what he would do." Ben bowed his head. "I'm sorry, I was distracted. I didn't see him this time until now. I can tell you that he's close and we have less than five minutes to get out of here. Maybe less."

"Okay." Ava said weakly. Her reality was completely out of whack. She walked dazedly to the counter, grabbed his bag and stood by the door.

Ben grabbed the cooler and the towel holding their wet clothes, stopping to jam it into the bag. He finished, taking it from her and nodded for her to open the door. He walked out first, looking both ways before motioning for her to follow. They walked quickly, trying not to draw attention, to the car to avoid suspicion. Once out of the lot, Ben stepped on the accelerator and the muscle car responded gladly.

"He's still following us." Ben's voice broke the tense silence. "He is faster than I thought."

"How is he following us? Who is this guy?" Ava didn't understand. She hadn't seen anyone watching them at the motel, she couldn't understand how he could still be following them.

"Peter has developed an ability as well. He's a tracker. If he touches something of yours, he can follow you wherever you go, like a bloodhound." Ben glanced guiltily over at Ava. "I'm sorry I didn't see him, I should have warned you sooner."

"Who says I would have listened?" She kidded, worried it had been her fault he'd been distracted. "Does everyone like you have a special ability?" Ava watched the mile markers tick past.

Ben shook his head, staring out the windshield. "No, father didn't know why some of us develop it and why some remain normal. It could be that it comes with age. It's hard to say because there really aren't that many of us. Maybe a hundred tops unless Bruder has converted more than I suspect, although his never last long." His hands slid up to the top of the steering wheel and back down, up and down while he explained. "My father developed something different. He had always been intelligent, maybe a genius depending upon your definition of the word. Then, a few decades before he died, he unlocked a large portion of his brain most people never touch. He was able to actually foresee events before they unfolded. He could see the future."

"Then why didn't your father kill off Bruder first? Why can't you see Bruder and track him?" It seemed so simple to her understanding.

"Bruder knows about my ability and was able to keep from being touched directly by me since it developed. I can't see him. And my father knew Bruder was intending to kill him, he didn't see the assassin he sent. Neither our conditions, nor our abilities make us invincible."

"Assassin?" Ava felt her stomach lurch. "Was it the same one he sent here?"

Ben nodded grimly, lips pressed tightly together. "Peter killed my father."

They drove south all night. Ava fell asleep despite her best intentions otherwise and when she woke at sunrise the engine was quiet. The car was parked at a gas pump and the cars around them mostly had Missouri plates. Ben was out of the car and when she sat up, his coat slid down off her shoulders. She caught it before it touched the floor.

Smiling to herself she touched it, feeling the rough wool. She raised it to her nose and inhaled deeply. It was strange to think he had been a part of her life since she was a child, protecting her just like he was doing now.

Ava was deep in thought when the driver's door opened. She startled, hitting her knee on the door panel in the process. "Ow!" She rubbed it gingerly.

Ben ducked his head to hide his grin as he closed the door and set the bag of goodies on the console between them. "I didn't mean to startle you. Did you sleep well?"

"I did, thank you. I didn't know I was that tired." She shifted in her seat. "Do we have a minute? I'd like to use the restroom."

"Yes, but be quick." Frowning, Ben scanned the plaza, searching. "He's not far and I don't want to underestimate him again."

Ava drew a few stares as she jogged through the station on the way in. It was one of those larger travel plazas and the restrooms were at the back. On her way out she walked past an aisle and felt something clamp onto her arm. Her momentum swung her around and into the shelves where her ribs banged into the wire racking with brutal force. A crackling pile of candy bars hit the linoleum.

"Don't say anything or we can do this right here." The blonde assassin's hand choked up on her arm, gripping her under her armpit, fingers digging in like claws. He marched her back toward the restrooms, through the employee only door and straight out the back to where his red sedan was parked. The engine was running and in less than a minute they were on the road going back the way they had just come.

Ch. 19

Ava laid her head against the window pretending to watch the scenery whip by while she stared at the side mirror, waiting to see the black Mustang appear. Hoping to see him, and afraid she would. She didn't want to but if *she* was going to die, she didn't want anyone else to needlessly be put in harm's way.

While the miles ticked past, Ava wracked her brain trying to think of ways to get rid of Peter. She didn't know where he was taking her or how long she had before he found a spot he liked. Given their previous meeting, she assumed he would have a plan already worked out. He was too meticulous to just shoot her and throw out the body. The idea of her end worked out so coldly made her shudder.

Instead of focusing on her death and when it would come, Ava considered the vital information Ben had given her. They could be killed in the same way as any mortal being and as long as they couldn't get a transfusion, it would be permanent.

Sneaking a peek sideways, she noticed something promising. Peter was not buckled up, while she was out of habit. Orchestrating a car accident could be a very bad idea although there weren't many other ideas coming to her. It was doubtful she could get his gun off of him, he was much stronger. And jumping from a moving vehicle at highway speeds was suicide. Ava made her choice and hoped for the best despite a little voice in her head reminding her she had already gotten a miracle once in her life. She might not be so lucky to survive her second car accident.

Ava watched the scenery, only now she had a different objective. She was looking for a sharp curve or forest with trees next to the road, something that would stop the car fast. She prayed the newer car had a passenger side airbag.

The road gradually curved downhill and up ahead Ava saw a sign for a series of sharp turns and some larger pine trees growing within a few yards of the road before it twisted out of sight.

Sensing the time was near, Ava worked hard to keep from revealing her anxiety. He had to be off guard if this was going to work. They went into the first curve and Peter didn't brake, opting to float across the centerline and cut through the curve. Ava felt the car holding its speed and her stomach fluttered in anticipation, a light sweat broke out on her skin as her adrenaline surged.

The second curve went the same way, the road turning into a bridge crossing over the small river below and Peter cut through the curve in the same manner despite the buildup of speed. They were going pretty fast as they went into the third and what appeared to be the final curve.

Just as the road began to cut back over the river, Ava lunged across the car and grabbed the wheel with both hands, pulling it as hard toward herself as she could. The car shot off the road with Peter, quickly recovered from being stunned, fighting to wrestle the wheel from her. He was finally able to though not before the outside tires hit the unpaved shoulder, skidding on the gravel and dirt. The quarter panel slammed into the metal guardrail and rocked the car back onto the road. The assassin fought to right the vehicle but it was going too fast. The back slid too far the other way, striking the guardrail on the opposite side. Ava heard glass shatter with an ear popping boom and the car was sent careening back over the centerline again onto the shoulder, only this time there was no rail to catch it. The front wheel was in the lead, caught on firm footing and threw the car over, sending it into a roll.

The car flipped over and over along the right side and into the woods. When it finally came to rest against a large pine tree Ava was hanging upside down in her seatbelt. The window beside her was smashed and she could feel something warm and wet running down her forehead. Putting her hand against her scalp, she saw it come away red with blood. Not surprising. Carefully, she turned her head to see how Peter had fared. He wasn't in the car.

Hurting all over but thrilled to be alive, Ava tried to figure out the best way to get free from the wreckage. She braced one foot on the dashboard, the other on the doorframe where the window used to be and unbuckled herself. Released, her body fell forward with only her feet keeping her from going through the shattered windshield.

Slowly she picked her way out of the car, trying to avoid putting any skin against the glass littering the area around her both, inside and on the ground surrounding the site. Once clear she stood up, paying close attention to how her body felt. She couldn't feel any broken bones nor did she see any injuries other than a few cuts on her arms and face, none of which were bleeding too severely.

Upright and relatively sure she wasn't going to die from her minor injuries, Ava started looking around for Peter's body. She had read about people being thrown hundreds of feet, and with their vehicle having rolled so many times, his trajectory could have sent him in several different directions. She walked back on the outside shoulder against the tree line, eyes scanning the road and forest floor beside her until she reached where their skid marks began.

Seeing nothing, Ava crossed the road and came back down. He couldn't have walked away, he had to be there. Movement up ahead caught her eye. The shoulder dropped off about twenty feet to the river surging below, and although it appeared relatively shallow, it was wide and moving fast. The movement she had seen was indeed a man pulling himself out of the water on the far side.

The guardrail would keep her from going straight down to Peter. She would have to overshoot his position by what looked like maybe a quarter mile. Fearing he might get away, she chose to go down the embankment on the nearer side forcing her to ford the stream on foot and bringing her right to him. Given how shallow it looked she was fairly confident she could manage.

As her feet hit the water, Ava gasped in shock. She'd forgotten that this time of year the snow was melting from upstream and joined the rivers in their rush downstream. In her haste to reach Peter, she had failed to consider the icy temperatures. And she saw that the water was faster than she had anticipated. It tugged at her legs, pushing her sideways as it rose to her knees. She looked ahead and saw him, army crawling his way out the water to pull himself to safety, his legs dragging behind him nearly useless. Ava hoped if *she* didn't get to him, he would succumb to exposure and shock. Her own toes had begun to tingle already, she would have to get through the water fast and try to stay as dry as possible.

Ava thought about going back just before she reached the middle and the water was nearly to her hips. She raised her hands to chest height and gritted her teeth against the cold. Seeing how far she had already come, Ava pushed on reaching the middle of the river, the current now battering her body turned sideways to provide the smallest obstacle possible. The water reached her waist and she had to lean into it to keep her footing, still feeling herself pushed downriver in increments.

The water had gone back down to her thighs as she crossed the middle and neared the other side when her foot slipped on a slippery rock. Ava's body was plunged into the water and her feet swept out from under her. Crying out involuntarily at the shock, she felt the water close over her head. Struggling to right herself, she got her feet back under her as she was rolled downriver.

Ava was a strong swimmer but the current was unswimmable. It was rolling her end over end until she was bashed sidelong into a large rock, stopping her violently.

Her arms shot out to wrap around the offending rock and pulling herself up, she brought her head out of the water.

Her body screamed for air while she choked on the water she'd already taken in. Ava's entire being shook as she coughed to clear her lungs and regain her breath. When the coughing eased, she looked up to find she had washed up only a few yards downriver on the other side of the bridge.

Nearly across, she had to force herself from the relative safety of the rock back into the water to reach the other side where Peter continued to crawl away. Thankfully, it was less than waist high and she was able to maneuver herself the rest of the way across with minimal lost ground.

By the time she reached the other bank, she was shivering violently. Ava walked the few yards upriver, carefully picking her way over the loose rocks, falling several times as her rapidly numbing feet became less certain. When she emerged from under the shadow of the bridge, grateful to feel the sun on her face Ava felt cheated that it was not enough to stop the clatter of her teeth. She wrapped her arms around her body, uselessly trying to warm herself. Glancing up, she scanned the rocky bank for Peter.

He had made it a few more yards and now lay motionless, facedown on the rocks. Ava heard a car pass up above. She anticipated that the driver would see the wrecked car and possibly come looking. Her eyes went to the still form.

If he was left here he would die without help. Given the nearness of the road, Ava feared a Good Samaritan could undo everything she had risked herself to accomplish. Unless she made sure he was already dead by the time help arrived. She pushed herself to move faster, watchful for a rock large enough to smash in his skull in case he no longer had his gun on him, or it had been rendered useless from its time in the water. Ava was determined, Peter was not going to walk out of this alive.

Eyes on the ground, Ava misjudged the incline and her unfeeling foot hit the side of a smaller rock. Unable to catch herself, she went down on her hip. In her mind her hands came out to catch her, only her brain failed to send the message. In reality, her shoulder was the only thing that stopped her head from striking the rocks.
Her mind was muddled, she knew she had the beginnings of hypothermia. She willed herself to get up, rolling to her stomach trying to get onto her hands and knees. Even crawling she was close enough to reach her target at this point. He couldn't be more than a few yards up.

Crawling on the rocks proved slow and tricky. The partnership between her eyes and brain told her she was touching them yet she felt no sensation in her fingers or body where her knees touched the rocks. As she inched forward, the sound of rocks sliding down from above reached her ears. Fearful her labors were soon to be undone, Ava struggled forward, shaking off the knowledge that a witness could send her to jail for bashing in a man's brains. She could claim post traumatic stress disorder. The idea brought a snort. From which kidnapping would she claim as the source, she wondered.

Hands were on her. She saw the black Italian shoes in front of her face. "Ben." She looked up and saw the concern etched on his face.

He nodded, trying to smile at her. "Seems like I'm always saving you Ava."

"He's not dead yet." Ava tried to chatter through frozen lips and pointed with her chin.

Understanding, Ben stood and walked away. Ava heard him cross the rocks and pause a short distance away. Seconds later, a loud pop rang in her ears and reverberated from the rocks.

He returned to her, scooping her up in his arms. "You're freezing."

She tried to reply only she couldn't, her brain even seemed like it was freezing over. Turning her face into his chest, Ava fought to stay conscious.

This bank was not as steep as the one Ava had gone down, Ben was able to carry her out with only a few stumbles on the uneven footing. The Mustang was parked on the far side of the bridge waiting for them.

They reached the car and Ben set her down in the passenger seat, adjusting his coat over her as best he could. "We have to get you dry and warm." He got in his side and she heard the engine roar to life, dials switching and the air blowing at maximum.

Ava felt sleep dragging her down, she closed her eyes and started to fade.

Ch. 20

Ben's hand reached over, shaking her roughly. "Ava, stay with me. You need to stay awake."

"Mmm hmm." She mumbled back, knowing he was right while lacking the strength to keep her heavy lids up.

He kept talking and she felt the car moving. Its quick maneuvering on the winding road tossed her around in her seat, keeping her from sleep. She managed to open her eyes, looking over at Ben. He was turning his head, looking around them on the sides of the road. She was wondering what he was trying to find.

She heard him mutter "perfect," and the car turned abruptly right, pushing her onto the emergency brake just as she saw a flash of a red and white realtor sign. Grunting uncomfortably was all she could manage. Her body too numb to right herself, she rode that way for a few minutes before the car stopped.

Ben got out, disappeared for a minute and she heard a bang. Immediately afterward, her door opened and he retrieved her. The coat fell off and she felt a cool breeze hit her wet clothes. Ava "hmm'd" her discomfort.

"Hold on honey, almost there." Ben carried her up a short flight of stairs and she heard his shoes scuff on wood. Above her, she saw the underside of an awning. Pausing long enough to push the door open with his foot, Ben swept her inside and at once Ava felt warmer air on her face.

They went straight through the square wooden structure into a back corner where Ben laid her down on a small couch. After running over to spin the dial on the thermostat all the way up and grab a blanket off the back of a nearby recliner, he hurried to undress her. Vanity wasn't an option, she couldn't raise a hand to cover herself if she tried. The running suit and shirt were off quickly and Ava lay cold and blue, shivering in her underwear.

Ben stood up and kicked off his shoes with his feet while he pulled his shirt over his head. Ava's eyes widened when she saw him unzip his pants.

"N..n..." She stammered.

Undaunted by her objections, he pulled them off so he was standing in his blue boxers, Ben was perfectly serious. "Skin on skin is still the best way to warm a body fast."

He lay down next to her putting himself against the couch back and his arms around her to pull her tight against his chest. He held her against him with one arm, the other working to rub her arms and back. Ben pushed his legs forward to rest against hers as well. Gradually, her arguments began to ease and Ava leaned into the warmth that was Ben. Her survival instinct had tossed embarrassment aside.

Sensation slowly returned to her limbs and her mind started to work again. Seeing she was no longer on the brink of freezing to death, Ben took a moment to better spread the quilt over them both and lay back down with her. His arms went around her again and she wiggled into his body, still a long way from being warm.

"Where are we?" Ava looked around, taking in the rough boards, sparse décor and minimalistic housing they found themselves in.

"A cabin." He shifted nervously. "There are tons of seasonal cabins in the area, this one is too small to be a year rounder so I figured it would be empty while it was on the market."

Ava shivered involuntarily.

"It's cold, they still have it turned down for the winter and the beds weren't made so this was the best I could do under the circumstances."

Ava chuckled, "It feels fine to me, even like this." She suddenly became painfully aware of the fact that she was virtually naked and felt her face coloring. "Oh boy."

"You know, we *have* known each other the better part of your life." Ben pointed out, trying to put her at ease.

"I don't consider our day together or your watching me from a distance, knowing each other." Seeing them from the prospective of the homeowner walking in, Ava giggled. "What if somebody came in right now? I feel like I'm in high school again, worrying when my mom is going to come home and catch us."

His chest rumbled against her as he laughed. "Did that happen a lot?"

Ava feigned offense. "No, it did not." Emboldened by their strange circumstances, Ava asked, "How about you? Did you ever sneak anyone in?"

Ben was silent. Ava looked up and saw that he was blushing. "I was in school a very long time ago. Things were different then. Women did not just come over."

"When did you graduate from school?" Ava asked, craning her neck to see his face.

He kept his gaze focused over her head. "I finished my studies at William and Mary in 1812 at the ripe old age of twenty."

Her mind flew through the numbers. "What was your major?"

"I wanted to be a physician like my father." Ben was quiet, introspective as his memories rolled back two hundred years. "He was already struggling with the acceptance of his peers and he wanted me to be more practical. I studied business instead. It was not interesting to me, nor did I like it."

"You've seen so much. Has it been strange to see the world around you change so much?"

"It has been a mixed bag of good and bad." His thumb rubbed her shoulder absently while he spoke. "When I was born horses, river boats and walking were the recognized modes of transport. Now no one walks, horses are pets and we have ships that can carry trains. It is absolutely astounding what we have done in such a short amount of time."

His thumb continued to roll over the ball of her shoulder, his fingers resting lightly on her arm. Ava grew steadily aware of every inch of their bodies now touching, which was a lot. Her breathing accelerated and grew uneven.

Ben's hand stopped and he bent his face down close to hers, brow furrowed. "Ava, are you feeling well? Are you going to be sick?"

She didn't trust her voice, instead only shook her head with her eyes pointed directly at the ceiling. Her awkwardness making her ears burn.

Ben pulled himself away as best he could. His eyes ran across her face. He must have seen something in her expression, because he got up and went to the cabinets on the wall opposite their nest.

The kitchen contained a counter less than three feet long and a few cabinets above and below. There was a ridiculously small fridge and no stove, they probably used a camping stove or the fire in the summer when they were here. Ben tested the faucet, finding the water was off for the season and turned to search the cabinets where he found a gallon of water as well as two glasses. He poured both full and brought them back to the couch.

Ava concentrated on the glass not on Ben, his scars or his tempting body she knew he would stretch out alongside her again in just moments. She choked on her first sip, coughed several times and then remembered how to drink liquid, tipping her head up to avoid wearing it. All the while pointedly ignoring Ben's nervous glances. He waited for her glass, taking it when she was done and setting them both on the lamp table before crawling back into their warm cocoon.

She was no longer freezing and could have told him so. Even if he saw this as mere necessity, she had moved beyond the "have to" of it and was having trouble not picturing some other possibilities. It had been a very long time since she'd had a steady boyfriend she'd been physical with.

He wriggled his arm back under her and rested the other above her hip rolling her back into him.

"You never answered my question." Ava breathed, sure he could tell what her body was thinking.

His hand shifted slightly, reminding her of its intimate location. "What question was that?" He murmured in her hair.

"Women. Did your parents ever catch you with any?" She kept her face forward, speaking to his throat.

His Adam's apple bobbed as he swallowed anxiously, feet twitching a few times before he cleared his throat. "You know a gentleman never tells."

She felt her lips curve enjoying finding some real tie to his past, when he was like her. "I don't doubt you are a gentleman, but none of those ladies are even alive anymore." Ava realized the callousness of what she'd said and instantly regretted it. "I'm sorry. I didn't mean to be so cold. I can't imagine what that must be like."

"What, burying everyone you've ever known? Knowing anyone you care about will die before you? Of course you can't imagine. No one can." Ben's anger coursed through his entire body. Ava felt his muscles tighten, readying to rise.

Ava put her hand against his chest. "I'm sorry. I'm just trying to learn more about you and I'm nervous." She spread her hand on his chest watching the short hairs rise around her fingers. "It feels like I'm at a disadvantage. You know so much about me."

Ben looked down and she glanced up, staring at his dark eyes and saw the storm passing. "I must apologize as well. It isn't your fault. I've grown used to the fact that I'm alone but not the number of funerals I have attended."

Ava was touched by his grief. "You aren't alone." Surprising them both, she stretched her face up and brushed her lips gently against his.

Ben retreated, eyes wide in alarm. "Ava, you don't understand. I was not trying to take advantage of you."

Lowering her head to rest on his chest Ava hid her eyes. "I don't feel taken advantage of, I wanted to do that." Her defense sounded petulant to her ears.

Ben didn't respond right away. "Ava," he began gently. "You are very dear to me, but I cannot be with you in that way." His body tightened again and this time he did get up. "We should get going."

He put on his pants, facing away from her in a silly attempt at privacy and was pulling his shirt back over his head before jogging out to the car to get his bag. Unzipping it to pull her other clothes out, he growled in frustration. "I don't know what's less wet."

Before he could offer her anything from his things, Ava shot up, wrapped herself in the blanket and stalked out the front door without a word. She could ride in the blanket for all she cared. All she wanted at the moment was not to be in the same room as him. His dismissal had been enough. Ava felt rejected and didn't want him to see that she was hurt.

By the time he had thrown their things together and was pulling the door shut behind him Ava had already slunk down in the backseat, her blanket stretched over her arms and wrapped tightly over her chest. She could only hope they didn't get pulled over. That would be difficult to explain.

Without a word, Ben put the bag in the trunk and slammed it shut. She couldn't see his face but assumed she had made him mad somehow with her clumsy attempt to kiss him, a fact she found even more mortifying than the fact that she'd done it all. He got in, spread her clothes on the passenger seat to dry under the vents and slammed his door shut.

After an hour or so Ava couldn't tell exactly since she didn't have a watch, she asked stiffly. "When will we be home? I need to call Elle and let her know I'm not dead. Yet." She knew they would send someone else once they discovered their first man was dead.

"Don't talk like that." He sounded angry though she couldn't see him without making an obvious effort, something her injured pride would not allow.

"It's true. They're going to keep coming after me and I can't keep gambling on surviving any more car accidents. I think two is more than most can expect to walk away from in a lifetime." Ava was being stubborn, she could hear it in her voice. She couldn't help it, his treating her like a child only served to remind her the position she was in. That of his ward.

Ben only just barely kept his voice from rising. "I will keep you safe. Have I not done so in the past?"

"You can't stop them all." Ava didn't mean it harshly yet that was the effect it had on Ben.

His tone changed from anger to defeat. "I know. But I have to try."

It tore at her to know she'd caused him pain. Subdued, she lay quietly, absorbed in her thoughts. Miles down the road, Ava sat up quickly. "Ben." She cried excitedly.

"What?" The car swerved as Ben startled. He glanced up in the rearview mirror and then took a longer second look before he tore his eyes away to direct them on the road ahead.

"Bruder is really tied to this potent blood theory, right? What if we follow a story of another surviving kid and wait until he sends someone out. We can catch the guy and find out where Bruder is hiding and go get him." She watched his profile for a change and saw none. To add insult to injury, he refused to meet her eyes in the mirror. "You can at least give me an opinion." Ava felt her own temper rising as his treatment of her bordered on rude.

His expression didn't change nor did he look at her again. "I have done exactly that a number of times. This time my options are limited. How do I keep you safe while I wait for him? We have no idea when that might happen."

"What about tracking the child crime incidents like you said before? That will get you to a smaller area, right?"

"He uses people to hunt for him now and spreads out his radius. Bruder can take children from anywhere without anyone being the wiser. I send people out to as many places as we can detect as quickly as we can. It's not always enough." His jaw tightening was the only change she saw during their entire exchange.

Ava liked to look someone in the eye when she talked to them and found his aversion irksome. "Would you look at me when you talk to me?" She fumed.

He flicked his eyes up in the rearview for a few seconds and she saw them darken. "Not until you cover yourself up."

She was at once aware that her arms were cool and saw the blanket lying pooled around her waist. Blushing hotly she realized it had fallen when she had sat up. Seeing his distaste for her naked form, Ava's initial discomfit rapidly turned to anger. He had turned her away twice in as many hours. One of those times it would have been easy to see someone looking, it wasn't anything any man would gladly steal a peek of and Ben had told her to "cover up," like she disgusted him. Feminine pride is a powerful thing. Ava's was bruised and she was furious with him for it.

In a huff she unbuckled and lunged forward to reach over the passenger seat, surprising Ben again. He jerked the wheel and she hit her ribs painfully on the headrest. "Dammit Ben, settle down. I'm just trying to get my clothes."

Ben's eyes went back and forth between Ava and the road as he straightened out the car in the correct lane of the empty road.

Ava grabbed at her clothes, unable to reach now that they had fallen to the floorboards during Ben's jerky driving escapade. She sat back, put her blanket up under her arms and crossed them over her chest. "Stop the car Ben."

Ch. 21

Once the car was safely on the shoulder, Ben put it in park and spoke sharply to her reflection. "Don't you know you can't do that? I could have crashed. You could have been hurt." His eyes were black with fury.

Rubbing her freshly bruised ribs, Ava shot back. "I *am* hurt! You're the one who told me to cover myself, so I try to and you nearly kill us both. What's with you?"

Instead of answering, Ben reached down and plucked her clothing off of the floor to hand it to her.

She tore them from his hands once they were within reach. Fishing through her running suit jacket and pants, she threw down the ball of them in a fit and whipped her door open to climb out.

Ben was out his door faster and caught her as she put her bare feet on the gravel and stood up to adjust her cover. He blocked her progress with his body, one hand on the open door, the other on the roof of the car.

"What the hell are you doing?" He seethed.

In a fine fit of wounded pride, Ava dug in. "I'm tired of being treated like a child. I am a grown woman whether you want to see it or not and I am fully capable of picking my own clothes. I want to wear a shirt, and I want to wear a goddamn bra like a grown up! Is that so unreasonable?" Her voice cracked. She was being ridiculous and knew it somewhere in her consciousness. However, her frustration at losing control of her life down to even what she wore had shoved her past the brink of what she could tolerate. Ava needed to push back, to feel like she had some control over something. Even if it was just a stupid shirt and a stupid bra.

Ben didn't understand. "Ava just get back in the car, I'll get it."

He gently pressed a hand on her shoulder to guide her back into the car and she put both hands on his chest, pushing him away. He took a step backward, hand coming off the car and she felt the chill on her skin where it was bare to the elements. Frustration continued to motivate her and Ava moved along the side of the car to the trunk. It was locked and she hit it with her fist.

Unfortunately it was her barely healed hand and Ava spun and swore, instinctively cradling it against her chest protectively, feeling her eyes starting to well up. The blanket was set on her shoulders and Ava bowed her head to hide her face.

She blinked back the threat of tears before they spilled out. Once back under control Ava straightened, turning to face her keeper. Calmly she asked him, "Will you please unlock the trunk so that I can get what I need?"

Ben did not speak, opting to return to the car where he retrieved the keys. Ava could feel the breeze on her skin where the cover left her centerline bare. She was past caring. In a pique, she left it like that to irritate him since it obviously bothered him for her to be "hanging out."

"Excuse me."

Ava stepped sideways to let Ben reach past her and unlock the trunk. When it was open he pocketed the keys and remained vigilant, scanning the road and farm fields surrounding them though no one was in sight.

She fished out both her bra and a hairbrush around whose handle she had fortuitously left a ponytail holder wrapped. When she stepped back, she shrugged off the blanket. Her pride was as damaged as it was going to get today she figured.

Sensing Ben starting to reach for it where it lay on the ground, Ava whirled. "Don't put that damned thing on me again." She kept her voice low though it trembled with underlying anger. "Who's going to see me?" She made a sweeping gesture with her arm indicating the nothingness surrounding them.

"I can." He replied softly bending down to retrieve it and toss it in the trunk haphazardly.

"So what? You already saw it all when *you* took my clothes off in the first place. It isn't bothering *me* to be half naked standing out on some road in the middle of nowhere. I don't even know where I am. My boss and my mother are probably under the delusion that I am on a romantic getaway with the man who stole me out from under their all too willing noses days ago." She stopped, not even sure how many days it had been. Everything was confused. "And do you know why they were so willing? Because it's been almost two years since I've even had a date. They're worried I'm going to waste my life away in that store.

They've made all my other decisions for me, I guess it's no surprise they would pick my love life too." The fire was going out of Ava to leave a hollow calm in its place. "I don't have the guts to figure out what to do with myself, following you was the first thing I actually had the nerve to try on my own. I was finally thinking I had the confidence to pick a future. Now," her voice broke, "now I don't know when I can go home, I don't know if I even *have* a future and I can't even get you to cop a feel when I offer it up." She stopped talking, her hairbrush and clothing still in her hands in front of her. She stared at them seeing them shake, willing them to stop.

"Ava." Ben put his fingers under her chin and she turned her head away. "Ava, look at me. Please."

She rolled her eyes and opened them wide to try to reabsorb the tears before she did as he requested. His expression surprised her. His furrowed brow made a line between his eyes now focused intently upon her face.

"We're in Wisconsin. I wanted to take a different route home in case Peter wasn't working alone. I was going to take you to my house where we have more options if they come." Ben shrugged. "Your phone's battery died last night, you can use mine to call whomever you want. It might not be a bad idea for them to think you are out having fun for a few more days while we figure out what to do. There's no reason to make them worry." The line in his brow lessened, his expression softening. "I apologize for not keeping you apprised of our situation, it was thoughtless and it won't happen again." He was treating her as though she was fragile, her breakdown not far from his memory. She could see it in his eyes, his need to manage her.

Not remotely placated and too tired to argue, Ava made an effort to get back in the car. Ben's arm went out and stopped her. "I want you to know that I *do* see you as a confident and attractive woman. When you decide to pursue a career or a relationship you will be successful I'm sure."

His too late assurance rang false and Ava called him on it. "If I'm so marketable why did you turn me down back there? I'm practically naked right now and you aren't even trying anything. What guy who thinks a woman is 'attractive' does that? You can make all the sweet talk you want, but in the end it's just words." With that, she pushed his arm aside and got back in the car to get dressed properly even if it was in wet warm up gear.

He stayed outside the car until she was finished. Ben got in, closed the door gently, and fished around on the floor of the car for a minute. Sitting back up he handed Ava his phone.

Ch. 22

Katherine had gone home to Mora believing her daughter had rejoined the dating world. Ava had a hard time lying to her mother and tried to weave enough truth into her story that she could convince her without feeling like a total heel.

"Yes Mom, it was a complete surprise. We went to a little place in Wisconsin for a long weekend, the cabins are rustic but it's romantic." She made an effort to keep the bitterness out of her voice when she answered her mother's questions. "No, it's not serious, we've only just started seeing each other again. I knew him a long time ago." Attempting a little damage control, Ava diverted her mother. "What about Robert? Have you been seeing much of him since you got back?"

Her mother nervously answered her questions without giving much extra information. Minus the alcohol she had in her system the last time they'd discussed him, Katherine was far more tight lipped about her beau. That was good, Ava took that to mean he was special to her and her mother really did deserve some happiness. She had meant it when she said it. It didn't bother her to think of her mother dating again, sixteen years was a long time to be alone. She wondered how long Ben had been alone and how much he'd dated, then got annoyed all over again.

Begging off, Ava promised to come home soon to have dinner with her mother and maybe Robert if her mother felt comfortable with it. Elle was the next call. It went pretty much the same way with Ava eventually steering the conversation to Bill and how Elle was doing with his leaving. Similarly, Elle soon begged off, not wanting to discuss it. Ava said she would like to use her vacation time to take a week off if that was okay.

Elle's life was a mess and business was good so her workaholic tendencies had gone into overdrive. She didn't even flinch when she granted Ava the time.

"You haven't taken a vacation in three years. Go and enjoy." She said as they disconnected.

Laying the phone on the seat between them, Ava sighed and rubbed her eyes grown tired from more than just scenery. "I hate lying to them. I hope this ends soon."

"Me too." Ben agreed.

"Then I suppose you'll pick up and leave again." He didn't respond and she didn't open her eyes to see if her words had an effect.

The miles and towns rolled by under their wheels. They drove up the western edge of Wisconsin, crossing back over into Minnesota at River Falls. Ben stopped at a gas station and they both took care of their needs. Ava remembered the last stop she had made and was sure to use the security mirrors before crossing through the tall racks. Ben emerged second having paid for the gas and held a bag in his hand.

He laid it down on the seat between them. "Snacks, help yourself."

Ava's stomach growled. She recalled Ben's synopsis of how he stayed young and realized he hadn't been sleeping or eating well since leaving Billings three days ago. She glanced over at him and stared at his face.

It was there, just becoming noticeable in the lines in his forehead and around his eyes. He looked exhausted and paler than usual, he looked older by at least a few years.

Concern for him pushed away her frustration at her bleak romantic prospects and dishonesty. "Ben, why don't you let me drive for a while. You should get some sleep."

He turned in his seat and looked at her, smiling mildly. "I'm okay. Thanks though."

"You look tired. This food can't be helping either." She pointed to the bag assuming it was typical gas station fodder.

Ben grew more somber. "You're right I can't live like this for long, I'm going to have to double up on my injections for the time being."

"Does that work?"

"In a pinch, yes. Long term I would age and die like a normal person if that was all I did."

"Is that what you're going to do eventually? After you get to the doctor, or are you going to keep living forever?"

He merged onto the main road before answering. "I would like to have a reasonably normal life, I think that's the right thing to do. We aren't supposed to live forever."

As promised, Ben pulled over once they reached a quiet section of road. He got out, popped the trunk and took care of what he needed to behind the cover of the trunk lid before returning to the car.

"That was fast." Ava commented in surprise when his door opened and he slid in.

His short laugh filled the car. "You get good at anything you practice for two hundred years."
She turned to look at him and was astonished at the change. His face was as smooth and unlined as the day she had seen him in the shop. "Oh my God. That is amazing." She laughed. "You should sell that. Women would pay a fortune for just a little bit of that."

His expression clouded. "Think of the casualties. How many children would it take to maintain the vanities of all of those seeking eternal youth? Bruder doesn't care, he creates more like us to serve his purposes but for each person he puts in 'stasis' at least one child dies, more are bled and drained for maintenance. As he replenishes his dying staff, the number of children who suffer grows exponentially."

Ava was silent, feeling she had made another mess of things by bringing up such a sensitive topic. She folded her hands in her lap and watched the terrain flatten during the last hour of their trip.

Ben called his attorney and by the time they arrived at Ben's condo and parked the car, the For Sale sign and lock box were gone. Sadly, so was the furniture and everything in the fridge.

Ava offered to go to the grocery store and Ben politely refused to let her leave.

"Now that I'm home, there's going to be some activity. We'll see how serious they are about eliminating you."

"You mean they might give up?" She hadn't considered that a possibility.

He shifted uncomfortably. "I burned some credit a few years ago, but if I have enough leverage left I might be able to get them to let you go." Ava perked, liking the sound of that. Though, as Ben continued, the idea became less attractive. "They would still follow you the remainder of your lifetime. They would be watchful of anyone you get involved with, a breakup would result in an untimely accident for fear you might have said something while he was with you. To have children would be terrifying. It isn't a decision to make lightly."

"Have you ever had children?"

Ben shook his head, his face a blank mask. "No, and it is no longer a possibility. Even my father's science could not overcome all the constraints of age or the limitations of living in a permanent state of suspended animation." He sighed, "My father's name ends with me."

Ch. 23

Ava was on her own while Ben ordered food to be delivered from a local organic market. He made another phone call to his attorney, who agreed to meet him at his home with a delivery of blood she had just received from his phlebotomist friend.

"Because I have to move so often, we have found it easier for her to deal directly with Jackie. She can ship it to me anywhere I need it."

The third call brought a visit from the movers she had seen take his things away only a few days ago. It seemed he kept some items warehoused somewhere nearby awaiting his return.

The house was re-outfitted with some of Ben's belongings, the rest to be delivered tomorrow. Food and the promise of a renewed blood supply were due by nightfall. The movers took Ava's key and promised to return with some of her things before lunch, she made them a list of what she needed.

Ben was busily preparing a small dinner of pasta and salad when the doorbell rang. Ava, having nothing else to do, had been skimming through a horticulture book at the counter and rose to answer the bell.

"Let me get that." Ben wiped his hands on a dishtowel. "Could you watch the sauce?"

She nodded, feeling he was keeping her out of his private affairs. Ava dutifully stirred the sauce and heard a female laugh in the entry. Curious to see this attorney, Ava stepped out of the kitchen and padded softly toward them. When she got close enough and Ben moved allowing her a clear view, Ava clapped both hands to her gaping mouth.

It was the woman from the photo on his dresser in Montana, the one in front of the courthouse. His attorney was like him, ageless.

Jackie spoke first with a soft southern drawl. Smiling, she stepped forward with her hand extended. "You must be Ava, Ben speaks of you often. I'm Jacqueline Guillome. You can call me Jackie."

Politely, Ava shook her hand glancing over at Ben to see if he was mad. Ben was avoiding her gaze, she thought his ears looked pink. "Ava Brandt. Pleased to meet you. I've heard a lot about you as well." She forced a smile.

Jackie raised her eyebrows, turning her face toward Ben. "Really Ben? Finally coming around after all these years?" She teased, enjoying his discomfort.

Ben found his tongue and when he looked at Ava, she saw that he was indeed blushing. "Jackie, would you like to stay for dinner? We were going to sit down soon."

Her features remained friendly but Ava saw a hint of something spark in her hazel eyes. She was considering it, then shook her head before answering politely. "Thank you but no. Tonight was a delivery run only." Her foot pushed a small cooler similar to the one Ben carried with him on the road. "I have a date this evening and I need to get ready." She winked conspiratorially at Ava. "Beauty is hard work."

Despite her jealous inclination to dislike the attractive woman who made Ben blush, Ava found herself smiling.

Laughing, she waved her hands at her less than flattering ensemble purchased by Ben in a rush at a discount store, now ready for a trash heap. Her hair had bee tucked back in a ponytail that she couldn't wait to wash. "Yeah, tell me about it. This took about three and a half minutes."

Jackie whirled on Ben, pointing. "Ben, you may have been out of play for a while but that's no excuse for not letting a lady have a little pride."

"I was busy keeping her alive." He bristled. Ava enjoyed seeing him squirm. "Which is no small task." Ben leveled a steady look at her.

It was Ava's turn to squirm and Jackie stepped to her rescue. She came over, putting her arm around Ava's waist and faced Ben alongside her. "Dinner can wait. Ava is coming with me and you can have her back when I'm done with her."

Jackie stepped away from her and took her hands, assessing. "You look like you could do with some spa therapy. I don't live far from here and you are about my size. Can I interest you in a shower and change?"

"You don't need to do that. My things will be here tomorrow."

"Let me ask you this. Do you want to sleep in that?"

"No." Ava wanted a shower and the thought of putting her filthy clothes back on made her skin crawl.

"Then it's settled." Again Jackie looked at Ben. "Objections?" By her tone, it was clear she expected none. Ava was guessing she was a formidable opponent in the courtroom, or across the table.

"It isn't safe for her to leave." Ben's apprehension showed in his pinched shoulders.

"Nonsense. Who better to have her with than me? I've been keeping you safe for decades, haven't I?"

Sensing her victory, Jackie turned her attention back to Ava. "Come on, we'll get ready together and I'll bring you back here on my way out." She spoke over her shoulder, not giving Ben any further opportunities to disagree, "We'll be back by eight."

They left a very troubled Ben standing on the doorstep, Jackie talking in her brisk manner the whole way out to her black Lexus parked at the curb. She lived a short drive away in a downtown highrise across the river.

Jackie's condo was elegant and displayed considerable taste in its contemporary décor. There was marble on the floor, granite and steel in the kitchen, sleek leather furniture arranged in the ample living room on a fluffy white rug. She led the way down the hall calling over her shoulder, "Shower's this way."

Ava trotted after her, eager to feel clean again.

"I'll just burn those." Jackie pointed to Ava's clothes when they hit the floor on her way into the shower. Ava did not disagree.

Ava pried herself out of a shower that ended far too soon, and wrapped her body in a thick Turkish bath sheet that hung below her knees. Jackie had provided her with the necessaries for hair and teeth, letting her know she could join her in her room when it was time to pick out some new clothes.

When she emerged amidst a rush of steam from the bathroom, the cool house felt good on her hot skin. She knocked on Jackie's partially closed door and was welcomed inside.

Jackie was in a black bra and panties sitting on the edge of her bed pulling a lace topped stocking up a shapely leg. She waved Ava in and pointed to a lavender set of underthings lying beside her on the bed. "They're brand new, I haven't even worn them yet."

Touching the material, Ava could tell they were expensive without even looking at the tags. When she did, her eyes popped. "I can't take these. They cost more than I make in a week."

Her hearty laugh was pleasant and Ava felt her lips turn up. "Don't worry about it. I'll charge Ben for them if it makes you feel better."

Even Ava laughed at that. She had been on a few sports teams here and there through high school so getting dressed in front of another woman didn't bother her. Ava dropped her towel to put on the offered pieces of satin and lace. They were nicer than any lingerie Ava had ever bought for herself. She had some nicer things, but had never justified going three figures on something only she was going to see.

She carried her towel into the closet to throw it in the hamper as directed. She was taking in the clothes hanging in the gigantic closet when Jackie joined her.

"Come on in. Let's see what suits you tonight." Jackie was already zipping into a black sheath dress and stepped into a pair of beautiful black and gray alligator shoes. Everything she wore described her, elegant and understated with only a hint of flash. She was the quintessential lady and Ava wished she could know her long enough to have some of it rub off on her.

Jackie eyed Ava, coolly appraising her form. When Jackie reached for a dress, Ava saw the scarring on the inside of her elbows. She was still staring when Jackie turned around.

Caught, Ava blushed but Jackie laughed again. "It comes with the territory dear."

"How do you explain it?" Ava thought about her date tonight.

She smiled broadly. "The same way I explain my need to eat organic and my aversion to alcohol. My bad kidneys." She held out her arms, "Dialysis."

It was ingenious, Ava admired this woman even more for having what her grandmother used to call moxie. Katherine did not have it, she'd never even tried anything remotely risky, preferring the safety of the known. And who knew if Ava would have. Her confidence had disappeared when she did, even Ben hadn't been able to bring it back from Bruder's lab. She promised herself right then that she would take hold of her flashes of newfound bravado and do her grandmother proud. Bruder couldn't take that from her anymore. Her life could be her own for once.

Jackie was holding up a dress for Ava to consider. Impatiently she shook it making it dance. "Hello, I need an opinion."

"Sorry, it's been a long couple of days." She grinned at being caught dozing.

"I bet it has. You don't have to worry anymore, you're safe with him. Ben will protect you to his last." She meant it to be reassuring, it bothered Ava.

"I suppose he does this a lot, protecting kids after he saves them."

Jackie's smile faded, the tightening of her lips was barely perceptible. "No, there's only you. He's a bit smitten if you ask me." She tried unsuccessfully to hide a hint of disappointment.

Ava snorted. "I doubt that. I thought he was going to turn himself inside out when I kissed him."

"You kissed him?" Jackie lowered the forgotten dress, her eyes sparkling.

Ava nodded, more than a little embarrassed to have brought it up.

She started laughing and Ava grew more uncomfortable, wishing she had some clothes on. There was something disquieting about being in your underwear while being laughed at.

Jackie noticed Ava's discomfort and stopped, wiping at her eyes. "Sweetie it isn't you I'm laughing at, it's Ben. He tries so hard to deny himself any pleasures. I don't know if you've noticed, but he lives like a monk. Saying no to *you* was probably the hardest thing he's had to do in a long time."

"No, he didn't seem to have a problem with saying no. As a matter of fact, I was just about naked that whole day and he treated me like a pariah." Ava declared bitterly.

"You were naked all day? *What* were you two doing while you were away?" She crossed her arms over her chest, brows raised.

Out of fairness, Jackie *had* opened her home to her. Ava figured she owed her something back. Relieved to have someone to confide in, she spilled. She told her about Ben

finding her in the hotel, falling in the river, how he brought her back from hypothermia and his distance the whole way home.
Jackie put her arms around Ava, pulling her in for a hug. "You are living a charmed life Ava Brandt. Do you know how lucky you are to still be breathing?" She pulled away, holding Ava's hands. "You are a strong woman. I see what Ben loves about you."

"What?" Ava didn't think she had heard Jackie correctly. "No, he sees me as a little girl. Ben's just protective, that's all."

Jackie's eyes searched Ava's looking for evidence of her sincerity, a hint of a smile on her lips. "You don't see it, do you?"

"There's nothing to see." Ava was growing annoyed with Jackie's persistence and restated herself firmly. "I told you, I made a move, he freaked. Whenever there was even a *chance* of skin, he was on me to cover it. Quite honestly, I had no idea *any* guy could say no that often." Jackie was right Ben *was* like a monk. It didn't make her feel any better.

Jackie held up her hands conceding defeat. "All right, you win. Ben's your long lost big brother." She made it clear she wasn't convinced although Ava appreciated the fact that she stopped trying to press her point. "Let's get you dressed, I need to leave soon and Ben is probably starving."

Ava's stomach growled and Jackie smiled. "You could use a good meal yourself."

She decided on her own that the dress she had was not going to do and Jackie put it back. Her fingers flicked through several sections until she reached a white garment bag. "Oh, I forgot about this one." She unzipped the bag and fiddled with the hanger for a minute. "Try this on."

Ava wanted to get back, Jackie had been more than kind and she was hoping to avoid any further intimate talk on the subject of Ben. Without consideration, she took the offered garment and stepped into it. Jackie helped her zip it up. Together they moved to stand in front of the full length mirror against the back wall of the closet.

"Oh wow." Ava murmured. She stared at herself in the mirror. The lavender slip dress was fitted in just the right places, the mild flare in the skirt brushed her skin a few inches above her knees. Thin straps complimented Ava's lean arms. If Jackie had wanted to make Ava feel beautiful, she had done it.

"I agree. It's perfect. Now let's get that hair and a little splash of makeup and you'll be ready to go."

Ava followed into the bathroom and took a seat on the edge of the corner tub. She let Jackie blow dry her layers into soft face framing curls that hung to her shoulders. The final touch was light shading accenting her unique tawny eyes and glossing her lips. When she looked at the finished product, Ava was astounded.

"I had no idea I could look like this." She declared.

Jackie put an arm around her and hugged. "I bet you've never tried."

It was true Ava hadn't tried all that hard, but in all fairness, Jackie had several lifetimes to perfect her look. She had a clear advantage. A pair of matching heeled sandals, a wrap for the freezing house and Ava was ready to go. Jackie grabbed a wrap for herself and they walked out with Jackie reiterating her promise to burn the outfit Ava had arrived in.

Ch. 24

Jackie drove as boldly as she spoke, texting furiously the entire way. It didn't help when Jackie reassured her she did it all the time. Blowing a parting kiss, Jackie pulled away just as Ben whipped open the door. Ava's fingers had scarcely begun to reach for the bell.

Ben's expression was unreadable when stepped back to let her enter and closed the door behind her. Ava felt her temporary pride in her appearance slipping away at his lack of a reaction. Crestfallen she moved past him, disappointed to have her point once again hammered home. Whatever Ben felt for her, it was most definitely not the attraction Jackie presumed.

Once inside the door Ava stood shifting uncertainly, her relative ease from familiarity with him and the house gone. Ava waited for direction.

Ben walked past her, calling over his shoulder. "Come on in."

She followed without speaking, listening to the echoing tap of her sandals on the tile. Ben moved out of the way as the kitchen opened in front of them and Ava saw the table set for a formal dinner, a bottle of wine open on the counter.

"I thought you didn't drink." Secretly she was thankful for the social lubricant, fearing an awkward evening ahead.

He poured a glass for each of them, "Not often." He handed her one, "I thought we could both use some given recent events." He raised his glass to her before lifting it to his lips. "It seems you've made quite an impression on Jackie." Ben nodded at the phone sitting on the counter.

Ava felt her stomach drop figuring out who Jackie had been texting, she could only imagine *what* she'd been saying. She took a swig of her wine thinking of everything they had discussed.

Ben was watching Ava carefully. "Jackie and I have known each other a long time. She worked in the offices of our family attorney in Charlotte when she got sick. When it was clear she wasn't going to recover, her father begged mine to help her. He knew what that meant and so did Jackie. She's been with us for over eighty years now."

"She's a great lady." Ava agreed. "She really cares about you." She hinted at the natural pairing she saw in them, the one Jackie clearly craved.

Ben took a small sip from his glass. "She hoped for a while we could have a relationship that was more than professional but that was a long time ago." He set his glass down and gestured toward the table. "Please, you're my guest and I haven't been much of a host until now. I would like it if you would let me make it up to you."

Confused at his change of attitude, Ava took the seat he pulled out for her. Two places were set; he put her in the one facing the kitchen making it easier for them to talk while he served.

"In your defense, you haven't had to be a host so much as a babysitter and we haven't exactly had a kitchen readily available. I don't blame you for not making me dinner before." She joked lightly.

Ben carried two plates from the kitchen and set one in front of her. They were filled with bowtie pasta tossed with mushrooms, small chunks of meat and peas with a light cream sauce.

"Pancetta?" Ava eyed the pink meat intrigued.

"Yes," Ben returned with their green salads tossed with vinaigrette, balsamic by the smell. "The recipe calls for proscuitto but I prefer pancetta for the texture."

"Thank you, it looks wonderful." Ava hadn't realized how much she was craving a real meal and this one promised to be fantastic. She lowered her head to inhale the smells coming from her plate. She smiled at him and raised her glass. "To your cooking."

He was just setting his napkin in his lap. Raising his glass as well he added, "To fresh starts."

They both drank and settled in to eating their pasta. Ava always had music in the background at work, at home and in the car. Ben's love for silence was a shock to the system.

"Do you like music?" She asked, swallowing her mouthful.

Ben nodded, buying himself time before taking a drink of his water. "I do, very much. You?"

"Yes, but I've never heard you play anything. Why is that? I have it on all the time."

"The world has become a noisy place. I find a calm car and home allow me to relax. While I've had you with me I haven't been working. Normally I'm at home very little and in noisy environments on a continual basis. I *need* the quiet by the end of the day."

"How often do you work on cases? How many do you work on at a time? I've never known anyone who does what you do." Ava was curious about his trade.

Ben shrugged, "It depends. I usually have one or two cases going at a time. That's really all one man can handle with any sort of competence. When the police are swamped they tend to shift some of their less severe cases over to me as a consultant and then I've had up to five or six."

"What kind of cases do police send to you? No offense but aren't there types of cases only the police can handle?"

"None taken. The police handle all felonies. Missing persons, petty crimes, harassment cases, that sort of thing is where my skill set can be of assistance. When they're busy they sometimes offer the client the choice of my services knowing I can usually devote more time to them and solve them faster."

"Do you always work as an investigator or detective? It suits you." When she'd found all of his listings she didn't remember seeing any other professions.

"Thank you, and yes I do. As I said, my father wanted me to pursue business regardless of the fact that it did not appeal to me in the least. Figuring out how the pieces fit together and following the clues where they lead has always been my strength and I find this career path fits me. When I learned what had to be done to save my life, it guided my decision to assist people, especially children. For as far as society has come, children are still seen as disposable. I try to use my resources to help them. It hopefully makes some amends for all that my father's discovery had done to them."

Ava found his penance admirable. She was also personally grateful for it.

"Does it bother you? What happened?" Ben sensed the direction of her thoughts.

She had a rare opportunity to discuss the details of her ordeal with someone who had been there as well. The fact that she was alive and able to talk about it was due only to him. "A little." She decided to open up, he had done so with her and this was, after all, their new beginning. "I have a recurring dream about it." She watched his eyebrows go up.

"You remember it that clearly?"

Ava nodded. "I remember the lady giving me candy and then the doctor in the lab. Although I have a confession." She fidgeted with her napkin. "I always thought the man who saved me in my dream was my father until I saw you in the store that day." She laughed nervously. "When I saw you, it all came back. I honestly thought I was going a little nuts."

"That explains it." Ben ran a hand across his eyes. "The look on your face when you saw me, I'll never forget it. You were devastated." He rubbed the bottom of his glass with one finger. "I knew you recognized me. I was worried you thought I was the one who took you."

It had never crossed her mind that Ben would be concerned what *she* thought of *him*. Seeing him susceptible to her judgment cast him in an entirely different light.

"What are you thinking? You look distraught. Is talking about this upsetting to you?"

Ava set her fork down and put her hands in her lap. "I guess I have to tell you that I've judged you unfairly. Until now, I've never allowed for you to have regular feelings. You're so much older, wiser in my head. I've always kind of admired it. So I naturally assumed you had it all figured out and weren't affected by what other people thought."

Ben was shaking his head, a wry smile twisting his lips. "I don't know about wise. Maybe resigned would be a better word. If anything, time has only taught me that nothing is certain. Patterns are predictable and people are not, especially under duress."

They had finished their meals. Ava stood and Ben rose with her. She flushed at being treated like a woman. She imagined the majority of his manners were based on how he was raised. There was much for her to learn about him if they continued their friendship, she looked forward to it. He was a good man.

“You did the cooking, let me clear.”

He started to argue.

“Please.” Ava was firm.

With a polite inclination of his head he sank back into his seat, watching her as she moved about the room. Ava was easily able to locate his containers to put away leftovers, she realized too late it gave away her knowledge of his home.

Ben chuckled, catching her pink cheeks. “I know you were here. Maybe *you* should pursue investigation as a career. It suits your nature far more than selling goods.”

Ava laughed, relieved he wasn’t angry. “I like to follow clues too.” Her work in the kitchen done, she returned to the table. Ben rose before she took her seat. “It’s helped me through my schooling, my aptitude for research is my claim to fame.” She tooted her horn halfheartedly. In truth, she wished she could work in the field except she had promised her mother to pursue a more reliable career in business. Ava had tossed around the idea of trying to merge her talent with her degree into a career researching companies for corporate mergers or something. Although that didn’t hold the same sort of attraction for her that helping people did.

He handed her the glass from her place and took his own as well as the bottle. “I regret that I find myself low on furniture for proper entertaining but I do have a couch and a coffee table as well as a very old collection of records.”

Ava’s laughter caught Ben off guard. “Sorry, but I think you’re the last person under sixty who still has records.” He shot her a look. “Okay, the only person who *looks* like he’s under sixty.” She was light from the wine and winked at him teasingly, taking the lead as they headed to the couch.

Ava kicked off her shoes and plopped down on the cushion, tucking her feet up underneath her. Ben sat next to her, finishing his glass in one gulp before pouring another.

"What will this do to you?" She raised her glass.

Ben pointed to his arm. "I have to double up for the wine I drink tonight and then I have to return to a normal routine. Our time on the road has taken its toll. I will start to age more than normal injections can repair if I continue to abuse my body like this."

"You *do* live like a monk." Ava blurted out.

Ben's hand hesitated before replacing the bottle on the table. "I what?"

"I'm sorry Ben, I shouldn't have said that." She was upset with herself for possibly ruining their evening.

Settling the bottle on the table and leaning back against the cushions, Ben regarded her seriously. "That sounds like a Jackie remark to me. I believe she has said those very words to me on more than one occasion." He shrugged a shoulder. "It's true you know. I deny myself most things knowing I have to stay strong long enough to find Bruder. All of this," he gestured to the wine and the room itself, "is superfluous. It's all distraction from what's really important."

The doorbell rang and Ben and Ava both shot to their feet. "Were you expecting someone?"

Ben shook his head, instantly on alert. "Stay here."

Stubbornly, she followed him to the door. When he started to argue, she raised her chin obstinately. "New beginnings. I am a grown woman and I am going to be involved in any decisions affecting me."

He snapped his teeth shut with an audible click but did not argue.

The door opened to reveal a tall woman, too dark to be Caucasian, too light to be Black, standing on the porch. "You must be Mr. Pearson or do you prefer to go by your given name, Benjamin Physick?" The light from the entry spilled out and reflected on a dark vehicle idling at the curb.

Her accent was out of place this far north. Ava had only heard that mixture of French and drawl in movies.

"I haven't used that name in a long time." Ben answered stiffly. One hand remained on the door, the other on the frame blocking her entrance. "To what do I owe this pleasure?"

She smiled, oozing sex even without her tight black pants and clingy sweater. "The Doctor sends his regards." She extended her hand and Ben took it briefly. Her almond shaped eyes slowly took him in from head to toe. Reluctantly tearing her gaze from his handsome shape, she glanced from Ben to Ava. Her smiled widened. "I did not know you were entertaining." Waving her hand dismissively, she went on. "Doctor Bruder has lost someone very important to him. You owe him."

Ben's voice rose, quaking in his anger. "The Doctor can consider it a small payment for all that he owes me. Now if that is all." He began to close the door.

Her booted foot shot out and caught it before it closed. "No, that is not all. The Doctor says you are postponing the inevitable." She stared at Ava while she spoke. "You are not honoring the agreement."

"My promise to Bruder has not changed. Our agreement stands." Ben growled out fiercely.

She didn't break eye contact with Ava, shaking her head slowly back and forth tossing her long, dark hair across her shoulders and smiling smugly. "Your offer is no longer attractive to him, your agreement has come to an end. He has sent me to collect what you owe him. Either you can give her to me or he will be forced to send a professional." The messenger did not completely hide her offense at being discounted as capable. "Things could get very messy."

So quietly Ava had to strain to hear, Ben responded through clenched teeth. "Ava is with me, she is under my protection. Tell Doctor Bruder if he wants her, he will have to come get her himself."

The woman gave Ava a dubious glance. "I would not dare the Doctor so. He is capable of causing you a tremendous amount of grief." Fear tinged the respect Ava heard in her voice. Her boot withdrew, and with a last lingering glance at Ben, she strutted away giving a show that would have made a normal man drool.

Ben had proven he was not normal and Ava was privately pleased to see him ignore her as well. He closed the door and they heard her heels striking the concrete steps as she descended to the street below. A car door closed and they heard it pull away.

"She was Creole, right? I'm guessing that means she's from Louisiana. So he's in Louisiana?"

Ben tipped his imaginary hat to her. "That's right. We have a day, maybe two tops before he sends someone more qualified to try to take you." Ben's hand rested on the knob, his head down as he planned. When he looked up, she saw the hint of a smile on his lips.

"Why are you smiling, because we have a day to start running?" That didn't fill Ava with the same sense of jubilation.

"No, I'm smiling because the good doctor has finally made a mistake."

Ch. 25

"I should have guessed." He mumbled to himself. "After Katrina missing people and missing kids are commonplace. Survivors would be a dime a dozen. It would have been perfect for him."

"So when are we going?"

"I am going after him as soon as I can get a flight out." He strode past Ava to the kitchen to his phone. Without delay, he logged on and started searching for flights.

His word choice was not lost on Ava. "What about me? Would you prefer I stay here or should I go home to wait for them to come for me?" She had followed him and stood in the doorway, arms crossed and glaring.

Ben cancelled his search and set down his phone. "I can send you somewhere. By the time he figures it out, I will have found him."

Ava rolled a shoulder. "That is assuming a lot. It's assuming you're right that you can hide me, and that you're able to find him and kill him. Something I hate to point out, but you haven't been able to do in two centuries. What makes you so confident now?"

"In all the years we've had dealings, Bruder has always sent messengers but he was always very careful. They were always instructed to keep their distance from me. As a result, I have never touched the messenger before. This was a first." He rubbed a hand across the back of his neck. "Bruder is paranoid, he doesn't instruct over phone or computer. His messenger will go to him to report back. I can follow her right to him."

In her mind's eye, she saw another assassin and felt the horror of being taken. The next one might not be so kind to leave Elle unharmed and who knew how long Ben's search would take him. "Don't leave me here." Ava said softly. She hated it, yet it was undeniable, she needed him.

"Ava, it's the safest way." Ben assured her, his eyes straying to his phone, clearly torn.

Ava refused to let him go, obviously she was seeing risks he wasn't. "What if you're wrong and he gets you first? I won't have any way of knowing. The first clue I'll get is when I see the killer at my door. No one can help me when you're gone." Her voice broke. "And I will have lost you again."

Ben frowned. "Like I said, when I left for Montana it was for your own good. You should have left things as they were."

"What about when I was fourteen? That's when you left before, right? I felt it when you were gone." Ava rested a hand over her chest, subconsciously showing him where she felt his loss. "I always felt safe with you here. When you were gone I was alone and I could feel it. That was when Mom gave me Dad's ring. She told me he would watch over me." She fingered the ring finding it a hollow comfort now.

"I took care not to let you see me. You couldn't have known when I was here and when I wasn't." Ben rubbed the back of his neck, troubled.

"You said it yourself, I'm an investigator, I notice things even when I don't know I'm seeing them." Ava rubbed her arms feeling the chill of the house. "Maybe you're not the only one who can sense things." She forced a smile and turned on her heel not wanting to be in the room while he made his plans to leave. She went back to sit on the couch and picked up her wrap where it lay on the arm. Her full wine glass beckoned and she took a drink. Ava swirled the glass, watching the wine slowly trickle back down the sides of the glass. It was slow to come down, Elle had taught her that was called "legs." That meant the wine was a good one. She was staring at the drapes, eyes making shapes of the shadows when Ben cleared his throat from the doorway. Ava glanced up impassively, she hoped if she acted like she didn't care she could somehow make it true.

"May I?" He indicated the seat beside her.

"You can do what you want." She kept her tone even, not wanting to hint at her feelings.

He picked up his glass as well and took a sip. Ava already feeling his impending departure, was unable to look at him.

Finally, tired of the standoff, Ben set down his glass and took hers from her hand to set it on the table. "I need you to understand something. This man is evil. He has taken everything from me and continues to murder children all over the world. This is the first chance I've had in over a decade to stop him. I have to take it."

"You say he's taken everything from you. You're wrong." Ava was quietly indignant. "He took your father, and yes he is evil, and yes he is hurting kids, and yes he needs to be stopped. But *you* are the one taking everything from yourself." She pressed on when he appeared ready to defend himself. "*You* deny yourself the simple human needs that make life worth living. Do you even *have* friends? Do you spend time with them? You may need to cut out excess to be the way you are, but there are pleasures you deny yourself for no reason. I think you find it far too convenient to blame your fears on the evils of one man. Who are you going to blame it on when he's gone, if you live?"

She rose and left the room, frustrated with false pretenses. Ben had shattered her illusions about her life when he'd come back, and yet his remained firmly in place. Ava was fearful of many things, but at least she admitted it and was trying to better herself. Ben wasn't. He was hiding from life, claiming he didn't want to lose anyone when really he was losing *every*one by not allowing himself to live. Even if it wasn't her, he had to let himself be close to someone, to find someone or something to make him happy.

Her eyes were tired and the wine was going to her head. Ava went up the stairway to the guest room. Of course the movers had only brought back one bed, his. She considered going home then decided he wouldn't allow it and she didn't have it in her to fight.

By her reckoning she had just as much right to a good night's sleep as he did and if she went home she would never be able to rest anyway.

Ben's voice behind her made her jump. "I don't know if I should thank you for your honesty or take offense at your rudeness."

Recovering herself, Ava faced him. "Well, you're welcome for the honesty and please excuse my rudeness. I'm not good at…" she waved her hand between them, "whatever this is. I can't do it anymore tonight. I'm exhausted." She piled her hair on her head in one hand and turned around, presenting her back to Ben. "Will you unzip me?"

"Why?"

"Because I want to go to bed and I don't want to sleep in Jackie's dress and ruin it." She craned her neck to see if he was moving. Ava dropped her hair and turned around. Ben stood rooted in the doorway, hands shoved in his pockets.

"I'm sorry," she sighed, sagging. "It was harsh and it wasn't fair of me to take my frustration out on you." She closed the distance between them. "Please understand that you aren't the only person who has ever lost anyone or who's afraid in this world. Keep that in mind when you're deciding someone else's life for them." She spun around and pulled her hair to the side again, repeating her request. "Could you please unzip me?"

She felt the zipper go down a few inches without his skin ever touching hers. It wasn't unexpected given his history with her body and a lack of interest, it still hurt her ego sensitive as she was to it. She had thought there might be an actual moment of temptation tonight, she had never looked better.

Guessing he would leave now that he'd said his piece, she walked away and reached behind her to finish unzipping herself and let the dress slide down her legs, scooping it up and tossing it on the bed as she walked, it was a practiced maneuver. "Ben, do you have a shirt or something I could sleep in?" She raised her voice assuming he would be halfway down the stairs. Ava turned to wait for his reply and was sent reeling backward as she bumped into his chest. "Ben, what are you doing?"

He grabbed her arms to steady her. "Ava, why do you keep doing this to me?"

Perplexed, she stared at him. "What, sleeping in your bed? Last time you put me in it and this time is your fault for only having one." She pointed at the large comfy bed beckoning her. "Do you want to share? It won't bother *me*."

"That is not what I mean. I'm trying to be respectful of you and you make it very hard."

Ava giggled, "No, I most definitely don't do that." She sniggered at her crude joke.

Ben groaned and rocked back on his heels staring up at the ceiling. "Do you have any idea the amount of control that took? Lying together…with you kissing me, it was very difficult to say no."

Shaking her head, Ava continued to deny it. "You said you don't want me and that's fine, I get it."

"I am doing my duty protecting you, I swore it the first day I saw you. I'm trying to leave you to live your own life and not to draw you into mine." His hands tightened on her arms. "I'm fighting a losing battle against the Fates trying to keep you away from me *and* out of danger. You heard that woman tonight. You are in danger being with me yet if I send you away they are sure to..." Ben's eyes burned and his voice was rough as he wrestled with himself.

Ava's eyes stung. "Do you hear yourself? You don't make any sense. All along you've told me you would be there for me. Jackie said you would protect me to your last breath and now you're saying you can't wait to be rid of me. If the Fates keep bringing us together, then maybe you should listen. We can be friends without me getting killed. Or we can avoid each other and I still might get killed. Or maybe the world will end tomorrow and we'll all be killed. The point is you can't control everything for everyone. It's too much, even for you."

She turned away to open a drawer. Finding nothing, she slammed it shut and opened another. "Damn it!" The highboy was empty, she moved to the low dresser and started opening and closing drawers. The second drawer had a short stack of shirts in it. "Finally." She murmured under her breath. Without a thought she reached behind her back and released the clasp on her bra with one hand, pulling it off and setting it on the dresser to pull the shirt over her head.

Just as she was tugging the hem down, Ava felt Ben's hands on her shoulders. The buckle of his belt was cold against her skin through the thin cotton. "Stop doing this Ava." His voice shook and his hands were too tight, his fingers digging into her skin.

"Ben, you're hurting me." Ava froze, she was afraid of his strength.

His hands disappeared in an instant and she spun around to face him, hand on the dresser to steady her trembling knees. His hands were on his head, clutching at his hair. She didn't recognize the look on his face.

"It doesn't work for me to be near you anymore. I can't do it."

Confusion and hurt hit her in a vicious double blow. Ava wrapped her arms around her stomach and leaned her hip on the dresser. "I have taken about as much of your abuse as I can handle. Jackie was wrong about you." She felt her control starting to slip. "She thought you loved me." Ava saw the stricken look on his face and held up a hand. "Don't worry, I set her straight. I told her you thought of me as a seven year old little girl still and you cared like a brother cares for a little sister. Only *I* was wrong too. I wouldn't want a brother if he was as cruel as you." She pushed herself away from the dresser. "If you're going to sleep here I want to know, because I would prefer to sleep on the couch if you want the bed. Sharing isn't such a good idea after all." Her cheeks were wet, her voice rough and she felt the beginnings of a headache. "I can't do it either."

Ava's knees wobbled as she took a few shaky steps and sank down on the bed, pulling at the edge of her shirt in a failed attempt to cover more of her legs. Giving up, she let her forehead fall into her hands. The mattress depressed beside her and Ava tried to ignore him. Ben patiently waited out her silent tears, putting his arm around her until her shoulders stopped shaking.

"You are wrong about a lot of things Ava."

"Do you think we could do this tomorrow? I don't know if I can handle any more tonight. You've got me so confused I don't even know what I'm saying anymore."

Ben ignored her request. "The first thing you are wrong about is that I think of you as the little girl I saved. The second thing you are wrong about is that I care for you like a brother and the third thing you are wrong about is that I don't want you."

Ava wiped her eyes and stared at the tears on her fingers.

"I know the best thing for you is for me to let you go and to keep my distance, but I can't do that if we grow any closer. If I can hold you and make love to you, I fear I will never let you go again."

Ava sniffed. "Then don't let me go." She let her eyes come up, seeing the decision in his eyes when he made it.

Ben's hands came up to cup her face, his thumb wiping a stray tear from her cheek. He kissed her gently, lips moving to her cheeks and down to the curve of her jaw, wrapping his arms around her to press her against him. Ava put her hands on the back of his neck and he groaned. Her other hand slid up into his hair and his arms tightened, pulling her over onto his lap.

Ava felt his hands at the edge of her shirt. She let go of him only as long as it took for the garment to clear her head, then reclaimed his mouth and her hold on him. Ava slid her hands down and grabbed his shirt to do the same, needing to be closer. When their skin was touching, Ava shivered.

"Are you cold?" Ben leaned back to ask.

Ava shook her head and drew herself back to him, determined not to be parted from him again. His pants came off, as did the rest of their clothing and nothing was left between them.

Ben slowed his kissing and tried to catch his breath, his hands rested on her hips, hindering her movements. "Ava, are you sure you want to do this? There are so many complications to a life with me."

His face in front of her, eyes filling her field of vision, Ava smiled. "Ben, I've never been more sure of anything in my life." Her lips touched his again as he claimed her body.

Ch. 26

Ava woke late, she could tell from the sun coming in the window. Smiling happily, she rolled over and reached out to find him as she had several times in the night. This time however, her hand touched cold sheets. When she raised her hand to the pillow and heard paper crackle, she felt her heart sink.

Dearest Ava,

To have you beside me would give me strength, though I could not bear to see you come to harm knowing I could have prevented it. I apologize for leaving you like this, please forgive me.

Be vigilant, things are not safe for you yet. I have provided for your protection in my absence.

Take care with yourself and know that I will be with you again as soon as I am able.

Eternally Yours,

Ben

Ben had done it again. He had made the decision for her and left her here like a child to wait and worry for his return. Fists clenched tightly, Ava sat up and punched Ben's pillow.

After she pounded the down flat she didn't feel any better and growled in frustration.

A pan clattered downstairs and her eyes narrowed. "That must be my babysitter," Ava grumbled nastily. She looked around the room for clothes and found the shirt from last night proclaiming Florida as the land of sunshine. It wouldn't do to storm downstairs looking every bit the abandoned one night stand in her dress. Digging through the drawers produced nothing better than a pair of athletic shorts. Making use of the drawstring waist to keep them up, she rolled them a few times to get them above knee so they weren't entirely god awful.

Shuffling out of his room, Ava was set to take out some of her anger unjustifiably on the babysitter until she hit the top of the stairs and smelled bacon. Their exertions from the night before had left her famished. She did not need to announce herself when she walked into the kitchen, her shameless stomach did that for her.

The babysitter was a well built, ebony black man with a shaved head and neatly trimmed beard and moustache. The strange picture of the man to be her sitter was made even more bizarre by the fact that he was wearing an apron with multicolored cats all over it.

"Good morning Ava. Waffles?" He motioned to a plate on the counter with a metal cover on top and a sizzling waffle maker nearby telling her another one was coming up shortly.

She was still trying to maintain a head of steam, feeling her anger dissipating quickly in the face of such pleasantness. Her stomach growled again and she gave up trying to deny breakfast. Explaining to herself she could convey her irritation even if she accepted the food, she reached for the plate.

"Oh, just a sec." He took the plate back and spun around to pull bacon off the stove and set it beside the waffles.

Handing it back with a smile, he revealed a beautiful set of pearly whites with a small gap in front.

Seeing the table already had butter and syrup, she sat down in the same spot she'd had at dinner to keep an eye on the chef. Waffles from scratch hot off an iron, and bacon. She was transported back to her mother's kitchen when she was nine years old. Restaurants couldn't duplicate homemade breakfast, nothing could.

A cup scooted in front of her, and Ava smelled coffee. The babysitter she was rapidly growing downright fond of was digging in the fridge.

"Orange or grapefruit?" He had a clipped British accent and a pleasant sounding voice which, on top of the cooking and physical dimension hinting at capable bodyguard skills, was probably why Ben had chosen him. At first blush there was nothing not to like.

"Grapefruit." Thoughts of Ben renewed her grump and she was mad at him all over again for leaving her behind while he possibly got himself killed.

Setting her juice down in front of her the sitter slash chef extended his large, long fingered hand, Ava noticed the manicure. "I'm Alistair. Ben is an old friend and has given me the very serious duty, of making sure you have everything you might need until he returns." His grip was firm, his palm calloused. Alistair, for all his polish, knew hard work.

"Thank you Alistair. These taste just like my mom used to make." She cracked a smile.

Alistair bowed his head in thanks and went back to the counter to retrieve his own cup of coffee. The cup was partway to his lips when he set it down and moved to the front door. She hadn't heard the bell ring but she heard the door open and voices she was starting to recognize. The movers.

Alistair allowed them in. They confirmed Ben had already given instructions on where they were to put everything. Ava imagined they moved him so often they probably had it down better than he did.

"When did you get here?" Ava asked when he retrieved his coffee.

"Just before six. Ben let me in and gave me my orders before he left for the airport."

"Have you been to that part of Louisiana before?" Ava tried not to sound too eager.

"When I first came to this country, I traveled extensively. I did enjoy Shreveport but Baton Rouge was better for cuisine. I had the finest shrimp etoufee in a little restaurant while I was there." He rolled his eyes up, closing them in a picture of delight.

Ava's eyes strayed to the clock behind Alistair's head. It was nearly nine now. Given post 9/11 regulations Ben would have to be there an hour early and it was twenty minutes to the airport. That meant if he left home around six his flight had probably left around eight. Ava's mind was busily sorting through what she knew and what she could deduce logically.

If Ben thought that the best thing for her was to stay behind and wait for news, he was wrong. She knew that she needed to be with him and she had proven she could take care of herself. Ava would control her own fate whether he liked it or not.

Finished with her breakfast, she sipped on her coffee until the door closed behind the last of the movers. "I'm going to wash up if you don't mind." Ava pushed back her chair. "Thanks again for a great breakfast."

Alistair was cleaning up, wiping down the counters. "You're welcome. It is always a treat to cook for an appreciative audience." He flashed her a quick smile.

She had started out of the room when Ava remembered her phone was dead. "Alistair, could I borrow your phone by chance? Mine is dead and I really should check in with my boss."

He fished in his pocket and handed her a complicated looking device. Taking it out of the room, Ava dialed Ben's number. It went straight to voicemail. He was probably still in flight. She hung up without leaving a message.

Impulsively she dialed the airline. Thankfully, they had one of those phone numbers that was a word and easy to remember. The next flight to Shreveport was scheduled to depart at eleven. If she hurried Ava could make it. Seat booked, she hung up and hunted for the app to find a phone listing. Five minutes later she had a cab and flight arranged.

Not having a plan from there, Ava only knew she couldn't sit idly by waiting for a killer while Ben's life hung in the balance. She had to try to reach him. It was possible *she* could track *him*. She had found him the first time, granted it was under less dire circumstances and with much more information than now, still she was compelled to try.

She hunted around in Ben's room and found the drawers were now full of clothes. A few shelves and hangers in the closet contained some things for her. It brought a smile to her face to see her things there, it made her place with him seem more real. Picking something cool for hot weather and a sweater just in case, Ava dragged her change of clothes into the bathroom and took a fast shower.

Twenty minutes later, she was ready to walk out the door. A glance out the window revealed the cab already waiting out front, she'd told him not to come to the door. Ava held her shoes in her hand and crept down the stairs. When her fingers touched the knob she heard a throat clearing behind her.

Busted, she rotated slowly to see Alistair leaned up against the wall, arms crossed and looking expectant. "Why the hurry? Do you have a plane to catch?" His stern face and thick arms were intimidating to say the least. There wasn't a chance Ava could get out the door if he didn't want her to.

She tried to appeal to his sense of duty. "Ben is going to have a much better chance of success if he has reinforcements. I can help him."

He shook his head unconvinced. "The boss said you don't go for any reason. It is too dangerous."

"Who is he to choose for me what I do with my life? He treats me like my opinion doesn't matter." Exasperation fueled her flaring temper. Her mother had always told her it was her downfall. She pushed thoughts of her mother aside.

His answer surprised her. "I think you're looking at this the wrong way. Ben is an old soul, he grew up in a time when men took care of their women. He loves you and doesn't want to see you hurt. He's only trying to do what he was raised to believe is right. Ben means no disrespect."

Alistair's straight answer cooled her head yet her objections remained steadfast. "I understand all that. Except that doesn't work for me. Women in *my* time are allowed to choose for themselves. My choice is to stand *with* him. If Ben dies while I sit here eating waffles and twiddling my thumbs I will never forgive myself. And whatever happens, I have to be able to live with myself."

He stared at her for a long time before his hands reached behind his back. Expecting some sort of binding device or weapon, Ava held her breath. Her air came out in a loud rush when she saw his apron loosen. "Let me get my hat."

The cab ride was short. Alistair's appearance drew some stares at the airport but they passed through security and the ticket line with ease. The flight was open enough for them to get two seats together. By the time they boarded the plane, Ava's anxiety was raging. She was walking into a large city she had never been to before with no idea where she was going, *actively* seeking a killer. She wasn't sure how much help she would be if she couldn't find out where the fight was. And now she had dragged Alistair into it, good sport that he was. Though who he was other than a good cook and a soft touch was undecided.

"Why did you let me go?" Ava asked when the doors were closed and he couldn't change his mind.

He opened the magazine he carried with him, a copy of a celebrity magazine rating the sexiest people alive. "Because as much as I respect the man and his ideals, I agree with you that it's your choice you have to live with. Not his." Alistair's large hand came to rest on her nervously shaking knee. "Relax dear, everything will be fine."

Now that they were doing this, her surety was failing. "I don't know if I can find him. What if something happens and I can't help because I can't even find out where he is?" Ava wondered at her impulsiveness.

Closing his magazine, Alistair twisted in his seat to aim his huge shoulders at her and asked her seriously, "Why do you think I came along?"

Shrugging, uncertain, Ava waited. "I wondered that too."

"Why did you think Ben chose me specifically, my cooking? He worried something might happen to you and he wanted to be sure someone could get you back if it did." He leaned in and lowered his voice conspiratorially. "I can do what dear Benjamin can do."

"What?" Her mouth hung open.
Alistair leaned back into his seat with a self-satisfied grin. "*I* can find him."

Ch. 27

They touched down and Ava nearly had to run to keep up with Alistair's long stride, he moved smoothly like Ben and she couldn't help wondering if that came with years of living in one's skin. At the rental desk Alistair insisted upon a convertible instead of the compact car Ava had reserved. Having the top down made the long ride a little more palatable, he argued. Alistair had to drive because he was using his "magic" to reach their mystery destination.

"It is not magic my dear." He corrected her with a sniff. "It is merely a heightened awareness that has increased over time. If you were to live two or more lifetimes you might develop some sort of knack as well. I would bet you've got it in you." He took I-20 out of town and headed due east.

"Did you have any strong tendencies during your normal lifetime?"

"What do you mean by 'tendencies'?" He raised an eyebrow over the rim of his dark shades.

"Were you good at some things and they got stronger with time, or did you get these after you, you know, changed over."

Alistair twisted his neck and lowered his seamless black sunglasses. "We aren't changed over to anything dear. We are using science to allow us to live longer. The same is

being done the world over in varying degrees, from things as mild as controlled diets and sleep manipulation, to terribly invasive procedures such as cancer treatments and transplants. Medical intervention is medical intervention any way you slice it."
Not the usual idealistic twenty-three year old, Ava was interested in the debate. "Right, but what about the cost? Even the kids that *aren't* killed are being drugged or bled without their consent to provide the blood necessary for others to live. It's exploitation." She thought of the loss of her confidence and security as well as her mother's peace of mind. Both had carried over through the remainder of their lives. "I was always taught that if someone has to sacrifice, it should be the adult for the child, not the other way around." Ava had been puzzling through the ins and outs of Ben's existence since she had learned about it. It was a conundrum further complicated by the fact that Ben's continued existence depended upon it.

On one hand, Alistair was right and it was the same as any other medical intervention. As humans, they all sought to better their lot and prolong their lives. Should it be up to another to stop them from doing just that? On the other hand, when one suffered for another to thrive, that couldn't be right. It had her morality in a tangle with no clear answer.

Alistair was quiet for a few miles. "My thought is this: One can live as one wants, long or short." He held up a finger as if anticipating Ava's argument. "*Until* that one's rights infringe upon another's."

"But they're not even fourteen. How can blood be obtained without infringing upon their rights when they're not old enough to give consent?"

"Extra blood is taken in hospitals for research all the time, this is no different. Maybe not the stealing the children in the night, thought that doesn't happen anymore on our end." Alistair frowned, then smiled knowingly. "Fourteen? Did Ben tell you there was an age cutoff?"

"Yes, he said he watched me until they wouldn't want me anymore. Ben said that was when I was fourteen." A prickling hint of foreboding crept into her thoughts, goose bumps rising on her arms. "Is that not true?"
"Well, I do know our man had to leave Minneapolis a while back." He eyed her speculatively and returned his face to the road. "You said you're twenty-three?" He tipped his head, thinking. "Yes," he nodded, "that would have been about right. Ben had an obligation to a friend and had to leave for a while. He's only been back less than a year."

"Right. Like I said, he left when I was safe." Ava repeated cautiously.

"You were safe, but it wasn't because of any age limit." He winked at Ava.

"Then why did Ben tell me that?"

"It's close, although not entirely accurate. Think about it, why would an arbitrary age be any sort of deadline? The cutoff is puberty, and that is different for everyone." He drove with his palms, tapping the steering wheel with his fingertips, collecting his thoughts. "You were a late developer?"

Her ears warmed. "Yeah, almost seventeen. They thought there was something wrong."

He nodded his head in some rhythm only he heard. "So that put our man in a bit of a bind. He had an obligation that required he leave and yet there was you." His teeth flashed. "So he did what was necessary to secure your safety in his absence." Alistair snapped his fingers. "It was no surprise that he returned here as soon as his obligation was fulfilled. It was a good thing he did, his truce with Bruder being void now leaves you out in the open."

Although touched, Ava again had to wonder at Ben's determination to keep her in the dark. He had claimed it was pure happenstance that had brought them together two weeks ago. Frustratingly, again his story rang false. "Tell me Alistair, would he lie to me about something so trivial as how he ran into me?"

Rich laughter erupted from his wide mouth, his polished teeth and vibrantly pink tongue flashed brilliantly in the sunlight. "That part is actually true! You cannot imagine how that one went over when he heard *your* shop got the antiques. It was hilarious." He guffawed again, slapping a thick thigh with his great hand. Ava caught a flash of his well manicured set of nails and watched the buffed surfaces shine in the open sunshine, a touch envious.

"So that was just chance?"

Still enjoying his amusement, he bobbed his head. "Said you were always there too. He couldn't call or it would put you ladies on alert that something was up. You were working all the time. He was watching for a day you wouldn't be there and saw you leave. He went in at lunch, said he was gambling on you being gone for a while." Alistair's accent was less clipped and more cockney the more he relaxed. "I saw him that day, nervous as a bride. Funniest thing I ever saw. Two hundred years and he's scared of a girl." His smile faded slowly as he collected himself and his speech pattern recovered its formality. "It was quite funny, really."

The change in her new friend's demeanor was significant and undeniably due to something that had happened after her chance meeting with Ben. Something else Alistair had said before was bothering her as well. She wondered what he could mean by Ben had done "what was necessary" to secure her safety. What had he done?

There was not an opportunity to pursue her curiosity further. Alistair was turning off the main highway at a town called Ruston to head southwest, his attention focused inward. "We are getting close dear. I think you should be prepared.

We are heading into the arms of a madman." When he turned to face her, gone was his jovial and friendly façade. Ava saw her first solid sign why Alistair was the sort of man Ben would leave behind with her. "You are sure you're up for this?"

Swallowing the lead ball of fear at the thought of facing her childhood nightmare in the flesh, she pictured Ben. She saw him when he faced the doctor for her as a child and saw his face from the night before when he had let his guard down with her. He'd carried far too heavy a burden for too long for her benefit. It was her turn to help him. Nodding, she said simply, "It's Ben."

Alistair's mouth twitched into a hint of a smile before he added his agreement with the sound of the engine growling into the next gear.

Ch. 28

The car stopped and Ava surveyed the scenery surrounding them, and felt her heart sink. They were in the middle of a wilderness area. It was beautiful, perfect for a hike and a hell of a place to track someone. Heavily wooded, leaf litter covered the ground dotted with Azaleas and Dogwoods beginning to bloom. Louisiana's spring was at least a full month ahead of her home state. The scent on the light breeze was a combination of fresh blooms announcing a forest coming to life and the pungent odor of damp earth and decaying leaves from seasons past.

Temperatures had to be in the eighties already with the humidity steadily making its presence hard to ignore. Ava wished she was back in the convertible with the breeze rolling over her skin to cool her. Already her shirt was promising to stick to her skin like a wet blanket before too long.

“This is it?” There was nowhere the doctor could hide the type of facilities he would require for his purposes on this undeveloped hillside. Ava felt cheated.

Her question drew a sharp glance from Alistair. She held her tongue.

He started to move steadily up a well trod path. The sureness of his stride led Ava to believe he remained on the trail. Perhaps this was not the doctor’s facilities at all. She reminded herself they were tracking Ben, who was tracking the doctor’s messenger. It was possible Ben and his quarry had not yet reached the lab, wherever that might be.

Invigorated by hope, Ava walked and jogged behind her large guide. They slowed at a marker informing them that the path to Driskill Mountain’s summit, the highest point in Louisiana, was behind them. Alistair continued on his path, leading them in the opposite direction. Ava kept quiet, trying not to distract Alistair, hoping they were close and she would see Ben again soon.

Their path angled downward halting at a freshly logged clearing. A sudden opening in the trees let the sun beam directly down and Ava was instantly enveloped in warm, wet air she wouldn’t feel at home for months. She held a corner of her shirt and flapped it, hoping to create enough of a breeze to cool her, or at least to peel her damp clothing away from her skin for a brief reprieve.

Ava watched Alistair, waiting for further direction but he was standing with his hands on his hips, head shaking while he stared at the ground.

“Is he close?” Her heart hammered from her hike. She told herself the shortness of breath had nothing to do with fear.

“He *is* close. There is something between us though, he’s muffled.” His accent was clipped and very sharp, a sign that he was worried. Ava had good reason to learn his tells fast.

She started to pace around the clearing, searching for some sort of *something*. She had no idea what, she could only hope for some sort of clue, some sign that screamed "Ben" that would lead them to him wherever he was. She borrowed Alistair's phone and called him again. It went straight to voicemail. Ava kicked at the ground and a chunk of wood debris went flying.

Clink. She heard the sound of metal being struck. Alistair had as well and their eyes met across the clearing. Excitement flowed through her, she fought it back not wanting to get her hopes up. Again she kicked, aiming in the same direction.

Clink. Both of them tuned in to where the sound came from. Alistair took long sweeping strides and Ava jogged to where they heard the sound. There, on the ground at the edge of the clearing was a metal lid easily slid aside to reveal a pit. A ladder's rungs descended into its depths. So well hidden had it been by the leaves and wood debris, it would not be visible to the human eye unless someone knew exactly where to look.

"This has to be it, right?" Ava looked at Alistair over the hole that looked just like a city's water access.

He continued to squint down into the blackness. "I've never trailed someone underground before."

Wishing for the first time in her life that she had a gun, Ava stared down the abyss as well. "Well, here goes." She took a breath and turned to step down.

"Wait a minute now dear." Alistair laid a hand to stop her, easily covering her entire shoulder. "There is no way I am letting you go down there first. I have my pride you know."

Nodding stiffly, Ava stepped back and traded places with him.

"My kingdom for a torch." He grinned tightly as he stepped down.

Ava detected the faintest trembling in his voice and his hand shook as he grabbed the rungs. She refrained from commenting out of respect. Only a spelunker wouldn't be afraid of *this* blackness, she thought nervously, watching Alistair's form disappear from the bottom up.

Together they descended, Ava counted the rungs. Thirteen, fourteen, fifteen. She heard scuffing on a rough surface and Alistair announced he had reached the ground. Her count had gone to twenty-six rungs. Face turned up, she took a long look at the clear blue sky before girding herself for the blackness.

Alistair's hand brushed hers and she took it. "It would be best for us to hold on to each other lest we become separated."

The warmth of his hand engulfed hers. Ava's clothes, wet with sweat, were cooling rapidly, accentuating the chilly underground temperatures. She shivered in her body's attempt to warm up, longing for the sweater she had left in the car, not thinking she would need it in this heat.

Farther into the tunnel they walked. Fortunately their path was clear. There was only one direction to go from the ladder. They followed the path side by side, free hands outstretched to touch the edges of the tunnel. It was about the width of a passenger car and, by Alistair's reckoning, about ten feet high. He could only just reach it with his fingertips if he stood on his toes. The ground was level and relatively smooth. How it had gotten here was a mystery, Ava said as much.

"My guess is that it is an old bomb shelter. They put them in some of the strangest places during the forties and fifties. There are tunnels under about every city and park in this country. Most are long forgotten, like this one."

It seemed an eternity they walked in the darkness, silent but for the soft crunching of their shoes on packed earth and an occasional stone. Eventually, Ava heard the hum of machinery, loud in the empty space. Alistair squeezed her hand excitedly and Ava squeaked. He had a firm grip. His free hand brushed her arm by way of apology. Ava took care to pick up her feet carefully, making as little noise as possible. Alistair did the same, no sound coming from his side of the tunnel.

The tunnel curved sharply left, Ava felt it on her side and pulled Alistair's hand to indicate direction. When they made the turn, the soft glow of track lighting hit their eyes. Distant, it gave them time to adjust as they followed it eagerly. No matter the source, they desperately sought refuge from the suffocating darkness.

Drawing near the light, Alistair pulled her behind him and she peeked out around his arm to see what they were walking into. The tunnel opened up on a cavern. It was dry and cool, lights ran along the flat ceiling and several computers were lined up on a table near a far wall. The sound they heard was the hum of a large generator running beyond the computers. She lost sight of everything else as her eyes fell on what was in the center of the room. There stood two metal beds. Replicas of the one Ava had laid upon so long ago.

The shivering from the cold turned to shudders and Ava felt her vision narrow until all she saw were the beds. Her legs buckled and she fell to her knees, losing her grip on Alistair's hand.

Feeling her slip he turned to her, his eyes anxious. Valuing their silence more than ever, Ava waved him off knowing she could go no further and her handicap would be a hindrance. Heart in her throat, Ava's eyes followed Alistair as he crept along the edge and followed the wall into the room where she lost him behind the computers.

Her eyes were drawn back to the tables and her mind went back. The wet shirt she wore became the cool metal against her skin. It was musty and stale in the cavern, the still air felt heavy and dry making her already strained lungs work harder to gain a breath.

Breath erratic, spots appeared in her vision and Ava put her hands down to brace herself. Dropping her head, she struggled to calm down. She heard herself wheezing loudly, deciding to hold her breath to keep quiet. Her shaking arms grew weaker, and, no longer able to support her, she fell to her side. Her upturned face watched the light fade as two pairs of legs rushed toward her, and gasping for air, Ava watched them fade into nothing.

***

Ava came to lying on the familiar metal surface. She felt it before she opened her eyes to stare at the yellow cast of lights, harsh in such a naturally dark place. At the edges where the lights were not strong enough to penetrate, shadows gave the illusion that they were alone in the world.

An involuntary whimper escaped her lips before she closed them tightly, not wanting anyone to know she was awake. Carefully, she tested her wrists and found they were unbound. Her legs were free as well. Ava mentally mapped the room and knew she could reach the tunnel in just a few strides. If she had the element of surprise, she could possibly lose her captors in the darkness, giving her a chance at escape.

Her thoughts turned to Alistair. If he was in here, she couldn't abandon him. Ava wrestled with her fear and remembered her vow to be stronger. She thought of Ben out there somewhere, maybe here, and in trouble. She took several deep breaths, closing her eyes to settle her nerves and remind herself she was no longer a child unable to defend herself. If she could move, she could get away.

Sneaking her feet over the edge of the table, Ava slid down on her back until she felt the ground against her toes, sinking down below the table. Once she was crouched on the ground beside the metal structure, she turned her head, taking in the room around her. The two sets of legs were at the computers, their backs to her. She saw no one else and dared to stand.

Looking behind her she saw only a pile of rags and medical waste shoved off to the side. Ava didn't see Alistair until she faced forward again and saw him standing with another man at the computers. Looking up, she could see the second man was bent over the keys, typing. She couldn't see him well, partially blocked as he was by Alistair and some other pieces of equipment in her way.

She could not hear their mumbling speech and because Alistair was an arms reach from the other, she could not get to him without also sacrificing herself. Ava knew she could find this place again with the police, and Alistair didn't seem in imminent danger. Ava hoped she could drive quickly and reach the police in time to save him. Closing her eyes and saying a silent prayer to keep her friend safe, Ava spun and started back toward the darkness.

Her foot crunched on a rock and she cursed herself. Fearing herself caught, Ava bolted. Three strides out, someone called her name and she slid to a halt. It was one she knew, and it wasn't Alistair.

"Ben!" She twisted her neck and saw him standing next to her big friend. Unable to contain her joy at seeing him unharmed, Ava reversed directions and ran just as quickly toward him like a fool.

His arms closed around her and she felt him rock back from the impact. Ben kissed her head and held her tight before he pulled away. "I specifically told you not to follow me." His expression was stern.

"And I specifically told you not to make my decisions for me." Ava shot back.
Alistair's calm voice of reason de-escalated the mood. "What's done is done Ben. If you want to bring Ava up to speed, I will keep looking."

Ben cast a glance back to the computer before he looked at Alistair and nodded. With his arm around Ava's waist, he guided her back in the direction of the table. Pushing her shoulder into his chest, Ava changed their course.

"Not there." She said flatly.

His arm tightened, giving her a half hug. "Of course." They walked around the offending object, giving it a wide berth, to end up between it and the computers. Ben explained, visibly agitated, that he had again been too late. "I followed the woman here. I couldn't have been more than a few hours behind her." He shook his head, "By the time I got here she was dead and the doctor had already cleaned house." He waved an arm toward the computers, shattered pieces of gray and black plastic littered the floor and worktable holding up what was left of the three computers. "We're trying to recover what we can but it looks like he tried to wipe the hard drives. Fortunately, he was in a hurry and unable to do a very thorough a job. Maybe he left us something. I was closer this time than ever. Her body was still warm."

Ava glanced around, not seeing a body. Confused, she looked askance of Ben. He nodded toward the pile of she'd noticed earler and Ava looked closer, seeing a hand and part of a black leather clad leg.

"I covered her up. He 'questioned' her before he finally killed her. It wasn't an easy death."

Ava swallowed hard. Poor woman, no one deserved that.

Alistair called out. "Ben, come here."

He turned and moved eagerly to the far end of the computer bank where Alistair had his head down staring intently at a partially obliterated unit.

"I don't think there's damage to the drive, just the casing. I think if we could get this to an expert we might be able to find something. Do you still know a guy?"

"I do." Ben pulled out his phone, checked it and frowned muttering about a lack of a signal. He shook it off, refusing to be brought down by the technical glitch. "Let's pull what we need."

Ben worked to remove the hard drives using some tools left by the retreating crew. Meanwhile, Alistair busied himself digging through the equipment and storage units looking for records of any kind. It seemed the doctor had taken all of those. Near the pile in the corner, Ben found a small canvas bag to stash the three hard drives in.

Glancing down, Ben spoke softly. "We should do something for her. We can't be caught burying a body up top." He nodded to himself. "We'll have to handle this down here."

Alistair and Ava joined him. Alistair fished in his pocket and held out a lighter. "Will this do?"

"Did you have that the whole time?" Ava stared at him in disbelief, recalling his hesitation in the dark tunnel.

"No, I found it over there." He inclined his head toward the remains of the rolling file cabinet that had "fallen over" in his thoroughness.

Ben reached out, taking it from Alistair's outstretched hand. He stood by the body and Ava saw his head bow. She and Alistair followed suit, bowing their own heads, while Ben said a few kind words. He knelt down and lit the rags.

The smoke rapidly filled the chamber and the trio moved quickly through the tunnel, single file with Alistair shuffling loudly in the lead. Now that they didn't have to worry about bad guys, they could make all the noise they wanted.

When Ava's hand touched the first rung of the ladder, she was gripped with a driving need to be in the light and rushed up to the top. A short time later, when she felt the sun on her back and the sounds of birds and insects again filled her ears, she sat on the ground and turned her face to the sky vowing never to go underground again.

Ch. 29

When it was time to part ways, the three agreed to meet at Ben's the next day. Alistair was the only one whose phone still worked, Ben's was dead from searching for a signal for too long and Ava's wasn't even with them.

Alistair booked his flight, bidding them adieu with a grand wave and a wink before returning to the convertible. Ava went with Ben to where he had parked at a scenic overlook a mile downhill. They walked without speaking, Ava was exhausted and couldn't have carried on a conversation and hike at the same time. Once, when her foot hit a loose rock, she skidded down a few feet on her butt.

Ben was a step behind her, offering her a hand up. "Are you all right? We can stop."

She stood and let go of him, determined to hike out under her own power. Her pride still stung from her short circuit in the tunnel. She was angry with her weakness, made even more blatant by comparing it to the bravery of both Ben and Alistair. Alistair had been scared of the tunnel yet he had gone down there. She, on the other hand, would have been no help to him if there had been someone other than a friend down there. Fainting soldiers rarely fared well, nor did their comrades.

"I can make it." Sheer stubbornness carried Ava the rest of the way to the car. Ben reached it first and, when he opened the door for her, she fell into the seat gratefully.

The engine turned over and Ben cranked the air conditioning in the SUV. By way of explanation for the unusual ride he rolled a shoulder, "I didn't know where I was going. Some of these roads can get a little rough."

Ava grunted her response. She let her head fall back on the headrest and let it loll to watch the rolling hills and beautiful scenery fly past her window as they backtracked the seventy miles to Shreveport.

Getting home proved a fiasco. Ben and Ava had to jump through some hoops trying to get a flight back that night when they finally reached the airport. In the end, they were able to get two seats on a red eye the next morning.

So, once again, Ava found herself filthy with no extra clothing walking into a hotel with Ben. "This is getting to be a disturbing pattern." She joked.

Ben glanced around the room and smiled. "At least this is a bigger hotel. We have some more options."

A hot shower sounded great after a day of sweaty hiking. When they had their keys, they went into the gift shop and bought enough to put themselves in decent order. Each of them got a shirt professing an undying love for Louisiana. Everything else could be washed in the room and hung to dry for morning.

Ava showered while Ben ordered dinner. "Do you have a preference?" He began to list off the choices.

Ava heard the first three and her mouth was watering. She hadn't eaten anything substantial since her waffles. "You pick, it all sounds good to me."

She had only her new shirt to wear after showering and Ben waited to take his, announcing she couldn't possibly answer the door as she was. Her ingrained feminism reared it head until she looked down and saw that her shirt barely reached her thighs. This *wasn't* a lonely country road where no one was going to see her. He won.

They had a table in this room and made use of it to spread out their feast. Alistair might have had better shrimp etoufee than this, but Ava doubted it. The flavors were incredible and she savored each bite. Ben enjoyed his as well, eating only a remarkably small portion.

"Is that how little you usually eat?" Ava's eyes went from her plate to his. A big eater by no means, she had taken nearly double what he did. Even his salad held only a hint of dressing.

He nodded, "At home I can eat a little more but restaurant food is much higher calorie and I have to eat very small portions."

"Doesn't that bother you? All the self-denial?" Jackie was wrong. A monk had more luxury than Ben allowed himself.

"Yes, but I've had a long time to get used to it." He eyed her slender form. "Do you exercise?"

Ava nodded, puzzled at the seeming randomness of his comment.

"Did you find it an easy habit to get into or do you have days when you don't want to do it?"

Ava tipped her head. "I see your point. It just seems like you give up so much. Is life worth living if it's always denying the things that give you pleasure?"

"A little food and alcohol are nothing to worry about. I did take a while to get used to the cooler temperatures. It would be nice to come home to a warm house or sit by the fire as long as I want on a winter's night." He admitted wistfully.

"Maybe after you've done what you need to, you can start doing that stuff again. You said you were going to let yourself age. Did you mean that?"

"Yes." He said without hesitation. "Two hundred eighteen years is a very long lifetime. It would be good to grow old." He stabbed a tomato.

Ava leaned back in her chair, laying her hands in her lap and eyed him steadily. "Speaking of doing what you need to do, what did you have to do when you left before?"

Ben's back stiffened, he eyeballed his impaled tomato. "What are you talking about?"

Ava maintained eye contact. "I'm talking about when you went away before, when I was fourteen. A little bird told me you made up the age moratorium and that you actually had to arrange something with the enemy so nothing would happen to me. Is it this deal I keep hearing mentioned that may or may not be called off? Could you tell me what they're talking about?"

Ben's jaw tightened and she saw anger flash in his eyes before he tucked it away. "Ava, what I have chosen to do for you was my choice and I don't want you to feel beholden to me for any reason. Can we please leave it at that?" He neatly slid his tomato off of his fork with his teeth.

Though she very much wanted to know what Ben had done, he made a good point. He *had* saved her more than once and there was a certain amount of karmic debt she owed him for that. Any relationship bore a certain amount of give and take although theirs was beginning to feel one sided, which might bode ill for their future.

Instead of answering right away, Ava chewed several more bites thoughtfully. When she spoke it was down a different avenue. “Why me?”

“Why did I save you? I already told you that.”

Shaking her head, Ava set down her fork and stared at him. “Why did you follow me all these years after you pulled me out of the lab? Alistair said you had to go away for a while and then you came back here, knowing I was safe. Why?”

Ben’s face flushed. “I will have to choose a mute next time I need someone to stay with you.”

She let his comment about needing a sitter again slide. “I like Alistair. He makes great waffles.”

Ben eyed her, Ava smiled expectantly.

He cleared his throat and took a drink of water. “I don’t know exactly, there was something you said.” His speech was halting as he reluctantly shared what was obviously a strong memory for him. Ben’s eyes implored her, “Do you remember what you said when I carried you out?”

Ava let her mind turn back to that night. Her recollection ended when she fell asleep, she didn’t remember speaking. “I didn’t say anything.”

“Yes you did.”

“What did I say?” She asked softly, willing her mind to find her own words.

Ben's face reddened and he looked away. Coughing, he glanced back at her, and some strong emotion choked his voice. "You called me an angel."

Just like that, Ava's mind gave up the memory. She was cradled in his arms and he was taking her out of that place.

He turned and his long stride rocked her toward sleep. Just before she faded, she remembered looking up and seeing the light blocked by his head. It looked like a halo. "Daddy sent an angel."

Her hand went to her mouth. "I did. I remember." Ava's eyes welled up. "I knew my father sent you because he couldn't come." How strange that she had gotten it confused when she'd locked it all away, to believe it had been her father. Ava's belief had come full circle, returning to what she'd originally thought after seeing him again. In her heart she still believed it. "That's why you've been with me for so long?"

"Yes." He took a sip of water, composing himself. "I had started to lose my faith. After the miss in Amsterdam I wasn't sure I was making a difference, I wasn't sure my end justified my means anymore. Then, when you said that to me, I knew I had made at least one small difference. I'd changed one life. I had to protect it."

It was a moving thing to hear about oneself, that she had made that great an impact and had essentially restored his faith in himself and his cause. All she could say was a simple, "Thank you Ben." And, "Give me your clothes."

"What?" He raised a brow at her.

Blushing, she giggled nervously. "I mean I'm going to wash them while you eat. I'm finished." Assuming he would disrobe, she walked a towel out to him and returned to fill the tub. A few minutes later, he knocked gently on the door and handed her his clothes, his pale, lean body wrapped only in a towel clinging low on his hips. Flushed as a schoolgirl, she took them and put them in the tub.

Having some experience washing stockings and lingerie in the sink, Ava knew what to do although it still took some time for her to wash all of their clothes. Finally she hung the last sock and stood, stretching her back.

Ava dried off her hands while she assessed herself in the mirror. She had inspired Ben to follow her and keep her safe for all these years. Was she worthy of that kind of devotion? He loved her, but how much of that was because of who she was and not what she represented for him. It was possible he loved the *idea* of her, a child who gave him validation when he needed it. Was she so different now, falling all over him the way she did? Was it some deep seated hero worship affecting her on a base level?

She questioned her worthiness of such sacrifice. Ava was not a great beauty, nor had she made proper use of the life he'd given so much to guarantee. It was a heavy burden for anyone to bear. And then there was the "deal" he had made with his enemy. What had the woman meant when she'd said it had expired?

He knocked on the door again, startling her from her harsh self-assessment. "I suppose you want to shower."

Hurriedly she moved out of the small bathroom and allowed him entrance, their bodies brushing as they passed in the doorway. Ava's responded instantly and she caught her breath as she shuffled out to clean up dinner. Ben had already done so, leaving Ava to put the trays containing all of their dishes outside the door making sure to back herself in to avoid any inadvertent peep shows.

The shower was already running when she locked the door behind her. The clean scent of soap wafted out on the steam billowing out around the partially closed door. As she walked from the front room to the bedroom, passing the bathroom in between, the shower controls squeaked off and the water stopped.

Ava plopped down on the bed and closed her burning eyes. Her body was rejuvenated after the hot shower, but her head hurt and her eyes burned. It was most likely a reaction to the dust and smoke in the tunnel and the unfamiliar pollens in the woods. She got up to turn the unit in the room from fan to air conditioning, not caring that it was going to get too cold for just a shirt. The filtered air would clear her head and help her eyes, the low temperatures would help Ben. Standing, she put her hands behind her hips and stretched her back again. The tub was exactly the wrong height to wash clothes and she could feel it.

Ava turned to see Ben standing outside the bathroom, running his hand through his hair. His scars shone silver against his skin, flushed pink from the shower. Catching the direction of her stare, Ben put his hand to his chest. "When the carriage flipped the door hit a rock and shattered. I was thrown out and landed on the broken pieces." Ben's fingers pointed to the inside of his elbows. "And this is what the conversion process and two hundred years of injecting oneself does. The scar tissue builds up and I've had to move my sites around a little." He looked up at her. "Do they bother you?"

She shook her head. "Not at all." Shivering from the cold emanating from the unit immediately behind her, Ava rubbed her hands on her arms and nodded at the counter across from the bathroom door behind Ben. "Do we have a coffee maker?"

Glancing over, he confirmed that they did. "Do you want some?"

Ava bobbed her head. "Yeah, I'm freezing."

"Why did you turn on the air? The fan wasn't as cold." He moved to fill the carafe with water.

She shrugged and aimed for the coffee maker, explaining her theory on filtered air, eye comfort and his longevity while she tended to the grounds and filter. Ava was attempting to open the bag of coffee grounds and couldn't get it. "They always make these so frustrating. It says, 'tear here' except it never works 'there.' Why don't they give you scissors in a hotel so you can just cut the damn thing?" Ava grumbled to no one but herself, tearing at the bag just waiting for it to give and spill grounds all over.

"Here, let me try." Ben reached around her to put the carafe on the counter and take the bag from her hand. One hand on either side of her put him directly behind her and she was intensely aware of his nearness. Thoughts of their night together flooded her mind and she felt the goose flesh rising on her arms.

He saw it and, having successfully torn the bag open with one try, ran a hand up and down her arm. "You're cold. Come get in bed. We can stay warm in there until our clothes dry."

Ava let herself be led to the bed where she proceeded to remove all six of the pillows she didn't need and climb into their King size bed. Without hesitation, Ben lay down beside her and put his arm across her stomach, the other hand propping his head with his palm so that he could look at her. When she laid her hand over his arm, she felt his heat and the other hand soon followed suit.

"Are you always this cold?" He slid his arm forward, hooking his hand on her hip and pulling her into him. "I thought *I* was cold."

Laughing nervously, Ava clarified. "In my defense, other than last night, you've only touched me when I was hypothermic so I don't think you have enough evidence to form a solid hypothesis."

“Last night.” He said softly. “It was awful of me to leave you like that. I hope you didn’t think that I just wanted to…” He let his voice trail off.

Ava chuckled at the ridiculousness of the suggestion. “I was mad you left without me, but no, I didn’t think it was a one night stand. If it was, you put a lot of work in for just one night.”

The corners of his eyes crinkled in amusement and he leaned down, his lips kissing her shoulder. “If you don’t mind, I would like to pick up where we left off.” He kissed her neck. “Unless you would like to sleep instead.”

“I can sleep on the plane.” Ava rolled into him, more than willing. “I had a few ideas of my own.” She slid her hands down his back, wiggling his towel loose with her fingers.

Ben moaned softly, his chest rumbling against hers. She shivered not from cold, but from pleasure and he growled, wrapping his arm around her back and flipping her on top of him. With one hand he pulled off her tourist garb. “Was this one of your ideas?” He teased, maneuvering them both to just the right position before stopping and holding her still. Teasing.

“You read my mind.” Ava wriggled herself loose and showed him exactly what she’d been thinking.

Ch. 30

Their flight landed during a spring shower at the Minneapolis/ St. Paul airport and before most people were awake, they were home. Though tired from getting very little sleep, Ava was positively blissful to be reunited with her new slash old love. She had been watching him closely, however. He was looking run down like he had on the road, she could see the bags under his eyes as well as new lines creasing his forehead and around his mouth from the strain. It suddenly became very real to her that if he were to lose access to the blood he needed, he would age and die rapidly. He wouldn't answer her queries as to how long exactly, though she had some indication from these past few days that it couldn't be terribly long, a few weeks maybe.

At home, Ben went straight to the fridge and she went upstairs. She understood what he needed to do, it didn't mean she could stomach seeing it. There it was again, *what he needed to do*. It continued to plague her. She warred with herself. While she agreed in theory with Ben that she didn't need to know each and every thing he had done over the years while she had been his unwitting charge, it ate at her wondering what he'd had to do and who had borne the cost of her survival.

When he joined her upstairs, she was picking out clothes from the stash the movers had brought with them. By her count, she had a few days more before she would have to check in with Elle and Katherine or go to her apartment to pick up more clothes. Given her good mood it tickled her to think of the women's reactions to seeing her with Ben so soon after hearing that she had gone away for a weekend with the blonde. Let them think it was feast time, there had been plenty of famine.

"What are you smiling about?" Ben slid up behind her, putting his arms around her waist and tucking his nose into her neck.

Chuckling, she shared her amusement with him. His hands loosened their grip and she twisted in his arms to see by his expression that he didn't share her glee. Ava took his face in her hands.

"What? Does it bother you that I mentioned him?" It didn't bother her, discussing a man she'd been intent upon murdering before Ben had done it for her. It had been self-preservation she told herself.

Ben shook his head, "No. Your mother and Elle." He continued at Ava's obvious confusion. "Won't they think less of you?"

Ava's forehead crinkled while she rolled the scenario over in her head. "Maybe my mother, but I did tell her it wasn't anything serious. I'll tell her I came home after one night." She shrugged unconcerned. "It's not a big deal."

His eyebrows shot up. "It won't matter how many lovers you've had, only their duration?"

Ava rushed to her own defense. "Before you start drawing the wrong conclusions, I think you should know that I have always been conservative in dating and my family has no reason to believe I'm that kind of girl." Her hands were back at her sides, fists clenching. "Not that I need to tell *you.* I would bet you know better than anyone who I've slept with."

Ben's face colored. "That is unfair. I would never intrude upon your privacy like that. Some of your gentleman callers did give me concern however, I did not feel it was appropriate to interfere. That was not my role." His manner had reverted to old fashioned formality. It was fascinating that he could flux between times much like Alistair when he was stressed. She wondered how old Alistair was. Ben put his hands on her arms, "I have never doubted your character. My concern is whether my timing will harm your reputation."

Her defensiveness was banking. "You don't have to worry. I'll find a way to explain it." She squeezed his hand. "Besides, once they meet you, they'll love you as much as I do." Surprised at her slip of the tongue Ava watched him, her eyes wide.

He smiled and kissed her softly. "Me too."

Ava leaned into him and Ben began to respond then cursed under his breath as he broke off.

"We have obligations first." His hands ran down her back, his preference plain on his face. "Alistair is waiting for us and we have someone to see about some hard drives. We can't let the trail get cold."

Sighing, Ava let go reluctantly and got ready to leave. Ben was already on his phone with someone doing a lot of talking and pointed to a coat closet in the entryway. Opening it, Ava found a light jacket for him. She pointed silently and he gave her a thumbs up, mouthing "thank you." She dug for one she could borrow, gestured to convey her request and Ben nodded. Both jackets donned, Ben still on his phone, they pulled the door shut and brought the bag with their precious cargo with them tucked carefully under Ava's jacket.

Alistair, it turned out, owned a small bistro in a trendy pocket neighborhood of Minneapolis at 48th and Chicago. He was sitting at a small table reading the paper and sipping on an espresso when they walked in, shaking the rain off their jackets.

"Ava." He greeted her like an old friend, rising to take her into an enormous bear hug. He shook Ben's hand heartily and slapped his back. Though smaller, Ben didn't flinch at the blows. He smiled warmly at his friend.

They were seated and Alistair waved for a server. They ordered espresso at his recommendation and were soon left alone to discuss their plan of action.

"The first step is to give these to Scott. I wouldn't trust anyone else with them." Ben started, taking a moment to fill Ava in. "Scott is someone I have known for a while. He is very talented with computers and I trust he will keep anything he finds in confidence."

Alistair was bobbing his head in agreement.

"Is he, ah, like you?"

"No, but his wife is. He has a daughter from a previous marriage. Needless to say, he disagrees with the doctor's tactics." Alistair informed her.

Their drinks arrived and the server asked if there would be anything else. Alistair raised his eyebrows at his guests, gesturing to either of them to order if need be.

Ava could smell the special, a spinach soufflé someone had been eating when she walked in, and she ordered one. Ben requested an egg white vegetable omelet. Alistair held up a hand to stop the server.

"I'll have the same. Both from *my* menu please."

Ben smiled at her. "Alistair has them convinced he's a huge health nut. He has a personal version of each item on the menu. It makes it very convenient to come here."

Ava was enjoying herself. Being with them was easy. "I love it here. I'd like to come again." She told them genuinely.

Alistair touched her hand where it rested on the table. "It would be a pleasure dear."

Sipping on one of the best espressos Ava had consumed in her memory, she listened to Alistair's entertaining telling of a trip he and Ben had taken to Louisiana a few years before Hurricane Katrina. It involved a woman of questionable virtue, a small man with a limp and three sailors on leave. By the time he had finished, Ava's eyes were watering and she had serious doubts that any of it was true.

"It most certainly *is* true." Alistair insisted, pounding the table in mock indignation.

She continued to disagree. "Things like that don't happen in real life. It sounds like a joke. 'Three sailors walk into a brothel.'"

"Who said anything about a brothel?" Alistair flicked up an eyebrow at her. "It was a gambling establishment."

"Yeah, it was certainly a gamble." Ben interjected with a laugh. "I didn't know if I would walk out with my wallet, my life, a clean bill of health or any combination of the three."

It didn't matter if it was true or not, Ava loved the story *and* Alistair. His fondness for Ben was clear to her as well, further endearing him in her eyes. Her accusation the other night about his friends turned out to be entirely false. He had at least one very good one, Scott was possibly another. It made her feel better about his long life to know it had not been entirely empty of human warmth and companionship. The stories continued over a delicious breakfast. Ava enjoyed hearing them, and even more than that, she soaked up Ben's ready laughter.

When he laughed and relaxed with his closest friend he was a different man than she had seen on the hunt and on the run. Ava hoped they had more time like this in store than the other. Her hopes rested on the three little plastic bundles of plastic and metal hidden in the trunk of Ben's car, waiting outside in the dissipating rain. The sun chose that moment to break through the clouds and Ava took it as a good omen for things to come.

After breakfast Alistair insisted he was not needed to drop off the hard drives and should put in some time at the bistro. Scott was most likely going to have to work with them for a while before he would know anything anyway. Ava hugged him good bye, his giant arms making her feel like a little girl. It was a cozy feeling and she sunk into it before letting him go. Ben shook his hand and they exited into the sunshine and warmer temperatures.

Ch. 31

Ava was expecting Scott to be in some secretive basement somewhere, working only for "the cause." She was shocked when they parked at Ridgedale Mall, a shopping mecca in the middle of upper class suburbia.

She looked questioningly at Ben.

"He works at Apple." He grinned at her expression. "Did you think he was living in his mother's basement, reading comic books?"

He wasn't far off the mark. "No, I know he's married." She shut her door and looked at him over the roof of the car. "I pictured him as more of a War Craft guy."

Ben threw back his head and laughed hard. Coming around the back of the car he took her hand. "Come on, now I really want you to meet him."

The mall was busy. They were just past Easter, a big time for retail and Ava was reminded of her own store with a guilty pang. "I should really think about getting back to Elle soon."

He slowed his pace to match hers. "Do you *want* to go back there?"

"What do you mean?"

"You can't have much of a future there."

Her hackles rose. "I suppose you have a different idea for my future?"

Ben did not see the danger until he'd already stepped in it. "I should think a woman with your mind and education would want more. I'm merely suggesting that you could excuse yourself from your job at the store and pursue a more meaningful career."

Ava stopped dead. Ben felt the tug on his hand when he reached the end of her arm. Their hands separated. "So you're suggesting I quit and leave my mom's best friend, my good friend, a woman who has been looking out for me for the past six years, shorthanded?" She held up her arms, palms skyward. "And what do you suggest I do for income during this pursuit for meaning in my life? I have bills; rent, cell phone, student loans that I'm not sure I can pay for even *with* my job."

"You could live with me." Ben said it quietly and then tensely watched her reaction, the muscle in his jaw twitching.

She reined in her temper, not wanting to say the wrong thing and hurt him. "Ben, I appreciate the offer but doing things for myself is important to me. So is Elle's happiness. I can't leave her in the lurch like that. I know I need to think about what to do now that I'm done with school, it's just that..." Ava ducked her eyes and admitted what she had not yet verbalized to anyone. "I'm a little scared. Having my entire future hinging on this one decision has me terrified." Petrified really, but she wasn't going to admit that even to him.

Ben had sterilized his expression so she wasn't sure if he was offended or not by her rejection. "I didn't know you felt that way about it, I apologize. Sometimes we have to do things not because of the opportunity, but because of the obligation." His brow furrowed in thought, "If you need any help once you decide on a career path, I do have contacts in a number of different fields."

"Thanks for the offer, we'll see what happens." Ava let it drop. She decided to press for an answer she needed to keep her perspective. "Speaking of obligations, what did you have to do when you left Minnesota? Where did you have to go?" She asked him softly. "I need to know."

He reached down for her hand again and raised it to brush his lips against her palm in an intimate gesture. Ava flushed. "I have a lab in Washington State. One of the scientists, a man I have a deep respect for, made a breakthrough and they needed a test subject for a series of trials. I volunteered." Ben frowned and a line appeared between his brows. "Some of the tests went better than others. When the results came back I was tied up for several years gathering the necessary talent to fill the gaps in our knowledge."

The Apple store was downstairs and crowded as usual. Most of the people milling about had ipod questions. Ben was approached by one of the "geniuses," the company's name for its associates.

"Hello Jenna."

The short redhead had holes in her face that spoke of a wilder evening life and sported a long sleeved shirt Ava was willing to bet hid a few spots of ink.

"Hey Ben. Are you looking for Scott?" She wore a huge smile that revealed big dimples and lent her expression a youthful air. She eyed Ava appraisingly and waved, low and quick at her. "He's in the back. Do you want to go see him?"

"That would be great. Thank you." Ben turned to Ava and she felt his hand slide up under her jacket.

Darting her eyes to where Jenna stood looking amused, Ava put her hand on his forearm. "Ben." She warned.

He gave her a quick kiss on her forehead and his hand went to her inside pocket to retrieve what he'd been after. Winking, he excused himself. "I'll be right back."

Ava moved to follow and Jenna held up her hand. "Sorry, I can only let one sneak back there. Do you mind?" She twisted her lips and raised her eyebrow, begging understanding.

"Not a problem." Ava flashed her a grin. Ben waited for her approval, she waved him off. "I'm fine. You know what, I do need something, could you help me?"

One finger pointed to the blue shirt sporting a white apple she wore as a uniform. "I'm told I'm a genius, I'll try."

Last winter Ava had slipped on the ice and her ipod had hit the sidewalk sustaining a good amount of damage. There was no longer a way to read the display, the screen was perpetually covered with tightly bunched horizontal lines. Because there was no way to read the screen, there was also no way to pick a song or playlist. The only thing she could do was turn it on and off. Eventually, Ava could no longer stand it and had put it on the shelf where it continued to collect a fair amount of dust. She'd been too busy with work and finishing her thesis that she hadn't been able to replace it yet.

Jenna laughed at Ava's sad tale. She had a good laugh, so many women shaped their laughter for fear of drawing too much attention or wanting to sound a certain way. Jenna's came from down deep, it felt honest. It made Ava happy just hearing it.

"What kind was it, do you want to replace it or try something else?" Jenna pointed and led them to the ipod table. She shouldered her way through the pedestrians and Ava followed in the wake she created.

Ava was eyeing the step up from hers. She had wanted to upgrade for a long time and liked the capacity for watching movies. In her dreams of her future, she had imagined taking a big trip when she finished school. Her trip account had taken an unexpected and fairly large hit recently.

Longingly, she fingered the one she wanted and Jenna picked it up.

"This one? It's my fave. Is that the one you had before?"

She shook her head, frowning. "No, I had the little one. I did tell myself I was going to buy the big one when I graduated though."

"What school?"

"Hamline, MBA." Ava responded without much enthusiasm.

Jenna's mouth twitched. "It was that awesome huh?"

She found herself laughing for the first time about it. "Yeah, I didn't even want it. I went because my mom wanted me to go for business and I figured if I kept going to school I would never have to actually *work* in the field. I can't imagine sitting at a desk all day dealing with reports and corporate bureaucracy that don't have any sort of greater meaning."

Again, Jenna laughed. "That is a very interesting take on how to avoid doing what your parents want." She pointed to the unit Ava wanted. "So, what do you think? Now that you've done what everyone else wants, how about what you want?" She looked over Ava's shoulder and tipped her chin up in greeting at someone.

Ava felt her time with Jenna growing short. She tried to release her. Waving her hand, she moved toward the old one she'd had. "No, I shouldn't. I want that one, but the old savings account has taken some unforeseen hits lately. I'll just replace the little one." She shrugged and smiled. "It was fine, I won't need the movie feature for the long plane ride I won't be taking."

Jenna's holey eyebrows shot up. "Were you going on a trip?" She rolled her eyes expressively. "I love travel. I go anywhere, anytime. Where were you going to go?"

Watching her fingers was easier than looking Jenna in the eye. She traced the edge of the white display table and answered, trying hard to hide the depth of the disappointment she was feeling now that she was realizing her dream trip wasn't going to happen. "Nowhere too exotic. I'm not as brave as you sound. I really wanted to go to Wales. It's where my father was from." The sound of her dejection rang in her ears and she shook it off. Forcing a smile, she pointed decisively to the replacement unit. "Next one will be the big one. I can take it on my fancy trip *next* fall. One year won't hurt."

Jenna gave her a sympathetic smile and smacked the table decisively, smirking when Ava hopped in place. "What color? You can change that at least." She pointed at the new colors.

"Bright green." Ava grinned back.

She reached down to unlock a case under the table and dug around to find the right unit. While she did Ava twisted to see if Ben was anywhere in sight and inhaled sharply, stepping back, surprised to see him standing directly behind her.

"Oh, hey Ben. Where'd you come from?" She felt her stomach flip, giddy at the sight of him.

The stocky Chinese man beside him smiled broadly revealing big, square teeth to go with his impressive biceps. "My wife used to look at me like that."

Ben chuckled. "Don't give me that Scott, she still does."

Jenna straightened, holding out the box for Ava. "You tell him Ben. You have it easy Mr. Fischer. I can make things more difficult for you if you want me to though."

"You're his wife?" Ava looked back and forth between them. "You're a…"

"Yep." Jenna bounced up and down on her toes. "I'm a."

"She didn't think you looked pure enough." Scott teased his wife.

She shot him a pretend glare before she looked back at Ava. Sweeping her hand in a circle around her face, she asked, "You mean because of this? A few holes and some ink don't make a lick of difference."

There was a grunt behind her. It did not sound like it agreed.

A hint of annoyance slid into Jenna's shining green eyes. "It only took a temporary boost and I'm done now." Her grin returned and she held out her arms, "The canvas is full."

Scott's pleasantly melodic tone brought Ava's attention back to him. "Ben said you were here. I had to put a face to the infamous name." Quickly, he flicked his eyes over to be sure he hadn't overstepped. Ben, though a touch pink, seemed pleased to be making the rounds with her.

Ava, however, felt at a disadvantage that they knew far more about her than she wanted. "I hope he hasn't said too much, you'll likely be disappointed." She quipped anxiously.

"Just enough to make me think of leaving my lovely wife, if you'll have me." Scott gave her a leering wink.

"You say that like someone else *would* have you." Jenna gave back as good as she got.

Ben stepped forward, hands up to cut through them and putting his arm around Ava. "I'd better get you out of here before I lose you or my friends."

"Just let me pay and then you can whisk me away." She had laughed more today with Ben's friends than she had in her recent memory and was reticent to leave.

"Did you two want to swing by for dinner tonight? Alistair was hoping we could get together." Ben asked them.

Husband and wife exchanged one of those long, detailed looks that only spouses are capable of in which they can have an entire wordless conversation. Scott answered for them. "That sounds great, but we have Patty." Jenna and Scott glanced at Ava.

Catching on, she answered their unspoken question. "That's fine, I like kids. I don't have much training or anything, but I'm game. How old is she?"

Scott, the proud father, laughed, "She's easy. Patty's nine and doesn't know she's a little girl yet so no attitude."

"I love the girl. She's a peach, but don't listen to her father about that whole innocent act. She has her days." Jenna rolled her eyes, shaking her hand.

"Let me continue to deceive myself. It's practice for when she's a teenager."

"How about eight?" Ben suggested and they agreed.

Ben steered Ava toward the door where she planted her feet, her eyes big. "My ipod. I'm finally here, I can't go without it." She stared at the sea of people beginning their lunch erranding now engulfing the geniuses. Scott and Jenna both were already occupied. "Why does everyone checkout at the same time? It never fails."

“I was hoping to take care of a few things before dinner tonight. Would you mind grabbing that for us and we’ll even up when you come over later?” Ben called over Ava’s head.

Scott nodded over his older woman’s head while she brandished an iPad at him. Ben was watching Scott closely, a crease in his brow.

Ava twisted her neck and leaned out to see what she was missing when Ben stepped out and looked down to grin at her, perfectly innocent.

“Not a problem.” Scott agreed cheerily from behind her.

“Do you want us to bring anything?” Jenna wanted to know. She excused herself from the gentleman wrestling his iPhone from his pocket.

“No. Does Patty still like mac’n cheese?”

“She’s a kid, she loves the stuff. We’re bad parents because we only let her have it once a week.” Jenna threw her hands up. “I just don’t see the draw.”

“Come on, it’s cheese and pasta. How can it be wrong?” Ava sided with the kid.

“Eight o’clock.” Scott confirmed and pointed at Ben before succumbing to his elderly customer’s questions, or risk her wrath.

Ben held up a thumb backing out into the mall.

Ch. 32

"Do you need to do anything today?" Ben asked as they strolled, hands clasped, past the colorfully advertised this and that stores working hard to convince people they needed things they most definitely didn't.

"I really need to swing past home. If you're having a dinner party I want something nicer from my closet and if I don't charge my phone soon, my mom is going to call the National Guard. What about you? I would assume you need a ton of stuff for dinner, right?"

He had a twinkle in his eye and sly smile as he pulled her hand up to kiss. "I have a secret, I cheat. Alistair's bringing everything. He does it all the time for me."

Ava laughed. "I was so impressed that you were going to get a dinner party together in a few hours and didn't even look worried. You've shattered my illusion of you as a cool character." She teased him.

"I hope not. Once you figure out I'm as boring as the next guy I'll lose you for sure." Ben's eyes were focused straight ahead.

She didn't want to make any false promises. There were still mysteries that held concern for her, things she wasn't sure weren't breaking points. Yet, she couldn't deny what she felt. Ava squeezed his hand and told him honestly, "Ben, I can't imagine loving anyone more than I love you."

He had a curious expression when he looked at her and squeezed back, his thumb rubbing the back of her hand.

***

They were not far from her apartment, the drive took only minutes. Ben followed Ava into the hall of her building, holding the doors for her after she removed her key. Her

unit was on the third of four floors and all the way at the end of the long hall. She liked the distance from the elevators for quiet, even if it made grocery shopping a logistical nightmare when she had more than two bags.
"I suppose you've probably been here before." Ava fished as she put her key in the lock.

"No." Ben was offended. "I told you I've always kept my distance. I have only intervened when absolutely necessary."

She stepped in and held the door, waving him inside. "Then welcome to my humble home." Her stomach twittered nervously. Thus far, her relationships had been fairly superficial and she had avoided bringing a man into her home since she had moved out on her own. Now, she closed the door and leaned on it, watching him crossing the threshold into her private life before following him through the small hall and into her living room.

A narrow set of wooden shelves from IKEA flanked the tv on one side, a small desk with her laptop on it sat on the other. The shelves contained the few pictures Ava had collected throughout her life. Overall she was not a picture person, never the one who brought a camera to an event or asked people to huddle and "capture a moment."

The pictures on her shelf were limited to three. One was of Ava with Elle in front of the restaurant where Elle had taken her to celebrate her graduation from college with her undergrad degree. The second was Ava and her mother when Katherine had taken her to "the Cities" to see The Christmas Carol at the Ordway and a fancy dinner afterward. Ava had been thirteen, it had been her first real trip to the metro area from their rural town. The third was her parents' wedding picture. Her mother's hair had been more auburn like Ava's then, not the flat brown dye she used these days. Her father's had been a rich chestnut. It was a close up so all she could see was the top of her father's tux and the ruffled edge of her mother's dated gown ringing her shoulders. Ava barely noticed the fashion, the reason she kept it up was the way they were looking at each other. Some kids had both of their parents, yet had to watch them fight and grow to hate each other. Ava would never know if her parents might have become that couple. She had the luxury of creating her own fantasy life for her parents. She liked to believe that if her father had lived they would still be married and he would still look at her mother that way. And her mother would love him like she did today, eighteen years after his passing.

Ben touched each picture and asked Ava to tell him what each was and its significance. She did as he asked on the first two but all she would say about her parents' picture was "it's the only good one I found of my father."

Self-conscious, Ava excused herself leaving him to pick through her life sitting out on display in the other room. She took a bag out of the bottom of her closet and grabbed her phone charger as well as a few essentials the movers had the decency not to have picked through too thoroughly. It was obvious from the order of her drawers and how she had left them that only the top few bras and panties had been brought to her. Now she took the time to make her own choices as well as something special she had bought and never worn for anyone. She was tucking the black lacy item into her bag when Ben knocked gently on her door.

As usual, Ava startled, whirling.

"Sorry," he held out a hand. "I didn't mean to scare you." His eyes cast about the room, taking in her sparse décor. Apart from the bed being outfitted in the most plush manner possible, there wasn't much else in the room. A plain dresser, nightstand and lamp were about it. She had never thought about it before but she lived a bit monkish as well. Not much of her personality was evident though what there was made her feel incredibly exposed. "You don't spend much time at home?"

Ava shook her head. "I've spent more time at the store and the library than I have here the last few years."

He stepped inside, his fingers trailed across the cover of a textbook on top of her dresser. "This is business school now, hmm? Is it any more interesting?"
"I doubt it." She closed the drawer, hiding her supply of doily work from his gaze.

"Is it true?" He asked her, tracing the cover of the book.

"Is what true, that business classes are boring? *I* think so." Ava reiterated.

Ben's eyes remained on the book though his hand had stopped its circuit. "Is it true that you spent the money you were going to use for a trip on unexpected expenses?"

Ava opened another drawer to pick through her shirts, embarrassed she'd been overheard. "How long were you standing behind me at the store?"

"Long enough to hear that I owe you something."

"You don't owe me anything. Everything I did, and chose to spend my money on, was up to me. If you were there, you also heard that I said I can go next year. Wales is not going anywhere and I've heard it's lovely in the fall." She closed the drawer not seeing anything she needed and turned to dig in her closet.

"That may be true, but I can't help but feel I am at least partially responsible. I would like to do something to make it up to you." He leaned against her dresser, arms crossed watching her.

Without looking back at him, Ava shook her head. "It's done. I don't regret it and either should you." She picked a light pink top with tiny posies on it and tossed it on the bed behind her. "What should I wear tonight?"

"We're a casual crowd. I would recommend wearing what makes you comfortable."

Ava turned halfway, enough to let him see from her expression, that she did not consider that an answer.
"To give you an idea, I'll tell you that Jenna usually wears jeans and a shirt that never gets tucked in. Scott will undoubtedly wear his cargo pants and a shirt with a pithy saying on it. Alistair will wear Armani." He shrugged. "It's a mixed bag."

She had been listening while she perused the contents of her closet. His friends were on opposite ends of the spectrum. Knowing their predicted attire gave her no more guidance than his suggestion. "And you?"

He shrugged, "I haven't thought about it yet. Does it really matter?"

Ava flopped down, sitting down on her bed in defeat. "I want to make a good impression on your friends. Getting to know them tonight is the closest I'm ever going to get to meeting your family." Ava would not get the chance to hear all the humiliating stories of his youth, watch him squirm when someone mentioned a past girlfriend, hear them tease each other in the way only family does. Ava had never had that large family experience, it had been only her mother and herself. She'd always hoped she could be a part of that big clan feel some day.

Ben pushed off the dresser and moved the suitcase to take its place beside her. His arm wrapped around her and she leaned in on his chest. "You have already met my closest friends and they all enjoy you." He kissed her head, "My father would have adored you. He always wanted a girl. He had urged me to marry, hoping to get one that way."

"What was he like?"

"Father was busy for much of my young life and I didn't see much of him. As I advanced in my studies, I often joined him in his offices to watch him work. That was where my fascination with medicine began. He helped so many in those early years and hoped that I would follow in his footsteps." Ben sighed, sounding tired as he went on. "All of that changed when he was shunned. That was then he began to steer me toward business." He chuckled softly, "We have that in common as well. My father pushed me toward business and I have yet to work in the field."

"You *were* eavesdropping." She teased, no longer embarrassed, and poked him in the leg.

"Can you blame me for wanting some insight into the mystery of your aversion to career change? I heard you mention it and took the chance to do a little reconnaissance work."

Really she didn't blame him and it was easier having him know than having had to tell him, if that made any sense. "I guess it's okay." She shrugged against him. "Honestly, I like working at the shop. It would be great if there was a way to grow my role, or use what I know to expand our services. I don't think I have the sort of visionary spirit to know how. The idea of being the boss doesn't interest me either. So many of my classmates wanted their degrees to start their own businesses or advance to the executive level. Not me. I just want to be a worker bee."

"Have you spoken to Elle about any of this?"

Her head rocked against his chest. "No, this is the most I've talked about it with anyone. The store is Elle's baby and I don't want to come in now and have her thinking I'm trying to show her how smart I think I am because I have the degree she doesn't."

"She didn't go to college?"

Ava's head rocked again. "And I know it bothers her. She stopped going to a women's business networking group for that very reason. They rubbed her nose in it."

His hand smoothed her hair, "You aren't giving her enough credit. Elle knows you better than that. Give her time and the opportunity will present itself. If you want to stay with her, you will find a way to make it work. I have faith in you."

His simple synopsis eased her mind, helping her with her perspective. "You're right. Why am I feeling like I'm on a cliff and I *have* to jump? No one's pushing me except me." She reached up, kissed him and patted his chest. "We've successfully sorted out the rest of my life, now could you please help me handle tonight?"

Ben walked over and stared at the contents of her closet. Without a word he reached in and plucked out a lightly patterned chocolate dress and complimentary pink crocheted sweater.

Ava raised an eyebrow. "That's one of my favorite outfits."

He held them out. "You were wearing it the first day I saw you, after I returned."

Butterflies fluttered in her stomach and Ava kissed him softly, taking the hangers from him to fold the items into her bag.

Ava was gathering her makeup and hair things from the bathroom when she heard her landline ringing. She came rushing out, cord from the iron dangling precariously close to her feet as she juggled her makeup bag and whatnot, barely making it to the bed before dropping the lot on the open suitcase. Ava ran back into the living room, catching it just after the machine caught it. Ben watched the mayhem looking amused.

Elle was just starting to leave a message. "Ava, honey, could you give me a call?" Her voice was shaky and Ava considered for a second not answering. She did sympathy much better over the phone than in person and figured she

could help more this way than if she heard about it face to face.
"I'm here Elle, what's wrong?" Ava forced herself to sound compassionate instead of fearful that she would have to comfort the woman, a task she wasn't equipped to handle.

When Elle heard Ava's voice, she broke down crying so hard Ava could barely make out the words. "Bill's been in an accident. I'm at the hospital. He's bad." She started sobbing.

"Oh Elle, I'm so sorry. Do you need me to come? Wait, what hospital are you at?" Ava's discomfort too a backseat to her information gathering. It gave her something else to focus on.

"No, you don't need to do that. He's at Mercy. I called Katherine. She'll be here by dinner."

"What can I do?" She figured Elle wanted her to take care of the store. She had guessed accurately.

Elle's voice stabilized when she had orders to give. "I could use your help with the store tomorrow. Are you back from your vacation, would your friend mind you cutting it short?"

"Yeah, I can handle the store. Don't worry about that, it turned out to be nothing." She spun around to see if Ben was listening but he had ducked back into her room, affording her some privacy.

"That's too bad. I hate to see you alone." Her voice cracked, "Even if you have your differences it's good to have someone to come home to."

"Never mind about me, you take care of you. And Bill." It was very much in character for Elle to put everyone else first. That was most likely why she and Bill had lasted as long as they had, despite the fact that he was a net zero to the relationship as far as Ava could tell. She stopped herself from thinking such things, they were no longer relevant. Soon Bill would be gone and Elle would be alone, something Ava knew she dreaded. "I'll take care of the store, you take as long as you need to be with Bill."

"Thanks Ava. I'm lucky to have you." She sniffed, Ava heard more tears coming.

"Go take care of things there. Call me or have mom call me with updates, okay?"

Elle agreed and Ava hung up, wishing her well.

The small apartment had not shielded much of the call from Ben, he emerged when he heard her hang up. "Is she going to be okay?"

Ava filled him in on what had happened with Bill and Elle before the accident, as well as Elle's dim prognosis for his recovery.

"That has to make it even harder for her. She might be telling herself he wouldn't have had the accident if he were still at home."

"But he left her." Ava didn't really understand how Elle could feel guilty. She hoped Ben was wrong.

Ben rubbed her back. "It doesn't matter. She will feel like she pushed him out, or she could have somehow prevented his leaving once he's gone. It doesn't have to make sense, it's how people feel."

"Do you really think he could die?" She turned her eyes up to his.

"It sounds like they're preparing her for the worst. Maybe he will make it, but if they are telling her this now, it doesn't look good."

Ava trusted his opinion given his medical knowledge, albeit practically ancient. In her eyes, his age and experience made up for that. He had seen more of death and labs that she ever cared to.

“Does she have someone who can be with her? Do you need to go?”

“My mom is coming down. Elle just wants me to mind the store tomorrow.”

“You don’t have to come tonight if you aren’t feeling up to it.”

Ava looked up at the clock. It was already after four. “Yes I do.” She couldn’t imagine being any help to Elle right now. She shrugged, embarrassed, “This isn’t really my thing. I can help best with the store. Mom will be with her soon, she’s way better at this sort of thing.” She thought about her mother driving down to be with her friend. “This is going to be really hard for Mom. Elle was with her after my father’s accident.” Ava couldn’t decide whether she should try to call her mother, or if it was better to leave it. In the end, Katherine would go regardless of how difficult it was for her. She would do anything for Elle. Knowing that, Ava left her phone in the cradle, not wanting to intrude on what was between the two women.

Ch. 33

A few minutes after eight, Ava was finishing setting the table when the doorbell rang. Ben swept her up to walk with him to the door. The symbolism was not lost on her. Ben was offering this evening as theirs, not his. Her mind was so overburdened with Elle’s crisis and surely her mother’s as well, she let herself be pulled into the illusion that they could live a normal life together with a house and friends the same as anyone else.

They opened the door to Alistair standing on the step in a flawlessly tailored suit Ava would assume was Armani as Ben had suggested. The light purple shirt was open at the collar, he had the look of a stockbroker letting his hair down. He shook Ben's hand warmly, offered him a bottle of wine and held out his arms to Ava as he stepped inside. She welcomed his genuine and effusive warmth. Ava appreciated his presence there that night especially. Alistair inquired if the caterer had been there yet.

"He was here an hour ago."

The catering van from Alistair's restaurant had dropped off salads, smoked ham and gruyere quiche, French bread, berry compote and of course a special container for their youngest guest. The only instructions he had left were to give the quiche and macaroni a bit of a warm up in the oven, everything else was ready to plate and serve. Ava had to admit she had never seen an easier dinner party to put together. She knew who to call if she ever had need.

"Where's your date?" Ben glanced around before shutting the door.

Alistair had Ava under his arm, cradling her against his solid side. "I have her. Where is yours?"

She smiled, throwing her arm around Alistair's back, so large she couldn't quite get her arm to the other side. "If things don't work out with Ben I'll let you know." Ava joked, but didn't let go until they had reached the living room.

Alistair took up the entire chair in the corner, jacket open while he reclined. Ben was still holding the wine when the doorbell rang again. Ava rolled it out of his hand and shooed him to the door while she went back to the kitchen to open the bottle with the barely legible label. She hoped it was good, then rolled her eyes at herself. Given the bearer, she should have known better than to have questioned its quality.

Scott, Jenna and Patty had already taken up their positions in the living room by the time Ava returned. Scott and Jenna sat on the couch together and Patty was on Alistair's lap, waving her hands animatedly as she told him a story of something that happened at school that day. Ava had picked up most of it from the kitchen.

Ben stood from his usual perch on the arm of the couch next to Jenna when Ava walked into the room. Scott and Jenna both smiled warmly at her. Patty eyed her curiously, arm possessively thrown over her friend's giant shoulder to stake her claim.

Scott introduced his daughter. "Patty, this is Ben's friend Ava."

She smiled politely, not making a move to let go of Alistair. "Hi Ava. Do you like dogs or cats?"

Because she had heard the majority of Patty's story from the other room, she knew the correct answer was dogs. Better yet, she didn't have to lie.

"I like dogs better, I had one growing up. How about you?" She handed off the two glasses to Scott and Jenna.

Graciously they accepted. Scott took a sip right away while Jenna held onto hers. Ava imagined being like Ben and Alistair, she would drink sparingly.

"Dogs are way better. They're smarter and you can train them. Plus, you have to clean a cat box. My friend Janice has to clean her cat's litter box and it's *really* gross. It smells *so* bad." Patty's charm was impossible to ignore. A bright faced, long legged version of her dad, she had slightly more Caucasian eyes and a hint of freckles across her nose, hinting at her mother's western European heritage.

Ava fell into the conversation with ease. "I had a Grandma who had a couple of cats and I never went in the room where they slept because that was where their box was and it smelled too. One of them was always hiding in there and if you tried to pet her, she bit you."

Patty smiled at her. Ava was kid approved. She grinned back.

"I'm going to grab some more wine, Patty do you want anything? I think Ben might have some good stuff in there."

Clearly not willing to give up her post with her favorite person, Patty said she was fine. Ava backed out and Ben followed her.

When they returned to the kitchen she poured three more glasses and had barely set the bottle down when Ben laid his hand on the small of her back.

"That was impressive, Patty is usually a harder sell. You have a way with kids."

The intimate gesture took her mind far away from the child in the other room. She rolled her head back and he leaned over to kiss her. Turning into him, Ava stretched her arms around his neck, pulling him down for more. Her fingers ran up into his hair. Ben's hands tightened on her hips.

Someone cleared their throat from the doorway and Ava immediately released Ben, he was slower to take his hands from her.

"What can I get for you Scott?" Ben grumped.

Undaunted, he walked up to them and set a box down on the counter. "I got so distracted I think I forgot." He winked at Ava and she felt her ears burning.

Ben pulled Ava closer. "My guess is it has something to do with that." He pointed at the box.

“Right, that was it. Delivered as promised. Now if you’ll excuse me, I think it’s getting too hot in here for me.” He tugged at his collar and left the room.

Ava picked up the box and saw that her purchase had been magically upgraded. She lifted it so that Ben could see it and whispered. “They messed up, how to I tell them I didn’t want this one?”

Ben moved off to scrape imaginary crumbs from the counter into his hand and fling them into the sink. “They didn’t mess up. That is a gift from me to you.”

“I told you not to pay me back.”

Ben held his finger to his mouth and replied, “I respected your wishes and did not pay you back. Nothing was said about gifts.”

Ben carried his and Alistair’s glasses leaving Ava to stare at the box on the counter. To fight about it would be purely out of stubborn pride. She felt the corner of her mouth twitch at Ben’s sidestepping of her request not to repay her. Scooping up her own glass, she followed Ben back to their guests.

Jenna was watching Patty stroke Alistair’s tightly trimmed beard while she tried to convince him why he was wrong to prefer cats. He, on the other hand, was describing the evils of dog drool. Ava sniggered picturing the man’s apron from the morning they met. The pride evident on Jenna’s face answered any questions Ava might have had about her feelings for her stepdaughter. Patty was a lucky girl. Ava felt a jealous pang she attempted to ignore as juvenile.

Being mature enough to recognize a childish and useless wish to have had two parents did not always make it easier to watch an intact family together. She reminded herself she had a loving mom which was more than some could say.

Ben, turning from delivering Alistair's glass to his side table, gave Ava a wink and slid his arm around her. He kissed her wrinkled brow. Grateful, she leaned into him and took a sip of wine. It was good and she took a small follow up sip, letting this one roll around on her tongue so she could pick up some of the nuances.

No sommelier, Ava had enjoyed a glass or two over the years and could recognize a quality bottle, which this clearly was.

"Alistair this is great. Where did you find it?"

Raising his chin and grinning, he replied, "I would be shocked if you had ever heard of it dear. I'm afraid the vineyard closed about thirty years ago." He winked. "This bottle has been with me for a very long time. I was waiting for the proper occasion to open it.

"What's special about tonight?" Patty asked him, taking his face between both of her little hands and keeping his eyes on her.

The man flashed his charmingly flawed smile. "It's Ben's birthday."

Scott and Jenna appeared just as surprised at his announcement as Ava. Patty however, took it in stride.

"Happy birthday Ben. Are we going to have cake later?" Her young eyes sparkled hopefully.

"I set a little piece of your favorite aside for after dinner." Alistair chirped cheerfully.

Ava pulled away to see his expression. "Ben why didn't you tell me?"

He cut a look over at his friend who was just as gleeful as his seat partner. "I really don't celebrate birthdays anymore."

"How can you not celebrate birthdays?" Patty was confounded. "They're the best thing ever. The last birthday I had, my friend lost her tooth in the pool and we had to dive and dive to try to find it. Janice found it, but that's because I let her use my goggles. She got an extra piece of cake."

"And it was very kind of you to share your goggles with Janice. Remember how happy your friend was to have her tooth back?" Jenna reminded her.

"Yeah, I guess." She agreed halfheartedly.

"Well, then happy birthday." Ava raised her glass to him. He tapped it lightly keeping his eyes on hers while he drank.

Scott stood up. "Does anyone else want to eat? I'm starving." He rubbed his belly and stretched.

"You should start keeping snacks in some of those pockets." Ben teased. He had indeed worn the aforementioned cargo pants. "You're always hungry."

"I have about ten pair of these and I'm going to wear them every time I see you because I know you love them so much." Scott patted his side pockets.

"And that would be different from any other day how?" Jenna sassed.

"Okay, that's it. If I'm going to be insulted, I'm at least going to do it on a full stomach." He took a few steps.

"Settle down Scott." Ben held up his hand at his friend's contrived anger. "I think dinner wouldn't be a bad idea. It's getting late and someone here has to get to bed early tonight."

Popping up from her perch, Patty's shrill objection rang out. "I do not have to go to bed early. We don't have school tomorrow and Mom said I can stay up." She shot Jenna a look of dismay at her apparent betrayal.

"No," corrected Ben. "*Ava* has to go to bed early, she has to work tomorrow."

"Oh." Patty adjusted her leggings back over her socks and trotted from the room, her vexation instantly evaporated.

Alistair stood and attempted to smooth his now irreparably rumpled suit coat before he gave up and slid it off to lay it over the back of the chair.

Ava and Ben led the way into the kitchen where Ben put the quiche in the preheated oven to warm while Ava set the salads on the table.

Patty joined them first. Ben asked if her hands were washed. This was an obvious routine. Patty held them up, flipping them palm out, then in for his inspection. Ben narrowed his eyes, studying them closely before giving her a nod of approval. Scott and Jenna both appeared as well, taking positions at the table without direction. Patty and Alistair sat on the opposite side leaving the head of the table and the position directly across for Ava and Ben. He pointed for her to take a seat and she chose the foot leaving the owner of the house the head.

Over salad Jenna asked Ava about work.

She explained Elle's situation and subsequent request and was moved by the offers of help and support from the others around the table. "Thank you. That's very kind."

"Do you know how long you'll be running the show?" Scott asked her, forking a chunk of salad into his mouth, chewing vigorously while he listened.

"I'm not sure, a lot depends on him. If she has to make arrangements it will be a while, but if he has a long recovery then who knows." Ava was pleased she had been dragging her feet on leaving. Without her, Elle wouldn't have anyone to keep her business running while she was out. Only she and her mother had ever worked there, and her mother had an equally important job being by Elle's side.

Ben excused himself to put Patty's dinner in the oven.

"Alistair's again?" Jenna busted Ben.

He faked confusion. "What are you talking about?"

The actual party responsible for dinner guffawed. "Don't worry Ben. Everyone knows you like to cook, just not for company."

"That's not true, he cooked for me the last time I was here." Ava didn't understand their jibes. Ben had never hesitated to cook, he seemed to like entertaining.

"You mean he made you a salad." Jenna corrected her with a knowing look she shared with her husband.

Stubbornly Ava shook her head. "No, we had salad sure, but he made pasta with a creamy vodka sauce from scratch. It was delicious."

The other three adults were watching Ben, waiting for confirmation that he had, in fact, cooked a meal.

"I *have cooked* for all of you." Ben grumbled looking both annoyed and uncomfortable.

Jenna snorted. "Yeah, but that was because we were snowed in and Scott kept complaining he needed more than toast and beer or he was going to eat his shoes." She laughed hard at the memory.

Scott feigned offense. "It's not my fault I'm the only one who eats around here."

“I’m turning over a new leaf.” Ben said sullenly.

All was silent for a moment and Alistair held up his glass, “To new leaves.” Even Patty held up her sparkling grape juice to clink glasses with those she could reach. Ava held her own for Ben to see, he tipped his head to her with a shy smile.

Her eyes stung when it hit her, this was the family she had been hoping for.

Ch. 34

Alistair had Patty on his lap, her dark hair spread out over her tiny face as she lay on his chest, sound asleep. Scott leaned back at the table while Ava cleared.

“I was able to spend some time on those hard drives after work today.” Scott had everyone’s attention at once.

Ben leaned in, “Did you find anything?” He failed to hide the eagerness in his voice.

Scott sat back, roughing his lips with the back of his knuckles. “Nothing that makes any sense. It’s all lists of personal data like height, weight and blood type. It reads like a hospital chart. So far that’s all I can get, the names are in some sort of code. Without a fame of reference it isn’t going to give us much.” Seeing Ben’s face falling, Scott hurried to add. “That’s just the first one. I’m hoping there will be some key to the code on one of the others. Maybe addresses to give us his operating range.”

Ben nodded, his lips tight. “Keep working on it. He feels like he’s close. I don’t want to wait too long and lose him.”

Jenna gave the table a quick smack, apparently something she did often to change the subject. “We should go. Patty’s tired and Ava needs to work tomorrow.”

Scott checked his watch and stood too. “I don’t go in until later. I’ll see if I can spend some extra time on them for you in the morning.

Ben rose and shook Scott’s hand. “I appreciate it Scott.”

Alistair handed the sleeping Patty to her dad. Jenna went around gathering the things a child discards in an evening. Sweater, socks, small handful of toys she insisted upon bringing and promptly dropped the second she crossed the threshold.

Hugs were had all around and the Fischer family left. Alistair retrieved his coat off the back of the chair and held out his arms for Ava. She couldn’t resist snuggling in for one last hug. He kissed her cheek and whispered in her ear. “You couldn’t know what this meant to him. Thank you.”

Ben shook his hand and closed the door, locking it.

“Care to finish your wine out here?”

“Sure, I’ll go get it. You’re the birthday boy and you’ve worked hard enough tonight.”

Returning to the living room, she found him in his spot. He touched the cushion beside him. She handed him his glass and sat.

“Well, I leave tonight to you.” Ben said, taking a sip. “You have to work in the morning and we forgot to pick up your car.” By his lack of concern, Ava could see he that he had no more forgotten the car than she. Carpooling was an inevitability they both wanted. “I can bring you home tonight or drive you in the morning, but that would mean you would have to let me pick you up after work.”

"Tomorrow's Saturday. I don't need to open until ten-thirty." She swallowed the last of her wine and set the glass down on the table. "I'm not tired. Are you?"

He shook his head. "No, not at all."

"Good, I'll be right back." Ava stood, Ben as well, as was his habit, until she had left the room. She enjoyed his look of confusion when he saw her go upstairs. He had surprised her with his secret birthday party during which she had thought up an impromptu gift for him. Quickly she dug in her bag, hoping he would stay downstairs long enough for her to change.

A few minutes later, Ava sashayed down the stairs and saw him glance up when her movement caught his eye. His features froze for an instant before it registered. The look on his face was exactly what she had hoped it would be.

Adding some extra wiggle to her walk, Ava made her way to where he sat on the couch arm and maneuvered herself to stand with his knees on either side of her waist.

"Wow," he murmured softly. "Is that for me?" He ran his hand down the front of the sheer black camisole, stopping at the edge of the delicate silver lace trim.

She put a hand on his arm, enjoying the tension she felt there, knowing she'd caused it. "You sprang the birthday on me so I had to make due. I hope you enjoy your present." She fingered a strap, "I barely had time to wrap it."

Ch. 35

Ava worked through the store, changing the floor configuration as best she could without help. Her conversation with Ben still fresh in her head, she tried to look at the store through different eyes. She knew there would be a way to grow into a more fulfilling role here. She merely wasn't seeing it yet. Ava told herself to be patient, like Ben said, the answer would come.

Ben. The thought of him made her smile. He would be there soon. The store closed in less than half an hour. She stopped staging a pile of hats when she heard the front door. Turning, she saw her mother walk through the doors.

"Mom!" She rapidly crossed the space, wrapping her arms around her excitedly. Katherine clung to her, taking strength in her daughter's rare display of affection. "How's Elle?" She finally asked, pulling away to see her face. Her mother had aged ten years since she'd seen her last.

"Sleeping. The doctors gave her a sedative. I got her tucked in, but she made me promise to check in on you. Honestly, I think she wants a break from everyone always asking if she needs something, or is she okay." She smiled weakly. "That did get to be a little hard to take."

Ava rubbed her mother's arm, finding it less difficult to empathize with her as she had in the past. She assumed it was because this time she *could* understand the pain both women were going through to some small extent. Ava couldn't fathom having to watch Ben die.

"Honey, is something wrong with your car? I didn't see it outside." Katherine changed the subject to one that was easier for her to handle.

Conversely, it was one that made Ava uncomfortable. "Um, well, I got a ride from a friend."

Her mother raised an eyebrow. "Really? Who? Someone you know from school? Elle said that man the other day was a no go."

Ava shook her head. "Yeah, that guy was from a long time ago." Closer to the truth than Katherine knew. "He just kind of appeared out of the blue and after one night of talking," you're welcome Ben she thought trying not to smile, "we figured out we wanted different things. Besides..."

The bell over the front door chimed and right on time, in walked Ben.

Ava couldn't keep the smile from her face when she saw him. "There was already someone else." She finished.

Ben's eyes scanned the store, stopping on Ava. His return expression was confirmation enough for Katherine as to why it didn't work with the blonde. Ava saw recognition light his eyes when he sighted her mother beside her.

He smoothed his face over as he approached. "I hope I'm not interrupting. I'm early. I thought you might need a little help, but it appears you have everything under control." Ben watched Ava's face, his eyes nervously flicked over to Katherine several times.

Ava's stomach twirled. "Mom, I would like you to meet Ben Pearson. He's that friend I told you about." Ava realized she was holding her breath and exhaled self-consciously.

Ben held out his hand and Katherine took it, eyeing her daughter's new beau. "Pleased to meet you Ben. I'm Katherine Brandt."

Ava ran her eyes over Ben, seeing him as her mother would. Six feet of lean muscle, dark features and pale skin. Casually dressed in faded jeans and the usual black shirt and sport coat, most likely hiding the gun Ava knew her mother could not know was there. He was a good boyfriend prospect.

"It is a pleasure to finally meet you Ms. Brandt. How is Elle bearing the strain?"

His formal manner of speech creeping out hinted that he was stressed. Ava's lips curved, she found it endearing that he was nervous to meet her mother.

"I was just telling Ava, she's resting right now." Katherine ran a hand over her eyes, exhausted from enduring a long day at her friend's side. "Bill's in a coma and they're talking about taking him off life support in the next day or two." Weariness left her sagging.

Ava squeezed her mother's hand. "Mom can I do anything? Do you need me to help out tonight so you can get some rest?"

Katherine shook her head. "No, I think Elle will sleep tonight. They gave her enough valium to tranq a horse." A shadow crossed her features then she brightened, "Maybe we could do lunch tomorrow. You're closed on Sundays still, right?"

"Yep. Do you want to do lunch?"

"Do you need me to pick you up?" Katherine was still under the false impression there was something wrong with her car.

Self-consciously Ava ran a hand over her hair smoothing it. "No, I can drive."

Katherine watched her daughter, making note of the change in her, the happiness in her eyes she hadn't seen in a long time. "Ben, would you like to join us?"

He started to beg off that he would be intruding on their family time until Katherine raised her finger. "I won't take no for an answer." She leveled a look at Ava, gauging her willingness.

Ben glanced to Ava as well and, hearing no objections from her, he agreed. "I would be delighted Ms. Brandt."

She waved him off. “Katherine, please.” Again she studied her daughter curiously. “I imagine we will be seeing a lot of each other.”

Begging exhaustion, Katherine excused herself. Ava hugged her good bye and Ben gave her a shallow bow, unable to stop himself from obeying the customs of his long dead era.

Alone, Ben and Ava looked at each other. She exhaled loudly. “Well, that was unexpected.”

“I hope it wasn’t too uncomfortable for you.” His eyes followed hers, searching for a sign he had misstepped by coming early.

“No, I think that went all right. She’s too stressed out to be hypercritical. That might bode well for you.”

“Do you mean to say that she would normally disapprove of me?” Ben raised a brow.

“No, no. Just that she’s overprotective and she might be easier on you right now than if she met you under more relaxed circumstances.” Ava grinned mischievously. “I don’t know if your nerves could take her on a good day.”

“Oh really? Do you think I was frightened?”

“Terrified.”

“I have faced down far more dangerous men in my time.” Ben’s voice grew dark and ominous.

Ava raised her chin in playful warning. “You’ve never had to impress my mom.”

“I have never had to impress *anyone’s* mother.” His tone softened.

“Seriously?” Ava was shocked.

In answer, Ben wagged his head slowly from one side to the other. His eyes never leaving hers.

Ava's face went hot and she smiled, flustered but pleased.

A car's engine revved outside and Ben glanced at his watch. "It's five. Do you want me to lock the door?"

"Please," she handed him the keys from her pocket, moving on to the cash register to prepare the deposit.

The bell chimed bringing her head around. Ava spotted a tall black man standing at the front door with Ben, talking quietly. Ben seemed to know him.

Examining the visitor, Ava guessed him to be a police officer. Even though he wore a suit and tie, something about him said law enforcement. His build was that of a thinner man although he had the beginnings of a paunch that came from too many hours at a desk. When he raised his voice, Ava recognized it instantly and froze. She had forgotten about him completely.

"Ben where the *hell* have you been?" The detective asked loud enough for Ava to hear. "Do you know how many man hours I've spent looking for you? I just drove by your house and it's back off the market. I was retracing your steps on the Tolliver case and came here." He scanned the store, nodding his head briefly in acknowledgement at Ava before his gaze slid past.

"I left you a message Al, didn't you get it? There was some unexpected business that took me away and I thought I would be gone for quite some time so I put the condo up. I apologize for the concern, I called you once I got things straightened out." He shrugged, confused at the detective's attitude. "I told you in my message that it turned out to be a false alarm. I only just got back a day ago."

“Two. I spoke with your real estate agent.” He shifted so that his back was to Ava and he lowered his voice for privacy.

Ava tried to be polite and ignore them. Her eyes found them several times of their own will. Ben’s expression had grown focused as he listened. Whatever Detective Sharpe was saying had him very interested.

The detective’s voice rose to an audible level. “So can you come by the station tomorrow around noon? You owe me a lunch. That last one didn’t count.”

“Yes it did. It’s not my fault you don’t like sushi.”

Sharpe shook his head, waving his hand. “Fish is to be eaten *after* it has been cooked. Not before.”

Ben’s glanced up at Ava. “I’m going to have to take a rain check on lunch, I already have plans.” He noticed the detective’s displeasure. “ I can come by after. We’ll grab a coffee.”

Ava smiled to herself bowing her head to her task, trying to appear absorbed so he wouldn’t think she’d been listening. Detective Sharpe’s bold voice got louder, he had turned around, seeking the target of Ben’s gaze.

“Oh, I see. Could this be the young woman who called me so anxiously looking for a missing Ben Pearson?”

Ava’s face flamed. She didn’t need to answer nor could she make eye contact with Ben.

“I should have known when she failed to check back. Whenever someone is that worried about a missing person, they don’t call once and give up. That was bad police work on my part.” The detective sounded closer.

Fully humiliated, Ava felt herself break out into a sweat at the detective's approach. When she was able to bring her eyes up, he was nearly to her.

Ben saw her discomfort and slid around the counter to stand next to her. He aimed to shut Detective Sharpe down. "Okay Al. I think you've embarrassed the lady enough."

It worked. Ava glanced up and saw Sharpe staring at her with that look police officers can't turn off. She didn't know how their kids handled it. It made her want to confess and she hadn't even done anything wrong. Not really.

"Sorry Miss. I was just putting two and two together. It isn't often I miss something like that." He held out a hand. "Brandt wasn't it?"

She swallowed, finding her voice. "Yes Sir, Ava Brandt. I suppose I should have called you when I heard from him."

"Yeah, you should have." He released her hand slowly, deciding about her. Sharpe turned his attentions back to Ben. "Tomorrow then. About three'ish? I'll move my afternoon around."

Ben nodded, the detective grunted. She could feel his eyes on her again though she was busily pretending to count out her drawer. The detective was escorted to the door and she heard the hum of their voices until finally the bell chimed and the lock slid into place.

Ava breathed out. "I don't like him."

"He's a good guy. He just doesn't like to be caught off guard. It's what makes him good at his job. Always looking for that angle he can't see." Ben walked back to her. "Al figures if he can see all the sides he won't be surprised. You surprised him."

"Well, he scares the hell out of me." She gave up on the money, laying it back in the till.

Ben wrapped his arms around her, unintentionally pinning her arms to her sides. "Were you really worried about me?"

She moved to free herself and he tightened his grip, trapping her. "I told him I had something to give back to you and I hadn't heard from you in a few days." Her pulse quickened.

His arms remained tight as he teased her. "It must have been more than that if you made an impression on him."

"I don't think so. I don't remember." Her voice started to rise. She struggled in his grasp needing to get free. "Ben, let me go." Panic crept in.

He dropped his arms and she stepped back, breathing hard.

"I can't… I can't not move." She put her hand over her face, upset with herself for her continued inability to get over her fear.

His low voice was nearly inaudible. "I'm sorry. I forgot." Tentatively he put his hand on the back of her shoulder.

Ava leaned into him, wanting his comfort. Ben slid his arms around her making certain he kept them very loose. She noticed and berated herself for her weakness yet again. So much for being brave. She recognized the fiery sting of failure.

Ch. 36

They spent the evening in and were cleaning up from dinner when Ben's phone rang. It was Scott. Ava didn't have to ask, she could hear the disappointment in Ben's voice. She heard him say the computer had overheated, warping the bearings and making it unreadable.

“There’s nothing anywhere to give you an idea of what the numbers mean?” Ben inquired desperately. “Could you print out what you did find? Maybe I can take a look and find something. Something might ring a bell with me.”

Ben settled in to watch the news before bed and Ava sat with him, yawning and tired from a long day. Almost at the end of the broadcast, there was a brief mention of a clinic specializing in teen pregnancies that had recently been shut down in Shreveport, Louisiana. Ben sat up at the mention of the city where Bruder had most recently been operating. Ava swung her feet off his lap.

“Authorities report that the clinic was heavily attended despite the fact that all the girls were under the legal age to seek abortions or receive care without parental consent. They credit its success to the low fees and promises of discretion doctors and nurses promised. Though the clinic did perform early term abortions, its purported specialty was in the care of mother and child through the term of their pregnancy.

Doctors handed out free prenatal vitamins and saw mothers once per week, an unusually high level of care for first and second term pregnancies. However, several girls have recently come forward reporting that things were not necessarily as they seemed. After reaching their second trimesters, *some girls* went in for their routine visits and were anesthetized, told it was for a routine procedure. Only when they awoke, they were told that not only had their pregnancies spontaneously terminated from the shock of the procedure, but the fetuses had already been disposed of and the mothers were unable to see them.

It was only after one of the girls came forward to local police officials that detectives were dispatched to the clinic. Police said they were met at the door by a nurse denying them entrance and demanding a court order. When officers returned with a warrant, the clinic doors were locked and the building abandoned.

Police continue to search for witnesses and seek any information on either of these suspects."

The screen flashed two composite sketches. One was a man with round glasses, small beady eyes, a hooknose and thin mouth. His hair was either gray or it was merely the work of the artist and he had a thin moustache ending just shy of the edges of his mouth. When Ava saw the woman beside him, she felt dizzy. The last time Ava had seen her, her hair had been longer. But the small, thin nose, almond eyes and full lips were the same. Her teeth would be slightly crooked on the bottom if her mouth were open. She remembered that from when she said the word "candy." Her lower lip had come down enough that Ava's young eyes caught the teeth. She had watched her mouth, thinking the woman's lipstick was glamorous.

"It's her." Ava whispered, her fears from that night coming rushing back. Her mind washed out the features of the man, putting a light on his head while illuminating the shape of his jaw and his hair. She knew even with her limited knowledge of him, that this was Doctor Bruder. The droning of the television faded away, leaving Ava with only the rushing sound of her pulse in her ears.

Ben said nothing. They both sat motionless while the programming shifted to a reality show about people who wanted to meet their Hollywood idols and the stunts they had to perform to win their prize.

He was speaking when Ava's mind reconnected with the present. She could hear him booking his flight. When he hung up Ava faced him with a blank expression on her pale face and waited.

“I was able to get on the eleven forty flight.” His voice was flat. “I have to go right now. I’ll be back when I can.”

She nodded her head and went back to staring at the screen, seeing what had been, not the false drama playing out on it now.

“What?” She made herself listen to what he was saying.

“Do you want to stay here? I don’t have time to drive you home, I could take a cab and leave you my keys. I’ll call Alistair and let him know I’m going.” He fidgeted, clearly distracted. “He and his people will keep an eye on you.”

“I’ll take a cab.” She tried blinking to erase the woman’s face from her vision. Seeing her image after all these years brought her warm voice from the dredges of her mind, like she was right there. It was etched into her memory in perfect detail.

Ava didn’t fail to register the fact that she would be under constant surveillance at Ben’s orders once more. It would be no different from the majority of her life thus far she reminded herself. Ben, her guardian angel, was always watching from afar.

He called her a cab and packed while Ava remained seated, motionless on the couch. The clunk of plastic wheels on tile alerted her to his return. Mentally she followed his progress, knowing by his sounds that his next stop was the fridge to inject himself, readying for at least a one night stay away from home, and his blood source.

On his way bay back down the hall the doorbell rang and he bypassed the living room to go straight to the door.

“Just a minute.”

Recognizing her need to go, Ava forced herself up and dazedly set one foot in front of the other. Her mind was a million miles away, mired in the echo of a fear so great her mind had hidden from it the majority of her life. Forcing her body to function helped remind her she was here, that she was safe. That woman was far away as was the doctor. They couldn't take Ava from her home, Alistair wouldn't let them nor would she. She was no longer a child so easily tricked.

Feeling disembodied and strangely floaty, she kissed Ben and let him pull her in for a tight hug good bye before walking her to the cab. With one more apologetic hug he packed her into the vehicle promising to call.

The ride to her apartment was brief. Upon arriving she found Ben had already paid and she'd left her things behind. Giving the parking lot a brief, distracted sweep, Ava let herself out of the car.

While trying to open her door, Ava's numb fingers dropped her keys on the hallway floor twice. After she was in, she locked her door and checked it several times. Finally believing it was somewhat safe, she headed straight to the freezer. Inside, she kept a bottle of Grey Goose for just such an occasion. It was only a few times a month she enjoyed a drink, but she wanted to put a barrier between her and the memories buffeting her shell shocked mind. She would rather have had wine, but given the fact that it would turn to vinegar in the temperatures of her unit, hard alcohol was all she kept.

A strong pour of Goose splashed with Cranberry juice over ice went down quickly. Ava's hand shook enough to make up for the fact that she had not taken the time to stir her drink her concoction. Sitting on the couch, sipping steadily on her house drink in the dark slowed her heart rate and trembling hands. When the first was gone, she got up to pour a second. The fuzzy feeling in her head began to uncoil the cold ball of fear that had spread from her stomach through her body, numbing her brain. As she got up to pour her third and, she knew from experience, last drink, Ava let her head loll back onto the couch and she watched the moonlight reflect off her balcony rails creating dark shadows like prison bars on her ceiling.

Woozy when she got up, the last half of the drink ended up in the sink. Checking the lock on the door again, and that the security bar was in place on the sliding door to the balcony, she stripped off her clothes and left them in a pile in the hall.

Ava could not get the shower hot enough for her liking. The heat made her skin itch and tingle, her lungs worked to move the thick air in and out while her head spun. She told herself next time to end at two drinks, especially if she was going to get in a hot shower. But the sensations were gifts. They helped tie her to the present, helped her know she was alive and that *these* sensations were real, not those ramming their way through her head trying to paralyze her with childhood terrors. When her legs got tired from standing she sat, letting the water hit the top of her head and run down her face, forcing her eyes closed while she held onto her knees tucked tightly to her chest. Finally, her fingers were pruney and she was having trouble keeping herself awake.

Turning the water off, she ran a cursory towel over her body barely drying herself and wrapped it around her hair before stumbling into her room and clumsily putting herself to bed. She did not dream of Ben saving her that night as she would have expected. Instead her dreams were filled with images of what would have happened if he hadn't. The feeling of having her blood drained was so strong she checked her arms when she woke. The memory of her life being stolen was still with her when the sun shone into her bedroom window the next morning, bringing with it a painful headache.

Ch. 37

By no means refreshed, Ava was at least functional after taking some aspirin. She didn't have to work, school was a non issue and she had no plans until she had to meet her mother for lunch.

Lunch. Ben was standing her mother up for their first real meeting. For his sake Ava concocted an explanation for her mother that was believable, held him harmless, and wasn't a complete lie

A quick call to her mother and they confirmed the details as to the when and where of lunch and Ava planned accordingly. She had four hours during which time Ava set about catching up on her chores. When her world had been upended she had fallen behind on things as mundane as laundry and housekeeping. It was good to settle in to the familiar patterns and seeing her little apartment returned to its tidy state. By the time she was done, she was in a hurry to meet her mother.

Driving fast, Ava made it to the restaurant in less than twenty minutes. It was a little fancy and far for lunch but Katherine wanted to try it since she and Elle hadn't gotten to go there the last time she was in town. Ava had tried it once before. She had been there on a date a few years ago after it first opened. The food was good, the date was bad and she was glad it had only been lunch.

She pulled into the lot and made a quick tour without seeing Katherine's car. Then, when Ava stepped out of the car and into the sunshine, she heard a honk from the street and looked up to see her mother's green Bonneville sitting at the light across the street. Waving, she waited beside her car.

Katherine's face was less pale than it had been the night before. Ava's anxious scan also revealed her light brown eyes had a bit more sparkle to them. Relief took the tension she didn't know she was carrying out of her pinched shoulders.

"Where's your friend?" Her mother scanned the lot. Her regretful countenance was sincere.

Ava hoped this wouldn't change that. "He was called out of town unexpectedly for work. He sends his regrets and says he'll be sure to make it next time." Ava started toward the door and stopped when she realized she was alone.

Looking back she saw her mother frowning at her hand while she fidgeted with her keys. Katherine shook the fob and pushed the lock button again. The lights flashed twice in rapid succession and Katherine dropped her keys in her pocket taking a few quick steps to join her daughter. "What does he do that he didn't know he was leaving yesterday?"

"Mom, would you get a new battery for that thing?" Ava was going to have to take the thing and replace the batteries for her frugal mother or she'd end up not even using it to avoid having to pay for a three dollar battery. "Ben's a private investigator. Things can come up kind of sudden."

Katherine's nose wrinkled. "He doesn't take pictures of people cheating on each other does he?"

Ava shook her head trying to picture Ben perched in a tree outside someone's bedroom window. She turned her head to hide her grin. "He works with the police a lot so he does more missing persons and stuff." It was impossible to keep the pride she felt at Ben's noble mission to help people from her voice. "The police came by yesterday and told him about a case. Today was the first opportunity he had to take a look at it." She shrugged. "With these things time is of the essence." Not a word was a lie, only two stories combined, yet Ava got a bitter taste in her mouth at intentionally misleading her mother.

Katherine wasn't watching her daughter while they talked she was busily looking around the restaurant, taking in the dark wood décor and the floor to ceiling glass enclosed wine storage behind the hostess table. The young blonde hostess looked expectant, politely waiting to avoid interrupting her guests' conversation. Ava held up two fingers and they were led to a quiet corner booth. It was slow since the restaurant had just opened for lunch. Ava was assuming things would get busy in the next hour or so and was glad they were on the early side.

Katherine Brandt was self-conscious in certain situations, like when there were a lot of people around, feeling inferior because of her factory job and small town life. Ava knew it and refused to give up on her, assuring her she fit in better than most people because of her respect and manners. Only her own discomfort set her apart. Ava continued to push her to go out while being sensitive enough to time their outings for off peak times.

Her protectiveness of her mother had increased when she'd gone away to school and Katherine was alone. Ava felt guilty for leaving her and put the responsibility for her mother's happiness on her own shoulders as a self-imposed burden. She watched Katherine accept the sparsely populated restaurant as they were paraded past the majority of the tables to a private booth toward the back.

"Has he been an investigator for a long time?" Katherine scooted into her side of the booth, obediently taking her menu from the hostess without comment or eye contact.

Ava slid in opposite her mother and took her menu with a polite "thank you." "Yeah, he's done it for a while. He really likes it, it lets him help people." She watched her mother nodding approvingly at Ben's reasons, feeling her anxiety dissipating at her acceptance. Ava was just about to change the subject to something with fewer potential tripping hazards when her mother floored her with an observation.

"I always thought *you* would do something like that." Her mother said it mildly, not taking her eyes from her menu.

"Really?" Ava didn't even try to mask her incredulity. "Me, a private investigator?"

"Well, why not? You always liked to figure things out, you never could let something go until you had the answer. Remember when your dad's brother Mike showed you that card trick?" She glanced up, laughing at the memory. "You followed him around all day asking him to do it over and over until you finally saw how it really worked. I always thought you would go into a science working in a lab or one of those forensic jobs with the police like you see on tv."

Ava couldn't believe what she was hearing, or how offhandedly her mother was telling her the last six years of her life preparing for a career *she* didn't want were a misunderstanding. "Then why did you lean on me so hard to go into business?"

"I wouldn't say 'leaned'." She waved her hand, "I said business was a smart choice because you could always fall back on it. *You're* the one who picked it." Katherine went back to reviewing her menu. "Have you ever had the Chicken Marsala here? It sounds good."

Ava's menu came down with a slap and she gaped at her mother, feeling the heat building within her. "I can't believe you're saying this now. I'm almost twenty-four years old and you're telling me *now* that the education you pushed for since I was fifteen is *not* what you wanted for me?"

"Ava, keep your voice down." Katherine glanced around them nervously at the empty tables, worried they were attracting attention. Her fingertips fluttered against the menu she pressed against her chest. "All I'm saying is that I think you would have done well in either field. It really isn't worth arguing about now, it's all done and over with."

But Ava wasn't ready to let it go. Nor was she able to keep her frustration from boiling over. Her emotions were already close to the surface from her worries about Bruder and his nurse hurting people and with Ben out there risking his life for the greater good. She lowered her voice and leaned over the table. "Yes, fifty-thousand dollars and six years later I have a degree I don't want. I guess it's not a big deal to you but it means something to me."

Katherine stopped her nervous drumming and worried glances to level a hard look at her daughter. It was easy to take for granted the strength of character Katherine held in reserve, she didn't often display the steel that had gotten her through her losses.

Ava watched it creep into her features when Katherine answered and she held her breath.

"You were an adult when you registered for each and every class. I might have given you my opinions but the choice was yours, not mine."

Properly chastised and recognizing who was in the wrong, Ava studied her menu to give herself time to cool down. Her mother was correct except she was missing a crucial piece of Ava's decision making process. Katherine was apparently ignorant of how important it was to Ava to please her. The futility of the argument made Ava's head hurt, she would gain no satisfaction in fighting her mother's sound logic.

"What do you think of the penne a la Toscana? I love roasted red peppers." Katherine asked mildly frowning at her choices.

Not wanting to further strain her overburdened mother, Ava took the olive branch. "It sounds good. I was thinking of something a little lighter, did you see the one above that with scallops and linguini? I might do that one."

The server came by asking about drinks and both women ordered iced teas, Ava's without ice. The server looked at her funny. Ava was used to that reaction. "Ice makes me cold." They went ahead and ordered lunch as well to minimize their interruptions.

When they were alone again Katherine folded her hands on the table and raised her eyebrows. "Since you bring it up, your birthday is coming. Do you know what you want to do?"

"I assumed I would do what I always do and come up to see you for dinner. Does the weekend before or after work for you? It falls on a Thursday this year." Funny that she and Ben had birthdays so close together. She snorted, the months were close. She couldn't hold a candle to his year count.

"You don't have any better offers than dinner with Mom?" She smiled shrewdly. "I somehow doubt that."

"I guess I hadn't really thought about it." She admitted.

Katherine continued to dig. "Does he have any suggestions or is he keeping his plans a secret?"

Shrugging, Ava wanted to divert. "We haven't talked about it, things have been a little crazy." Ava changed the subject abruptly not caring how obvious it was. "How are things going with Robert? Will he be joining you this trip?"

Her mother tried to hide her discomfort. "I don't think so. I'm here for Elle."

"Right, but what about you. This has to be hard for you too Mom." She meant it sincerely. "Let him be there for you, you don't have to be alone anymore."

Katherine pushed her fork around with her fingertip, putting it exactly perpendicular to the edge of the table. "It is hard keeping it to myself, but I don't know how he would feel about it. Helping me with my husband's ghost is a lot to ask of any man."

"I guess I hadn't thought about it that way." Ava tried to put herself in that place. Would she be able to help Ben through something similar if it meant watching him mourn someone he'd loved before her? She wanted to think she would be gracious enough although she had to admit it made her uncomfortable to even think about. She shrugged off her personal doubts to support her mother. "Mom if he cares about you won't it be *harder* for him to know you're having a hard time and not be able to be here with you?"

Katherine tipped her head and watched her daughter, a strange smile twisting her lips.

Ava squirmed, not wanting to know what her mother was thinking. It was undoubtedly some sort of keen observation only a mother can make about her personality or appearance that makes a daughter want to shrivel up or crawl under the table. Ava averted her eyes signaling she had to be done.

Katherine recognized the sign and gave her peace until the food came. When it did they had a quiet meal, only commenting now and again about their food or an aspect of the restaurant one found interesting. Both had a lot tying up their thoughts.

Lunch didn't take long since neither one was interested in lingering. Katherine demanded Ava let her pay and Ava relented, fully aware her mother wouldn't take no for an answer. Then, when Katherine got up to use the restroom, she quietly slipped a twenty dollar bill into her mother's purse. They walked out together, hugged, and Katherine agreed to keep Ava up to date on any changes in Bill's condition.

Ch. 38

Two important calls came in that afternoon while Ava tried to occupy her mind with a game of solitaire the old fashioned way, with real cards.

The first was from her mother. Katherine was crying and Ava knew at once what it meant.

"Bill's gone. He passed away shortly after I got back to the hospital."

"Do you need me to do any shopping or make any food?" She couldn't limit her assistance to running the shop anymore. Ava was starting to feel impotent. "Anything?"

Surprisingly, this time she was not refused. "You know, we could use some essentials at the house like milk and juice."

"I can go right away. Can I make anything or do you have any special meals you want, maybe lasagna or pasta salad?" Ava tried to think of what people made for grieving families when they're in no shape to cook. It seemed like it was always something they could reheat and eat off of for days.

"Sure, if you could do a lasagna or something that would be perfect. Why don't you come by about dinner time and I'll have her home by then? She's not going to be very good company tonight but it might do her good to see you."

"I don't plan on staying. I'll just drop off and go." She was already making a list.

"Thanks baby."

"No problem Mom."

As soon as Ava hung up she was on the move. Her now fully charged phone went in her pocket, keys and purse in hand she drove to the store to get everything she needed.

She was putting the lasagna in the oven and measuring out rice for the next dish when her phone rang again. One hand catching the oven door from slamming, she snatched the buzzing device off the counter before it went to voice mail without checking the caller id before answering.

"Hello?"

"Hi Ava, it's Ben."

Ava's face lit up upon hearing his voice. Then she smiled thinking it cute that he'd announced himself as if she wouldn't recognize his voice. "Hey Ben." She toned down her excitement in hopes of not sounding as desperately in love and needy as she was to have him back with her. "How's Louisiana? Have you been able to talk to the police at all?"

"Yes, I had Sharpe make some calls for me and I was granted access to the case files but they honestly don't tell me much. Like they said on the news, the girls are all underage and there are some privacy issues and the fact that they don't want to say too much in front of their parents. It's pretty frustrating."

"Isn't there a way around the privacy issue? Was Sharpe mad you had to cancel with him today because you went out there?"

"He's fine putting it off but I had to promise to meet with him as soon as possible. Sharpe has some pull down here and was able to get me in on the interviews even though technically I can't be *in* them. The lead detective can't get me in the interviews in front of the parents, but they have an interview room with a one way mirror and they'll let me sit in unofficially. That should be enough to get me what I need."

"That's great Ben." Ava missed him. Leaning on the counter she wrapped her free hand around her middle and closed her eyes, picturing him standing in her kitchen with her. "Do they have any ideas where the doctor might have gone? Have any tips been called in or anything?"

He snorted. "There have been quite a few calls. None of which hold any promise." Ben sighed and growled his frustration. "How about you? Did you have a pleasant lunch with your mother? I hope she was understanding about my having to miss it."

She struggled to keep her voice upbeat. "Yeah, she was actually kind of impressed that you work with the police. We talked about that and then I ended up blowing up about college, which is pretty dumb since I'm done now and she made me mad because she was right." Somewhere between layers of noodles and cheese, Ava had let go of her childish anger.

"What was she right about?"

"That my degree was my decision so I have no one to blame but myself for not liking what I ended up with."

Ben gave a low whistle. "I guess you did have it out. How did things end?"

"Quietly." Feeling like a first class heel was partially fueling Ava's cooking frenzy. She hoped it might make up for being a brat. "I'll apologize when I see her later tonight."

"Are you having dinner together too?"

"No, I'm dropping some food off at Elle's." She sighed, catching him up on her end. "Bill died today. Mom's taking her home soon, she's kind of out of it." Ava was not looking forward to walking into the house with so much raw pain. She would be in and out, as promised. Katherine was much better at this than she was.

Ben expressed his sympathies. "I'm sorry I don't have good news for you. I don't know when I'm going to be home, this might take a few more days. Have you seen Alistair yet?"

"No, should I have?"

"I doubt it. He doesn't have to see you to see you." He tried to keep his tone light.

Ava sort of understood that and didn't want to ask too much about her babysitter's skills. Right then she just wanted Ben. "That's cool." She tried to hide her disappointment with some lighthearted joking. "I have enough to keep me busy here. *Someone* gave me a fancy MP3 player that is going to take a brain trust to figure out."

"Whoever did that must think you're exceptionally smart to figure that out all by yourself," Ben teased back. "Really honey, I wish I could be there for you right now. Are you sure you're okay?"

Ben's distress tore at her already heavy heart. He was possibly near the end of a decades long search, Ava would have to be incredibly selfish to even think of asking him to come home. Even if she broke her leg she wouldn't have the heart to call him off his hunt.

Ava smiled, willing her voice to sound happy while her hand splayed over her stomach and rubbed up and down like her mother used to do for her when she couldn't sleep. It usually brought her some comfort. At present it did nothing. "I'm fine Ben. Do what you need to do there and keep yourself safe okay? I don't want to hear something happened because you were distracted worrying about me." She meant it and tried to convey the seriousness of her request.

"I promise." He said soberly.

They said their good byes and Ava hung up. She turned around and leaned on her elbows against the counter to reconfigure her thoughts.

"Hurry home Ben." She said a silent prayer for him and pushed herself off to dump the rice in the water. There was a lot for her to do here.

***

At six o'clock when Ava rang the doorbell at Elle's, dark had fallen and there was a chill in the air. Ava had been too busy shuttling dishes and bags from her apartment to her car to grab a jacket. She shivered, waiting for Katherine to get the door.

"Ava, thank you so much." Her mother's weary eyes were red. Her mascara, so carefully applied for their lunch, was smeared, wiped and smeared again, giving her an eighties band look that would have been hilarious under different circumstances.

Hands full, Ava leaned in to give her mother an armless hug over the casserole dish she cradled. When her mother's arms wrapped around her Ava whispered in her ear. "I'm sorry Mom, about earlier. You were right and I'm a jerk."

"Oh baby, I hadn't even given it a second thought." She gave Ava an extra pat on the back and rubbed her arm before she let her go.

They both knew that was false, Ava had been her mother's world since her father died and she could easily wound her with a word. Deny it as she might, Katherine needed the apology as much as Ava needed absolution. When they parted, both faces were just a little brighter.

"I have a few things in the car." Ava pointed with her chin over her shoulder. "If you'll take this one I'll grab some more."

She handed over the dish, feeling the cold of the outside air when she no longer had the warm ceramic against her palms. Empty handed, Ava trotted back to the car and put the handles for the cloth grocery bag over her shoulder before dipping down for more. Carefully she angled the meatballs and rice dish, a Minnesota comfort food staple, crossways with the brownies. Elle loved Ava's brownies. She hoped they brought her a little joy now.

Katherine met her at the doorway gaping at her burden. "Wow, you must have been cooking all day!"

Ava slowly mounted the front steps, tasty load balanced precariously in her arms. "It was nice to feel like I was doing something to help." She twisted her upper half sideways and carried the cargo inside, straight through to the kitchen. The house was mostly dark and quiet.

"Where's Elle, is she resting?" Ava asked her mother in a whisper when they were standing in the dim kitchen, illuminated only by the light over the sink.

Katherine pointed up, to Elle's bedroom above. Ava nodded and moved back to the front door.

"Are you leaving already?" She stage whispered at Ava's retreating back.

Shaking her head, Ava turned so she didn't have to get any louder. "No, I have more."

"*More*?"

Indeed she did. In addition to what she'd already carted in, Ava also had scalloped potatoes but they were boxed so she would only accept partial credit. Katherine pooh poohed her deflection. "If you mixed them and baked them, then you made them."

She also made extra rice, a strata with ham and broccoli and a batch of chocolate chip cookies. Her grocery bag had staples like milk, juice, butter, sugar, coffee, fresh fruit and the makings for salad. She had no idea she had gotten so out of hand until it was all sitting on the counters and Ava sat back with her mother, surveying the bounty piled all over every flat surface.

Katherine was standing, arms crossed and shaking her head. "I haven't seen you cook like this since Dusty died."

"I loved that dog." Ava agreed, staring at the unbelievable mountain of food. "Cooking gives my hands something to do."

"I guess I didn't realize how upset you were by this." Katherine started shuffling some of the things in the fridge while Ava handed her dishes.

They were able to get everything but the cookies inside. "Do you need any dishes back right away? It's going to take a while to eat this down."

"No, I just need to get this stuff back before Thanksgiving. I think I used every baking dish I own." Ava chuckled. "Think Elle would notice if I took a cookie?"

"Grab a few and I'll pour a couple of milks."

They sat down to have their milk and cookies at the kitchen table. Both of them taking comfort in each other's company in that rare way only family and very good friends have. They could sit together, not needing to fill the silence with trivialities.

Ava was chewing a bite of her cookie when her mother's troubled voice broke into her thoughts.

"Baby, I don't mean to pry but you aren't yourself. Is everything all right with you?" She laid a hand on Ava's hand where it rested on her milk glass. "I know you didn't really like Bill."

Her direct request threatened to break the floodgates, barely holding Ava's fears at bay. "I'm worried about Ben."

"Is he doing something dangerous?" Her eyes widened.

Nodding, Ava set down her cookie and rubbed her fingers together, rolling crumbs off onto the table. It gave her something to fixate on less intrusive than her mother's stare.

Katherine's hand tightened over her daughter's getting her to look up at her. "Can you tell me what he's doing or is it some sort of secret?"

Ava glanced up and made eye contact with her mother only briefly. "It sort of is and I won't feel better until he's back here."

"You really like him, don't you?" She watched her daughter push the crumbs into a pile and press her fingertip on them to make them stick only to roll them off again and start the whole pointless process over.

"It's that obvious?" Ava laughed at herself and risked a glance at her mom.

Her mother nodded her head, grinning. "I'm glad to see it, I was starting to worry about you." Her grin broke, her expression changing to one of consternation. "Sometimes when things happen to people, they shut off the part of themselves that lets them feel. I thought maybe you did that when you blocked out what happened to you."

Ava started to disagree, stopping when her mother placed a hand flat on the table to let her know she wasn't done.

"When you were ten, your friend Ruby fell and twisted her ankle. You brought her ice and a piece of candy, but she kept crying. Once you saw you couldn't fix it, you just got up and left. You weren't mean about it, but it made you so uncomfortable, you just sort of detached. I saw it a hundred times over in different ways. And on the rare occasion you would bring a boy home, it was the same thing. No spark. I worried you would never let anyone in."

Ava's ears were beginning to burn. Discussing her emotional ineptitude was something she really didn't think she could do on a good day, and today was definitely not that. Sensing her daughter had reached the end of her tolerance, Katherine eased up.

She rubbed the back of Ava's hand. "I'm just saying I'm happy for you to have found someone that makes you happy. It is so important to find someone for your heart to love. Whether it's a partner or a child we all need it, it makes us whole."

Her thoughts constantly looping back to Ben, Ava finished her cookie and washed it down with milk feeling all the while like she was back in school when things were bad. She and her mother would go into the kitchen if they had a fight and they would share a treat, refusing to go to bed until they had reached some sort of an agreement. Some nights Ava had given in due to a stomach ache more than any sort of break in her position. Katherine was equally distracted and grabbed an extra cookie.

A little after seven, Ava stood and stretched before rinsing her glass in the sink. "Tell Elle I'll take care of things as long as she needs me. When will you know about the service?"

"It should be in the next couple of days. I'll call you when I have the particulars." Her mother came up and rubbed her back. "Let me know when Ben comes home. I want to get to know the man who finally made my little girl fall."

Ava agreed, keeping her moist eyes out of her mother's sight line lest she see how hard a time she really was having keeping herself together. She walked her out and Ava waved when she pulled out of the driveway. It was going to be a long, lonely night.

Ch. 39

Monday morning broke rainy and gloomy and it suited Ava just fine. She hadn't slept well and ended up showering late the night before, which was the cause for the mess on her head. What was less obvious on the outside was that she had a headache from lack of sleep and the constant worrying that she was going to get a call that Ben was hurt. She wondered if she would know somehow if something happened. For the millionth time in the last twenty-four hours, she pushed her negative thoughts roughly aside.

Concerns for her own safety were non existent. Ava automatically trusted in Ben's ability to keep her safe whether he was here or far away or it was him directly or Alistair doing the watching. It left her to go about her business without any extra precautions beyond keeping the typical watchful eye for suspicious characters lurking near her home or the shop. That was something nearly every single woman does as a habit.

Ava was guessing Elle would be gone for at least another few days, beyond that she wouldn't venture a guess. Workaholics usually cope with stress by working, so Elle might be in right after the funeral. Given her time allowance Ava appraised the shop, trying with her new perspective to see if there was anything she would want to do or thought might go well for the store. If there were any dramatic changes she would make if it were hers.

Seeing nothing obvious, Ava got out the laptop and started researching a few pieces Elle had received while Ava was on vacation. Digging for a particular piece, she found a comparison piece on an internet site and had a thought.

Elle was in the business of selling items and most of their items turned over within a week. The store did not pay the sellers until the item sold and then the store took a commission. It was a very straightforward, typical resale setup. However, it was limited by floor space and the ability of customers to bring their items into the shop.

What Elle's had working for it specifically was its location. It was right in the middle of a bustling area of mixed commercial and residential buildings, providing it with a significant amount of traffic. The result was a busy store every day they were open. That was a lot to say for a consignment shop.

Ava pondered the possibility of having an online addition to the store. A virtual store that would maintain Elle's reputation for having higher end merchandise by requesting an appraisal or some legal documentation confirming the authenticity and value of the piece. It would be more specific than the other online sales sites too, catering to those wanting to find that particular piece for their collection, not just an inexpensive table or entertainment center.

The idea grabbed her and she started digging. She looked online all day between customers. When her lunch came from the sandwich shop Ava ate it at the keyboard, completely wrapped up in what she was reading. It sounded like she might have an interesting niche that could fit them quite well. No one else had anything like it yet, and it would allow Elle's to grow without having to split into two stores or move away from their prime location and loyal customer base. At first blush, it was looking like a viable option.

Knowing Elle wouldn't want a business plan, Ava went about preparing her idea for sale in a different way. She made a flow chart showing how the online furniture brokering portion of the business would take in new customers, how their information would be verified, and how payment would be made. When she felt her goal was complete, it was near the end of the day. She set the paperwork she had created aside for the day to be looked at with a fresh set of eyes in the morning.

At six, Ava was hungry for dinner but did not want to eat from the delivery place she always got food from. Their limited menu was beginning to get old. Digging through their pile of take out menus, Ava thought about how much takeout she was going to be eating this week. Working twelve hour days wasn't going to leave much time for shopping and she didn't feel good after fast food for one day, much less several.

Inspired, she went back to the laptop and in minutes had the information she wanted. She asked the phone order girl for Alistair. The girl was very polite, asking her to hold please.

Within a minute of being put on hold, Ava was greeted by Alistair's booming voice.

"Ava! How are you my dear?"

His welcome warmed her even over the phone. "Hi Alistair. I'm okay. I won't take up too much of your time, I know it's dinner rush right now."

Interrupting her with a sound from his lips like gas escaping from a balloon, Alistair stopped her. "That is why I pay these fine people. They will handle the rush and leave me to talk to my favorite customers. Why do you think I have a restaurant? Where else am I going to go all day and talk to people about food?"

That was why Ava liked Alistair. He was so jubilant, it was hard not to catch some of his joy for life. "Thanks. I was actually wondering if I could contract your services."

"What do you need from me dear?"

Ava quickly explained about Bill and Alistair offered his sincere condolences. "While Elle is out handling everything for Bill I'm the only employee. I can't close the shop and I don't want to go grocery shopping at ten at night after work. So my proposal is this: do you have a daily menu I could see online and order from to get delivered here or is my store too far from you? I'm going to be eating two meals a day here for the next few days, possibly longer depending when she's ready to come back. Could that work or no?"

"Could it work?" He made an odd symphony of noises she didn't even understand. "Of course it will work. Let's do this, tell me what you want for dinner. I already know the address." She should have realized he would know the store's address, Ben would have given him that already. "We'll send you a menu good for the next few days and you can fax or email your order. Just give me an hour's notice before you want it. I can't have you starving. Ben would have my head."

At mention of Ben's name, Ava held her breath feeling her good humor evaporating.

Alistair lowered his voice, also suddenly sober. "Ava dear, he's okay. I would know if he wasn't. I would tell you."

"Do you promise?" Ava told herself she was being silly to request such a thing from a grown man, yet she waited for his response.

"Of course I would. Why wouldn't I?" Without waiting for an answer, Alistair dialed into the crux of her apprehension. "Dear, I have known our man for a very long time and I know what you mean to him. And, if I may be so bold, I can see that you are equally fond of him. I will not keep anything from you, don't you worry."

His gentle voice and trustworthy nature soothed her nerves. Alistair's honesty worked to subdue her doubts, though it did not erase them. "Thank you Alistair. I can't tell you what that means. I've been going out of my head."

"No worries dear. Now what can I get you tonight?"

Not half an hour later the doorbell chimed and in walked Alistair sporting a black fedora and trademark Armani. His restaurant could not possibly be paying for his wardrobe unless there was something she didn't know about the food industry.

Ava was helping a woman choose between two dresses for an outdoor graduation party. On her way up front, they stopped at the hat and accessory table. Despite her attempts to rush her, it was another ten minutes before she was rung up and on her way.

"Thanks for waiting." She rolled her eyes and wiped the back of her hand across her forehead where a few strands of hair had come loose and were tickling her nose.

Alistair held out his arms and Ava gratefully fell in.

"You feel lonely dear." He gave her a squeeze, "You can feel free to use me for your daily dose of male companionship until Ben comes home."

Knowing Alistair's giving nature, Ava took his offer at face value. "Thanks Alistair. Had I known I was going to have you for my deliveryman I would have ordered for two." Ava motioned toward an antique table at the front of the store with clothing on it. "I could have set the table."

He laughed heartily. "What are you doing for dinner tomorrow?"

Ava held out her hands to the edges of the shop.

"Consider it a date then. I'll bring you dinner myself and we'll enjoy a meal together." His brows pulled down. "We can't have you alone all day *and* all night. Left to your own devices for too long, you will start to borrow trouble."

She laughed and wiggled her brows at him. "Then you'd better watch out. I'm alone a lot, I'm very good at that sort of thing. But yes, until someone comes back to me at work or at home, I'm going to be depending on my customers for my social needs."

Tsk, Tsking her Alistair unpacked her dinner and set it out on the back counter behind the register. "I would rather see you eat it here while it's warm than hide it in back where it will get cold."

While he was reassembling his thermal bag, Ava asked if Scott had been able to untangle the data he had retrieved from the hard drives.

"We aren't sure." He stroked his goatee pensively, shaking his head. "It looks like there is a more complete database on this last one although it's huge and encrypted. The data he found only had partial information on it."

"I wish I could help. It's hard to feel so disconnected all of a sudden. I need to be here for Elle and I want to be helping you and Ben too." Alistair was easy to talk to, she found herself telling him things she normally wouldn't say out loud.

His large hand covered her shoulder. "Everyone wants to be a part of this but we draw more attention traveling as a pack. There is no indication the doctor is still in the area. Ben is probably in the safest place possible right now. When it comes to fact finding, there is no one better than Ben."

"So that's all you think he's doing, fact finding?" She was relieved to hear he wasn't putting himself in danger with a higher contact manhunt. Suddenly, a new idea popped to mind. “Do you have those printouts Ben wanted? I wonder if *I* could take a look at them. I’m pretty good at fact finding myself.”

“Scott has them but I can get them. I’ll bring them to you tomorrow.” He put his hand on the insulated bag and checked his watch on the other. “I must be off, restaurants don’t run themselves you know.” Alistair kissed her head and strode to the front door where he stopped with his hand on the bar. “Don’t forget our date tomorrow dear.” He winked and walked out.

Ava picked up the laptop and started to search.

Ch. 40

In her element, Ava felt confident. Research and fact finding were two things Ava was more than proficient at. In the past she’d been able to find what no one else could from sources all over the world using only her computer. Her brain put things together that often escaped others, and her luck with difficult searches had earned her the automatic point position on information gathering in any and all group work projects in school.

There was limited time during the evening store hours for her to dig into what she had thus far, and she hurried through closing duties in a rush to get home. Once in for the night, Ava set the coffee maker and sat down with her trusty computer.

First she searched for what she knew; the clinic in Shreveport. There were a number of hits in local papers and some blogging activity offering nothing new. Then she tried searching for other clinics that catered to teenagers. The sheer number of them was surprising. The volume of religious sites discussing the evils was predictable and cumbersome to dig through. But it was the clinics that drew her. She searched for open versus closed within the last forty years, keeping in mind that the ageless doctor had been rumored to be working on something for roughly that amount of time. Ava hunted for a link to the clinics.

She hooked up to her printer, running off copies of several articles of interest conducted by Pro-Choice groups. They showed a trend of clinics peaking in the late seventies and early eighties. It wasn't the numbers they showed, it was the locations she found most interesting. Most were in large urban areas with high poverty and immigrant rates. The findings led Ava to wonder if this was the population the doctor had been targeting.

It would follow that a group of young women without resources or those who could not speak the language would find themselves at the mercy of a clinic that offered free care regardless of reputation or rumors of pregnancies gone bad like those that eventually closed this latest clinic. How many other clinics had the doctor run over the years. Her mind started to churn out ideas and she put pen to paper to capture them, intending to run down each one.

It was after midnight when her burning eyes halted her pursuit for answers. Glancing at the clock, she sighed. She had meant to try Ben before it got too late. Disappointed in her obsessive tendencies, Ava brushed her teeth and went to bed.

Morning came and Ava went to work, using slow periods to follow her idea on the online store. Her work for Ben was now too involved to dip in and out of between customers. She was busy with a steady rush of customers from ten on and hadn't even thought about eating when she said good bye to the last person in the store at one for a mini break in the action. Her stomach growled and she looked at her watch.

"Damn." Her shoulders slumped and she rubbed her empty belly, thinking it too late to call in an order. She was starting to prepare herself for the long wait until dinner when the bell over the door chimed and a woman entered.

"Can I help you?" She asked the young Asian woman pleasantly.

The newcomer smiled as she approached and Ava saw the white polo shirt she wore bore an insignia with a familiar name. "Alistair, I love you." Ava breathed.

"He thought you might have gotten busy, so he took the liberty of sending you something." She grinned, opening the bag.

Ava took the containers, blushing awkwardly when her stomach announced its impatience.

"I'll take that as a thank you." The delivery girl giggled closing her bag. With that, she started toward the door.

"Wait, I need to pay."

Waving her off, the girl said, "The boss said to settle up when you're done."

"Thanks." Ava waved and took her prize behind the counter to find out what he had sent.

Seasonal, fresh and healthy seemed to be Alistair's claim to fame. Today was no different. Scents of asparagus soup and a ham and brie Panini wafted up to her. It was just the right amount and the store was shockingly dead for long enough to let her eat in relative peace.

Several hours later, her cell phone rang. Ava snapped up her phone and saw the number was not the one she wanted. She made her voice more cheerful than she felt.

"Hi baby. How's it going there?"

Ava limited her topics to those she could talk about without getting too personal. The other night had pushed her boundaries and she didn't feel up to a repeat of that. "Fine Mom. How about you? Did Elle have a hard night?"

"It's hard to tell, she was out cold from a sleeping pill the doctors gave her. She's up now and doing all right. Thanks for the egg dish by the way. Elle hasn't eaten a good meal for days and that went over really well this morning." Katherine sighed, sounding tired. "I was calling to let you know she's scheduled the service for Thursday, day after tomorrow, at ten a.m." Before Ava could ask, Katherine continued. "Elle said to close the store for the day."

"Okay."

The chiming at the door drew her eye and she saw a group of women walk in. She recognized the company name listed on their prominently displayed ID badges as one from an office park the next street over. They would be pressed for time and would expect efficient help.

"Mom," she started to say.

"I heard the bell. I'll let you go."

"K, bye." Adding hurriedly, "I love you Mom."

***

Ava had her head down replacing the register tape when a booming voice from across the counter shattered the silence of the empty shop.

"Ava, my dear!"

Startled, she jumped and dropped the register tape hearing it hit the ground and roll off somewhere under the cabinet behind her. "You sure know how to make an entrance." She tried to be crabby only his bubbly personality wouldn't allow it. She found her lips twitching in spite of herself.

The insulated bag dangled where he hefted it over the counter. "Ready for our date?"

"Sure. Elle and I actually have a little table set up in back. I hope you don't mind, the ambience is more than a little lacking." She pointed toward the curtained doorway. "It's on the dock."

He waved a hand. "You're scenery enough dear. Lead the way." The big man leaned forward and whispered conspiratorially, "I don't know when I'll get another chance to get you alone." His teeth flashed.

Ava laughed and picked up the tape. "Okay, just let me put this in. If you want to head back there I'll join you in a minute."

He backed away from the counter and bowed with a flourish. Ava laughed again and reached down to grab the tape from the floor. She hurriedly tore off the unspooled section and clicked it in. By the time she reached the dock, the little table was already set. An envelope with Ben's name on it sat at her spot.

"Real plates and a metal fork? You know how to make a girl feel special." She teased, surveying the spread he'd put out. Her fingers were already prying open the flap of the envelope.

"Ah, please. Pleasure before business." He directed her to her chair and waited for her to be seated before taking his own.

Ava set the envelope back down, hiding her disappointment. "Thanks for lunch too. I'm sorry I didn't call in. I lost track of time and honestly, the first time I even got to think about eating was when your girl came in."

Alistair was dishing up the food between their plates, not looking at her when he said in an unusually serious voice. "You know you've got their tongues wagging at the restaurant with what you said."

"What do you mean?" She felt her face fall. Wracking her brain, she couldn't remember saying anything controversial to anyone."

"Word got out that you're in love with me." Setting down the dish, he reached out a hand.

Reacting automatically, Ava reached out to give him one of hers, her face frozen in shock.

Alistair stared into her eyes, his expression sincere and in a low, seductive voice that sent goose bumps up her arm said, "I love you too my dear, but it is not to meant be."

She started to object and he held up a finger.

"I can accept being used for my cooking. People do it to me all the time. But eventually you will want more, and alas, I cannot give it." He kissed her hand and winked playfully. "Not to only *one* woman."

Ava blinked a few times before she started laughing, hard. The stress of the store, Elle's loss and Ben's absence were forgotten for a few minutes while she laughed at her own expense. Alistair seemed quite pleased with himself.

"I thought you needed that. If you don't mind my saying so dear, you are an easy target."

Her laughter abated, she wiped her eyes. "I told you I don't get out much. You're right, I did need that."

"Ben is family, and now so are you. I will do my best to look after you while he's gone." He raised a paper cup with sparkling water.

Ava raised her own expectantly.

“To love, my dear.” He winked.

Ch. 41

Ava was entrenched in her work shortly after she got home, taking time only to click on the coffee pot before diving back in. Scott and Alistair were right, the contents of the folder were difficult to figure out without more information. To the best of her ability, Ava deduced that the clinics were testing blood types of both woman and fetus. There was something funny about the data for the mothers’ blood types though, part way through the tests, it changed. Ava couldn’t figure out how that was happening. It had to be corrupt data. She had put it aside for the time being to do checking into blood history and types when the phone rang at nine.

She grabbed it without peeling her eyes from the lines she was comparing. “Hello?” She answered distractedly, finger to the screen to hold her place.

“Hi Ava.”

“Ben.” She sat back in her chair, her lips curving into a soft smile. “It’s good to hear your voice. I miss you.”

“I was hoping you would say that, me too.” He sounded worn out.

“Is everything going okay there?” She wanted to ask when he was coming home but restrained herself. “Have you found anything?”

Sighing heavily, Ben gave her a run down. He’d been able to shadow the police thus far in their investigation and had been given “consultant” status thus allowing him access to witnesses and files. They had interviewed nearly all the girls who had come forward. Their stories were the same. They were given prenatal vitamins as well as a shot on each visit. The doctor and his nurse told them it was an additional vitamin shot. All of them reported that it made them ill. Only after the clinic shut down and the shots stopped did any of them improve. Never seeing or speaking to anyone about their conditions or treatments, the girls assumed the illness was related to their pregnancies.

All of them came from questionable home situations with no adult guidance to speak of and were on their own to handle their pregnancies. Most kept their condition secret even from friends, and the clinic was set up with patients being escorted directly into the waiting rooms. They never saw each other with only one exception. One of the girls had arrived early and recognized the girl leaving as a fellow student in her school. Embarrassed, she hadn't said anything. The girl she'd recognized left the school shortly after. Ben had tried to follow up with the mystery girl with no success.

She had stopped coming to school several weeks ago and he had yet to reach anyone at her home number, a few stops at her house had yielded no results either. Tomorrow he was going to her house with an officer who could gain entrance if need be. He took a deep breath. "How about you? Have you been taking care of yourself?"

"Business has been crazy and we would have been busy with *two* of us. With just me here I've barely had a chance to breathe. I don't know what I would do if it weren't for Alistair, he's been great." As the words came out of her mouth, Ava feared Ben would think the worst of the situation.

"Oh? What's he been doing?" Ben inquired mildly. Feeling guilty, Ava stammered. "Um, I asked if he could bring food over for me since I'm working so much. And then last night we had dinner in the back." She rushed to defend herself. "The curtain was open and customers were in and out all night. We were barely alone."

Ben was quiet for a few seconds before he started laughing. "Ava, honey, I've known Alistair for over eighty years. You might not know it since he won't commit to one, but he has very firm beliefs about relationships. The thought that either of you would do anything like that hadn't even crossed my mind."

Telling him had taken a weight off her shoulders. She hadn't felt guilty about anything she had done or said, yet she didn't want him to think there was something there when there wasn't. His comment about Alistair's attitude about anything long term intrigued her. "He so sweet and he obviously *loves* women, why *doesn't* he want to get involved?"

"I'm not exactly sure. Alistair is a private man and we haven't discussed it. I would imagine he has his reasons. Maybe he's been burned, or maybe he doesn't want to watch someone he loves die." Ben's voice told of his own unease with the idea.

Ava didn't want to go down that dark and uncertain path tonight. She missed him too much just having him gone for a few days. She couldn't even think about letting him go for good because of their "age difference."

Ben avoided the topic as well. "I suppose you're locked in at the store for the rest of the week?"

"We're closed Thursday for the service. Maybe in the next few days Elle will get an idea of when she wants to come back, but yeah, until then it's just me." She couldn't help the yawn that escaped her.

Ben heard it. "You sound tired. Why don't you get some sleep? You have to take care of yourself while I'm gone."

His voice softened. "I promise I'll take over when I get back."

"I will." His kind sentiment put a lump in her throat she had trouble talking around. "This is just short term. Things will be back to normal soon enough. Thanks for worrying about me, it's kind of nice." His comment brought up her fears for his condition. "Are you getting what you need out there?"

"Yes, I'm practiced at handling things on the road. Jackie sent me a package this morning. Now get some sleep. I love you and I'll call you tomorrow. I'm hoping to be home soon."

"I love you too Ben."

***

The day of the service was a blur of activity. Ava's mother called her in a panic at eight. It seemed the caterer for the service had lost the order. When she'd called to check on it, he told her he was sorry, but he could not possibly be ready in time.

"I might know someone who can help." Ava got the essentials, like how large a service and what, if any, gatherings would take place afterward. "I'll call you back."

Ava called the restaurant and the only person in was the baker, they didn't open for another two hours. He said he would call Alistair and see what he could do. Hanging up, Ava cursed herself for not getting Alistair's number before. In minutes, she had him on the phone.

He conveyed calm as usual, but there was tension in his voice and very little kidding around. Even Alistair, miracle worker he was, saw this as a huge challenge.

"Alistair, I understand if you can't do it. It's a lot. I can always go to the store and get some deli and veggie trays or something."

Offended at the thought, Alistair's voice steeled. "Don't you *dare* serve them grocery store snacks. They're grieving for God's sake." He didn't *slam* the phone down, but firmly placed wouldn't be an exaggeration.

Ava made another call to her mother who anxiously picked up on the first ring. She breathed a little easier when Ava told her a friend of hers was handling the food. He promised to have it to them by ten at the latest. Katherine wasn't completely convinced it was going to end well, then again, neither was Ava.

She went to Elle's house intending to ride with them to the service, helping out where she could. Ava hadn't seen Elle since before she went on vacation. It had been two weeks yesterday, by her count. When she came downstairs in her black pantsuit, Ava tried to hide her shock.

Elle had always taken great care in her looks. She wasn't vain to a flaw, though she said it was always smart to put your best foot forward. You never knew when you were going to run into your next boss or ex-boyfriend on the street and you always wanted them both to take a second look.

She had prepared her clothing with as much care as ever. It was neatly pressed and tucked and yet her clothing hung on her body. Ava would guess she had lost at least ten pounds, her skin sagging from the weight loss. Elle's flesh tone was gray, her face blotchy from too much crying and stress. Red eyes told the same story.

"Elle, I'm so sorry." Without hesitation, Ava stepped forward to hug her.

Her boss who often moved heavy display tables stubbornly without waiting for help hugged her limply back.

"Thank you Ava. Has it been a mess at the store? I should be back Monday." Her voice was slightly slurred. Between the glazed look in her eyes and her speech affect, Ava assumed she was heavily medicated.

"Don't worry about it. I can cover as long as you need me."

"Okay, well, we should get there." Ava noticed Katherine didn't say funeral home. She wondered if Elle was processing much of this through the medicated haze. "We need to see if everything is in order and I have the florist coming soon." She checked her watch. "Yep, we need to get going."

All three women piled into Elle's Mercedes to go to the home together. Katherine drove. When they arrived, the florist was already talking to the funeral director. He broke away to clasp Elle's hand supportively.

"Mrs. DiMarco, I would again like to extend our deepest sympathies. We have a beautiful service arranged for your husband. Would you like to see him before we begin?"

Elle nodded, dismissing offers from both Katherine and Ava to accompany her into the next room. The service was to be closed casket due to the nature of his injuries, although it was not unusual for a spouse to have a final look to say good bye.

Ava sat on a chair at the back of the room watching Katherine speak with the florist. He shook her hand, nodded and left the room. Returning a few minutes later, both he and his young female helper were burdened with large arrangements of cream colored roses and hanging ivy. The positioning, even the colors of the arrangements were similar to a wedding. A minor detail that struck Ava as disturbing.

Pots were placed on several stands around the room, at the entrance, and one large one waiting on a chair to be draped over the casket. Elle's touch was evident in the choices; the tone being one of simple elegance. Elle was still in that overmedicated husk somewhere, Ava took heart in that.

At nine forty-five, Ava was watching Katherine sign the florist's receipt while she tried to keep out of the way of the milling mourners trickling in. She was debating waiting outside when a large hand touched her shoulder.

"Alistair!" She exclaimed in a loud whisper, glancing around to see if she'd disturbed anyone. Only her mother seemed to have noticed and had glanced up. Eager for one of his hugs, Ava threw her arms enthusiastically around him, clinging a little longer than usual.

Alistair welcomed her just as warmly. "How are you doing dear?" Leaning back, he frowned, searching her face for evidence of her mood no matter what she might say.

"I'm fine. I expected it to be hard, him dying the way my father did." She shrugged, "It isn't. I think I feel worse about not feeling anything." She motioned with her arm toward the door leading to where Elle was reviewing the body. "It means a lot to Elle that we're here though. She's in rough shape." She shook her head. "I can't imagine being in her shoes." The thought of going into that room to take a final look at Ben's face before he was taken from her forever was sickening.

"*You* won't ever have to my dear." Alistair said gently putting his head next to hers.

Ava had a sudden flash of Ben standing over *her* casket and felt the same nausea. To know that he might be forced to bury her someday gave her a new understanding of Elle's and her mother's pain. Alistair sensed where her thoughts had gone and tightened his arm around her back, offering what he could for solace.

He had his arm around her shoulders when Katherine approached. She had been watching them, keenly interested.

"Ava did you want to introduce me to your friend?"

"Mom, this is Alistair. Alistair this is my mother, Katherine Brandt."

Alistair held out his hand to shake Katherine's gently. "Alistair Downing madam. I am pleased to have been able to assist in your time of need."

Katherine blinked and looked to Ava for clarification.

"Alistair is our caterer." She informed her.

Bobbing her head, Katherine smiled faintly. "Oh, of course. We appreciate the help Alistair. Thank you." She was staring at the them, arms entwined. "How do you two know each other? Did you meet at Hamline?"

"No Ms. Brandt, Ava and I have a mutual acquaintance, Ben Pearson. Have you met him?"

Katherine's lips tightened a fraction, the first sign of trouble. Ava knew by the squaring of her shoulders, that she had her dander up about something.

"Yes, I have met Ben. Did you say the two of you are friends?"

Ava caught wind of what was troubling her mother. Eyes going wide, she lowered her arm and felt Alistair's slip away out of respect. "Mom, we're just friends, really."

Katherine's cheeks flushed. "I'm sorry Alistair. I'm afraid it's been a long week." She confessed, putting a hand to her head.

Alistair smiled broadly. "It's no trouble Ms. Brandt. Your daughter is a special girl, I would be protective too." He leaned in and Katherine's eyes got big. "I'll tell Ben he's well thought of." He winked.

Katherine's cheeks flushed again but when he straightened up she was smiling. She too was falling under Alistair's spell. "So, ah, were you able to put something together? Ava said you have a restaurant?"

Alistair smiled again, his joie de vivre was back in full effect with his successful delivery of the near impossible. "Come with me," he instructed. Arms held out to maneuver them, he wheeled them, one on either side, into the attached reception room where the brunch was to be served. Two of his employees were walking in with trays piled high with sandwiches, vegetables and fruit, a large container of green salad, and a platter of cookies and sweets.

"I didn't think you carried cookies." Ava stood on her tiptoes to see what kind.

"Even the best of us need a little treat now and again dear." He teased her.

"Do you think you could put one in my lunch tomorrow?" Ava explained her ongoing arrangement with Alistair to feed her while she was working like a dog.

Katherine thanked him. "It's good to know someone is keeping an eye on her while she's all alone."

"Mom," Ava declared embarrassed. "I'm not four."

The funeral director approached them, placing one hand gently on Katherine's shoulder as seemed to be his way. Ava suspected it was a habit stemming from a job of constantly comforting those in grief.

"We will be bringing out the casket now for the service to start. Please take your seats."

Katherine's eyes found Elle immediately, rushing to join her. The poor woman looked unsteady on her feet. Alistair guided Ava to sit beside Katherine who joined Elle in the front row. Apart from Ava, the two widows were the only family either one had to speak of now. They sat together, Katherine holding her friend's hand in silent support, and Elle, staring unblinking at the box containing her husband.

Ch. 42

After the service, those who wanted to pay their final respects at the casket were invited to do so. Ava didn't feel the need to approach. There was nothing she hadn't said to Bill in her mind during the service, and she moved with Alistair out to the reception area to get a coffee. Slowly, the others filed out. Speaking in hushed tones about the beauty of the service, they moved on to fill their plates in the time honored tradition of feasting in honor of the dead.

Glancing around her at the faces of those she did and didn't know from a life intertwined with Elle and Bill, Ava saw that they were appreciative of the reception. Grateful for Alistair's meal time rescue, Ava drew up beside him.

"Thank you Alistair. You really came through for us. I owe you." Ava smiled at him, laying her hand on his thick forearm.

"You would do the same for me dear. That is what friends do." Seeming to remember something, he tipped his head. "There is something I was supposed to ask you. Serendipitously, Jenna called me this morning right after you did. She was wondering if I was going to see you again. Due to it being such a leisurely morning," his face twisted into a coy smirk, "I was able to find out what she needed so that I could pass along her request. She informed me that both she *and* Scott have to work on Sunday and Scott's mother who usually sits for Patty wanted to go to an indoor garden show. They were hoping you might be available to help. It seems she was quite taken with you the other night and offered you up herself."

That was her only day off for a week and it might be her only day off for another. But, like the man said, "That's what friends do" and these were Ben's and now her friends.

"Sure. When do they need me to come get her? I can bring her back to my place." She hoped it was a nice enough day, her apartment would be awfully small for an active nine year old on a rainy day.

Alistair produced a house key and dangled it in front of her. "They thought you might be willing to watch her at Ben's since it is bigger and both of you are familiar with it. You know how children are sometimes in new places." He jiggled the key. "Are you game?"

She didn't want to admit that the opportunity to be in his house held great appeal to her, missing Ben as she was. And if he came home, she would already be there and they could handle daycare together. Grinning, she snatched it from his hand. "What time?"

Elle was exhausted after the service and Ava could see the effects the medication had on her. She was barely functional by the time most of the attendees had filed out. Katherine had her hands full trying to maneuver Elle out to the car and it was clear there were some cleanup issues with the tables requiring attention which was not something the funeral home handled. Seeing her mother guiding Elle, Ava knelt down to scoop up some carrots that had rolled onto the floor. When Katherine came back from getting Elle situated in the car like a tired toddler, she bent over to help.

"Leave it," Alistair stepped in, crouching down between them. "I have staff coming for that and I will stay to be certain all goes off." His arm wrapped around Katherine, helping her up and ushering her to the door. Ava watched her brows go up as he whispered something in her ear.

"Really?"

He nodded confirmation and Katherine thanked him with a tired smile, dragging herself off to the car.

"What did you tell her?" Ava asked him upon his return.

Frowning, Alistair let his distress leak out. "I told her I'm sending some things over for Elle. She's been on those drugs for far too long now. Her body is not handling it well." Alistair's eyes flashed in anger, Ava saw a very different man than the one she adored. She didn't doubt that he was capable of dark things. "These doctors prescribe drugs so quickly. It isn't good for a body to expose it to such substances, especially for an extended time as with your friend. They do far more harm than good."

Ava saw a flash of sun on glass as a car turned out of the parking lot, abruptly cutting him off realizing she'd been in her own world. "Oh no, I have to go. They're my ride." She started for the door.

"Don't worry dear you can get a ride with me if you can wait for my people to arrive."

"Are you sure that isn't too out of your way?" She asked, worried she was asking too much of him after what he'd pulled off already.

Shaking his head, Alistair checked his watch. "Not at all. I have loads of time before I'm due anywhere."

Shortly, his staff arrived to begin cleanup. He thanked them and kept things light, his employees happy while he took inventory that all the necessaries were still present and being loaded up.

Returning to Ava, he held out an elbow. "Have to make sure no one took the good silver you know." He winked. "Ready?"

Her hand covered only a tiny portion of his jacketed arm. "Yes Sir."

***

Alistair dropped her at Elle's to get her car, waiting politely for her to start the car before following her out of the neighborhood. Levity aside, she caught him scanning the streets the whole time. Ava had invited him to stop for a drink which he regretfully declined. There were "things that need doing," he'd said, leaving her to have a drink by herself.

In her apartment, drink warming her belly, she found herself exhausted and unwilling to get off the couch. Whether the cause was the constant strain of the last two weeks or the alcohol didn't matter. She pulled off her dress and slipped into her jammies, happy to lay on the couch with her favorite blanket and an Elvis movie on AMC. It was one of her favorites, Elvis and Ann Margaret were fun to watch even if she had seen it ten times already.

She dozed off for most of the movie and woke in time to see the second half of Roman Holiday with one of her favorite actors of all time, Audrey Hepburn. Watching the chemistry of Hepburn and Gregory Peck made her long for Ben. She thought about picking up her phone until, as the premise of the movie unfolded, she found it dampening her desire to call him.

The two main characters, a newsman and a princess, share a wonderful evening in Rome together. In the end, even though they fall in love, they both have to go back to their real lives, obligations demanding they remain apart.

Early as it was for them, Ava loved Ben with all her heart. And with that love had also come the fear of his loss. Not even considering the inevitable separation Ava's death would bring, Ben had pursuits that could tear them apart. His search ruled him. It would always take him away from her.

She had seen it twice already. When there had been a hint of Doctor Bruder's trail, Ben had left without a thought. Knowing where his passion lay, she could not rightfully ask him to change.

Her eyes burned. She turned off the tv, tossing the blanket back on the couch in a heap. Rubbing her eyes, she wandered, shuffling off to bed for the night at a few minutes after seven. Ava lay there staring at the ceiling, waiting for sleep a long time before it finally came.

***

The next day as Ava was opening the store she heard her phone beep. Pulling it from her purse she saw she had a message. "Weird," she mumbled. She hadn't turned it off. "I must have been really tired." After she put her purse down, she punched in her password.

"Hi Ava."

She sighed unhappily. She had missed Ben's call.

"We've spoken to the family and no one at her address has seen the missing girl for weeks. I'm checking out the last few ideas I have before I come home. I hope to get out tomorrow on the mid day flight."

That was today! Her heart skipped a beat.

"I'll call when I get in." Hearing that he was coming home put an extra bounce in her step. Ava went about the shop grinning like a fool thinking Ben might be home today, her concerns from last night cast aside in the bright light of day.

Morning was slow and she moved some pieces around, dragging out the last of the antiques from the dock. It was a woman's makeup vanity from the early thirties with only a small amount of scuffing on one back corner. Ava staged it with a small chair with a brass back and embroidered seat. A hat and some glass bottles on top set the scene perfectly.

Ava was adjusting the last small bottle when the doorbell chimed, in walked a young couple holding hands. The woman made a beeline for the vanity and Ava knew it was sold. From there she didn't stop until lunch arrived unbidden again at one. Then, when dinner came at six thirty, it hit her. Ben hadn't called.

Dinner smelled delicious, but Ava only picked at it. Most of it ended up in the garbage. Making matters worse, work slowed down to a crawl by seven. Needing distraction, she logged on and went back to her search for clusters of young missing women. She had a theory and was hoping to share it with Ben soon. In the back of her head was the flicker of hope that she could help him finally put his long quest behind him, leaving him to live out the rest of his natural life in peace. Maybe even with her.

They didn't have a printer hooked up to the laptop at the store, so when Ava found what she was looking for she began taking fastidious notes. Her pen flew for over an hour before she felt comfortable she had the most important details captured. When she shut down, she had several pages as well as a number of clusters she wanted to compare with the printouts she had captured already on the clinics.

Ava looked at her notes before putting them in her purse to fish out the keys to lock up. She straightened and counted the register. The lock turned on the front door exactly at nine and she was ready to leave. In her mind she was already starting to formulate a few speculative theories. So distracted was she that she forgot to scan the area before stepping out. Because she didn't, she failed to see the car parked on the far side of hers under the light in the lot.

The steel service door swung shut and she followed its arc to lock it when a voice made her jump and drop the keys.

"Hi Ava."

Forgetting about the keys, Ava whirled to see Ben, standing at the bottom of the metal stairs. "Ben!" She could neither hold back her smile nor herself, and she bounced down the stairs to throw her arms around him.

"Sorry I didn't call, I barely made the plane and once I was on it, I decided to surprise you." He returned her embrace just as fervently, almost desperately. "Did you miss me?" Ben teased giving her an extra squeeze.

Unrepentant for her enthusiasm, Ava answered with a giggle. "Can you tell?"

He pulled back and lowered his face. She stood on her tiptoes to reach his mouth and Ben grasped her tighter lifting her to him. When she pulled away Ava slid her hand down his arm to grasp his hand as she studied his face.

"You look tired. Didn't Jackie get your, ah, supply to you?" Her eyes searched him eagerly, seeing more signs of strain. "Do you need to get home?"

Ben ran his hand through his hair. "She did what she could, but that heat does a lot of damage. Anything over seventy for more than a few days takes its toll."

"What do you do in the summer when it's ninety degrees outside?"

Snorting, he smiled crookedly. "I'm pretty much nocturnal, and in the worst of it I limit how much I go out."

"No wonder you stick with this line of work. You can do most of it at night and inside."

Ben ran his free hand up the inside of her arm. "Are you tired, or could I interest you in coming over?"

Shivering, Ava peeked up at him and rested a hand on his chest, still adjusting to the realness of him there with her. "I work tomorrow. Do you?"

Shaking his head and throwing his arm around her, Ben steered her to his car. "Nothing that can't be done while you're gone. How about we take my car and I'll bring you back tomorrow."

Not wanting to let go, Ava agreed.

Ch. 43

Ben threw his keys on the counter and Ava fished out the one Alistair had given her. She put that one up too. Ben looked at it questioningly.

"Alistair gave it to me yesterday at the funeral. Scott and Jenna need a sitter on Sunday and they think it's best if I watch her here, so he gave me that." Her finger nudged the key's silver chain, swirling it around itself into a coiled metal snake.

Ben's finger nudged it back. "Why don't you hang on to it in case I have to go somewhere while you're here? I would hate to think of you two standing outside, cursing me for not being home."

Of course she saw through his transparent explanation. "Okay." Her finger slid under the chain, hooking it and redepositing it in her purse. Seeing him in the better light, Ava's consternation over his condition increased tenfold.

Ben's skin had a gray cast, his forehead and around his eyes held new wrinkles. The speed at which he aged when his body was stressed was alarming. "How many times can you do this to yourself?" She rested her hand on the side of his face.

His new wrinkles came together when he frowned, he looked like he was five years older and had spent a lifetime in the sun. "I'm not sure. My father hadn't tracked that very well, and I'm not willing to ask someone to do it on purpose out of curiosity sake. From my *personal* experience I can tell you that I've stressed myself on a minor scale such as this a number of times and each time, it takes a little longer to recover than the time before." Ben was careful to keep his tone noncommittal. "I would assume there *is* a breaking point."

"When was the last time? When *we* went to Louisiana?" She hadn't noticed as dramatic a change that time.

"No, I wasn't gone as long nor did I spend as much time in the heat. The last time I put myself under any sort of extended stress was when my father was killed. I was following several of Bruder's people and ran down three of them before his trail finally went cold. It was summer, took several weeks, and I was on the move so my access to Jackie was limited. When I was finished I had to go directly to the lab for a total blood exchange."

Ava tried not to think about all the little kids who had unwittingly contributed to Ben's successful recovery, telling herself he was doing this to save a great number of them from a worse fate. "What do you need to do first? Can I do anything for you to help?"

Ben's gaze flicked to the fridge and Ava, conflicted about the process, offered him some privacy. "I'll give you a minute."

She walked out of the kitchen and at the end of the hall her eyes settled on his bag still by the door. Seeing it gave her an idea of how she could help. Ava's least favorite part of traveling was unpacking at the end. She grabbed the handle and hefted it up the stairs where she threw it on the bed to unzip and unpack.

Unpacking someone else's bag is more personal than one might initially think. The first thing that struck Ava upon opening the bag was the musty smell of high humidity and the faint odor of sweat. Louisiana in the spring is warm. She had experienced that herself not two weeks before. The smell didn't bother her and she took out the clothes, tossing them in the closet hamper. Next came the shoes, shaving kit and a stack of papers. A cursory examination gave her the impression they were his notes from his investigation. She set them on top of his dresser, laying his change dish over them to keep them together.

Ava partially zipped the now empty bag to let it air and returned it to the closet floor with the shoes. The kit went into the bathroom on the counter. When she walked out into the main part of the bedroom she nearly ran into Ben, clearly finished in the kitchen. His face already looked less lined, though the change was not as total as before when they had been on the road together.

"Thank you for unpacking. That couldn't have been pleasant."

She shrugged her shoulders unbothered. "I don't mind, I like having something to do."

He moved aside to allow her to pass by him. Ava reached the bed and turned, lifting her leg under her to sit on the edge.

"So I saw your notes over there. Did you find anything with the missing girl?"

Ben followed her path, sinking down beside her and tipping backward to lie flat. He rubbed his face. "No one has seen her for a while. I think it's at least a possibility that we should be looking for a body."

"Do you think they killed her or it was an accident from taking the baby?"

"I don't know. I was reading my notes on the plane and in the morning I'm going to call Detective Sharpe to have him check with the detectives down there to see if they've gotten anything from crossing their Jane Doe's with the girl's file."

It felt wrong to be talking about the dead girl without giving her the respect of a name. "Who was she?"

"Adelphia Williams." He answered softly, one hand coming up to rub her back.

Ava tipped back too, rolling over to lay her head on his chest. It felt good to be back with him, to feel his chest move and the vibration of his voice against her body. There were some other things she missed too, but she hadn't a clue if his recovery time included that.

Ben's arm around her back pulled her in close and he kissed her head. Craning her neck, Ava offered him her lips. Kissing her softly, Ben's hand moved down and he pulled her up toward him. It turned out he did not need extra time to recover enough for that.

The sound of a gentle spring thunderstorm woke Ava just past seven. She reached over and was alarmed when her hand touched only cool fabric. Without noticing what she was doing, Ava's hand searched the pillow while she listened for the crackle of paper. She found nothing and exhaled in relief.

Used to sleeping in a virtual oven, Ava swung her legs over the edge and sat up without a stitch of clothing on. The carpet kept her feet from freezing on contact, but the air that touched her skin was not so forgiving. She began an immediate search for a sweater.

Searching in the closet, Ava greedily snatched an old U of M sweatshirt off "her" shelf and a pair of jeans to hold off the immediate threat of freezing to death indoors. Ben said he liked it cold, he wasn't kidding. He must have kept the thermostat up higher for her before, but being in the shape he was, he couldn't afford that now. Ava swallowed any comments about the temperature. That was part of being with Ben.

He was in the kitchen. She heard the fridge door shut when her feet hit the tile. When she walked in, she found him brewing coffee and popping down a piece of bread.

"Hungry? Alistair used up the last of my flour, I can't do waffles."

She pointed to the yogurt he had open on the counter. "Do you have another one of those and another one of those?" She nodded at the toaster.

Smiling, Ben seemed pleased. "That is for you," he pointed to the toaster. "And this," he fetched another yogurt from the fridge setting it on the counter in front of her, "is for you." He pulled put another piece of bread down for himself.

"Thanks." Ava skirted the counter to put her arms around him, he pulled her in tight to his body. "Mmm." Ava groaned. "I don't want to leave."

His chest rumbled against her cheek, "I don't want you to either. I am based out of here today with some review of my notes and phone calls. I'm going to see what I can put together, see if I missed something."

"Oh, I totally forgot. I've got some paperwork I wanted to show you but only half is in my purse, the other half is at my apartment. What are you doing tonight after I close? I can show you what I found."

Ben's eyebrows rose under his remaining wrinkles. "What have you been doing while I've been gone?"

She smiled, excited to show him what thought she might have found. "You can't expect me to sit idly by while you're off tracking the ultimate bad guy. I did some fact finding of my own and Alistair gave me Scott's printouts from the hard drives for reference."

He watched her appraisingly. "Ava, have I told you how lucky I am to have you?"

"No." She went up on her toes to kiss him. "But you're right. You are lucky."

The toaster popped and they had their breakfast standing at the counter. After eating her yogurt and drinking a second leisurely cup of coffee, Ava could put off the inevitable no longer.

"I have to shower or I'm going to be late."

"Want any help?" Ben asked suggestively.

Sighing, Ava declined. "I can't be late and you know what would happen if we tried that one."

Ch. 44

Saturday was typically a busy day at the store. This one was no different. If anything, it seemed busier than usual. Ava was grateful for the work, it kept her from counting the minutes before she could be with Ben again. She was excited to show him what she had found.

At lunch Ava was pleasantly surprised when she had a different delivery boy. Ben walked in with a bag for her. The store was swamped with customers all around, and she kissed him in front of all of them when she took it off his hands. Who was going to tattle on her for kissing on the clock? She giggled, feeling like she was getting away with something.

"I heard you needed lunch, and you tip well. I guess I heard right although I'm not sure how I feel about you giving that kind of tip to just anyone." He grinned.

Ava playfully pushed his chest and rolled her eyes. "Don't remind me. I feel bad, I've been leaning on Alistair so hard this week. This is going to cost me a fortune, but I just couldn't face shopping and cooking plus all this."

"Don't worry about being too much work for Alistair. He lives for this stuff." Lowering his head, he rested his forehead on hers. "I'm taking over from here. Consider it a point of pride. Alistair can't escort my woman all over town without starting rumors."

Ava giggled. "That reminds me, my mom thought I was cheating on you with Alistair when she saw him hug me at the funeral. She got pretty upset with him." She swiped at a cluster of water droplets on the sleeve of his jacket. "I do believe she likes you." Waving a finger at him in mock discipline, Ava added, "I still wouldn't suggest missing another lunch date."

He held up both hands, palms out. "Not if I can help it."

Yet another batch of customers came in and Ava sighed. "Duty calls." Raising the lunch bag, she wagged it back and forth. "Thanks for the special delivery."

He gave her a chaste kiss good bye and she had to return to work, longingly watching him walk out. Lunch would have to wait. Indeed it did. It was consumed in quick passing bites until finally Ava gave up and threw the rest away. Dinner went much the same way with the delivery by the young Asian woman from before.

"Ben, huh?" She gave Ava a long look. "I'd love to know how you pulled that one off." Her smile was a little less friendly than it had been before.

Ava's claws came out. "I didn't pull anything off. *He* came after *me*." That was entirely true, she fought the urge to laugh at the girl's gaping mouth. "Thanks for dinner." She raised the bag and the girl, Cindy according to her name tag, stormed out.

After an eternity all the customers were gone, the register counted out, and the store cleaned up. Ava didn't have to return for an entire day. She was looking forward to her day off with Ben, even if they did have Patty with them. Ava assumed Ben would be waiting out back again and locked the front door first.

She had been correct in her assumption. Ben stood outside in the light rain waiting for her.

"Ben, you could have waited in the car." Ava put a hand up to touch his wet hair. "You didn't need to wait at the door, it isn't a date."

"I like the rain." He looked hurt. "Who says this isn't a date?"

Ava laid her hand on his face. "It's not a date until we are in *one* car." She tipped her chin toward her much abused blue car in the distance. "I've left that thing out here one night already, I'm not pushing my luck. The last thing I want to waste my money on is a new window or paint if some kid decides to take a whack at it. We have to take it home."

"Ava I'd like to, except the heat," Ben started to object. thinking she wanted to stay in the toasty apartment. He was right to worry, the temperature in her apartment would probably tax him more than he could handle right now.

“My notes I want to show you are there. I need to stop in and grab them.” She looked up at him through her black eyelashes. “And maybe grab some things if I’m going to stay over again. Remember, tomorrow’s the big babysitting day.”

Ben’s expression was pained. “Oh that’s right. I forgot all about that. We’ll have to keep our hands to ourselves while she’s there. Scott would furious if we taught her about the birds and the bees.”

“Do you think she doesn’t know?”

He was horrified. “She’s nine! Why would a nine year old already know about sex?”

Seeing his dismay, Ava downplayed it. “You’re right, she’s a good kid. She probably doesn’t know yet.”

“I know children are learning about it and having it far sooner than when I was young but when I look at them, I just see them as children. They’re racing through their lives so fast.” He brushed the water out of his hair.

She couldn’t disagree with his logic, yet having grown up in a different time she was more pragmatic. Not that *any* age would be acceptable for sex if *she* ever had a child. Her hypothetical child would not have a boyfriend until she was of legal age to drink. Maybe. “Since you won’t tell me how many lovers you’ve had, will you at least tell me how old you were when you were first with a woman?”

The direction change made him stumble. “Why would you want to know *that*?”

“Because I’m curious about your love life. You know plenty about mine. I’m just trying to level the field.”

“You’d better get in your car, you’re getting soaked.” His hand guided her toward her car.

Left unanswered, his imagined stable of women grew in her mind. Jealous, Ava stomped in a puddle on the way to her car. She was glad it splashed up her pant leg, soaking it through. It gave her something other than Ben to be annoyed with.

When they got to her apartment, Ben parked his car and got out to follow her in. They didn't speak until they were inside and Ava excused herself to her bedroom to get changed.

She was into dry jeans and a long sleeved shirt, preparing to don a fleece pullover when he spoke from the doorway.

"You don't have anything to worry about."

Stopping with her pullover poised over her head, Ava answered over her shoulder. "You can't tell me that. I know you've been with more than a few women. I'm just asking you to tell me when was your first time. I get to know *some* stuff about when you grow up even if you keep your adult life secret."

"Why does it matter?"

"I don't know. There's very little I know about you or where you came from. It would make me feel like I knew you a little better if I could know some personal things about you. Were you a jerk when you were young? Was there someone special you had to leave behind after your dad changed you? I want to know." She pulled her sweater over her head and turned around. "Do you still want me to spend the night?"

Ben's face was blank. "Of course I do. Do you want to?"

"Yes." She grabbed her bag off the closet floor and was putting a few things in it for tomorrow. Spring weather had a number of possibilities and Ava tried to pack for most of them. She wandered out of the room to grab her papers before she forgot. When she returned and put them in her bag, Ben spoke firmly.

"Yes, no and twenty."

"What?"

"Yes, I was a jerk when I was young, though I ask you to take into account my lack of parental guidance. No, I did not leave anyone special behind, and I was twenty when I had my first experience with a woman. I was with friends, I was drunk, and she was a prostitute. I am not proud of any part of that night."

Blinking at him, Ava regarded Ben for a moment. "Thank you." She zipped up the bag and carried it past him to set it by the door, reaching past him for a raincoat from her closet.

"And you?" He asked.

"Do you want to know or are you asking because *I* did?" She couldn't read his expression.

"I saw you on a date once, I checked in when I came back for a brief time several years ago. You were nineteen. You had grown into a beautiful woman while I was away, I saw you differently that time. It was difficult to think of that boy touching you." The memory of the event effected him; his jaw tightened. "I wanted to follow you inside and toss him out."

"Seventeen." She flinched at his look of shock. "I was lonely and I thought it would help. He didn't love me and I knew it. He never called me after that." It had not been her proudest moment, though it wasn't her worst. She had gotten over it long ago.

Ben stared at her, she could see his mind working to justify her giving herself to someone "unworthy." He was having visible trouble taking Ava down from the pedestal where he had kept her for so many years.

"My grandmother used to say you couldn't love someone until you knew something about them you didn't like. Once you knew that and got past it, you could say what you had was worth something."

She could see him rolling that around in his head. Not being a guy with incredibly old fashioned values or the old double standard let Ava be unburdened by Ben's confession. He might have trouble accepting hers, but she had answered his question honestly and that was something she lived by.

Jacket in hand, Ava stood by the door. "Ready?" She issued it like a challenge.

He nodded and she opened the door for him.

Ch. 45

It was more than a little uncomfortable in the car ride over. Ava was rethinking her overnight stay when Ben came downstairs into the living room where she had been analyzing her findings. Her theory was gaining momentum and she was eager to share it. Ben's footsteps on the tile pulled her out of her zone and made her uneasy.

"Ava," he rested his seat on the couch arm. "I must apologize for my behavior. There are times when my upbringing clashes with what is acceptable today. It isn't fair for me to judge you by outdated standards."

Having the ability to look past the possible inference, she took no offense at his mixed apology. He was clearly struggling, and that *he* was willing to come to *her* meant a great deal in her eyes. She understood what that took, being a prideful person herself.

"And I should work on my delivery. Sometimes I forget about people's feelings. I'm sorry too."

Ben extended a hand, expression perfectly serious. Ava held hers out expectantly. Ben took it and shook it once firmly. "Truce?"

Breaking out in a grin, Ava answered. "Truce."

Pointing to the paperwork spread out on the coffee table and in her lap, Ben asked, "What is this, your research?"

"It is. I wanted to show you my theory, only first I need to start here." She shuffled her papers, putting them in several neater stacks."

"I hadn't figured you for such a slob." He teased, knowing it wasn't true.

"I am *not* a slob. Research is messy business," she shot him a half serious glare. Finished with her sorting she scooted over and he slid down to sit beside her, getting a better view of the pages. "Okay, I used the timeframes you gave me for Doctor Bruder's research. Assuming he started working on this shortly after he spun off from your father in the fifties, I started there." She pointed to the heading for a chart she had found on one of the Pro-Choice sites. "I started looking for clinics serving pregnant women, specializing in those under eighteen. See how there aren't that many until twenty years later, peaking about 1982." She shuffled in the stack in front of her on the table. "Now, I looked for clusters of missing women and children."

Ben was fascinated.

She felt her chest swell with pride that she had found something new. "You can find anything on the internet." Ava grinned. "If you take these clusters and cross them with the clinics, specifically those that were only open during the times of peak missing persons reports, you see that there have been only about ten, maybe twelve clinics. Each was open roughly two years, then closed down with no new reported locations. None of the clinics is affiliated with any of the usual political backers like Planned Parenthood or Family Services. That's odd in and of itself, and they all fit the same criteria of specializing in early term abortions and care in young women's pregnancies. Like the clinic in Shreveport, all of these were in low income areas populated mostly by families operating below the poverty level and had large immigrant populations."

She handed Ben the page she had written her final comparison notes on. Ava let him review her summary before pulling her last page with a map she had printed to mark her findings.

"Each of these highlighted areas indicates the locations of the clinics, coinciding with significant reports of missing persons matching Bruder's clientele." She shrugged when he looked up curiously at her use of the word.

His phone rang from the kitchen while he was studying her papers. "Would you mind getting that?" Ben asked her glancing up distracted. "This is wonderful." He mumbled as she walked out of the room.

"Sure." Buoyant, she trotted into the kitchen. Reaching for his phone she saw the name pop up and called, "It's Detective Sharpe," before answering.

"Hello?"

The detective hesitated before speaking. "I would assume this is Ms. Brandt?"

"Yes Sir. Ben's just in the other room taking a look at something. Would you like to speak with him or do you need me to pass along a message?"

Again he paused. The detective had a habit of thinking through each sentence methodically before speaking. It made it seem like he was on a time delay. "Could you tell him I will be working tomorrow and I expect to see him at nine thirty sharp. There's been a development on that case I need him on and it can't wait."

"Will do." Ava wondered if it would be a breach of police protocol if Ben discussed the case with her. The thought crossed her mind briefly of what it would be like working with the detective or Ben. She wanted to think she would be good at it.

Returning to the living room, she saw that Ben had dug through her piles and now held several pages she recognized. When he heard her, he looked up, his eyes troubled.

"This coincides with the reports I've had from our people and my findings as to locations and clusters. Until now we hadn't known about the clinics. It all ties together. He's been hiding under our noses operating as a legitimate doctor." He laid the pages on his lap and sat back to rest his head on the cushions. "I can't figure out what he's doing with these girls and their babies. I wish we knew what that data Scot pulled off the hard drive meant."

His lined face and ashen pallor compounded his beaten mien.

"If the girls are pregnant, we know he isn't after *their* blood. They're too old."

"Is it the babies?" Ava asked, feeling sick to her stomach.

He shook his head. "Not in Shreveport anyway. There weren't enough girls and the pregnancies terminated were in the first few months. There wouldn't be enough blood to make them worthwhile."

Ava tried to look at it clinically and not see them as young scared girls or babies, it was very difficult. She thought of Ben's missing girl from Louisiana, Adelphia Williams.

"Do you think the missing girls are patients who figured out what was going on and threatened to talk?"

"I don't know. Maybe. Or maybe something went wrong and he had to dispose of the bodies." Ava's revulsion was plain on her face. "It wouldn't be unheard of for an abortion to go badly, it would be easy to hemorrhage. If they weren't prepared for it or didn't make a great enough effort it's a possibility to lose some of the mothers." Ben closed his eyes.

Ava watched his chest rise and fall so slowly it was sometimes hard to tell if he was alive. Part of being in his "state" required lower levels of respiration. She had seen both Ben and Alistair physically alter their breathing like a yogi or something. Ben was more practiced; he could do it nearly anywhere with little conscious effort. Ava noticed he often slowed his actions and breathing while cooking which seemed reasonable, it was a meditative practice. She enjoyed sitting and watching him, finding it calming to her frenetic mind.

"I almost forgot, Detective Sharpe wants you in his office tomorrow morning at nine thirty sharp. He said there's been a development in the case and he wants to talk to you about it."

Ben cracked an eye and looked at her. He held an arm out and she scrunched down to lay on him. He tucked her in close. "Do you think if we stayed right here and didn't move, tomorrow wouldn't come?" He asked hopefully.

"Mmm," she closed her eyes and let her head rise and fall with his slow breaths. "Let's try."

Ch. 46

Tomorrow, in all its stubbornness, did come. At nine, Ben left to see the detective and Patty arrived.

Jenna was apologetic when she dropped her off. "I'm sorry Ava, I heard Ben *just* got back. We really appreciate it. So does Scott's mom. She usually takes Patty when we both work, but today was her once a month free pass. Thank you so much."

Ava waved off her apologies, "Don't worry about it. Ben had to work for a little bit and Patty and I are going to have a fun girl's day." She looked down at Patty, tall for her age and nearly at Ava's shoulder. Another thing she had not gotten from her father, Ava thought with a smirk. If the poor had girl inherited her father's build she would be short and thick, good thing her mother balanced that out.

Patty was smiling shyly, her purple backpack appeared stuffed full with backup entertainment should time with Ava prove to be less than satisfactory.

Jenna said her good byes and kissed Patty on the head. "Be good." She shouted, waving as she jogged off the porch and out to her car. Scott waved from the driver's seat. Ava waved back as did Patty, closing the door after they pulled away.

Inside, Patty set her backpack down at the door. She was unsure of herself without her usual people around her.

"Have you eaten breakfast yet?" Ava started going through her repertoire.

Patty nodded. "Yeah, at like seven though."

Ava took the opening. "Panera is just down the block. Can I interest you in a muffin and a cocoa or something?"

She nodded her head, a nervous smile cracking.

"Great. I *haven't* eaten. I'll buy."

Patty slid her shoes back on and Ava took her credit card and some cash, leaving her purse. She paused, checking for Ben's key in her pocket before pulling the door shut behind them. She didn't leave a note thinking they wouldn't be gone long. Kids eat fast.

The muffin and cocoa loosened Patty's tongue and she told Ava all about her friends, especially her best friend Janice. Ava remembered the name from Ben's birthday. It sounded like Janice was a very good friend until recently when she'd started ignoring Patty in favor a new girl in class and now Patty was mad at her.

Ava told Patty how she'd had a similar experience in the seventh grade and that it had turned out all right. With pulling the story out of her backlog of memories, Ava tried to recall what had happened to that particular friend. When along the line had that friend, and several others, fallen away? It had been before she'd gone away to college, she couldn't blame it on that.

As she looked back, Ava only saw a long line of friends she had kept at a distance, never getting close. Each time growing apart as those friends sought confidants and companions who would share secrets and dreams. Ava had never been that girl; it hadn't bothered her because she hadn't wanted it. It could have been the loss of her father or seeing how that loss had cut her mother so deeply or her inability to trust stemming from her long buried trauma. No matter the cause, the result was exactly what Katherine had mentioned the other day at lunch. Ava *had* closed off that part of herself until now. She had missed so much out of fear. Maybe she shouldn't have been so hard on Ben about being afraid to connect with people. By her figures, he was ahead of her on that one.

“Ava, what’s wrong?” Patty’s sweet voice brought her back. “You look sad.”

Forcing a smile, Ava cleared her mind. “I was just thinking about something Ben and I were talking about yesterday.”

“Are you going to marry him?” Patty asked, licking whipped cream off of her spoon. Ava hadn’t seen her touch the cocoa yet she had devoured the whipped cream in a way that made Ava sick just thinking of the ball of sugar sitting in her stomach.

“Uh, um, I don’t know. Are you done with your muffin?” Ava busily started clearing their table, stacking napkins and food remnants on their round tray.

Patty sensed she had struck a nerve. Either from innocence or manipulation, both possible at her age, Patty hung on tenaciously. “I heard Dad and Mom talking. They said Ben loves you and when people are in love they get married.”

Patty wasn’t so cute in Ava’s eyes anymore. Ava hadn’t been around kids enough to know they could so easily see through the smoke screens adults allowed each other to maintain certain illusions. Patty wanted to cut through Ava’s little bubble and make her think about things she didn’t dare.

“Some people do get married, but Ben and I haven’t talked about that.” She kept it simple.

She tipped her head and, just like that, pursued another line of questioning. “Are your parents married? Jenna’s not my real mom.”

“My parents were married. My dad died when I was a little girl though so my mom raised me.”

“That’s sad. Didn’t you get a new dad?”

“No, my mom was kind of like my mom and my dad.”

The idea was strange to Patty and she wanted to talk about how a dad can't be a mom and a mom can't be a dad while they dumped their remnants in the trash. The girl liked the way her dad and she were always silly together. Jenna was good at helping her do her hair and snuggle and stuff she said. Her real mom was kind of serious but they did lots of cool stuff together like go to fancy restaurants and plays.

Ava told her that her mother had done all of those things.

"She must have been tired." Patty observed.

"I bet she was." Ava hadn't thought of it that way before and decided to do something for her mother, maybe get her a day at the spa or something. It was no wonder she hadn't dated when Ava was young. She didn't allow herself the time, and most likely didn't have the energy to do that sort of thing for herself. Katherine deserved tons of credit Ava knew she hadn't given her.

Patty reached for Ava's hand when they walked out. Feeling touched by her innocent affection and easy acceptance, Ava felt a connection to the girl. Ava's eyes stung, her heart warmed to Patty and she had an urge to pull her into a hug. Figuring it would probably scare the kid, she refrained.

It was such a beautiful day they decided to continue their girls' day outside. The area was home to about a four block stretch of boutique shops interspersed with some tiny restaurants and ethnic markets. They window shopped, Ava bought Patty a small bracelet with a tiny dog charm on it that she had pointed excitedly at when they passed by. Ava bought nothing for herself in reality though when Patty asked why not, she explained she had bought several things in her mind.

Confused, she wrinkled her nose and twisted her mouth to one side. "How can you buy things in your mind? You can't bring them home that way. They aren't yours."

Laughing, Ava told her how she and her mother would do that sometimes when they were out. They would each point at the things they most wanted and they would tell each other what they would do with it or how they would wear it. Later Ava figured out they did it because they didn't have much money and yet she never felt like she wanted for anything, her mother made her feel special by having the experience of "buying" anything she wanted. It was the fun of the shopping and imagining having the thing sometimes more than the thing itself that she had found attractive.

Patty liked it when she heard it described that way and they finished shopping together, mentally buying up the entire window of a jewelry store. They were laughing when they came around the corner, Patty dragging one hand along the short rod iron fence surrounding Surdyk's parking lot, and approached the condo.

Ava saw them before Patty did, instantly recognizing the aggressive posturing. Heart racing in the sudden adrenaline surge, she watched the car's reverse lights get closer as it flew backward around the corner, following the men who were now running toward them and closing fast.

Thinking quickly, Ava yanked her hand from Patty's and grabbed her under her arms, lifting her over the fence. "Run inside and find someone with a name tag. Tell them to call 911. Tell them there are bad people at Ben's house. Don't go with anyone until the police come. Okay?"

Patty's eyes were wide as she clung to Ava in terror and confusion. "No."

Ava struggled to separate Patty's hands from her sleeves, glancing over her shoulder at the men who were nearly on top of them. She felt the need to protect the child and was frustrated at her for not understanding the danger they were in.

“Patty, let go of me. Run.” She broke her hold and pushed Patty away.

Patty stepped backward, crying, and Ava saw her mouth form a little “o” as one of the men’s hands closed on Ava’s arm. The little girl scuffled backward and fell on the curb. The other man, taller and long legged planted a hand on the rail and easily threw his legs over to pluck Patty off the ground.

Surdyk’s liquor, the main portion of the store was closed on Sunday, not the adjoining deli. Two customers were walking out and heard the commotion.

“Hey,” one woman yelled. “Hey, let go them!”

The woman with her was digging in her purse for her phone. Ava didn’t watch for long. Her eyes were glued on Patty, now struggling and screaming against her captor. The tall, fair, Nordic looking man tried to pin her arms to her sides and control her kicking legs while he dragged her to the car waiting at the curb.

Patty’s panicked cries, “Ava! Ava! Help me!” hit Ava like barbs and she felt the tears running down her own cheeks.

Ava’s shorter attacker was brutally strong. His fingers were hard pincers, digging into her flesh as he pinned them behind her back. She reached a foot back to kick at his knees, except he was quick. He held both of her wrists in one hand, guiding her toward the car with the other. Ava dug her heels into the curb and pushed back against him. He raised her arms and she felt a searing pain in her shoulders as they threatened to leave their sockets. She stopped and threw her head back, trying to hit him, and he punched the back of one of her overextended shoulders. Ava felt her knees sag as her vision narrowed and she saw dancing spots.

Ava felt her shins hit the metal bottom of the door frame a second before her face skinned along the cloth seat. Patty landed on top of her, slamming Ava's head into the window and the two passenger side doors slammed shut. Ava felt her body roll back, bouncing roughly off the back of the seat and was dimly aware of Patty crying on top of her as her world faded away.

Ch. 47

Ben was discussing the case with Detective Sharpe. It was a missing person, the third young black girl in a month. They lived in a forty mile radius stretching beyond Minneapolis and into Shakopee. All went to different schools. One of the girls' friends said she was pregnant although no one knew for sure. No one knew if the other two were pregnant.

It had taken all of Ben's self-control not to tear the file from the detective's hands and see the information for himself as opposed to having to wait for him to slowly dole it out, piece by deliberate piece.

Ben felt the familiar tugging at his being that told him Ava was moving. He knew she was not alone, she was with Patty. He smiled inwardly, thinking of them having their girls' day together.

Ava had proven to be so much more than he had dared hope. She was a strong woman even if she couldn't see it in herself yet. Sometimes he saw glimpses of the frightened child he had carried out of the dark lab so long ago. Her mind was brilliant, her ability to make connections others might miss was truly extraordinary. She might very well have found the missing piece of the puzzle in his quest to find the doctor. He had been trying to think of something special he could do for her on the way here this morning. Maybe that trip she wanted when this was finally over.

Ben was hit with a sick, lurching feeling as he sensed Ava starting to move fast, more than just a little jog into a store or up the stairs. Alarm bells went off in his head. His ability did not let him see all the details, it was as if the people he could "feel" were in a fuzzy bubble only extending a few feet out from their bodies. What he did sense cancelled out everything the detective was saying. Ava was lying in the back of a moving vehicle, a sedan, and Patty lay on top of her. Ava wasn't moving.

He shot up out of his seat, pausing only long enough to tell Sharpe he had urgent business. Ben's exit plans were abandoned when he heard the call come in on the scanner. He could feel his phone ringing in his pocket simultaneously. A quick glance told him it was Alistair. He declined the call already fully aware of what was happening, and frozen in place by what he was hearing on the scanner on Sharpe's desk.

"All available units, possible double abduction on the corner of East Hennepin and University. An adult and child, both female. Witnesses report they were put into a dark vehicle by force. Vehicle is a dark newer model sedan, possibly black, with heavily tinted windows. License plate is unknown."

Ben texted Alistair to follow him and bring "reinforcements." Alistair would be able to track Ben as easily as he could Ava.

Detective Sharpe had stood up when Ben did, taking in his alarm, and not missing the fact that Ben was up *before* the call went out. "Ben what's going on? How did you know…?" The fact driven detective did not know how to put what he had witnessed into words that fit into his compartmentalized vocabulary.

"It's Ava. I don't have time to explain." His thoughts flashed to the resources available to the detective and made a split second decision. "This case with the missing girls here, Ava being taken and the case in Shreveport are all related. Come with me. We can talk about it in the car." Ben saw that Sharpe was thinking it through and spoke harshly. *"I am leaving now."* He spun, moving rapidly to the door. Having to hold back on his speed in the station was painful.

Sharpe stared at Ben. Just as he was about to leave him behind, the detective reached behind himself and grabbed his jacket. "I'll drive." He jogged to catch up.

Ben told Sharpe about Doctor Bruder, referring to him as a physician conducting medical research on young pregnant women. He was truthful when he confessed that he did not know what the doctor was after in his experiments. He explained that when the doctor moved a clinic into town, some of the women disappeared as did some local children. The children were also sometimes found alive and weren't being linked with the other cases.

Detective Sharpe was driving fast, making his way to the crime scene, frowning at the road in front of him as he listened. Ben was leaving out a lot, wanting to give Sharpe enough to inspire him to listen and follow Ben's lead, not enough to reveal himself. He would if he had to though. He would do anything to save Ava. His concerns for her eclipsed everything else.

With a heavy heart Ben dropped his head in his hand. "I have to call Patty's parents." Taking a deep breath, he pulled out his phone and dialed Scott.

Several minutes later, a sober faced Ben hung up.

"I hate that part." Sharpe said darkly, not turning his head. "The call that changes their lives forever."

Short tempered in his fear for his love and his friends' child, Ben roared at the detective. "Don't give up on them. If you are, drop me off now you'll only slow me down."

Sharpe turned his head, watching the man he respected enough to call peer curiously. "I'm not giving up on anybody Ben. You need to keep your head or you won't be any good to either one of them."

Ben made several efforts to slow his breathing, to calm his mind but every time he closed his eyes he saw Ava lying so very still, Patty hunched over her. He could see the girl's little face, pale with fear, hair soaked with tears stuck to her cheeks. His rage kept boiling to the surface and he was glad he had been injecting around the clock. Not only had he recovered, it would give him strength and stamina he was going to need.

Ch. 48

Ava was aware of someone grabbing her roughly, pulling her head first from the car. She could hear Patty crying, the sound was moving away. Shaking the fog out of her head, Ava tried to locate Patty as she was hauled to her feet.

"Settle down, you're both going to the same place." The short muscle bound thug grumbled, steering her by her good arm. Somewhere in their transport, her other arm had gone numb. It was obvious from the way it hung that it was no threat to him.

Seeing Ava behind her, Patty was quieted and let the tall Norseman drag her along. Ava shook her hair from her eyes and looked around her to see if she could recognize where they were. Should they get out, it would make an escape attempt easier.

The car was parked at the base of a rocky cliff. High walls rose on either side with only a dirt path marked with tire tracks leading from the car off into the wooded area beyond. Ava knew of several locations somewhat nearby with this kind of terrain. She guessed that she had been out under an hour considering it wasn't that much darker outside. She pricked her ears, listening for water. It would help her to limit the possibilities. She heard only birds and the breeze rattling last year's yet to fall dry oak leaves.

Muscles, the little thug, dragged her with him along the path a few yards before they walked into a gap in the cliff face and the sun disappeared. Once inside the cave Ava could see a light bobbing ahead. She assumed it was the Norseman with Patty. She trained her eyes on the light and sped up. The thug beside her, content to follow his partner's flashlight, let her set their pace.

They reached Patty quickly, her short legs and the fact that she was getting tired from trying to keep up with her tall escort made catching her easy. Ava slowed when she came abreast of the girl. Her dead arm was toward Patty and she flicked her fingers to touch the girl's thin arm. Patty shrank away, relaxing when she saw it was Ava offering her a smile and some comfort. Weakly she tried to smile back, sniffling and taking Ava's limp hand in her own.

Ava slowed her pace for Patty and their captors allowed it, in no apparent hurry now that they were out of sight. Ava knew that it was the doctor's men who had them and as soon as they entered the tunnel, she realized that the doctor was *here*. This place bore an eerie resemblance to the bomb shelter in Shreveport, as well as the room she remembered being taken to as a child. Now she knew why he preferred these places. It was the cooler temperatures that they needed to survive, in addition to the solitude that let him do whatever he wanted without detection. Angrily, she wished this one would collapse and crush the bastard.

A new light source, much brighter than their lone flashlight, shone up ahead. It was hard to tell how far without anything on the walls visible to mark distance and depth. It turned out not to be far at all, they were there much quicker than she had hoped.

When they walked into the larger, hollowed out area of the cave, Ava saw the doctor had replicated his lab yet again.

Her stomach twisted painfully when she saw the tables with the padded leather restraints lying open and waiting. Patty craned her neck, looking to Ava for reassurance. Ava swallowed her own fright to try to be strong for Patty. She could tell she didn't succeed, the girl's grip tightened on Ava's weak fingers.

The blonde woman had cut her hair, it was chin length now and she wore it straight. Ava easily recognized the almond eyes that slid out from around a tall bank of medical equipment mounted on shining, wheeled metal carts, the likes of which they'd seen in his Louisiana lab.

Ava saw that she was talking, although she didn't hear anything. She was staring at the crooked lower teeth, she heard herself whimper and her knees wanted to buckle. She told herself she was grown up now, no longer a defenseless child. She could get them out if she kept her head.

They took Patty first. Her cries of protest rousted Ava from her shock as she felt her little fingers slipping away. Ava willed her hand to hold on, it failed to listen.

"Leave her alone." Ava demanded, working to free her restrained arm.

Muscles grabbed her shoulder with his other hand and jammed his thumb into her bruised collarbone, bringing her to her knees.

Patty kicked the Norseman in the shins when he picked her up, biting his hand when it got too close. Ava struggled in vain against the man holding her as she too was hauled over and laid on the table, the overly strong blonde nurse helping Muscles to strap down her flailing limbs. Her body strained against the cold metal and stiff straps, back in place after so many years. The prick and burn in her arm too was familiar. She heard Patty grow silent as the drugs dulled her brain.

"No! Let her go!" Ava shrieked in protest when she saw them wheel the machine over to Patty. They were going to take it all, Ava knew that. They wouldn't let her live after she had seen where they were. Ava was cold with fear and fuzzy from the drugs rapidly taking effect. The fact that she could think clearly made her think they'd unwittingly given her a child's dose, not enough to incapacitate an adult. She was slow and wouldn't be any good in a fight, but she might not be completely useless.

Ava had faith. Ben would come soon. He always came for her, her father had sent him to protect her. Her foggy mind was blurring timeframes. Mixing now with long ago, it was making her thoughts a jumble, blurring the line between reality and fantasy.

Sure, they were going to kill her. Ben and Alistair had told her as much. Then, her aged blood being no use to them, Ava was surprised when the blonde woman wheeled a machine over to her. She focused on that face, only slightly altered by the years, and time blurred again.

"Hello Ava, do you remember me?'

She nodded and replied in a small voice. "You gave me candy."

The crooked teeth showed when she smiled. "That's right. You've come back to us and afforded us a rare opportunity. We have been watching and you continue to lead a charmed life. You might be more special that we first thought." Ava saw a syringe flash in the light. "But first, a little test. We need to be certain you haven't gone and contaminated your blood with chemicals, or developed some sort of illness." A hint of a frown crossed her brow, "Those things happen with time you know."

She felt the needle go in and slight pressure on her arm for a few seconds before the cotton ball was affixed with a strip of tape.

"We wouldn't want to waste any." She smiled, patting the tape secure before walking away.

Alone, Ava let her head fall to the side facing Patty and was relieved to see she was not plugged in yet. Thus far, the attention had been directed at Ava. She intended to keep it that way for as long as she possibly could. "Patty, it's going to be okay." Ava slurred.

Patty's eyes fluttered. She was alive, that was what mattered.

The drugs blurred Ava's vision as well as her mind. As she stared at the lights on the ceiling, she watched the halos and spectrums of light dance in and out of focus. Unlike the drug soaked candy she'd been given as a child, this one left her conscious. Never having tried more than a few drags off of a joint now and again, Ava had never experienced the hallucinations of harsher drugs. Thankfully the fog of the drug kept her from panicking at being tied down. Like recreational drugs, it seemed to inhibit her fears.

The lights made her eyes sore and she closed them, seeing their images burned into her lids. They made a night sky, the darkness punctuated by the orbs of yellow light. The darkness went from one shade of black to lighter grays intermixed, and she saw a city skyline only she wasn't sure what city it was supposed to be.

When her eyes had been closed for long enough for the orbs to fade her mind wandered into a dreamlike state, painting different images on her lids. She saw her mother and Elle at a funeral. Following her mother when she went up to shut the lid, she saw herself in the casket. Ben and Alistair were putting flowers on her grave and Scott and Jenna wept at Patty's. In her mind's eye she put their graves next to each other just like they were now. Unable to do anything else, Ava clenched her fists making her nails cut into her palms, pushing back the haze. Stubbornly, she forced her eyes open to see if Patty remained untouched. She was, for now.

Ava heard two voices. One was the blonde nurse and the other had to be the doctor, she recognized the accent from her dreams. Adult Ava knew it was German. She couldn't make out what they were saying but the doctor sounded excited.

The light above her head was blocked and she saw a short man with round glasses and gray hair looking down at her. He had a pencil thin moustache and a hooked nose. His introduction was unnecessary.

"Hello Ava. I am Doctor Gerhardt Bruder. It's been a long time."

Ch. 49

Ben arrived at the bluffs above the river hidden inside the Minnesota River Valley Wildlife Refuge. It was not open to public vehicles and Detective Sharpe gave Ben one of his long looks when he told him to turn in.

Thus far the detective had not said a word since asking Ben how he knew where the girls were and refused to drive on until Ben told him he "saw things." He was sure the detective didn't believe in psychics, though thankfully, he didn't question it. Ben's perceived premonition of Ava's abduction had spooked Sharpe and bought Ben a little leeway. For the time being.

Ben and Sharpe were a few yards inside the cave when a sequence of familiar sounds reached them. That of an engine, a car door and a shoe scuffing stone, each closer than the one before. Sharpe turned, Ben didn't need to. He already knew it was Alistair. He did stop to wait, putting a hand on Sharpe's arm and holding up a finger to let him know it was okay.

Sharpe accepted, somewhat hesitant. Ben could see him methodically trying to figure out the details as they continued to elude him. His investigative skills were unrivaled however, this was something he would never see coming and Ben knew it.

Alistair caught up to them and the detective started to object to the arsenal he carried with him until a shotgun was placed in his own hands. Alistair had another for himself and handed Ben a second handgun to back up the one he already had holstered on his belt. A leather bag slung across his chest also opened to reveal a box of shells for the shotguns and several clips for Ben.

Properly outfitted, the three stepped forward to stop a madman.

***

"Do you remember me?" The doctor was asking her.

She mouthed the word, her throat had gone dry. "Yes."

His lips pulled back revealing the kind of imperfect smile unheard of in America today in the land of whitening strips and braces. His canines were slightly longer than was typical and his front two teeth were short, further accentuating the illusion of fangs. Age had thinned the softness in his face leaving his bones prominent, his skin was stretched tight over his cheekbones and sharp chin.

In Ava's drugged mind, she saw the image of a vampire. It was just as Ben had said in the beginning. The legends of the modern vampire could have been written about this man. Where Ben and Alistair were pale, the doctor was bone white. White like he hadn't seen the sun in decades. Ben had told her he was strong and fast, depending how much he blood he was using, and according to Ben, it was a lot. He was the strongest of all of them. However, unlike the vampires of myth, this one could be killed.

"I have always thought of you as the one who got away. It was a shame Physick took you from me. But history repeats itself and here you are again."

At first, Ava didn't understand who he meant. Her lethargic thoughts taking time to catch that he was referring to Ben by his given name.

"The boy has been a problem for me from the start. He distracted his father and slowed our research. Then, finally, we had the process confirmed and he convinced Doctor Physick that I could not be trusted. They hid Physick's notes with the proper sequencing, leaving me with nothing. I was young and acted impulsively. It was a terrible loss to have to destroy the man, his mind was beyond compare. It was a shame his blood held no special properties either." His eyes were off. There was too much white around them and his cheek twitched in a subconscious nervous tic.

Ava could see that he was indeed quite mad.

He held up a finger. "When his blood failed, I wasn't ready to give up. I experimented with consuming tissues from his brain to see if his strength was there." Bruder's voice swelled in frustration. "Nothing. There was nothing, he took his brilliance to the grave with him. And now, I am aging *faster*. It is Physick who is responsible for my losses. He knows what is missing and he is going to tell me." His tittering laughter sent a chill up her spine. There was no sanity in his eyes and she feared for Patty and herself. "Because now I have you."

This man was stark raving mad. He had crossed over from injecting blood from young children to consuming the brains of his former colleague. There would be no reasoning with him. She clung to the hope that he was narcissistic as well as a nut and she could draw out his speech, buying them time. The longer she could keep him from hurting either of them, the better chance they had of being discovered.

"Your research with the pregnant girls. What is that? What do you want with their blood?"

He brightened and nodded excitedly. "That is a pet project of mine. You see I have been working with some exciting chemical compounds I've constructed out of antigens. This particular compound is very special. Once introduced, it attaches to the patient's red blood cells. It tells the body's immune system to attack itself until it is so weak, any outside germs can cause the patient's death. It is an engineered immunodeficiency virus, easily transmitted once the skin is broken. It acts quite similarly to HIV."

Unable to comprehend how someone could willingly engineer something so devastating to their own kind, Ava stared up at the mad doctor.

"What about the children? You need them for your survival." She could not see him committing a slow suicide by killing a necessary source for his longevity.

Bruder grinned again, canines making dents in his lower lip. "That is the brilliant part." He tittered again, setting Ava's teeth on edge. He smiled, quite pleased with himself. "We have finished our testing and can say with certainty that unborn children are resilient. When the virus is introduced to the mother alone, the fetus dies. However, if a secondary antigen is introduced, it has the same effect as a shot frequently given to mothers with Rh factor conditions. The secondary antigen lasts for several months, protecting them both until the child is born. When the child is removed, so too is the barrier between the compound and the mother's immune system. The virus attacks and she dies. All of those orphans will need care. Who better than myself? I am one of the rare few who can see children for the value they add to our lives." Wild eyes scanned the darkness surrounding them. "I can finally operate in the light, no longer hiding in the bowels of the earth in these abandoned holes."

Suddenly the doctor's body stiffened and he bared his teeth like an animal. "He's here." He hissed. His eyes were wild when they settled on Ava. "He's found you much faster than I anticipated." Bruder's head swung around, looking for something. "He's gotten stronger."

He quickly unbuckled Ava's arms and legs. Her limbs failed her they were unresponsive to her dull commands. Doctor Bruder yanked her off the table and held her to his side as easily as he would a doll.

"Thomas, Mitchell, do not let anyone through that entrance." He growled at the two thugs.

The nurse, unruffled by the chaos breaking out, moved about the lab in an orderly fashion conducting their apparent exit protocol. She stacked several log books in a pile before stuffing them into a messenger bag she threw across her chest. Then, with an ease that belied her relatively small body, the nurse picked up one computer after another and dropped it on the ground, smashing them beyond recognition. She had just raised the last unit when the roar of a shotgun echoed in the tunnel.

Spinning her head, Ava saw the Norseman fall, knocking the occupied table over onto its side with the little girl hanging suspended. Patty's small form dangled from her restraints facing away from the tunnel mouth. Muscles had armed himself and lay on his stomach next to the metal frame, firing in rapid succession into the opening. Panicking, Ava shouted to the tunnel entrance, "No! You'll hit Patty!"

The gunfire from the tunnel stopped immediately. Muscles lay unmoving, his gun trained on the dark opening. Ava rolled her ankles one at a time, concentrating on getting her blood flowing and making her body respond to her will. She did the same with her good arm and was rewarded with tingling as feeling returned, the other remained dead weight. The drug was still showing its effects, but she could move, though it took far more concentration than normal.

The nurse's task accomplished, she joined Ava and the doctor near the wall. Ava felt a flutter in her chest knowing Ben was blocking the only entrance. This time the doctor was trapped. It was finally going to be over.

Ava was watching the tunnel, fearing Ben would walk out and into a bullet. Worried she would see him fall, unable to look away and miss him, Ava was staring at the black hole in the wall when something streaked in toward them.

Muscles cried out and was jerked up off his stomach. There, holding him by the throat was Ben. His other hand flashed out, easily disarming the thug. Ava heard the crack of bones and the lifeless body fell from his grasp. Ben immediately began to scan the room for other threats.

"Physick." He didn't yell, he didn't need to. The sound of Bruder's voice froze Ben in his tracks.

He spun and stopped when he saw Bruder, standing with Ava pinned to his side. Ben was not so far away that Ava missed seeing the color empty from his face and his eyes grow black with hate.

She could hear the satisfaction in Bruder's voice when he spoke. "You are stronger. Have you been breaking your own sacred rules? Are you taking more than what is *absolutely necessary*?" He mocked.

Ben's voice was cold and hard, Ava barely recognized it. "I am as strong as you now. This time I will stop you, with or without a weapon."

Bruder shifted Ava on his hip, calling attention to his possession. "No, I don't think you will. You see that I hold all the cards this time, and you have nothing."

"I am still willing to honor our agreement."

Bruder's grip around Ava tightened and she cried out involuntarily. "I no longer have need of your resources through you, I have my own in." He lifted his chin arrogantly. "Now, I am going to walk out of here, and if you do not want this one to die, you will not follow me."

Ava saw Ben's shoulders tighten. His jaw and fists were clenched helplessly.

"Ben, you can't let him go. He's going to…" The arm holding her tightened again, squeezing the air from her lungs. Her words wheezed out.

"It is your choice Benjamin. Is your father's killer worth losing the child you have protected for so long?" He clucked and wagged his head, never taking his eyes from Ben's. "It would be a shame to lose her after all the time you have invested. Now, if you behave, I will let her live."

As far as any of them knew, Bruder didn't know Ava and Ben were lovers. He assumed Ben's commitment was purely protection. She kept her mouth shut, knowing Bruder would not let her speak again while in her head she willed Ben to act. She saw in his eyes that he would not. Her body went limp, weak in defeat. So many people were going to suffer if this man got away now and there was nothing Ava could do to get away from him. He was far too strong. Wrestling against him was like wrestling a machine, with about as much mercy.

Bruder swung around and Ava's hopes crashed. There was another entrance. The doctor pushed aside the standing tool case beside the computers. He waved his nurse past and she dutifully fell to her knees to crawl inside. Bruder dropped Ava and she fell onto her knees. Roughly, he shoved her toward the hole in the wall, less than three feet tall. Ben remained motionless, helplessly watching his nemesis again move out of reach, this time taking his love with him.

The nurse was up ahead, Ava could hear the bag scraping on the rock wall. Inspiration struck her as her hands hit the ground. She had a very real ability to slow them down. The doctor pushed her to make room for himself in the tunnel and she made a show of her useless arm hanging to the ground, bearing no weight at all. She took a few slow, ambling hops to make her point. Injured and drugged, she would be a hindrance.

He crouched down beside her and spoke in a harsh whisper. "*I* am getting out of here. You can either figure out a way to make *that* work and live, or I will shoot the child *and* you before I make my escape. It's your choice." His breath was stale and hot on her cheek.

He didn't appear so insane now. The doctor's eyes were level and his hands steady. Ava didn't see a gun however, she had no doubt he had one on him.

Ava pleaded for Patty's life. "Please, leave her alone. I'll go with you. I won't fight you."

The doctor smiled pleasantly and waved her into the tunnel, giving her a shove with his foot to send her face first into the floor of the small tunnel. Ava's face felt like it had been rubbed on a cheese grater. It stung and was beginning to bleed if the wetness she felt was an indication. Her weight bearing hand now sported a torn palm and each time it hit the rock, it was rubbed raw as little pieces of dirt and debris ground around inside it. She felt the doctor behind her, heard him humming something pleasantly as he crawled, occasionally giving Ava a shove to keep her moving.

With each random shove she pitched forward, unable to catch herself. Her hand on the ground was torn and bloodied, the one she dragged beneath her had been rubbed raw where the top scraped the tunnel floor. Her knees had gone past painful to numb. Only his constant prodding kept her going, and fear for Patty. The more distance they put between the doctor and Patty, drugged but unharmed, the more likely it was she would live.

After she had fallen three or four more times, Ava concentrated on each hand and knee placement. She distracted herself with thoughts of the little girl behind them. The drugs would clear her system with few ill effects and she would be back with her parents soon. Ava felt relief wash over her knowing that Ben and Patty both were safe.

Up ahead, Ava saw light around the nurse's form and eagerly moved toward it, glad to be free of the darkness in the cramped tunnel. For good measure, another violent shove came from the source of the constant humming behind her. Ava was not sure, but she thought she heard something behind them, someone else in the tunnel. It was difficult to hear over the humming doctor and their grinding progress to be sure.

At long last, Ava reached the light. It was a series of rungs leading up to a round hole in the ceiling, exactly as it was at Driskill Mountain.

The second she stood to go up the ladder, Ava swooned. The drugs slowing her body left her unable to catch herself before she fell to the ground, breaking her fall by hitting her head on the side of the ladder.

Grunting in frustration, the doctor picked her up and carried her hanging face down under his arm and climbed steadily out of the tunnel. He had been humming to himself again, stopping suddenly when he reached the top. The bright sunlight was disorienting but felt good on her cold skin.

Ava turned her head and saw the nurse kneeling next to them, also very still. The messenger bag lay on the ground in front of her and, when Ava was able to twist her body, she saw the nurse's hands on top of her head. Ava tried to crane her neck to no avail, the cause for the nurse's predicament was too tall.

“Put her down Doctor.” Demanded a very calm, very angry voice she knew well. His accent bore no resemblance to the jovial, gentlemanly Englishman she adored. It was pure East Ender, and the threat behind it left no room for argument.

The doctor did exactly as requested. Ava was unceremoniously dumped on the ground, landing with a distinct thud and groan.

“Ava dear, can you make it over here to me?”

Now that she could roll over, Ava did so and twisted her head to see Alistair glaring at the doctor and nurse over the barrel of a large shotgun. He couldn’t afford to look away from them, so couldn’t see her nodding her head. Her answer came out as a squawk. “Yes.” Painfully, she tried to stand and her legs failed her. A few more yards of crawling wouldn’t kill her she told herself. At her first “step” she questioned her certainty. It hurt just as bad going over leaves and sticks as it had over rocks.

When she reached Alistair, Ava flopped herself over on her side like a dead thing. She was safe now and didn’t have to move, which was good because she didn’t think she could if she wanted to.

With Ava safe, Alistair could return to his demands of the two scientists.

“You Girlie, toss that bag over here. One handed, that’s it. Thank you.” Alistair hunched down to grab the bag and slid it to Ava. When he did, he saw her bloodied face and unfocused eyes, and his eyes lingered.

That was what the doctor was waiting for. Two shots rang out and Ava watched Alistair’s face contort with pain before he pitched forward. He lay very still with his face in front of hers, his body facing the other way. His upside down features filled her field of vision.

Ava's hoarse scream filled the echoing silence that followed the shots. She wriggled to him where he hit the ground, reaching her hand out to touch his face. He smiled once and winked before he closed his eyes. She couldn't see him breathing, Ava knew his body was too quiet. Tears leaked from her eyes, spilling onto the ground.

Ch. 50

Feet crunched on the ground coming closer to her, and she saw the doctor's hand reach down to remove Alistair's hand from where it lay on the bag to take it back. Ava again felt herself lifted off the ground, this time ending up slung over the doctor's shoulder. She heard his voice and the nurse's, but wasn't listening to the words. Her mind was back there, on the ground, hoping like mad that her friend was alive and that someone would get help for Alistair before he was gone forever. The thought of his smile gone from this world left a hole in her heart. A sob rattled out of her chest as she was bounced along, watching Alistair's prone body disappear from her sight as they walked into the tall brush.

The doctor slapped Ava's leg, getting her attention. "I gave that one his life, it was mine to take back as I pleased. And I pleased." He snorted at his wit and picked up his conversation with his nurse again. "Physick has taken too much time and energy from me. I was not joking, our deal is expired. I will have no further need for the completed formula when I have an endless supply of donors. I will be able to take as much as I want, and think how strong they will be. Survivors from the start, all of them." He patted her leg and Ava flinched away from his murderous touch. "This one's blood work intrigues me. I wonder what secrets *that* development might hold."

Nurse said, "Are you sure you want to break your truce? What if you can't sell the virus? The research is so close and he's promised you all the we might need of the synthetic blood. It will solve the problems we have had with the shorter, weaker conversions. We can go into full stasis without needing to take so many."

"You believe his promises so easily? They are nothing." He scoffed. "His team's research will not succeed as long as I have *her*."

Ava didn't understand how *she* kept Ben's lab from a breakthrough, who else could the doctor mean?

"Once the world sees the potential for what I have created, countries will be clamoring for my virus."

That god awful laugh of his brought a hint of bile up Ava's throat.

He gloated. "A virus that can bring down an entire population, no one will be able to be without it. They will be too afraid. It is the next nuclear threat."

Ava couldn't see in front of her to know why they had stopped until she heard the locks pop on a car. Her strength was coming back, though against the superhuman power of the doctor, she didn't know how she could manage to free herself.

"Bruder!"

As soon as she heard his voice, Ava went wild. She knew Bruder would not hesitate to kill him this time. She kicked and twisted and did everything she could to keep the doctor busy so he couldn't hurt Ben the way he had hurt Alistair. "Ben no! Get out of here!"

"Be still." He slapped her butt and it stung, it did nothing to stop her gyrations.

She straightened her body, nearly standing up in the arm he'd wrapped around her thighs, and threw herself backward, trying to wrench him off his feet. With little effort Bruder reached up with his free arm, wrapped his hand around her throat and brought her down in front of his body as a shield. On the way down, Bruder twisted her to face away from him, so that Ben could see her face.

His fingers pressed against her throat, compromising her air supply. Already panting from her exertions, within seconds Ava was gasping for the small amount of air he was allowing through. "Put it down Physick."

Ava could see Ben held a gun pointed at the doctor, except now that she was in the line of fire he was lowering it. "No Ben, you have to shoot him. He killed Alistair!" She screamed at him, trying to make him angry enough to pull the trigger. She had seen it in him. He had killed before and he could do it now. This was the man responsible for everything he fought against. "He killed your dad and he's going to kill you." Her choked voice broke, "Please shoot him."

The doctor giggled. "He won't shoot. Will you Benjamin? Her life is so precious to you. The one you were able to save, I see what she represents for you." He put his nose right against Ava's ear and she squirmed, trying to get away from him. "I suppose I should tell you Benjamin. Her life is doubly valuable now."

Ben's brows knitted together in confusion.

"Did you know she is pregnant? Your dear angelic Ava is not such an angel."

Ava saw his face blanch. His gun hand wavered. "What?" He muttered, almost to himself. "That isn't possible. We can't...the process doesn't allow it."

"It's yours?" Bruder licked his lips eagerly. "How fascinating. The child will be even more intriguing." He wagged a finger at Ben. "Your father's testing was not thorough, he died before he could finish. The *females* cannot grow a fetus because they are in stasis. However," he held up his hand. "Males are not as limited. As long as they partner with a healthy female, they can reproduce. And you have. Congratulations. I see that it is a surprise."

"I can't be. We haven't been…" Ava's voice trailed off and she ticked back the time. They had been together several times over the past few weeks, she wasn't even late. If it was, it was just barely.

Bruder confirmed it. "Blood tests like the one I ran are very sensitive. You are approximately two weeks pregnant. I ran it twice."

Ava stared at Ben. He was ashen, but he appeared to be strong and ready to fight. If she wasn't in the mix, she knew he could finish the man finally. Now was the time for her to be brave. Bruder was stronger by far, not taller. Ava took one deep breath and leaned her head forward before she threw it back as hard as she could.

Crunch went his nose and Ava felt the blood running down the back of her shirt. His hand came off her throat and Ava fell to the ground. The doctor was temporarily blinded.

His nurse saw what was happening and, with the selflessness of a true devotee, threw herself in front of her master just as Ben brought his gun up and squeezed the trigger.

Bruder was able to see well enough through his watering eyes to take hold of Ava's arm. He dragged her around the front of the car. On the other side of the vehicle Ava saw the cliff edge and, realizing what he was about to do, tried to plant her feet to no avail, he was too strong. Bruder grabbed a handful of her shirt and held her out, over the edge.

"Ava!" Ben followed them, his heart stopping painfully in his chest when he saw her dangling. "Bruder! You can't do this." He pleaded. "We had a deal. You promised not to hurt her."

"Put the gun down." The doctor replied flatly. "I told you, I don't need your synthetic any more. I will have my own ample supply soon. With so much of the real thing at my disposal, why would I need your *imitation* blood?" He spoke the word with distaste. "All of your tests have show it is not nearly as powerful, we would be no better than *them*." He sneered.

Ben's gun hit the ground at his feet where he stood, by the grill of the car. Ava, hanging absolutely still and not daring to move, felt the doctor shift and turned to see his other hand reach behind his back. The sun flashed on the black barrel tucked into his waistband.

"Ben, gun!" She shouted right as Bruder let go of her, pulled his weapon free, and fired.

Ben was fast, almost as fast as the doctor as he dove behind the car. Several more shots rang out as he pulled into a ball behind the tire, avoiding them all.

Ava was crying as she clung to the scrub and rock, Ben could hear her from where he crouched. He had to rush the standoff, he didn't have time to wait for the doctor to lose patience and make a mistake.

Ben held his gun at the ready as he crawled over the nurse's body, looking over the hood for the doctor to go with the feet he had just seen. Only the rest of the man was nowhere to be seen. Ben glanced up at the rocky outcropping that would afford the doctor a perfect sniper's position and recognized the trap he'd laid. The doctor had set himself up to take Ben out when he came to help Ava. He thought fast, time was against him.

The nurse's body lay by the passenger door, the keys were in her pocket. Ben went back, opened the door, and climbed inside sliding over to turn the key. He put the car in reverse and backed it up to the only cover, a tall pile of lightly colored limestone rocks and put the car back in park.

With the cover of the car and rock behind him forming a small V of safety, Ben scurried out keeping his head low and dove for the hand barely clinging to the nearly bare face of the rock. His heart in his throat, he grabbed Ava's wrist with both hands and pulled her up.

***

Ava was ready to fall, her fingers were slipping. Her precarious toeholds in the rock face were crumbling and, as much as she tried to will it, her damaged arm would not budge an inch to help her. She heard the shots and a car start. Fearing the worst, Ava stopped crying, her mind going blank.

First Alistair and then Ben, Bruder was destroying everything she loved. And now he was leaving her there to die too, with Ben's baby barely starting to grow inside her. Ava didn't notice her muscles relaxing. With a strange detachment she watched as her fingertips lost their purchase and she felt her body starting to fall backward. Closing her eyes she waited, wondering if she would feel it when she hit the ground below.

Strong hands clapped around her wrist and Ava's eyes flew open. The sun was behind him, his head casting a shadow over her face and Ava smiled through the tears coursing down her cheeks. Her words from childhood came back to her, as true now as they were then. *Daddy sent an angel.*

Ch. 51

The sound of sirens reached Ava but she didn't release her death grip on Ben. He held her with one arm, his spare gun in the other remained trained on the sniper position, waiting for signs of his enemy. When he heard the sirens Ben knew he was gone.

Ava had wrapped her arm around his neck the second she could and would not let go. When the sirens got closer, Ben tried to stand.

"I can't get up." Ava whispered into his neck. She could feel Ben's hand moving up and down her body searching for injuries. "Nothing's broken, I just can't stand." She told him.

"Did he give you something?" He twisted her arm to see the puncture mark and cotton ball taped to the inside of her elbow.

Ava nodded.

His hand stopped at her shoulder, his fingers gently probing.

She flinched.

"It's dislocated. Who did it?"

"Muscles." She used the nickname she'd given him.

Ben kissed her head, mumbling in her hair. "Good, *I* got that one. Alistair got the tall one."

Mention of Alistair put the vision of his dying eyes in her mind. "He's dead, Ben." She told him, her voice flat. "Bruder shot him right in front of me."

"I don't think so." He brought his hands up to loosen her grip and, exhausted, she finally allowed it and sat back. Ben studied her face, worried at what he saw there. "Detective Sharpe went behind you in the little tunnel, Alistair went back out the main tunnel with Patty. He dropped her off at the car and ran and around to catch you at the top. We'd seen the hole from the satellite images Sharpe pulled once we knew where we were going. After Driskill, we knew what to look for. Sharpe is with Alistair now, he called me and an ambulance when he found him and Patty is sleeping in the car."

"Do you think he's going to be okay?" Ava was confused. Her mind was still annoyingly bogged down with the effects of the drugs. "Wait, the detective is here?"

"I was with Sharpe when I felt them take you. He has resources we don't. I told him enough to get him to come along."

Her mouth fell open. "How did you explain how you were tracking me?"

"I'm fairly certain he thinks I'm psychic." Ben smiled grimly. The kind of attention Sharpe was going to direct his way was not going to be easy. If he stuck around, he might have to go into a new line of work.

"Speaking of psychic, did you know why you caught up with him this time? The doctor I mean." She couldn't take her eyes off of him. Ava had been so sure she was not going to see him again and now here he was.

Ben was watching her with a queer look on his face. "Yes, I caught him this time because I was following you."

Ava wagged her head deliberately. "He's like you, he can see you coming. He said you were really fast to get to me, faster than he thought. He said it was because of me. I'm like your natural male enhancement." Not being dead was making her punchy. She giggled at her own joke.

Ben put a hand on her head, leaning in to study her eyes. "Are you feeling all right?"

"I can't feel my arm, my knees hurt, I might have lost a friend and..." She ended abruptly, not saying the other thing, the thing that was weighing the heavy on her mind. She was pregnant with the child of a man who would outlive them both. Ava wasn't ready for any more big decisions at the moment and here was another one falling in her lap. She wasn't even twenty-four years old. Not for four whole days.

Ben heard what she wasn't saying. He was suspiciously quiet as he went on examining her cuts and scrapes. "We'd better have someone look at these. It looks like there is some gravel and debris in them." His head was down looking her knees and Ava could see the side of his face. Features pinched and lips tight, Ben was not happy.

She tried to comfort him, feeling more than a little responsible for Bruder's escape. "We'll catch him Ben. He can't run forever."

He didn't look up from his task, she heard the heat in his voice without seeing his expression. "That man is toxic, he destroys everything he touches. Look what he did to you." Ben's hand touched her leg above her chewed up knee. "Now that he's broken our agreement, you aren't safe anywhere and I don't know how I can protect…" he started to touch her abdomen and stopped himself. "How could I have done this to you? He'll never leave you alone now. I'm sorry, I never thought this could happen."

Ava choked at the thought of Bruder laying his hands on her baby. Ben was right, she would never have peace now. For Bruder her blood was special, Ben was ageless *and* the son of his great rival and now they had made a child. It was like honey to a bee. Her pulse picked back up, her breathing started to accelerate. Ava's heart hammered faster and faster until all she could hear was the rushing of her blood in her ears as her thoughts grew jumbled. Ava started to see spots in her vision, she touched her head where it began to pound.

"Ava, Ava, look at me." Ben's eyes were all she could see as he took her head in his hands. "You have to calm down. We don't know what he gave you, but your body is having a hard time regulating itself. I need you to try to take a few deep breaths."

A heavy weight on her chest made it hard to breath and her stomach was roiling. Her eyes started to roll back and Ben raised his voice, panicking.

"Damn it, look at me. I need you here with me, breathe Ava." He fought to get his own respiration under control. When he saw that Ava was trying he took her hand, holding it to his chest and helping her to focus on the rhythm he was able to regain from years of practice.

She had herself under control for the most part when the detective came up from below the hillside.

"Jesus, what did they do to *her*?" He stood with his hands on his hips, eyes bouncing between the two of them. Fresh scrapes on his knees and hands as well as a few marks that were going to be good sized bruises had started to swell on his face and beneath his clothes. The small tunnel was not built for a man his size and Sharpe had barely made it through in several spots. Blood that didn't belong to him marred his light colored shirt and pants where he'd wiped his hands.

Ben shot him a warning glare.

"Sorry." He offered Ben. "Sorry Ava." Adding softly, "She doesn't look good Ben. I'm going to call another unit." Detective Sharpe walked off to call a second ambulance.

Ava heard him talking and zoned him out. She was so exhausted, all she wanted was sleep. Leaning forward, she laid her head on Ben's chest. "I'm tired." She was no longer hyperventilating, yet she remained lightheaded. Her blood felt like sludge in her veins, her body was not getting enough oxygen. A sense of foreboding grew at the edge of her consciousness.

“They’re a few minutes out, can you keep her awake until they get here?” Sharpe sounded uneasy.

Ben didn’t answer the detective, Ava felt his hand under her chin pulling her face up to his. She let him raise her head keeping her eyes open even though hers wanted desperately to close; they burned from dirt and tears and sweat.

“You can’t go to sleep. Not until the medics check you out. Don’t close your eyes, Ava.” Ben spoke rapidly. He began to ramble, shifting against her, anything to keep her awake.

Ava was sort of listening, and as he went on she was captivated by the sing song cadence to his prattle and she began to drift. She heard him talking about Alistair being on his way to the hospital, telling her they were both going to be okay. It was all far away like a tv in the other room. She couldn’t make sense of his words but she liked the sound of his voice. It was a strong, warm voice, the kind that made you want to listen. He would tell great bedtime stories Ava thought.

“You would be a good dad.” She mumbled sleepily.

Ben closed his mouth and blinked at her.

“You would. I think you would do great stories, it’s the voice. You have a sexy voice.” She smiled lazily, losing her battle with fatigue.

Another set of sirens sounded in the distance. Detective Sharpe came back from where he had been speaking nonstop on his phone to other law enforcement agencies. They were continuing their search for Bruder by helicopter as well as on the street, they’d set up a perimeter and were bringing in dogs. Sharpe had faith in his department. Ben and Ava were more realistic, they knew how long Bruder had been doing this. Without someone with special skills, nothing the force had on staff, they would never find him.

The ambulance turned off its siren as it got close. When the medics got out they brought their gurney for Ava to sit on instead of the ground. They tried to push Ben aside, explaining that they needed to move around Ava freely to do their jobs. Grudgingly, he gave up his position beside her to hover nearby.

Detective Sharpe stood with Ben, describing the extent of the search grid he had set up and Ben nodded, grunting to show he was listening. But when one of the paramedics filled a syringe he stepped in, cutting the detective off mid-sentence.

"What is that?"

The medic, probably used to well intentioned loved ones telling him how to do his job explained, "It's just something to calm her Sir. It'll make it easier to reduce the shoulder."

"She's pregnant." He said it without feeling. Ben's monotone declaration fell heavily on Ava's ears.

The medic nodded and put the syringe aside. "We'll see if we can't get by without it for now."

"Thank you." Ben stared at Ava, not bothering to pretend he was listening to Detective Sharpe at all anymore.

Ava watched the medics buzz busily around where she sat. Her answers to their questions were lethargic and dull. Her only real response came when one of them tried to raise her much abused and very swollen arm. She jumped and screamed, protecting it with her good one.

"Ma'am, the longer we wait, the more it's going to hurt." The medic tried to reason with her.

Ava looked to Ben for help, her chin quivered. She was at capacity for pain and stress, no longer wanting to be here or have anyone touching her. "Tell them no, Ben."

Ben knelt down in front of her, his expression a mask of serenity. "Ava, they need to fix it. It's only going to hurt for a minute. You've got to let them do it," he reasoned with her like she was a child. It worked. Ava grudgingly released her grip on her arm, watching Ben as he stood up and backed away.

One medic held her body while the other began raising her arm until she screamed and it rolled forward, slipping itself back into its socket. They put a sling on and it was done. Her face was red and wet with perspiration as she panted. The entire time, she had stared at Ben. He kept his mask in place for her, only the tiniest of flickers crossed his features when she screamed.

Detective Sharpe stood beside him, patting his back at one point. "It's okay buddy. She's going to be okay." He stared at the activity in front of him and lowered his voice. "Your man in the other rig is in rough shape. Big guy though, and they said he's strong. He has a fighting chance." Sharpe changed the subject, lowering his voice. "You know, I have kids."

Ben looked at him, non reactive.

"Three of them. First one took us by surprise too." Detective Sharpe kept his gaze aimed at Ava. "Glad we did it though. We thank God for those kids every day. They probably saved my life." He nodded to himself, hands going into his pockets. "I was wild before the first one. Took chances, always the first one in a house, always willing to take on a suspect. Now I'm smarter. I think of them first. Now I let caution help me make the *smart* choice, not always the *ballsy* one."

"Sir, we're going to move her now. Would you like to ride with her?" The medic asked.

Ben nodded and followed the gurney. "I'll see you Al." He reverted to using the detective's first name, not something he did when they were working together. "Thanks for today." He stepped up into the ambulance after they loaded Ava and the medic waiting to close the back door motioned it was time.

Ch. 52

When Ava was resting comfortably Ben borrowed her phone to call her mother. She was there in minutes. Standing over her daughter, Katherine was beside herself. At first she blamed Ben, sure it was some case of his that had gotten Ava in trouble. Al was there and rose to Ben's defense.

"Mrs. Brandt, Ben's quick thinking and knowledge of the suspect are the reason your daughter is alive. You should be thanking him."

Cutting her eyes at Al, Katherine rubbed her hands together. Not entirely convinced, she offered a weak smile to the accused. "I'm sorry Ben. It's been a trying week and now she's *here*." Her eyes were wet and her lips trembled. "The last time she was in the hospital she was so young." She sniffed. "The bed makes them look small no matter how old they are. When she was younger and disappeared, I thought I was never going to see her again." She held a hand over the blanket tucked around Ava's feet, afraid to touch her.

"Excuse me Mrs. Brandt. You said she was taken before? When was this?" He shot Ben a sideways glance.

"It was a long time ago, she was seven. Someone took her out of the yard at our apartment after school. She was found early the next morning, unharmed except for a needle mark in her arm. She was missing a lot of blood. The police said it was an odd case." She rubbed a hand up and down her arm. "They never found out who did it or why." She wiped a tear from her eye. "When the police tried to question her she shut down. It was scary, the doctors wanted to institutionalize her or give her medications. She mostly recovered except she blocked it out until recently." Katherine sniffed again. "And here we are again, and I'm afraid she won't come back to me this time." She choked and put her hand over her mouth. "If you'll excuse me." She left the room to regain her composure.

After Katherine left Al whirled on Ben, out of supporting mode and back into detective mode. "What the hell is going on here? What aren't you telling me?"

"I didn't think it was pertinent that you know she was abducted as a child. This is a different case." Ben stared at Ava. The strain of the day was making itself apparent in his features.

"Is it? It sure sounds an awful lot like the same case to me."

Ben didn't answer.

Sharpe monitored Ben closely. "Child abductions where they take blood and let the kids go? I've never had an abductor take a kid for just blood before. That would be a very strange coincidence. We don't know if they intended to let the girl go because we intervened. They had all the equipment for some sort of medical procedure, blood would be a definite possibility." He stared at Ben, suspicion written all over his face. Pointing to Ava Al asked, "How old is she?"

"Twenty-three." It came from the bed.

Ava had heard her mother and struggled to break free from the heft of her lids keeping her eyes closed. Her mind was still resisting and her body weighed a thousand pounds. It was as though she had run a marathon during finals week. She was spent. Then she'd heard her mother's distress and fought her way up, through the blanket with which her mind had carefully enshrouded itself. Now as she opened her eyes, feeling the stiffness of tape, bandages and raw skin welcoming her back to herself, she answered the detective's question. Seeing Ben so close Ava automatically reached out her hand and he moved up beside her to take it.

"I was worried about you." He smiled gently at her, thumb stroking the back of her hand.

"How's Alistair?"

He couldn't completely hide his concern. "He's in surgery now."

Surgery would mean more lost blood. Any blood they would give him wouldn't be enough. Alistair was going to need a special kind they wouldn't have here. Alarmed, she opened her mouth then shut it when she saw Detective Sharpe staring curiously at her.

"They have everything he needs to get better right here." Ben's eyes told her what he couldn't say out loud. "He's going to pull through. Alistair's a stubborn man and I've seen him come through worse.

She concluded that meant they had a way to smuggle his blood into the hospital. It would make sense. They were still human and humans sometimes found themselves in need of medical help. They would have to have an inside man for just such an occasion.

Sharpe stepped forward, "Good to have you back Miss Brandt. I take it you heard our conversation?" He sat familiarly on the edge of the bed.

Ava afforded a quick glance at Ben and saw a storm gathering there. She thought it would be best to hurry things along and send the detective on his way. “Yes, I was taken when I was young. That was a little different, this man showed more interest in me than the child. I think he just took her because she was a witness. He drugged Patty but otherwise didn’t touch her.”

“That’s speculation. Who knows what he would have done if we hadn’t stepped in.”

Gulping, Ava did think of what he would have done. Clarity was returning to her, giving her access to her mental faculties again. “I don’t think that kind of differentiation is uncalled for in an investigation, do you? Some crimes can seem to be exactly the same except for a few details. Don’t you use those very details to catch the correct criminal all the time?”

The detective had been resting his hands on his thighs, tapping his finger as he thought. He watched her, silent for another minute then got up so suddenly Ava flinched. Sharpe made for the door and turned back, one hand on the doorframe and said, “You sell a good story but there’s something you aren’t telling me. I’ll figure it out.”

When he was gone Ben came to sit beside her. His hand stroked her hair, brushing it away from her face. “Nice job with Al.”

“He’s not going to give up, is he?” She didn’t want to think what Ben would have to do if he lost his source of income or raised suspicions about himself any more than he had already. He would most likely have to move away.

Shaking his head and putting on a false smile, he assuaged her fear. “No, he’s a consummate professional. He won’t let his personal doubts get in the way of our business relationship. His greater concern right now is catching our runaway.” His brow furrowed. “I don’t think he will.”

Ava couldn't disagree with what Ben was saying as much as she wished they weren't even having this conversation. She wished things could be different.

"So, do you want to talk about it?" He kept his eyes on her hand, tracing the edges of the bandage covering her scraped palm.

"I don't think I'm ready." She watched his profile, both of them too uncertain to look the other in the eye. Ava was still reeling from Bruder's pronouncement and, by his reaction, she guessed that the discovery was unwelcome for Ben.

As is always his only choice when a man isn't married to the mother of his child, Ben told Ava the only thing he could. "I will support you in whatever you decide."

Predictably, Ava saw that as an indication that she would have to make her decision alone. "Okay. Thanks." One of her eyes twitched. "What did they give me?"

Ben latched onto the change in subject. "They didn't give you anything. I told them about your, ah, condition."

Noting his inability to say the word Ava frowned, her doubts confirmed. "Maybe it's what he gave me. I feel really strange and I'm having trouble remembering much after we got out of the tunnel." She strained to fill in the holes. "I remember Alistair's face after he was shot and I remember Bruder talking to the nurse." Frowning, she shook her head. "It's so hard to think."

"I wonder if the doctors could add a toxicology screening to your blood work. We should find out what exactly he gave you. It might, you know. It might have long term effects." He was nervous and uncertain. It would have been charming if it wasn't for the fact that it pertained to the single most important decision she had yet to face in her young life. Now she found it exasperating.

Saving Ben a trip and an uncomfortable silence, a doctor walked in to check on her. "Good, I heard you were awake. I'm Doctor Carlson. How are you feeling?" He picked up her hand, checked the contact on the sensor on her finger and watched the screen. Then, he looked sternly over at Ben who had returned to the foot of the bed to allow the doctor room to work. "Are you trying to make my job more difficult?" He pointed at the monitor and stared severely down his nose at Ava. "You are here to rest. That is what this place is for, healing. Whatever you two are talking about, stop. It can wait. Your blood pressure is too high and your pulse is erratic. You don't need to be getting upset right now."

Ava flushed and turned to look out the window. "What time is it?" When they had left the bluffs it had been early afternoon, the sky outside her room was fully dark.

Doctor Carlson checked his watch. "It's seven thirty, which reminds me, you missed dinner. Would you like to have a tray sent up?"

She shook her head. Her stomach was churning, she didn't trust it to hold food."

Ben snapped out of his sullen silence. "Doctor, Ava says the drugs she was given are still affecting her. I was wondering if you were running a tox screen in your blood work. If not, could you, before it clears her system?"

"Is that true?" The doctor was on instant alert, snapping his wrist with the watch over to reach into his breast pocket. He pulled out his penlight and checked her eyes, checked her pulse the old fashioned way, with his fingers and watch and did a thorough breathing run through with his stethoscope. "Tell me what symptoms you're experiencing."

Ill at ease with the doctor's pointed interest, Ava poked at the lint on her sheet. "Well, my body feels like it isn't really listening. It's hard for me to get my arms or anything to move without a lot of extra effort. My brain is the same way. A lot's missing. I told Ben, I'm having trouble remembering what happened in there."

"You were in shock when the paramedics treated you. That can cause those types of symptoms." Doctor Carlson explained, his concern visibly subsiding.

"No," Ava shook her head. "It's more than that. When I was trying to talk to the paramedics I knew what was going on and what I wanted to say, only it was like," her eyes moved around the room as she searched for an adequate description. "Like I was dreaming. Have you ever had the dream where you're running away and you're in quicksand? It was like that except it was everything. I was trying to think of words and I couldn't find them. It's getting better but it's still harder than it should be."

The doctor was listening carefully as Ava described her symptoms. When she finished, he clicked his penlight several times while he thought. "I'm going to send a nurse in and draw some more blood right away. We *are* running a full workup, although I do have some things I would like to test for separately. I anticipate we'll have some answers for you soon." He turned and began to walk out of the room.

Ava raised her voice in time to catch him at the door. "Doctor Carlson? Could you run another test for me?" She looked down at her hands, fidgeting with the bandage sticking out of her sling. "Could you run a pregnancy test?"

He was confused. "Are you concerned this incident might have put that in jeopardy? We will be able to tell you more about the possibility of that once the results are back on what you were given."

She hid her eyes, she could feel both men watching her. "It's just that I didn't know until today, and I'm not sure if what I was told was true." Ava flicked her eyes up at the doctor and back down. "I wanted a second opinion."

The doctor nodded his head, giving her a warm smile. "I'll have them run it."

"Thank you Doctor." Ben answered.

Ava smiled tightly.

Left alone again, Ben and Ava found themselves without much to say.

"Would you care for me to run out and get you something to eat? I would assume you prefer not to eat the food here." He was formal, anxious.

Ava wanted to be by herself. "Sure. That would be great." She tugged at her sling, straightening it against her side.

"Do you have something specific in mind?"

"Pick anything."

"Very well. I will return shortly."

She heard his leather soles on the floor tiles, listening as they softly brushed out of the room to be lost amongst the other sounds in the hallway. Somewhere, an elevator dinged and she just knew it was for her. Frustrated, Ava laid back and closed her eyes.

Sure enough, the sound of someone trying to be stealthy entered her room. Her smell wafted in with the breeze she created. Out of kindness, Ava cracked her eyes but maintained her sleepy countenance. She had to show her mother she was okay, even if a long emotional conversation was beyond her.

"Hi Mom." She said weakly.

Katherine smiled broadly despite her blood shot eyes, leaning in to kiss Ava's forehead. "Oh baby. I was so scared." Her hand shook as she touched the scrape on her cheek.

"It looks worse than it is. Only some scrapes and bumps, it'll be fine in a few days." Ava tried to alleviate her mother's concerns.

"Don't tell me when to worry. I'm your mother and worrying is my job." Ava could see exactly where her temper came from. It was rare for her to show it, but Katherine had a hot streak too.

"All right mom. Fret away." Ava didn't want to argue. "How's Elle?" She steered the conversation away from herself.

Flashing a smile Katherine sat on the edge of the bed and folded her hands in her lap, not sure where she could touch her daughter. "Your friend, Alistair, he sent over a great care package. It had some vitamins, fresh juices, that kind of thing. Elle's stopped taking the sedatives and her color is coming back. She's looking a lot better. She's even talking about coming back to work tomorrow." Katherine frowned, surveying Ava from head to toe. "I guess there'll be no stopping her now."

Ava disagreed. "She just has to open. I'm sure they'll let me out tomorrow. I can spell her after lunch. She should rest." Ava wanted some sort of distraction. The idea of being alone with Ben *or* herself right now was unbearable.

"So should you." Her protective hackles were up. "Speaking of which, where's your boyfriend? He should be in here fluffing your pillow or doing something kind for you."

No one had called him her boyfriend before and Ava bristled. Yesterday she would have said it wasn't nearly enough to cover what he was to her, today was another day. Now she worried he wasn't going to be with her much longer. She had seen the look on his face when Doctor Bruder told him about the pregnancy. He looked like he wanted to be sick. That was not the reaction of someone who was going to stand beside her through pregnancy and child rearing. Her mother had done it alone, she could too.

She studied her mother, wondering what her reaction would be to the news if it proved to be true. "He ran out to get me some decent food. It's fine, he's being plenty helpful." She lied.

Her mother was dubious.

Thank goodness for the efficiency of hospitals. A nurse came in to take two vials of blood from Ava's arm. Katherine paled.

"It doesn't hurt Mom." Ava was getting tired of everyone's concern. She wanted to close her eyes.

"I know, but a mother doesn't like to see her baby's blood." She rubbed Ava's leg, smiling at her own weakness.

The nurse finished up and announced visiting hours were nearly over. Ava's yawn wasn't feigned.

Katherine took the hint and kissed Ava's head. "I'll be back in the morning." She pointed her finger and looked stern. "If they tell you to stay, you stay."

"Yes Mom."

Ava fell asleep for real after her mother left. It was a fitful one filled with visions of Alistair's frozen smile and crawling through an endless tunnel, surrounded by darkness. She dreamed she *had* fallen from the rock face, plummeting through the air as Ben stared at her from above, his face expressionless as he watched her fall.

She woke up with a jolt. Her room was dark and quiet. She was alone. Very alone, she reminded herself. Ava rolled over, pulled her knees up to her chest and breathed a huge shaky sigh. Tears wet her cheeks and her body shook as she cried as quietly as she could. Nurses passed up and down the hall outside her room. Mercifully, no one ducked in.

"I brought you dinner." Ben's gentle voice came out of the darkness.

Ava froze and held her breath, ashamed to have been caught.

Ben went on, his voice hoarse as he tried unsuccessfully to hide his inner struggle to master his own feelings. "I brought you soup thinking you could take small bites. That way you don't reopen the cuts on your face." His voice came closer. He was behind her, nearly at the bedside. "I have to apologize." He laughed bitterly. "I seem to do that frequently with you." His voice was serious. "I do owe you an apology for my behavior."

"It's fine." Ava didn't want him to feel like he had to lie to her.

"No," his voice was firmer. "It's not fine and I would like to explain myself. It's important for you to understand why I reacted the way I did." He cleared his throat, uncomfortable yet determined. The anonymity of darkness lends strength and people often reveal things they cannot in the light. Ben used it to gird his courage.

"I never knew my mother. My father was distant until my later years. My only lengthy experience with children has been with Patty. My hunt for Bruder has left no room in my life for a family." Pausing, Ben was either letting that sink in or he was thinking.

Ava waited.

"My life has taken a number of strange turns, not all of which have been good. A family would only distract me and they would always be in danger."

Her eyes were still watering and Ava could feel the sting where her salty pillowcase stuck to her scraped cheek. "You don't have to explain. I get it. I can figure this out on my own. We might not even have to worry, it could be a lie."

Ben snorted. "He is many things, but he is not a liar. If Bruder says he found it, he did."

Ava felt her heart sink.

"What I want to explain to you is that everything changed for me that day you kissed me. I had been telling myself that I came back here because it was a good place for me, because of my connections within the police department, and that I would be able to stay away from you. Then my case brought me to your store, and I saw you." Ben's voice sped up, suddenly in a rush to get it all out. "When you recognized me I told you I feared you thought I was responsible for your abduction. It ate at me. I tried to go away, I knew it would be better. Then Peter took you and I knew I had to keep you safe, my job as your protector was not through. I knew I was too close to you, but like a fool, I believed I could keep my feelings for you closed off, that I wouldn't let them affect me. That was over the day I pulled you out of the river bed. When you lay beside me and I was finally able to touch you," he took a deep breath, "it was nearly impossible for me to hold myself back. And when you kissed me, I knew that I had been a fool."

She barely breathed, not sure if she was more afraid of him stopping, or continuing.

"It has been torturous to be with you, worried that somewhere, sometime you will be taken from me. *This* has only served to prove me right. A child of my own," his voice broke, "out there, exposed, it terrifies me to my very core."

He bent over, his lips at her ear. "The thought of you having our child is everything I could have ever wanted." He rested his forehead against the back of her head. "The thought of you both being taken from me, is my worst nightmare."

Sniffling, Ava rolled over and reached out her hand to touch his arm. "I'm scared too. I can't even figure out what I want to do with *my* life. Now I might be responsible for someone else's? Part of me hopes the test comes back negative but part of me hopes for the opposite too."

Ben pulled away to grab a chair except Ava asked him to lie with her. "I don't want to hurt you."

"You won't." She assured him, scooting over and rolling on her side to give him room.

He lay down facing her, carefully wrapping his arm around her waist. Ava scooted in, not able to get close enough to him and closed her eyes. He kissed her forehead, then lay his head down next to hers and whispered, "Good night Ava." This time, her sleep was untroubled.

Ch. 53

"Coffee?" The smell hit her nostrils, pulling her from the depths of a deep sleep. Ava started to stretch and stopped with a wince. It had been real. The parts she could recall anyway.

"And breakfast." She heard the paper bag crackle when he set it on the table beside her bed. Ben helped her to sit up.

Once up, Ava regretted the movement. Ben saw her pale and was anxious.

"What's wrong? Are you still feeling sick?"

Shaking her head, she looked up and smiled when she saw his face. "You went home." His features were smoother.

"The first night nurse let me stay, the second was rather severe." He frowned at the memory. "I took the opportunity to go home, change and get you an edible breakfast. You never ate dinner last night."

"You did something else too." Ava pointed to his face. "I can tell. You're almost back to normal."

"You are a keen observer. Remind me never to lie to you." He joked, opening the bag and taking out a container.

Snorting, Ava shot back, "You *have* lied to me and I didn't believe you then."

"Touche." Ben was in a good mood, his humor had been restored. His smile faded when he saw Ava's look of consternation. "There's something wrong, isn't there? Should I call a nurse?" Ben reached for the call button and Ava stopped his hand.

"It isn't a big deal. I just need to go to the bathroom." Her cheeks pinked.

He straightened back up, "Oh. Do you need help?"

"I would rather do it myself. I'm not really to that place in our relationship just yet." She flashed a nervous grin.

Relieved it was vanity and not pain, Ben helped her swing her legs over the edge and made her sit for a few minutes before letting her stand. "You don't want to faint." He justified his overprotective gesture.

Feeling fine, Ava stood and wobbling only on the first step, ambled to the bathroom just outside the door. The movement brought back the sluggish feeling in her veins, she was panting before she reached the bathroom. When she returned, her stomach growling like mad, Ava startled at her unexpectedly crowded room.

"I heard you didn't have a roommate and I made a request that I be allowed to move in." Came the deep, somewhat weaker, British accent she'd feared she wouldn't hear again.

The nurse helping to move his wires and tubes stepped aside and Ava saw Alistair's pale, very much alive, face.

"I'm flattered that of all the rooms in here you would choose mine." Her eyes welled up with the joy of seeing her friend joking around. Apprehensive they were telling her Alistair was going to be okay so as not to stress her, she had not fully believed them until this moment. She was overwhelmed.

Ben was standing at Alistair's shoulder, his features relaxed. "I told you he was tough, even if he is a bit of a dandy."

"There is no reason a man *cannot* be as pretty as me. It is merely difficult for most to carry off." His laugh was cut short by a wince.

Ava was back to her bedside and Ben came to help her get in. The light sheen of sweat covering her face didn't escape his notice. Under the guise of tucking her in, he slid his fingers to her wrist, holding it for several seconds to check her pulse. Ava knew what he would find, she could feel that it was racing. When she compared herself to Alistair, she was embarrassed to be receiving any attention, and tried to wave Ben off.

"You have to let him dear. It's easier than fighting with him." Alistair was fully within view, his nurse was checking his monitor on the other side. "I've told you, I am fine madam. Your kindness is appreciated but can a man not get a moment's peace?"

The nurse was severe, "Keep in mind Mr. Downing, your being in this room is a privilege easily taken away if you misbehave."

Alistair's obedient salute did not win him a smile. When she was finished, his nurse spun on her heel and scowled as she left the room. On her heels, Doctor Carlson came in carrying a manila file. Ava felt Ben's hand tighten on her wrist.

"Ms. Brandt, I have your toxicology report here." He raised his folder to show her. "I was wondering if we could discuss it in private." He frowned at her unexpected roommate.

"It's okay," Ava assured him. "Alistair's a friend and I want him in here." She didn't miss the way the doctor exchanged glances with Ben. Ben gave a barely perceptible nod of his head indicating he was okay with the arrangement. "I saw that." She busted them. "For the record, it is *my* room gentlemen." She pointed out flatly.

"Would you like me to come back?" The doctor asked Ava, uncertain what domestic situation he had walked into, or caused.

"No, they can both hear whatever you have to say." She nodded at the doctor's questioning glance. "I'll end up telling them anyway, they might as well hear it from you."

"Okay," Doctor Carlson opened his file and began to flip through it, brow furrowed and all at once looking very serious. Too serious.

Ava's heart fluttered and breakfast suddenly didn't smell so inviting.

"First let me say that your test came back positive. You *are* pregnant. Congratulations." He glanced up, checking to see if that was a good thing.

Alistair bellowed. "You're what?"

Ava and Doctor Carlson ignored him. Her chest was starting to hurt.

"This other data is a bit more confusing. Whatever it was you were given, it's something we haven't seen before."

Ben and Ava exchanged glances. Ben was confused, Ava more subdued. She felt the walls closing in, her field of vision narrowing until all she could see was the doctor's mouth. She watched it making the words, not surprised when she heard them.

"It has similar effects on the system to morphine, except there was something else we don't see anymore." He rubbed the back of his thumb against his nose. "I mean, I know what it is from textbooks, but it's something that went away with blood typing at the turn of the last century."

Ava swallowed. What she had overheard the doctor and his nurse discussing came back in snippets. "Were there antigens in my blood that were incompatible with my blood type?"

The doctor didn't hide his shock at her knowledge, instead he bobbed his head. "The plasma in your blood is destroying itself. It's the worst case of transfusion reaction I've ever seen." Then, he frowned. "There's more though, it isn't limited to the blood."

She didn't see any harm in telling the doctor the little bit she could recall. "The man that gave this to me, he was developing a bioweapon. It's a virus that makes the body's immune system attack itself." She turned her head to see Ben and Alistair staring open mouthed at her. Ben's knuckles were white from him gripping the bottom of Alistair's bed. She smiled without humor. "The funny thing is, it won't hurt the baby." Ava could hear the doctor and nurse in her head. "That's what he was testing at the clinics.

He was checking how sick moms would affect the babies." There was more only she couldn't remember. Ava's head felt light. She stood up. Her legs ached when the blood flowed down into her feet again.

Dr. Carlson snapped his folder shut, rushing toward her, hand out. "Ms. Brandt please, lay back down. We want to run a few more tests."

Ava was shaking her head. "No, there's nothing more you can do for me here. I want to leave. I'll sign any forms you need me to sign that I'm going against your wishes." Ava pushed off the bed and swayed, catching herself on the rail. She went to the closet and took out her bag with the hand not in a sling, then used the bad one to push her luggage to the bathroom. Ava kept a hand on the wall for support the whole time, she couldn't trust her balance.

The hospital gown ties, keeping the sling in place, plus the fact that she was only one armed made dressing tedious. A nurse waited in her room with Dr. Carlson to inform her, again, that she should not leave. They could run some more tests, they said. They could try to find some way to help her.

Taking pen to paper, Ava signed. "This man has been working on this for years. There is no way you're going to find a cure in the weeks or months I have left. Thank you for all that you've done for me but I can't spend the time I have left in a hospital."

"Leaving me here alone, are you?" Alistair found his voice, fare more toned down than was his usual.

Turning to look at him, Ava felt a catch in her throat. "I can't stay here."

His great, bald head caught the light as he dipped it in agreement. "I understand. I would not have my last meal be in this place."

"*Can* you eat this?" Ava thought of his special diet.

The wide grin crept across his face. Her lips curled unconsciously. He would be getting exactly what he needed here. Who could say no to him?

"I have my food brought in, of course. Hospitals are very accommodating now for special diets."

The nurse "harrumphed" behind her. Ava stifled a giggle. Alistair could make her smile no matter what. She was relieved he had made it, Ben was going to need him after she was gone.

"Hurry home." She reached out to touch his arm.

Her friend winked, "I will be there in a few days. Watch for me."

Ava signed the forms and walked out with Ben's arm around her.

Ch. 54

"Where do you want to go?" Ben asked softly, staring straight out the windshield, his hands clutching and unclutching the wheel.

"I don't know. It's so final. I've been trying to remember what he said it would do. How it would go, if it would be hard or if it would be gradual, sudden, what." Ava watched the trees they passed. The green was vibrant, the bright pea green of spring blooms. Her last spring. "As best I can remember, he said it would take some time and death comes from outside infection. *His* virus only weakens the immune system, leaving it open for other bacteria and germs. A hospital is probably the worst place for me if you think about it."

His jaw was tight, "Do you recall his mentioning a cure?"

"No."

They kept driving, Ava recognized the roads. "You did it again, you're making decisions for me."

"Do you mind?"

"No, not this time."

He carried her bag up the steps in let her into his home. Ava didn't complain. Alistair was right, he would be impossible to stop.

When they were seated in the living room, Ava's thoughts turned to Alistair and his seeming rapid recovery. "So you have people in the hospital? I noticed Alistair looks good for someone who just got shot and lost a good bit of blood. He doesn't look much older and his color was coming back already."

Ben's lips twisted into a thin lipped smile. "I don't know how I ever thought I was going to keep anything from you."

Ava gave him a weak smile, she was tired. "Is my phone in here? I should call my mother. She was going to come by this morning and it's almost visiting hours. I should tell her I'm not there."

Rising first, Ben motioned for her to stay seated. "I put it in your bag while you were getting dressed." He found it and brought it to her.

Katherine answered on the first ring. "Ava, did you leave the hospital?" Her tone was accusatory. "You're calling me on your cell phone. I know you're not in the hospital."

"Guilty." Ava rolled her eyes, unable to stop the little smile her mother's chastising brought with it. "There was nothing they were going to do for me that I couldn't do at home." Her voice cracked and she cleared her throat to cover it.

"Why don't I come stay with you? I could at least help you out until your arm gets better. Elle's back to work, she doesn't want me in her hair."

She felt bad she hadn't given Elle a thought since last night. "Are you sure she's okay to work? The store has been really busy."

"It's the best thing for her. You know how she is when she's upset." Katherine dismissed Ava's concerns. "What do you think? I'm already in town, I can do some grocery shopping or help you around the house for a few days. I have the vacation time."

"Um, actually Mom," Ava hesitated, nervous what her mother would think. "I'm staying with Ben for a while, he's going to help me. Thanks though." She added hastily.

"Oh." Katherine was crestfallen. "Well, that's awfully sweet of him."

"Why don't you come over?" Ava looked up at Ben questioningly and saw him nod his approval. "We could have that lunch we never got to have." And we might not have again she thought to herself.

"Today?"

"Sure, I can give you directions."

Ava's mother was always a little hesitant about driving into the city and Ben lived right in the heart of it. While she was giving directions, Ava heard her mother growing anxious, recognizing the direction she would be heading. To her credit, she didn't say anything. Ava felt bad, Katherine was giving this a real effort if she was going to come here without saying boo about it.

It was settled, "One o'clock." She told Ben upon hanging up, handing him the phone to put on the table.

"Should I call the restaurant?" Ava didn't know what he had available for an impromptu lunch.

Ben surprised her, "No, I want to cook. I have to go to the store anyway." He rose from his seat on the arm, coming over to sit by her hip. Reclined as she was, she had taken up most of the couch. She shimmied over to give him room. "Why don't you rest while I'm gone? You look tired."

"You aren't going to start treating me like an invalid because of this are you?" Ava wasn't sure which "this" she meant.

His expression was pained. "If our time together is limited, I would like to take care of you." He saw the beginnings of an argument. "Consider it my consolidating all the days when you were going to be sick during our lives together. Certainly you would not have been too stubborn to accept my assistance on *all* of those occasions." He reached up to brush her long bangs out of her eyes, tucking it behind her ear. Combined with the raw look in his eyes, it was an incredibly intimate gesture.

Ava found herself unable to meet his gaze. "Okay. I'll agree for now, but you have to remember, this is my time too and if I want to do something, you can't argue."

In place of verbalizing his acquiescence, he leaned in and kissed her. It wasn't passionate, nor was it chaste. This one conveyed both love and pain. Ava's eyes were damp when Ben pulled away and she saw him blink, ducking his head when he stood up.

His voice was shaky. "I won't be long. Do you want anything special?"

She started to say no then stopped herself, admitting shyly. "I do have a guilty pleasure. I don't see any point in denying myself in light of everything."

"What is it?"

"Fig Newtons."

Ben smiled. "Funny what you learn about someone when you live together." He said wistfully.

After he was gone Ava yawned. Ben was right, she *was* tired. She wandered upstairs and lay down in what was for now "their" bed. Only she lay on *his* side, breathing in the smell of him from his pillow as she let sleep pull her down.

Ava startled awake. She glanced at the clock and saw that it had been less than twenty minutes since Ben left. He couldn't be back already yet she could have sworn she heard the door close.

Creak. Ava froze, her breathing stopped while her heart beat double time. Someone was in the house and she was certain it wasn't Ben. He might be quiet so as not to disturb her, but he wouldn't sneak, and this was definitely sneaking. Whoever was in the house did not want to be heard.

Having been in the bedroom a few times before had its advantages. Ava knew Ben had guns in the house, she even knew where. She carefully slid the nightstand drawer open, disappointed to find that Ben had taken that one. It made sense. The Browning was his favored weapon. Her next place to look was in the closet. Lying on top of one of the shelves in the back was a box. She'd seen it when she'd gone looking for what all the movers had brought for her.

Thank goodness he didn't have kids and didn't have to keep it locked. Ava felt a pang at that and kept moving. It wasn't time to feel sorry or for self-pity. The shiny silver of the Heckler & Koch flashed in the light. Ava didn't know if it was loaded, she hoped not to have to go that far. She was only hoping to frighten the person away or hold them until Ben could get there.

Creak. The intruder was at the top of the stairs, he or she would be in the bedroom in seconds.

Ava was already in the closet, the entrance of which was partially hidden when the bedroom door was open as it was now. She slid behind the door and held the gun up one handed, straight out front, mimicking a movement she had seen in the movies a thousand times.

Clothing rustled just outside the door and Ava parted her lips, trying to make her breathing silent as she willed her nerves to stop humming. The profile of the stranger's face showed itself, not quite a full head taller than hers, as he passed in front of the door. Ava glanced down and saw that his hands were at his sides, they were empty. That didn't mean he was unarmed, she reminded herself.

Waiting until he was fully inside the room, past the door was the longest few seconds of her life. By some miracle the intruder turned his relatively narrow back to her to investigate the bed, rumpled from her nap. She could see how he might think there was a body within the fluffy mess.

When he took a step toward the bed, Ava pushed the door out of her way and pointed the gun, suddenly huge and heavy in her hand, at the man's back. She wished she had use of the other hand to steady it.

Putting all of her energy into keeping her hand steady and her voice firm, Ava announced herself. "Stop and put your hands on your head. I have a gun."

The man did stop, and slowly raised his hands to rest them, fingers intertwined on top of his head. "Take it easy. Don't shoot." His voice was level, he didn't sound the least bit frightened.

“Lay down on your stomach and keep your hands together, behind your neck.” Ava’s mind raced as she tried to think things through. The intruder followed her instructions without argument.

One handed she couldn’t bind him and the only things at her disposal were in Ben’s closet anyway. She had a thought and backed into the closet, using her fingers sticking out of her sling to reach under her gun arm and tickle a belt off the hanger. She used her fingers and propping the metal buckle against her side to loop the leather through the metal in a large noose.

“Put your feet together.” She commanded.

He did as he was told, turning his face to the side. “He just wants to study you.” The calm voice tried to soothe her.

Ava slid the noose over his feet, fortunately hanging over the bed and, using the side of her leg for resistance, tightened it to the nearest hole. She nodded to herself in satisfaction. Even if it slid it would delay him long enough she could run.

“Who?” She played dumb to buy time. Glancing at the clock on the nightstand, she prayed Ben would come back soon. The market was close, although she had no idea how long he would be there and if he had to make a special stop for her cursed cookies. Mentally kicking herself for not bringing her phone up here she felt the gun wobble, drawing her attention back to her captive.

His hands were slowly sliding apart, his shoulders shifting, readying for action.

“Stop moving. Put your hands back together.” Ava repeated the command firmly.

“Easy now.” He spoke to her soothingly. She detected a drawl as he drew out his words. “I don’t want to hurt you.

The doc sent me to see if you wanted to go for a little parlay. That's all."

"Well, I'm not interested in parlay with anyone. If you really wanted to talk, you would have knocked." She pointed out the gigantic hole in his statement.

He changed his tactics. "Why don't you let me sit up and we can talk face to face, like civilized people?"

"Civilized people don't break into other people's houses and sneak into their bedrooms. I think I'll keep things as they are, thank you." Ava was starting to get jumpy and her arm was shaking hard.

"I think we got off on the wrong foot. What if you let me up and we make this a more friendly sort of discussion?" He again tried to slid his arms out, taking his hands off his head.

"Stop that. Hold still or I'll shoot you." Her shrill voice cracked.

Ava's nerves emboldened him.

"I don't think you will." His hands were down and he was in a push up position, raising himself up and rolling over. Staring right at her he smiled easily, completely relaxed. "There, now isn't this better?" His eyes were gray and cold, with not a flicker of fear, or any human emotion at all for that matter. The shaggy dark brown hair on his head was sticking up in front from laying on his face, he otherwise looked the part of a business man on his way to the office. His dark gray pants, light gray shirt and tie fit his narrow, lightly built frame well. He was dark, his skin wrinkled from sun. While it made it hard to age him, Ava was of the impression he was in his mid thirties. She wondered if he was one of them. If Bruder had changed him.

Taking a full step back, Ava rested her shoulder against the side of the bedroom door in an effort to steady it.

"That .45 looks awful heavy. Why don't you set it down? I won't hurt you." His smile did not touch his eyes. They remained coldly detached. "I have a job to do and that's to bring you in so my boss can have a few words and take a look at you. If you want to be difficult," he pointed a finger at her stomach, "he's got other places to put that that don't involve you."

She didn't trust her voice, barely managing to shake her head in silent protest. Bruder was prepared to put her baby in a surrogate or lab dish if she didn't come quietly? Ava's horror grew tenfold. She didn't want to pull the trigger. She didn't know if it was loaded. If it wasn't, it would end her bluff. If it was, she would be shooting a man point blank while he looked her in the eye. Ava didn't know if she could do that. Even if he was prepared to do the same to her.

There was no denying these were the eyes of a killer staring at her, daring her to pull the trigger. In the face of his challenge, she found her nerve lacking.

The sound of the front door opening broke the silent standoff, both heads turned and the killer lunged to his feet.

"Ben!" Ava shrieked.

The killer's feet hit the ground and he stumbled before he caught himself on the footboard, pushing himself off and jumping the rest of the way to fall to his knees, face inches from hers.

"I'll take that." His hand closed on the barrel of the gun.

More of a twitch than a conscious effort, Ava's finger pulled the trigger. *Click*.

The killer chuckled and easily wrested the gun from her hand. He reached down to unbuckle the belt around his feet, and in one swift motion was free. Ava listened for signs that

Ben was in the house and heard nothing. A paralyzing thought came to her, the killer wasn't alone.

Her captive turned captor grabbed Ava by the back of the shirt and dragged her, too fast for her to gain her feet, toward the bathroom. The sound of metal sliding stopped everything. Ava turned with the man holding her, Ben filled the bedroom doorway opposite them.

"Let her go." The ice in Ben's voice chilled Ava nearly as much as the look in his eyes. The killer did not immediately respond and Ben raised his gun hand. "This one is loaded." Ben assured him.

Ch. 55

One hand went out, palm up, the other gave up its hold on Ava's clothing and rose as well.

"Ava," his voice was softer, a hint of the grit behind it still apparent, "could you go to the top right drawer in the dresser and grab my handcuffs?"

She got unsteadily to her feet and kept her back to the furniture on the wall as she eased past the dead eyed intruder to do as Ben asked. She stumbled once, shaking her head to clear it.

"Thank you." He said as she removed the cuffs with a clank from the drawer, and he pointed at the man's hands sticking up over his head. "Could you put those on him? He will be a perfect gentleman and help you by putting them both behind himself so you don't have any trouble. Isn't that right?"

Not speaking, he did as he was directed, allowing Ava to restrain him with limited effort. "What are you planning on doing with me? You can't keep me here, and you don't have a silencer on that thing so you can't shoot me." He sounded sure of himself.

"I'm going to turn you in to the police." Ben's hand slid into his pocket and fished out his phone, hitting a series of buttons without looking. "Detective, I've caught an intruder in my home. Could you send someone to pick him up?"

After Ben hung up and replaced his phone, the killer smiled and looked smug. "You should have killed me when you had the chance. I'm not going to talk, you know that. In a few hours I'll be out and next time you won't see me coming."

Ben remained cool, "I don't think you'll be out so easily. You're a person of interest in an ongoing investigation who has proven himself to be a continual danger to my guest and myself. I believe I can have you charged and held without bail."

The killer was riled. He moved to get his feet under himself and froze when Ben rushed in and brought the gun down against his head. His body crumpled and fell to the floor.

Once he was out Ben flicked the safety with his thumb and replaced his gun in its hiding place behind his back. Ava reached for him as he stepped around the body between them and her legs balked. He put his arms out when she wobbled. Weak, she sagged into him and he pulled her in tight.

"Are you okay?" He pulled back, looking for signs of injury.

Ava bobbed her head, not wanting to tell him how the foreign compounds in her body were already affecting her. "I heard him come in and I found the gun." She pointed to the closet, "I hid in there until he came in and then I made him lay on his stomach."

He shook his head, smiling in admiration. "I think you're right. You *should* be doing this for a living. You're a natural."

She didn't answer, not wanting to go down that road right now. No reason to keep thinking about her impending demise.

Ben slid his arm around her shoulder and guided her to the door. "I'll drag him downstairs where we can keep an eye on him. Could you go put the groceries away?" When Ava blinked at him in confusion, Ben explained, "Your mother will be here in less than two hours. We don't want to alarm her."

Unable to argue, and at the same time amazed to see how calmly he handled a killer in his home, Ava understood his admission that asking a woman to share his home and his life was impractical. Granted, not all women would *draw* trouble like Ava did, but Ben probably had his fair share considering. The doctor might have honored a truce on the surface for myriad reasons, yet Ava was willing to bet Ben still had his share of attempts on his life over the years.

Reaching the bottom of the stairs Ava saw the grocery bag lying on the ground. He had dropped it when she yelled. Picking it up carefully she carried it to the kitchen, hoping he hadn't bought eggs.

A few items into the unpacking, the doorbell rang. Ava shuffled into the hall but before she could go more than a few feet, it opened, and Ben was greeting Detective Sharpe.

"Ben." Sharpe was stepping in as Ava came down the hallway, her hand on the wall for balance.

Ben closed the door behind the detective.

"You've got to let me in on this, whatever it is you've got yourself mixed up in. I trust you, I've known you a long time but this is getting hard to explain to my superiors." The detective was animated in his annoyance. "You've been nothing but solid until a few weeks ago when that girl showed up. Now you skip town, come back like it's nothing, the girl and your friend's kid get abducted in broad daylight, and you have an intruder in your home the next day? I'm thinking this girl is bad news. She's got you into something and you don't want any part of it, baby or no."

Ava stepped out of the hall and into Detective Sharpe's sightline. His head jerked toward the movement, his eyes went wide. "Ava, I thought you were in the hospital."

"Why, for this?" She pointed at her sling and shrugged. "Even if I left, Ben would be in trouble. The doctor wants us both."

Ben eyed her for a long time before he turned back to Sharpe. "Al, you might want to sit down." He motioned toward the living room.

"What about him?" He pointed to the limp form sitting propped up against the bottom step.

"He's not going anywhere." Ben replied. "Come on."

Sharpe fell into step beside Ben, Ava followed as they passed her. She was curious how much he would share, and if Sharpe would think them both crazy, or offer his help. Ava didn't know if she would be able to believe it if she hadn't had her own firsthand experience with the doctor.

Sharpe was the only one who sat. Ben stood, fidgeting with his hands and Ava remained at the threshold, leaning against it and watching them both. Her legs held for the time being.

"Well?" The detective was anxious.

"It's complicated," Ben started.

Sharpe cut him off. "I'm not an idiot. Shoot." His features were clouding over. Ben was going to lose his willing audience and have a hostile crowd soon.

Ben sensed the same thing. "The doctor's name is Gerhardt Bruder. He's a scientist who has been working on genetic research for decades." He was blurring what he could. "When Ava was younger, she was taken as a test subject. The doctor took samples of her blood like he does with many children and young women. I've run across him repeatedly in my missing persons cases and have been tracking him for a while. Shreveport was the first real evidence I've had of his location in years."

Detective Sharpe shifted in his seat, he was listening attentively, no signs of disbelief thus far.

"What we've recently discovered is the purpose of his research and after what Ava found, we might be too late to stop him."

The detective shifted his focus to Ava, his suspicion fading.

Continuing, Ben drew Sharpe's attention back to him. "The doctor has developed a virus he intends to sell on the black market. It's essentially an engineered form of HIV. A simple infection can kill the victim once they're exposed."

Detective Sharpe was thinking, his eyes on Ava, his fingers tapping his leg. "Why were they after her *this* time?"

"She remembered him. That makes her a witness. When they came after her this time I got involved, and now he wants her for another experiment."

"Why?" The light flickered in his eyes. "The pregnancy?"

Ben was growing agitated. "He was going to kill her before he pulled another sample of blood for his data. He's obsessed with his research. He ran a test and found out about the baby. Now that he knows it's mine, he wants her alive." He frowned, "I don't think he wanted to kill her at the bluffs, that was desperation."

Ava felt her throat tighten hearing him mention the baby.

"He's given Ava the virus." Ben choked on the words.

Detective Sharpe shot up. "He exposed you? How much of this stuff does he have? Can he realistically sell this on a large scale? If it needs to be injected how can he weaponize it?"

Ava cleared her throat and took over, letting Ben regain his composure. "I've been thinking about that. He needs to get it into the bloodstream. He can use bullets if he wants to keep it small scale, or if he wants to affect the most people he could make a dirty bomb. Anyone who doesn't die from the shrapnel would die from the virus." Ava had been gradually putting together the pieces of what she had heard, her memory reluctantly giving it up bit by bit.

"How do we find this guy? You've been tracking him you said?"

Ben shook his head and rubbed the back of his neck. "I don't know. He moves his labs, he stays out of sight. No one really knows how much he has. The only reason we know what we do is because Ava heard it."

"Is there a cure? Did he mention an antidote or something?"

Again Ben shook his head, Sharpe looked over at Ava and she did the same.

"What about *this* guy?" He jutted his chin toward the entryway. "Is he muscle or do you think he knows anything?"

"Not sure." Ben answered truthfully. "He's a professional, *that* I can tell. Maybe he's got a record. Could you hold him for a while? I don't want him coming back."

The detective smiled. "The first call I'm making is to Homeland Security. They're always willing to lose someone."

Ben sighed, "Thank you, Al. I want to keep things as calm around here as possible for a while." He didn't need to say any more. Al and Ava both understood what he meant. Ava was to be left in peace.

"I'll help any way I can. Call me if you need anything. Want me to call you if I get anything from this guy?"

"Yes, that would be helpful." Ava knew Ben didn't mean it. The killer wasn't going to give up anything and there would most likely be others following in his footsteps.

Detective Sharpe was right, he wasn't an idiot. He walked past Ben, placing a hand on his shoulder. "You take care of her. I'll keep someone posted here for the next few days. Call me if you see anyone else suspicious." He looked over at Ava. "I'm going to do what I can Miss Brandt."

She forced a tight smile, not trusting her voice. Telling the detective made her future feel more concrete. This was really happening. A tremor shook her knees.

Al reached the man in the entry who was just beginning to stir. "Hi there. Ready to go for a ride?" He grabbed the cuffs holding his hands behind his back and roughly pulled him to his feet. The killer grunted and stood, resting his shoulder against the wall while Detective Sharpe read him his Miranda rights walking him out the door.

True to his word, the detective's promised squad car parked in front of the door within the next fifteen minutes. Ava peeked out the drapes several times to see them still there.

Ben was in the kitchen putting together a Margherita flatbread pizza and a salad topped with mangoes and papaya. "Would your mother want wine?"

"She'll be fine with the sparkling water." She pointed to the bottle he had set out on the table. "She's a wine with dinner kind of a girl." Ava wanted something to occupy her mind and her hands. Unfortunately, Ben had dinner under control.

He noticed her antsy mood. "I have this. Do you want to go soak? It might relax you."

"I don't know." She traced the veins in the granite counter top.

"Why not? I thought you loved water when you were upset."

"You're pretty observant too." Her features lightened with the first real smile she'd managed all day. "Honestly, I've avoided mirrors so far and if I go in the bathroom it's going to be tough."

Ben laid down his knife and his mango, wiping his hands on a towel. He came around and pulled her up against him. "Your mother said I needed to help you, right?" He didn't wait for an answer. "It's important to me to make a good impression on your mother. How would it look if the moment she walked in she saw you jittery and needing your hair washed?" Ava pulled back and he nodded, pretending to be serious. "You're beautiful honey, but I can see the sand in your hair from here."

She blushed. "How could you let me walk around like this?"

"I was going to tell you before we went anywhere, then you invited your mother over." He kissed her forehead. "Now come on."

"Why?" She let him lead her toward the stairs.

"I'm going to wash your hair." He pulled her upstairs.

Ch. 56

"Are you sure you've never done this before?" Ava asked him while he massaged the soap into her scalp, using the hand held sprayer to rinse it. She had never had anyone wash her hair before, it was luxurious.

"No. Am I doing it right?"

The warm water ran down her head, Ava felt her tension going with it. Being still let her pulse slow and she could clear her head. The weakness she was feeling only seemed to affect her when moved around. She felt her worries going with the sand. "Mmm hmm." She kept her eyes closed.

Some amount of movement had returned to her arm. It remained a challenge to use it. Ben took the washcloth she'd been trying to soap from her without a word. She sat up leaning forward, giving him access to her back, and he proceeded to help her wash the grit, both physical and mental, from her body.

***

By the time one o'clock arrived they were ready for Katherine. Ava was clean and had only been mildly upset when she saw how roughed up her face looked. The rugburn on her cheekbone was pink and the broken skin was covered by the several inches of raw, abraded skin running from below her eye to the corner of her mouth. Two little scrapes marked the skin on her nose.

Normally, Ava wore a sweater at Ben's given the low temperature however, with Katherine coming, he had turned it up and she only had to wear a long sleeved shirt allowing the sling fit better.

The doorbell rang a few minutes after the hour and Ava moved away from where she had been helping Ben to set the table. Ben stepped in front of her.

Guessing what he was going to say, Ava rose to her own defense. "There are officers outside." She reached up on her tiptoes to kiss his frowning mouth. "If they happen to let someone through I'm not worried. I know how fast you are, and I know how strong you are. You could be there before anything happened." She flashed him a knowing look.

"I don't know what you're talking about. I'm no faster than any other man." His brows knitted together feigning confusion.

"I'm observant, remember? I've seen how fast you can move when you want to. You picked me up in a dead lift off a sheer rock face. It's the extra blood and I know it." She winked at him and moved around him to answer the door. She was careful to go slow, keeping her pulse steady.

"Mom, hi." She put out an arm to hug her as Katherine stepped inside.

Ben was a few feet away in the living room, trying to be unobtrusive, close enough to move if he had to. Ava pretended not to notice.

Katherine stepped in, head on a swivel making her assessments. Ben stepped forward to offer her his hand. She shook it, scanning the room around him. "Hello Ben, did you just move in?"

"No, I've been in for about a year." He looked around as well and made a show of frowning at what he saw. "I must confess, I've been working long hours and until recently haven't found a reason to be at home much. I'm afraid my decorating reflects that."

Katherine darted a sly glance at her daughter. "I can imagine."

"Ben, do you mind if I give Mom a tour?" Ava asked, thinking it would give her mother time to say whatever was on her mind. She looked like she'd swallowed something unpleasant, Ava wanted her to get her complaint out without Ben having to hear it.

"Be my guest. I have some things to finish up in the kitchen." Ben smiled politely, turned and left them together.

"So, this is the living room." Ava pointed at the room beside them. On they went upstairs to see the loft area, complete again with bookshelves and pictures.

Doing exactly the same thing Ava had upon seeing it, Katherine picked up the photograph of the man in the truck. "Is this Ben's grandfather? He looks exactly like him."

"Yeah, strong genes, huh?" She moved on to point into the bedroom, making a point of not stepping inside. Even if her mother assumed they were intimate, best not to rub her nose in it.

Too late, Katherine stepped into the bedroom and saw Ava's bag on the floor. Completing a panoramic spin around the room, including a long look in the closet, she stopped and took a long look at her daughter, crossing her arms. "Is there anything you would like to tell me about this arrangement?"

"What do you mean? I told you Ben was going to help me for a few days. We were here today and invited you to lunch." All true and not even close to the whole picture. Ava smiled trying in vain to placate her mother.

"Baby, if you think I buy that then you take me for a fool. You're moving in? Really Ava, you've just met this guy. You don't know anything about him."

“Mom I’ve known him a long time, we’ve just started *dating* in the last few weeks.”

“Well, I can’t believe it’s too serious. It wasn’t long ago you were sleeping with that other guy.”

The false story about Peter, the dead assassin, had slipped Ava’s mind. “I never told you I slept with him. I said I went with him to a B&B to see if we could work things out. After one night I knew we couldn’t, and I left. I didn’t sleep with him. Case closed.”

Her certainty shaken, Katherine frowned. “Why did you let me believe you’d slept with him.”

“You’re my mother. I don’t make it a habit to talk about who and when I am sleeping with anyone. I didn’t know that I should clarify that when you see me with someone.” Ava’s blood was up, “Well, for the sake of clarity Mom, I am sleeping with Ben. And yes, I am staying here for a few days.”

Once the words were out of her mouth she regretted them. She saw the impact of her sharp words before her mother put a false bravado in place and forced a polite smile.

“Well, I hope things work out for you.” Katherine wheeled from the room pretending to finish her tour solo, wandering in and out of each room.

Ava felt foolish. She flopped backward on the bed and put her hand over her face. “I am such an idiot.” She muttered under her breath.

“Yes, but I love you anyway baby.” Her mother, having returned, sat beside her and patted her leg.

“I shouldn’t have snapped. Things have been a little strange lately and then after yesterday, I guess I’m more shaken than

I'd like to admit." It helped to confess that to her mother even if she didn't lay out all the details.

Katherine didn't answer, she lay back with Ava and put out an arm. Ava snuggled onto it. Katherine curled it around her back. "Did you know this was the only way I could get you to go to sleep when you were a toddler?"

"I remember you used to do it when I was older, after he died." Ava didn't say his name. She never did.

She rubbed her daughter's arm. "Oh, it started long before that. You always wanted to lay on me even as a baby and then when you were getting into your big girl bed you got clingy again." She patted her, "That was when this started."

"I hope you don't feel like you gave up too much for me." Ava worried about her mother being alone. Her whole life had been built around her daughter.

Katherine dismissed it, "No, no parent thinks they give too much. It's usually the opposite. Later, when we look back, we worry we didn't give enough."

"I'm just saying, I hope you and Robert work out. You deserve something for yourself."

"Thank you baby." Katherine replied tentatively. "I hope so too."

There was a knock on the door frame. "Are you ladies hungry or would you like me to hold lunch while you catch up?"

Katherine gave Ava's head a kiss and sat up.

Ava had to roll onto her side to push herself up off of the soft bedding.

"No, we're ready. I was just explaining to Ava how lucky you are."

Ben chuckled softly, "No need to tell me Katherine."

"I'm her mother. It's in my job description." Standing, she turned and offered Ava a hand.

***

Lunch was light and tasty. Ava enjoyed the meal and the pleasant conversation. They were lingering at the table when the discussion turned more serious, at least for two of the three parties.

"Ben, can I ask how the little girl is who was with Ava when, when you know." Katherine couldn't say the words.

"Patty? She's fine. She was a little shaken up is all." Ben tipped his head to Ava, "She has a new hero though."

"What? I didn't do anything." Ava truthfully couldn't remember having done a single impressive thing. If anything, she figured she traumatized the girl by yelling at her.

"On the contrary, she said you were very brave." He popped a piece of pineapple into his mouth and winked. "She said you were a great shopping buddy too."

That made Ava smile. She felt the scabs on her cheek pull and winced, laughing she remembered their "shopping spree."

"I taught her how to shop in her head." Ava grinned at her mother. "Do you remember when we used to do that?"

Laughing, Katherine said that she did. "When did you meet her? I don't recall you talking about babysitting anyone's kids lately, she must be someone new.

“She’s the daughter of some of Ben’s friends I met here last week at a dinner party.”

“Oh? What was the occasion?”

“It was my birthday.” Ben answered.

“Really? That’s odd, you and Ava are so close together.” Katherine pointed out. “You should have coordinated birthday parties.

Ben turned to see Ava beside him. “When is your birthday?”

Uncomfortable with the inconsequential event being dragged out, Ava answered him with only the one word. “Thursday.”

Katherine jumped on Ava for her lapse in disclosure. “Baby, I thought you said he knew. Why wouldn’t you tell him about your birthday? You aren’t old enough to start lying about your age yet. Ben’s older than you, isn’t he? And he told you.”

Choking on the laugh that erupted spontaneously, Ava told her mother most definitely, “Yes he is.”

Ben walked away from the table, taking the empty bottle of water with him. “Can I get anyone anything?”

Katherine politely declined and Ava shook her head.

Ben fished around in the pantry for something before returning. When he did, he reached over and touched Ava’s hand under the table. She glanced up and gave him a small smile.

“Well, I can see that Ava is starting to fade.” Katherine broke in on their stolen moment as she rose. “Ben you know how to show a lady a good time. Thank you.” Ben and Ava both rose with her. She was solemn coming around the table, "Thank you for everything you've done for Ava."

He flushed and answered tightly. "I have not done nearly enough Katherine."

"Yes you have," she assured him. "You saved my little girl."

Which time? Ava thought, wishing she could let her mother in on the joke while a part of her was pleased that Ben could finally collect some credit for what he'd done those years ago.

They walked into the entryway, Katherine slid into her shoes. Ben opened the door after she hugged Ava good bye. Behind the door sat the highly visible squad car.

Katherine pointed at it with a thumb and tried to sound unconcerned. "Is that for you?" She asked her daughter.

Not seeing the point in lying about it, Ava nodded. "It's just a precaution."

Looking like she wanted to say something, Katherine glanced from Ava to Ben. Moving in, she put her arms around Ben. At first he was taken aback, and then he lifted his arms to return the embrace. "Take care of my baby, Ben. Promise you'll keep her safe."

It was a good thing Katherine didn't see Ben's initial reaction. His own fear naked on his face would have sent her into cardiac arrest. "I will do everything in my power Katherine. That I can promise you."

They said farewell to her mother and when the door shut, Ava sat down on the bottom step. She put her head on one of her knees and mumbled more to herself than to anyone else, "This is going to kill her."

Ben growled at her. “Don’t talk like that. I’m not giving up and you can’t either.”

She was afraid to look up and see him so furious yet she couldn’t let him delude himself either. “Ben, we have no cure and we have no way to track him. I am just trying to be realistic. My mother doesn’t have anyone except Elle and some new boyfriend, and who knows if he’s the real thing. I don’t want her to be alone. At least if there was some way we could get the baby far enough along she would have a grandchild.” Ava stopped and closed her eyes, concentrating. She heard his accented voice in her head, she strained to remember. What was it he had said about the fetuses? The haze clouding her memory began to lift and Ava’s eyes popped open.

“What?”

“There isn’t a cure for me. But there *is* one for the baby.” She had Ben’s full attention. “It all comes back to the blood. He said they treated the compound that causes the virus like the Rh factor with pregnancy. If they gave the mother a second shot of something, I don’t know what,” her features clouded briefly, “it let her survive and she would live until the fetus was viable. It must mask the negative effects of the virus from the immune system for a while.” Ava was hopeful, she turned her face up to him. “Can we find a way to keep me alive long enough for the baby to survive?”

Ben answered, starting out slow then gaining momentum. “Yes, we can keep you alive long enough to *raise* the baby.”

“What are you talking about Ben?”

“Antigens, of course. I can’t believe I never thought of that. He’s mad but he’s a genius. So much like my father at the end.” Ben was talking more to himself than to her. He started to pace up and down the entry, his stockinged feet making a hushed noise that sped up with him as he picked up tempo. “If it’s in the blood we can flush it out. Keep it at bay for as long as we need. We have access to equipment the common populace does not. He thought he was giving you something we couldn't handle. He's given you the one thing we *can* handle." Ben laughed, Ava worried he'd cracked.

"What are you talking about? Antigens aren't something you can take out of someone, not completely. They're attached to my blood." She tried to reason with him.

Ben shook his head stubbornly. "I'm saying we can do *exactly* that. It's called an exchange transfusion. We can take out all of your blood and replace it with compatible blood."

She nodded silently, less than enthusiastic about where she anticipated the blood was coming from.

He sensed her hesitation and came to a halt in front of her, holding up a hand. "We're getting close on the synthetic blood we've been working on. The version we have now has its flaws and isn't by any means a final solution, but it would buy us some time. They were conducting another rounds of testing the last time I checked."

Ava felt the idea take root. She sat up, eyes flickering in excitement only to dim. "Will it hurt the baby?"

His enthusiasm didn't wane. "Not if we do it slowly enough. It won't shock the body as long as we use the right type."

"Where can we go? Is there a hospital that will do it? Do you have to sneak in the blood?"

Ben was shaking his head. "It's too risky to have you weakened in a public place. You would be too exposed and he's shown us he isn't done yet. I have a place we can go."

Ava raised an eyebrow expectantly.

"Have you ever been to Washington?"

Ch. 57

They left that night. Detective Sharpe was told Ben might know someone who could help her and the clinic was out of state. Sharpe said he would hold off Homeland Security for now, but to save some of the contaminated blood for testing. If this were weaponized, the damage would be greater in the impoverished populaces worldwide. There would not be enough blood in the world to give everyone affected a total blood exchange, nor could they conduct them quickly enough for those who could. Homeland Security would want to try to develop a vaccine to counter the antigens or teach the body to ignore them if that were possible. Sharpe admitted, "far smarter people than he" were going to work that one out.

Ava slept on the plane assuring Ben she was fine, only a little bit tired. It was easy to relax when he was there keeping vigil over her. No normal person could beat him. The fact that not all of those sent by Bruder were normal people didn't bother her.

The plane landed as the sun was setting. Ben had been on his phone until the moment they took off and was back on the second they were down. Ava was having trouble walking and leaned heavily on Ben, explaining away her weakness as exhaustion from the strain. He apologized for having to take a commercial flight, explaining that the company owned plane was tied up. Smiling weakly, Ava waved off his concern again.

The rental was waiting, having been alerted to the "medical emergency" Ben was handling. The employees of the airline blatantly stared at them both like they were wearing their skin inside out as they slid into the Mustang.

"What is your affinity with this kind of car?" Ava tried to alleviate some of her own nerves by focusing on something unimportant like Ben's single mindedness when it came to automobiles.

He afforded her a sideways glance. "It's my favorite so far. Don't you like it?"

"It's fine, I'm just curious since this is all you drive wherever we go. I guessed there was some sort of story there."

Ben stared straight ahead. "The first Mustang came out the year my father died. He liked it, said he was going to get one except he never got the chance. I guess it's just a silly thing I do to remember him."

"It's not silly." Ava replied softly. She'd been too young to have a memory of a special thing about her father. That was why she was going to live to raise their child. Her child was going to have a mother *and* a father if Ava had anything to say about it. No matter what Ben was planning, she was on board if it was for the baby's well being no matter the cost. Strangely unconflicted, she dozed on the way to the lab.

***

Physick Enterprises' research lab was not the kind of lab Ava was expecting. Instead of having a parking lot and a front entrance with a receptionist and tons of glass, it was an underground parking garage with an elevator. An elevator that went down to a level that shouldn't exist, and *didn't* unless you had a special key, which Ben did. He slid his key card into a slot on the side for security badges. The ramp elevator took them down two floors below the lowest level to a place unlike any she'd seen before.

The walls were all see through, glass with aluminum frames partitioned out the space. Only a few areas had opaque walls. The floors and ceilings were dark gray, nearly black shiny tiles. Track lighting was everywhere giving it a bright, sterile appearance. Everyone there dressed in scrubs as if they were in a hospital, a number of them wore face masks.

When they entered, Ben was greeted by name by everyone they passed. He knew theirs as well, despite the anonymity of their garb. Ben took Ava by the elbow. Beginning to feel as though her legs and arms were weighed down by concrete, she was happy to have the support. They came to a glass door and it opened automatically. A tall, thin man with rectangular glasses and flaming red hair stepped out reading a clipboard, glanced up, pausing only for a split second when he saw Ben.

"Mr. Physick, perfect. I heard you were here. I wonder if we can discuss some matters during your visit."

"Sure Liam, but first, have you set up a room for the exchange transfusion?"

The way Liam examined her was entirely clinical. He tipped his head, taking mental notes and finally nodded. "I'll have Lynn take her into three, we're set up in there." He looked over Ava's jeans and long fitted sleeves. "Do you think we could get her into a gown?"

"I'll take care of it and meet you in ten minutes."

Ben walked her to a room on the dark sidewall. The doors had been hard to see until they were up close. There was one on either side of an ordinary drinking fountain, one door for men and one for women.

"Locker rooms. When you go in, there will be drawers on the far wall. In the top drawer should be hospital gowns. Take one, change and put your things in a locker, and take the key. Meet me back out here and I'll walk you over to where you need to be."

Head swimming, Ava did as she was told. Minutes later when she emerged, Ben was waiting anxiously. Her skin was clammy and bathed in sweat. Ava was seeing black holes in her vision.

Ben took one look at her and inhaled deeply. "You aren't you're tired, are you?" Having guessed at her ruse, he was angry with her.

She tried to explain herself. "I didn't think it would help to talk about it because there wasn't anything you could do, and then when you mentioned this," she shrugged, eyes rolling lazily, "I figured it didn't matter."

Ben kept his mouth closed, silently fuming as he supported most of her weight with an arm around her waist. Ava's feet barely touched the ground as he whisked her to room three.

"I will stay with you the entire time." He tried to force a smile only it came out a grimace.

They stopped at a glass door, opened promptly by the tall redhead. Liam didn't wait for the door to close before he started asking questions. "Ms. Brandt I would like you to describe for me what you are experiencing." He glanced at his file, pointing to the bed for her to have a seat.

Ben lifted Ava up to sit on the bed, her feet dangling without so much as a twitch over the edge. Ben stood just out of the doctor's way, watching every movement. Ava misunderstood Ben's interest as a lack of trust in Liam's ability. She started to hyperventilate.

"Ms. Brandt, you will have to calm down if we are to proceed." Liam cautioned her.

Ben stepped in, "Liam, a moment please."

Obediently, Liam stepped back and studied his clipboard.

"Ava, you need to be honest with him so he can help. We need to know how this is affecting you to counter any effects already underway. The exchange will stop the virus progressing, it won't undo any damage it's already caused."

"Why do you look so nervous? Is there something you aren't telling me?" Ava slurred, dipping her head in an exaggerated effort to keep her eyes focused on him. Pieces of his face were hard to see.

Ben glanced around guiltily, lowering his voice and leaning in. "I told you it is safe as long as we go slowly. But do I get nervous when the woman I love is about to undergo a procedure more severe than a haircut? Yes. Truth be told I don't trust *anyone* with you except me. And even that is in question at present." He gave her a tight smile. "Liam is the best man I have. You need to tell him everything."

Ava was not much relieved by Ben's admission. She was watching Ben twitch and pace at the side of her bed and told him he had to try to calm down or she was going to have a full blown panic attack. He said he would and backed away to allow Liam free access to her.

"Mr. Physick has informed me that you were given an injection of incompatible antigens mixed with an immunodeficiency virus, is that correct?" Ava nodded. "Can you tell me what symptoms you are experiencing and if you have noticed any changes since the initial onset?"

Shooting a guilty glance sideways at Ben, Ava laid it out for Liam. "The only thing I felt at the start was the morphine. It made me slow and dull like you would expect. I had some problems thinking clearly and talking to the paramedics but I still thought that was morphine. When I woke up in the hospital a few hours later I could kind of think sometimes, my body was really tired. By morning when I got up and moved around, my legs were getting achy and painful and now it's everywhere. The more I move, the worse it gets."

"Your pulse is high, is that just when you move around or do you feel dizzy or notice your heart racing more often?"

"It's when I move. I can actually feel the blood trying to pump. It's like mud in my veins." Ava was as honest as possible with him. "When I stand up I feel like I'm going to have a heart attack, my chest hurts. I'm dizzy all the time and now there are black spots in my vision."

"Spots in your vision? Do they move or are they similar to holes in a screen and move with you?"

Testing it, Ava focused on Liam's clipboard and turned her head from side to side, keeping her eyes on the same spot. "Stationary."

Setting aside the clipboard, Liam touched the cuts on her face and those on her knees. His mouth pinched and he glanced up at Ben. "Ava I am going to have my assistant Lynn double check your blood type and get a reading of your vitals. I need to discuss some details with Ben and I don't want to be in Lynn's way. We will be right back."

Knowing they were keeping something from her, Ava wanted to object when she saw the way Ben had stiffened when he heard about the spots in her vision. Her heart began to gallop and her vision narrowed to pinpricks of light. She felt like she was going to pass out any second, she couldn't control her breathing.

Lynn, the assistant she had heard come in during her interview was rubbing her arm. "Ms. Brandt? Ms. Brandt? Are you feeling faint Miss?"

Ava nodded, struggling for breath. She heard the door open and Lynn calling the doctor back.

Ben called to her asking her to look up. He wanted to see her face. She couldn't respond. His hand grabbed the back of her neck and forced her head up at him.

"I can't see. What's going on? I can't see." Ava mumbled, her tongue felt like it was growing too thick for her mouth.

Just before she lost consciousness, Ava heard Liam say, "It isn't ready, she's too weak for what we have. We have no choice, it is either that or we lose her."

When she woke it was in stages. First she could hear. They were talking about getting more Type B blood and confirming it was the right kind. It seemed redundant to her that they would need to clarify type for synthetic blood. Wasn't it universal?

Gradually she became aware of the blood in her veins or rather the fact that she *wasn't* aware of it; it was no longer sludge pushing its way through her system. Her heart rate was down and she could breathe more easily. After what seemed an eternity, Ava's vision finally returned and she blinked at the lights above her head.

Liam stood over her, checking her eyes with his penlight. He glanced behind him when he saw her flinch. "She's back with us."

There was some scuffing of shoes, Liam stepped aside, and Ben was there. His eyes scanning hers, hand reaching down to her wrist to check for himself. When she tried to sit up he stayed her with his hand. "You don't want to move around. You have catheters in both arms. Are you feeling all right? Do you have any numbness in your fingers or toes? Can you feel your lips?"

His concern was even greater than hers, it struck her as funny that she could be the calm one. For his benefit she wiggled her fingers and toes and made a popping noise with her lips. "I think I'm okay."

Ben stopped asking questions, remaining close as Lynn, the tiny waif of a research assistant, scuttled around Ava taking readings from the monitors and writing copious notes.

Using one of the catheters, she inserted a syringe to take a blood sample and returned to her microscope to prepare a slide.

Ava and Ben watched the activity in the little room without a sound until it was time for the next round. The process went on for the better part of the night. Ava got hungry but was only allowed water and ice chips for fear of nausea and vomiting. She urged Ben to go get something, which he adamantly refused. Several times she did see a clinician come in and hand him a large syringe for his own uses. His outward appearance was back to normal so his continued large volume injections puzzled her yet she didn't want to ask in front of everyone. He was obviously the boss and the girlfriend didn't grill the boss in front of his employees.

Finally, Lynn's slide revealed only undamaged blood with no intruders and an exhausted Liam pronounced the process complete. The catheters were removed, holes patched and Ava was eased into an upright position. Once she was sitting she felt woozy and had to wave off her helpers' efforts to help her stand.

"She is too pale." She heard Ben's apprehensive voice.

"Sir, you are aware the side effects. She will be in a weakened state for a short time and should be kept calm. The pregnancy is a complication that will extend her need for rest but only by a day or two." He flipped through his notes. "Ms. Brandt is in good health and I do not see any reason for you to be concerned. She has handled the process better than could have been expected."

Ben grumbled although it sounded like there was no real reason except frustration and nerves. Ava's head cleared and she slid down to her feet. Ben stepped in before either of the other two could move to be at her elbow, steadying her.

Glancing up at him, Ava gave him a knowing look. "No faster than any other man, huh?"

His tight jaw hinted at his mood. Ava said no more on the subject.

She refused to be wheeled in a chair anywhere. "Let me keep the tiny amount of pride I have left." She insisted.

They compromised, ending up with her leaning heavily on Ben's arm as he walked her to the onsite clinic.

"What did he mean 'I've handled the process better than expected'? Have you done many of these? I thought you were still in the experimental phase with synthetic blood."

When he didn't answer right away, Ava twisted her neck to see his face. She noticed her eyes were clear, really clear. The lights beyond Ben's face were almost too bright to look into. She put her hand up to block the glare.

"Your body was processing the virus faster than anticipated. The infection in your cuts had entered your bloodstream." Ben refused to look at her. "We were going to lose you."

"What does that mean?" Even with a clear mind Ava was unable to comprehend what Ben was saying.

He stared straight ahead, "It means you're okay for now."

Arrival at the clinic doors deprived them the pain of any further discussion. A tall, dark haired beauty met them just inside. The embroidered name on her white doctor's coat said Jillian, no last name. Jillian's large doe eyes had unbelievable lashes which she used to peek out from under as she aimed a sultry stare at Ben.

Ben nodded politely. "Hello Jillian. You have a bed for Ava?"

Irritated that he hadn't noticed her attentions, Jillian spun on her heel. "This way." Her heels clicked on the hard surface of the floor. She stopped at a bed in a quiet corner away from the other two out of the ten that were occupied.

When Ava caught on to her obvious isolation, she looked askance of Jillian.

She was matter of fact. "I understand you have some special condition? We don't want to risk infection."

Ava didn't say anything. It was too soon to be telling people she was pregnant, there was always a possibility of *any* pregnancy terminating in the first three months. She knew that. Plus, again these were employees. Ava didn't want to be the one to let them know the boss got his girlfriend pregnant by accident. What if he didn't want them to know about the baby?

Ben moved past Jillian who stepped out of the way as he helped her into bed pulling the standard white hospital linens over her to cover her. Ava watched his face, waiting for him to make eye contact, curious when he wouldn't. Although fairly certain he wasn't trying to be distant to hide their relationship, she mirrored his attitude and kept her face impassive.

Scared and alone, she hid her fear relatively well under her guise of disinterest. Half lidded eyes covered up the fact that Ava wasn't sure this was going to work and complications could hurt the baby. Her unfocused stares revealed none of her fear in knowing experimental blood ran through her veins. She couldn't help but think that she might have just done more harm than good to her baby all to buy *herself* more time.

"Why don't you rest for a while?" Ben finished straightening her blankets. "You've been up all night. I have some housekeeping I need to take care of." He kissed her on the forehead before straightening to leave. "Call me if anything changes." He turned to Jillian. Ben's tone left no room for argument.

Jillian gave him a blinding smile. "I will Sir."

Ava's eyes followed Ben down the row and out the door. He always had a commanding presence and it seemed even more so here. It was as if he tried to operate under the radar "outside" whereas here he didn't have to hide what or who he was.

She drifted without sleeping. The other two beds were occupied with patients sick with some sort of flu. One was hallucinating and calling out for people by name, and the other kept kicking off his covers, thrashing wildly. Occasionally, both of them screamed.

When Jillian came to check on her vitals, Ava inclined her head toward the beds. "What's wrong with them?"

Without flinching, she replied. "It's a reaction to the blood."

Feeling her stomach drop, Ava's eyes widened. "What blood?" But she feared she already knew.

"The synthetic blood we're developing. We were able to get past the coagulating problem, but now we're having trouble with it reacting with the red blood cells in the recipient's blood stream. It keeps getting rejected after a few months. They have both had partial transfusions to alleviate the reaction." She glanced over her shoulder at the sound of one's cries and looked back, unaffected, "Apparently it feels like their veins are on fire." She reported while calmly taking notes from the monitors.

Ava was appalled. "You test on your own people?" She knew Ben would never use normal subjects like Bruder but, she'd never thought he would experiment on his own people. She began to wonder at the intelligence of offering herself up so quickly to be an experiment as well.

Lowering her clipboard, Jillian stared at Ava as if she was a moron missing something very simple. "All the people here want to find an alternative to live donors. Most of us are only maintaining our own stasis until a solution is found. That is the only reason Mr. Physick allows anyone to be converted."

"*Ben* made you like this?" She found it hard to believe that Ben of all people would have increased the need for donor blood by even one, much less by the fifty or so people she'd seen already and who knew how many more were out there.

Jillian had obvious doubts about Ava's mental state. "Mr. Physick feels very strongly about saving lives. Each person here has proven his value to the company and when the time comes, his contribution is weighed against the cost of the addition. Mr. Physick has taken each person's conversion very seriously and has a strict rule that no one under any circumstances is to handle their requirements on their own. His arrangement through the medical community has provided for everyone here to now."

Mouth closed, Ava stared at the ceiling to contemplate what Jillian was saying. Nothing was black and white. Ben had to do some questionable things to achieve his end goal and he was still not living a consequence free life nor were those around him. She felt some relief at knowing it was hospitals providing the blood they lived on until the synthetic was developed. At least it hadn't been obtained in the manner Doctor Bruder had, by draining one child completely for each person he changed over.

A small sound beside her caught Ava's ear. Turning her head, she caught Jillian staring at her chart aghast. Failing to hide her jealousy, Jillian gritted her teeth as she asked, "Who is the father?"

Ava wasn't willing to lie about their baby even to spare Ben some discomfort. It felt wrong to lie about it when asked directly. "Ben is."

She watched Jillian's face redden and her beautiful features twist into something far more ugly than jealousy. Just as quickly, Jillian brought her features under control and she very professionally slapped her clipboard to her side and spun, heels clicking until they disappeared beyond the sliding glass doors with a soft whoosh.

Left only with the tortured utterances of troubled patients with whom she shared quarters, Ava stared at the ceiling and gave up any attempts to sleep.

Ch. 58

It seemed like forever before Ben returned. While she waited, Ava retreated into herself and listened closely to her body making note of its suspicious silence. She noted the lack of burning in her veins as well as the clarity of mind, she felt not just well. Ava felt great.

His voice by her ear drew her back from the inner sanctuary where she'd fled to in an effort to block out the nearby noises unnerving in their suffering.

Looking around, Ben appeared anxious. "Where's Jillian?"

She ignored his question needing her own answered first. "I know that wasn't synthetic blood you gave me." She watched Ben's face go blank confirming her suspicions. Voice dropping to a harsh whisper, Ava gaped at him in horror. "Did you put a child's blood in me?"

Ben flinched at the disgust in her tone. He put a calming hand over hers.

Ava jerked bodily away from him. "How dare you! How could you decide that for me?" She put a hand over her abdomen. "What will that do to our baby?"

"I did what I needed to do to save your life." Ben rubbed his hand over his face, his expression one of agony. "*And* our child. The synthetic wasn't as far along as I'd hoped, you weren't strong enough to handle it. You can't fault me for what I've done. It was the same process you would have had in a normal hospital only the blood was different."

Ava started to speak and stopped when he looked her squarely in the eye.

His surety in what he'd done was absolute. "No one died for you, no one dies for any of this." He blinked. "The plane's been all over the country collecting blood from every available source, it's been going non stop since last night."

Ava believed him. Relieved not to have been the cause for some mother's loss, she took solace in the knowledge that she would return to normal after her body replaced the blood they had put in, she would not be a slave to the process like Ben or Alistair or any of the people living on borrowed lives. Their baby would remain an innocent as well.

She waved a hand at the doors and answered his query about the missing doctor. "After she read my chart and saw what my special condition was, she stormed out." Ava teased him, hoping to show him she understood the difficulty of the decision he'd made for her. "Do I have a reason to be jealous?"

Surprisingly Ben laughed, he'd clearly been unsettled knowing she would eventually figure out what he'd done and relief showed in his lighter expression at her forgiveness. "Not likely. My interest in Jillian is purely for her mind. She came on board a few years ago and has been a great asset to the company. We have utilized her knowledge in nearly every facet of our research. No one knows the ins and outs of this project better than she." His shoulders rose and fell. "She's let me know that she would like more and I have let her know that's not possible." He stared pensively at the door, "I feel bad that she was upset."

"I just hope it won't get in the way of her making sure I don't die." She joked caustically. "Seriously though Ben, when can we go home?"

He turned back to her, dark eyes inches from her face. Ava felt her body respond to his nearness. "It's near dawn now, if all is well in a few more hours we can go. Because we had to move faster than expected, we need to monitor the baby for a little while longer." Ben's gaze was serious. "To be sure the baby's blood is clean we'll most likely have to do this again before it's born. Next time I want you to keep me abreast of any deterioration you might experience so we don't have to come so close." Ben stared evenly into her eyes making his point. "Okay?"

Embarrassed she'd given everyone such a scare, Ava nodded.

He brightened. "I have some good news. Alistair is getting out today."

"Isn't that early? Does he have someone who can stay with him?" Ava worried he would fall or hurt himself and no one would be there to help him.

Ben put his hand over hers, this time she leaned closer. "I think he has several offers on the table right now for nurses."

"He's really that popular with the ladies?"

He gave her a look. "You say that like you're surprised. Alistair may be a rogue, but he knows how to treat a woman."

Ava giggled. "I've never met anyone I would call a 'rogue' but you're right. Alistair would be one."

"Are you hungry at all? I could smuggle in something for you." He smirked. "I know the boss, he lets me break the rules now and again."

Her stomach answered him, eager at the mention of food. "How about something small, just in case?" She didn't want to throw up here, she had no idea where the bathroom was and cringed at the thought of humiliating herself in front of Jillian, if she ever came back.

Ben gave her a kiss, promising to return with something tasty and bland.

No sooner had Ava settled back in than Jillian's clacking heels could be heard reentering through the clinic doors. Ava tried to pretend she didn't notice her.

"Ms. Brandt, I am afraid we got off on the wrong foot." She put her hands on the bedrail beside Ava's head, leaning over her so Ava got a clear view down her shirt.

Mentally comparing, Ava figured *those* weren't how Ben picked his women or she was a distant second choice. Ava attempted to make amends. Ben had to work with Jillian and it sounded like she was of great value to the company, Ava didn't want to be the source of any awkwardness between them. "I'm sorry you had to find out like that. It's all been kind of sudden for all of us."

Jillian's posturing was confrontational, her muscles tight. "I would just like to know what you're playing at."

She snorted, "I'm not playing at anything. It just happened."

"It just happened," she mocked. "You can't tell me you managed to trap a man like Ben Physick on happenstance." She sneered. "You've become a minor celebrity around here for what you've done."

The skin on the back of her neck was tingling. Ava had a strong feeling Jillian was not going to let this go. She rolled back her blanket and tried to sit up.

"Ah, ah, ah. The patient must rest." She chided, placing a firm hand on Ava's chest and pressing her back.

Fear made her strong and Ava pushed back. "I really need to go to the bathroom. I haven't gone all night." She jiggled her legs to show she was serious.

Jillian eyed her suspiciously before she lowered her hand. She had a low opinion of Ava's intellect which could be a benefit. "Be quick, we can't have you getting lost."

Ava nodded obediently, sliding down onto her feet. She walked out and started to follow the path she'd seen Ben take when the sound of the doors sliding open behind her stopped her.

"Ms. Brandt, the restrooms are the other way. Why don't I help you?"

Facing her, Ava saw her beautiful features set in the most serene of expressions. How she could fool people into thinking she was kind was easy to see. Ava wouldn't doubt few people saw the other side of her.

"Thank you." She tried to sound grateful.

Jillian walked beside her to the restroom located on the other side of the sliding doors. She started to follow Ava inside when, turning around, Ava tried hard to look self-conscious.

"I've been poked and prodded and had a ton of people all over me the last few days. Could I have a minute of privacy?" Jillian looked reticent to give her even that. "I'm coming right back out, promise."

Jillian waved her inside looking annoyed.

Ava stayed in the bathroom far longer than was required to complete her business, wanting to give Ben more time to get back so she didn't have to be alone with that woman anymore.

Eventually, the syrupy sweet voice called through the bathroom door. "Ms. Brandt, we really should get you back to the clinic. I need to check your levels."

Sighing, Ava washed her hands and opened the door. Jillian was staring the other direction and Ava did the same hoping to see Ben coming around the corner. Her shoulders sagged. There was no sign of him.

She shuffled alongside Jillian. The time on her feet had made her truly was tired. Not that she would admit that to the bitter woman beside her. Jillian helped her into bed and left her to attend one of the other patients finally resting quietly. Ava watched the doctor open a cupboard on the far wall and take somethings out, her arms moved in front of her. When she left Ava felt her pinched shoulders ease and her muscles releasing their tension. She watched the woman work hoping she was done with Ava for a while.

It was only minutes before Jillian turned around. She happened to be in Ava's sightline and she saw a flash of metal. Were it not for her time with Ben, that quick flash would not have told her anything. However, she *had* spent a lot of time with Ben and had seen that particular item a lot lately. Jillian was coming back to her with a syringe. That wasn't what had Ava breathing hard it was the fact that she was hiding it, that couldn't be could.

Ava was off the bed and around the other side like a shot. "Stay away from me."

Flashing her teeth, Jillian smiled sweetly. "You poor dear. You're delusional. Here, let me give you something to calm your nerves."

"Not that way." Ava pointed at the needle held down by her attacker's side. "You aren't supposed to give me anything. I know that."

Annoyance chinked away at her kind façade. "You need to lay down and do what I say like a good girl. We can't make you well if you don't do as I say."

"If you're *supposed* to give me that, then why don't we wait until Ben gets here and see what he says."

Ava had guessed right. Jillian's eyes narrowed, her mask of pleasantry gone as she lunged at her, hand grasping at her gown's sleeve. She held on tight but Ava wasn't going to let vanity get in the way of her safety. Putting her arms up, she backed away and let the gown slide off leaving her in her camisole top and underwear. Jillian fell back several steps. Cursing, she recovered herself and, putting one hand on the bed, flung her legs across to land on the same side as Ava. Barefoot and indecent, Ava took off heading straight for the doors. At least she was likely to catch somebody's eye out there so she wouldn't have to fight the nutty doctor by herself. She was going too fast for the electronic sensor on the doors and slammed into them with her arms. She pounded on them, waving a hand for the sensor as she waited for them to open, watching Jillian gaining ground, running behind her, syringe in hand.

Just as they opened, Ava shot out still staring behind her and hit something solid. She screamed and started hitting it too. A bag smacked the ground and her hands were loosely restrained in his.

"Ava, slow down. What happened?"

Ava didn't have to explain. She still had her head craned back to see Jillian who had slid to a stop a few paces behind her, syringe in hand. Her beautiful face was unrecognizable in her rage.

"What the hell is going on here?" Ben demanded, taking control of the situation.

"She was having a reaction to the treatment. I was trying to subdue her." She carefully tried to put herself back together for appearances sake, straightening her coat and smoothing her hair.

Ben was furious and didn't believe a word. "Under what circumstances is chasing a woman with a needle considered subduing?" He wrapped an arm protectively around Ava.

She continued to stare at Jillian, dumbfounded by her Jekyll and Hyde personality. "Ben I want to go home." She said it quietly.

"Let's get your things." He started to turn, wheeling Ava with him and stopped at the change in Jillian wielding the syringe like a weapon.

Jillian was beside herself, she screeched shrilly. "What is it with this stupid little bitch? Everyone wants *her.* Why?"

"What did you say?" Ben froze, Ava felt the tension building in his body and his flesh went hard beneath her fingers. Jillian's performance was drawing a crowd, where she and Ben were standing in the doorway kept the doors from closing so everyone could hear. Ava noticed a few larger men in suits, not scrubs, coming toward them.

She continued, hanging herself with every word. "You were supposed to be with me. I was hand picked. Look at me. No man in his right mind would turn *me* down. But *you* did. You did to be with *her*?" She scoffed.

While she ranted Ben slid in front of Ava, shielding her body with his. "Jillian, calm down. You're valuable here. Your knowledge has been crucial to our advances, let's not lose sight of that."

"*Our* advances? What a laugh. We have been working for years while you dole out the blood like a drug. You keep us locked away in this basement, beholden to you. You're undermining the *real* progress going on out there while all of these other discoveries we've tried to put into use are bogged down in years of medical trials waiting for approval. None of it will ever see the light of day. I gave up my career for this." Her eyes narrowed and she stuck her hand in her coat pocket. "Doctor Bruder would have let me use it a long time ago. If it weren't for that one tiny little piece of the formula you have hidden away somewhere I could have killed you and been able to sell my findings on the open market. I was supposed to seduce it out of you, it was going to be so quick and easy. It's been six years!" She shrieked. "You would rather have that stupid little *nothing* and now she carries your bastard, her hooks are in for good. I'll kill you both for what you've cost me." She lunged, the old fashioned syringe flashing in her hand. She was nearly as fast as Ben.

To Ava it looked like Jillian was tied to a tether and hit a brick wall before being yanked back, sliding along the floor. When she saw the woman's head tilted unnaturally to the side and Ben appear ten feet in front of her, she realized what had happened.

Her legs felt weak, Ava slid down to sit on the floor. Ben stood over Jillian's body staring down at it. The large men entered and Ben wiped his palms on his jeans.

"Take her to the morgue. Have her computer checked out. I want to see everything she has sent and received to any external addresses. Double the security up top, no one without proper clearance comes anywhere near this facility." Ben commanded the attention of everyone within range. He pointed to the shattered syringe on the floor. "I want an analysis of whatever was in that and check those men for any unusual substances." Ben indicated the men mercifully calm for the moment in their beds.

He pulled his jacket off and draped it around Ava's shoulders. "Can you walk?"

She nodded, too shocked to talk. Ava let Ben help her to her feet and guide her to the locker room where he helped her dress. She left the sling off, preferring to put her hand in her pocket to keep it from hanging. Ava was tired of appearing weak and being treated like a victim. She was tired of being attacked at every turn. She felt a justified anger simmering within her.

Stopping only to grab an attaché from a clinician holding it out for him near the exit, they rode up in the elevator to the outside world and the rental in the parking ramp. Ben drove quickly to the airport. Instead of going to the main terminal, they went straight to the smaller hangar behind the airstrip reserved for private aircraft.

Ben answered her curiosity grimly. "We're done taking chances."

He was on his phone as he guided Ava through the hangar to a small jet. The pilot held up a hand to Ben, he nodded and they boarded. Ava fell exhausted into the plush leather seat.

Ben was heatedly discussing the chemical makeup of whatever was in the syringe. Ava, who didn't understand most of it, was tired. She hadn't slept all night and was having trouble keeping her eyes open.

She heard Ben growling out more orders. "Get every one of them in for a full evaluation in the next twenty-four hours. Destroy every vial that woman touched." He snapped his phone shut.

"What's going on Ben?" She mumbled sleepily.

He was working hard not to explode. "That woman," he spat the word, "put trace amounts of neurotoxins in our samples after they were cleared for test subjects. Do you know the kind of pain they've gone through just so she could sabotage our research? She had another dose of the toxin in that syringe meant for you."

That kind of cruelty was something Ava couldn't comprehend. It was such a waste of what had been a great mind. Now she was dead because of her vanity and greed. Ava drifted off, dreaming of needles and bodies on fire.

Ch. 59

The descent made Ava's ears ache. She woke, yawning automatically to clear her ears. Ben was back in control of himself, busily typing away on a laptop. Her stirring caught his eye.

"Did you sleep well?" He closed the lid and slid it into his bag.

Nodding, Ava stretched her stiff limbs. "I can't wait to sleep in a bed again." She took stock of his appearance. "You look pretty tired yourself. You can't keep running yourself ragged. You're using blood like speed. Aren't you going to crash?"

He kept his expression blank. "It is a short term necessity. I can maintain it for a while longer."

"Don't be so sure, you look worn out." Ava didn't mean to sound so harsh yet the truth of what she was saying could hardly be denied. Ben bore an uncanny resemblance to a middle aged man who had just come home from a three day bender in Vegas.

Chuckling, Ben rubbed his eyes. "Now *that* is a fair assessment. But fear not, dear lady. I shall not perish quite yet."

"Did you ever really talk like that?" Ava tried to imagine Ben in the clothing she had seen in pictures from the end of the 1700s when he was born. She stifled a giggle with the back of her hand.

Inclining forward in his seat, Ben affected a solemn demeanor. "Why yes, I did, madam. Do you find that it suits me or do my intonations offend your delicate ears?"

Ava couldn't hold back her laughter. "That is so hard to imagine. Men just didn't seem very manly then. Not like now. You fit in today much better."

"I am the same person as I was then." He ran a hand through his hair. "I prefer jeans to breeches and hose as well however, on the whole I disagree with you. When I was a young man any offense to self or family was handled privately, even duels were held at specific times and places to limit interference and injuries to innocents. Now, men exchange words or bullets on street corners in front of women and children without concern for whom else might be harmed in the process. I do not see that as 'manly' in the least." Knuckles roughed his jaw line in his agitation.

"I didn't mean to offend you. I'm sorry." She apologized sheepishly.

He took a breath and closed his eyes. "My temper is short at present. I should not take it out on you. I apologize."

Ava left him alone, he was upset and strung out. He needed to rest whether he admitted it or not.

They landed and drove home without even discussing where that might be. It was a given she would be going with him. When they arrived, the squad was already out front.

Ben called Alistair while Ava freshened up. He came in while she was dressing. "Alistair is coming for a visit. He said that he has something very important and he wanted to tell us in person."

She felt her heart leap at the prospect of seeing the big man. "When is he coming?"

"He's on his way now." The doorbell dinged. "Speak of the devil and he shall appear." The side of Ben's mouth twitched up. He could not hide his fondness for his good friend. Ava wondered what had brought the two of them together, her memories fully restored from her time with Bruder, she remembered the doctor telling her Alistair had been one of his.

Ava thought she beat Ben downstairs until she opened the door and he sidled up beside her. Alistair greeted her appearing to be in tip top health. She flung her arms around him before he could take a step inside the door.

"You know how to make a man jealous Ava." Ben teased from behind her.

Self-conscious, she pried her arms from her friend and stepped back to let Alistair enter. He winked, "Don't listen to him, I like the attention. It speeds my recovery."

"I'll bet it does." Ben grinned. "How many nurses are paying attention to you these days?"

Alistair eased his body gingerly into the chair in the living room. "A gentleman never tells."

"Ben tried that one on me, I think it's an excuse to be a pig." She raised an eyebrow archly at him.

"She will give you a run for your money Ben. You'd better hope for a boy or you will be sorely outmatched."

Hearing him talk about the baby and knowing it was a possibility she was really going to be a mother gave Ava pause. "Does anyone else want a water?" She rushed from the room.

Alistair's voice rose and Ben's response came from the hallway, moving back into the living room. He had tried to follow but Alistair was giving her privacy, bless him. By the time she returned, three waters in hand, Ben was giving him a rundown on all that had happened.

Alistair rubbed his goatee deep in thought. "We know how to beat this virus. Now we need to find a more efficient way to spread the cure should it hit the market. Otherwise, only the few with access to large, ready blood supplies will survive. The way he's planning to use it, I'm guessing he'll drop it in a highly populated area for a showy test. We are looking at massive casualties. Did you get a sample for your detective friend and the CDC?"

Ben bobbed his head and continued to sneak glances at Ava. "I did. It's already been sent to him at the station where his Homeland Security counterpart is waiting for it. I also took the liberty of sending one to our friend at the CDC with instructions to contact me. It would be good to have another set of minds working on this."

Leaning forward, he changed the subject. "Now, what was it that was so important you had to tell me in person?"

Alistair settled back and folded his hands in his lap looking pleased. "We got him."

Ben's froze. "What do you mean we got him?"

Alistair's eyes were dancing with barely contained excitement. "I mean we got him. What was the one thing keeping us from following Bruder before? Why couldn't we ever just go get him?"

"Because no one's touched him. He's a ghost." Ben held up a hand as if to grab air. "We can only follow what he leaves behind."

Grinning, Alistair leaned in and whispered dramatically. "He touched me."

"What?" Ben jumped off the arm of the couch.

"He touched me after he shot me. He had to move my arm to get the bag from under it, you see? I can track him." A shadow crossed his face. "And I wanted to come here to tell you because he's moving around you. I want to be here when he comes."

"He's coming here?" Ben swiveled his head as if the mad doctor was in this very room.

"He's heading toward you. I don't know if he's alone but he is beginning to close in. If it's all right with you, I would like to stay here to act as a security system of sorts." The same deadly serious expression Ava had seen when Alistair faced down the doctor slid into place, he got even bigger in her eyes. "We can end this."

It was agreed Alistair would stay and the police would go, assuming their presence was keeping the doctor from making his final approach. Ben called Detective Sharpe and told him the squads were making Ava nervous and could he call them off. Ava didn't mind the detective thinking she was a Nervous Nelly if it meant they could finally catch the bad guy before he killed a whole lot of innocent people.

They each kept a firearm on them wherever they went in the house. Ben gave Ava his 9mm, it was the lightest weapon they had. He showed her how to load a clip, put the safety on and off, and the easiest way to point and shoot.

"Point it like you would point a finger." He said.

Ava tried a couple of times, refusing to even try until he took all the bullets out and showed her by pulling the trigger. She flinched, closing her eyes, expecting more than the empty click as the hammer struck an empty chamber.

He reloaded, showed her how to cock it and gave her a shoulder holster to put it in. It chafed and she was constantly aware of its weight. Ava feared the gun would go off at any minute and she would shoot herself in the butt or someone else by accident.

Alistair found her hypersensitivity hilarious, roaring with laughter every time she moved and the gun shifted against her causing her to jump.

"I used to like you." She told him sardonically at dinner.

"You said you *loved* me. I have a witness." He mocked kiddingly.

Ben had thrown together a simple meal none of them really tasted. Alistair said the doctor was close, he was possibly waiting to be sure the police were really gone. They stayed in, waiting for him to come to them even if it meant a slight delay. Ben wanted home field advantage.

He was comfortable fighting in close quarters and the size of the house limited how many people could come at them at a time. The natural pinch points the hallways afforded would slow the doctor's speed and possibly provide Ben with enough of an element of surprise he could overpower him if it came to physical prowess versus gunplay.

They were sitting at the table, plates cleared while they made superficial and meaningless conversation about nothing any of them were interested in, just the sound to fill the silence when Alistair's body stiffened. "He's here."

"How many?" Ben's pleasant expression evaporated and he was all business.

Alistair shook his head, brow knitted. “I can’t tell. It’s not right.” He closed his eyes. “He’s got someone interfering, it doesn’t feel right.” He sat bolt upright in alarm. “He’s got a jammer with him. Get her upstairs!”

Ben shot up from his seat sending it crashing behind him, Alistair did the same. He drew his gun from his belt, pulled the shotgun he favored off the floor by his feet and cocked it.

Ben snatched Ava off her seat like she was a doll, holding her tight against him while the world shifted around her. She felt air move and before she made sense of it, she was in their master bathroom standing in the tub. She looked at him baffled by what had just happened.

“A jammer’s just like it sounds, we can’t see around him. Bruder must have figured out we could see him. He’s set us up to get us all together.” His expression had gone dark in his fury. “Get down, the tub’s bulletproof. Don’t make a sound unless someone comes in. Then just point and shoot when they come through that door. Alistair and I will announce ourselves so don’t hesitate thinking you’re going to hit one of us. Understand?” His eyes had gone black and hard, ready to fight. He pulled her up against his muscles hardened from the incredible amounts of blood he had been injecting. It was working like body builders who “juice” for extra power. His kiss was as hard as his body.

Ava was afraid at his desperation. She couldn’t make herself ask him to stay yet she was terrified that he would leave her alone up here. When he pulled away, he saw it on her face.

“I have to do this. I’m your guardian angel, remember?” He grinned, flicking an eyebrow up playfully at her belying the palpable tension in his body as he strode just as quickly out the door.

Dumb from fear, Ava shakily got down on her knees in the tub and slid down on her side, elbow propped on the ledge so only her forearm and head stuck out with the gun aimed at the door. Figuring a body would be a bigger target she aimed for the middle instead of high for a headshot. She thought of the safety and flicked it off, 'red is dead' Ben had told her. She looked at the red dot several times, somehow expecting it to have changed while it sat waiting in her hands.

They didn't come in with guns blazing. She heard the front door open with no fanfare to announce what was to come. The open entryway and tile were a fantastic security measure. She had a passing thought that had been as intentional on Ben's part as the cast iron tub in his decorating choices.

Someone's shoe scuffed on the tile below and she heard rushed footsteps followed by a loud crack. Her stomach twisted and she fought down the picture in her head of Ben or Alistair lying in their own blood.

"It isn't one of my boys, it isn't one of my boys." She found herself repeating in her head.

Another short series of cracks echoed through the house. Her breathing sounded loud enough to give her away. Ava forced her lungs into a slower pattern feeling the fuzzy edges closing on her periphery as her oxygen levels dropped. Alistair's frozen face all too easily came to mind.

A loud boom sounded from deeper in the house and hid the sound of his approach. Ava's ears still echoed with the sound of what she assumed was Alistair's shotgun when a dark form appeared in the door. She took aim and pulled the trigger. Nothing happened. Cursing herself, Ava realized she hadn't cocked the gun. She reached her other hand up too slow. She found herself easily disarmed before she could even begin to defend herself.

"Hello Ava. I thought I would find you here." The doctor's beady eyes filled her vision. He reached down and plucked her by the shirtfront out of the tub, propelling her in front of him as he moved out into the room.

Bruder positioned himself with his back to the wall and Ava in front of his body with his hand crushing her windpipe preventing her from calling out, he waited for Ben, his gun aimed at the doorway.

Alistair's shotgun boomed again from the interior, maybe the kitchen. Ben's gun was silent. Ava's ears were ringing from the gunfire and her impending suffocation. She didn't hear Ben approach. One minute the doorway was empty, the next he was there.

Ava felt her heart flutter when she saw him standing there unhurt. Her eyes welled at the realization none of the gunfire below had touched him. For a split second she stared at him, her heart nearly bursting with the love she felt for him. Then, in the next blink, it started hammering in her chest again when Doctor Bruder fired a shot just over his head sending a sliver of wood into his cheek, slicing it open.

"I am not going to waste time with ultimatums. You know what I want and I have the leverage to get it from you." The doctor spoke evenly. He did not shout. He was calm and collected. Ava was guessing he had been dreaming of this moment for centuries.

Ben stared at Bruder, his handsome face clouded with frustration. By his very own words this was his worst nightmare. Ava wished for the strength to be noble and tell him to think of everyone else, not to stay his hand for her. At the same time she feared she *would* beg him to spare her, to give Bruder what he wanted. If she died, their child's life ended with hers. But the hand tightening around her throat took the pain of the decision from her. She could only stare mutely at Ben, watching him suffer.

Ava had experienced firsthand how strong Bruder was and knew she could not wrest herself free, yet she also knew he was arrogant. He would assume she was no threat because he was stronger. Most of his attention would be focused on Ben now.

Ava could think of no way to help Ben save one, to remove herself from the equation. So, by increments, she let herself go limp. Almost immediately she was rewarded with the desired response, Bruder relaxed his grip. He wouldn't willingly let her go, she knew that and prepared herself by adjusting her feet and getting a solid stance to give her better leverage for maximum effect. Her hands eased into one fist, the other wrapped over the top against her stomach to avoid moving her upper arms.

Just as she was settling her weight into her heels, she saw Ben's eyes flick down to hers and he figured out what she was going to do. Instead of being fearful or angry with her, the corner of his mouth twitched, the only sign he wasn't listening to Bruder. Ava felt a rush of pride at his acceptance of her capability.

"You said you didn't want anything from me anymore. We have too many problems with the synthetic." Ben didn't mention that he had found the source of the problems and eliminated her.

"You're closer than you think to a solution." Bruder shrugged airily. He still thought he was in control.

Ben waited, ready to follow Ava's lead. She mouthed "on three" and counted "one, two." Instead of saying "three," she spun into the doctor breaking his hold and swung her elbow into his side.

He was fast and able to twist and deflect the shot that would have easily broken ribs if it had been able to fully connect. Instead the point of her elbow grazed along his hip, her momentum carrying her off balance and spinning wildly into the bathroom doorjamb. She lay unmoving on the ground, staring at the scene unfolding and unable to breathe while Ben's life lay in the balance.

While the doctor had turned his face to avoid Ava's blow, Ben had closed the distance lightening fast. He was in Bruder's face when his head came back around. Ben knocked the gun from his hand and launched a blow of his own, rocking the doctor back into the wall, his head making a hole in the sheetrock.

The doctor was equally fast. He shot back with a fist to Ben's ribs and there was a distinct crack. Ben fell to his knees, gasping for air. Bruder took the cheap shot and sent three fast kicks to follow his punch.

Ben rolled away and the doctor followed, preparing to launch another attack. Ava looked around and saw the gun Ben had given her on the floor behind her in the bathroom where Bruder had dropped it. Another boom from downstairs gave the doctor pause. She saw Ben hop to his feet and land another punch in the middle of the doctor's chest. Bruder went down to his knees as his heart took the blow and stuttered. Ben followed with another straight at his nose.

Ava army crawled to the gun and fumbled with it in the bathroom doorway. This time she remembered to cock it and the sound of the gun chambering the bullet stopped the brawlers in their tracks.

Ben's face bled from the cut on his cheek and he held an arm to his side, gasping for breath. The doctor's nose was at an odd angle, blood pouring from his nostrils and upper lip.

Ben smiled tightly at her, "Nice work honey," he started to step around the doctor to relieve Ava of the weapon. Another pop from downstairs rang out and Ava jumped, her hand bobbling.

The doctor saw it and reached behind himself. Ava saw the steel as he pulled the large blade free from a hidden sheath.

Her eyes widened, seeing the blade swinging toward Ben's side. "Ben!" She shouted stabilizing the gun in both hands, any pain in her shoulder forgotten.

Ben jumped sideways at her warning, away from the knife, a thin line of blood showing against the light blue of his shirt.

Ava squeezed her finger on the trigger.

With two of the three cracks coming from her gun, Ava saw the doctor's body jump. Blood immediately stained his chest and stomach as his knees buckled and his body slid down to land on his face.

Ava's hand shook and she no longer wanted the gun except she was afraid to put it down, fearing it would go off again. Ben stepped past the doctor, no longer able to harm anyone, and gently removed it from her hand. She stared at the body at her feet unable to look away, letting Ben put his arm around her shoulders.

Movement at the doorframe made her jump and Ben reassured her. "It's Alistair." Of course, they could sense each other so there was no fear of shooting each other.

"Well done dear." Alistair bend down and checked the doctor's pulse with an appreciative nod. "Ding dong, the wicked witch is dead."

Faint sirens pierced the sudden stillness.

Ch. 60

Detective Sharpe led the charge when the squads arrived. The trio of survivors sat on the steps within full view when he arrived. Their hands were empty and they were within sight so no accidents would occur. Ben and Alistair were eerily familiar with this part of the process.

Ben dissuaded Ava from going anywhere else in the house. Even if she had wanted to, Alistair had agreed with Ben that it would be "highly disagreeable to go meandering about just now."

Sharpe called the coroner and informed them they would need four body bags. Ava shuddered, Ben tightened his arm around her and she leaned heavily against him. Each bag dragged out by the police contained a person who had come there to kill them. Ava sat in wonder at the unconscionable hatred that man had inspired and was glad he was dead.

An ambulance arrived to glue Ben's cut cheek and tape his three broken ribs before they departed. Amazingly that was the extent of the injuries the three had sustained.

When all the questions were answered and the police had completed their necessary procedures they packed up and left Ben, Ava and Alistair in the deafening silence of the home.

"What about the rest of them?" The doctor was the head of the snake, but what about the body, she wondered aloud. "What about those other people who worked for him? Even if they don't want to keep up with his crazy experiments or sell his virus, don't they need to keep taking blood to stay ageless?"

"If Bruder's gone I think we will find many of his ilk willing to work with us on meeting their needs. Without a madman driving them, it will prove to be the far more attractive option."

Ben's phone rang, quiet after the barrage of gunfire that still echoed in Ava's ears.

"Hello?" Ben listened silently for several moments.

Ava's ears caught a faint hum of excitement on the other line. Her recovery time was definitely faster after the transfusion. By rights she shouldn't even be able to hear after the gunfight.

"That's fantastic!" He was quiet again, listening but Ava could see his eyes alight from whatever good news he was getting.

Both of them stared at Ben, eagerly anticipating his news. Finally he snapped his phone shut and slid it back in his pocket.

"Well, what is it?" Alistair prodded.

Unable to contain his enthusiasm, Ben slapped Alistair on the back. "We've got it. Once the neurotoxin was exposed and its pure form available for comparison it was easily isolated in our synthetic formula. Liam's been able to separate it in small batches and is going to start working on the rest of it." He beamed, the tension flowing out of him left him looking years younger, more than if he'd just given himself one of his renewal injections. "We have a pure synthetic. We can neutralize Bruder's virus in any population should there be a need." He ran his hand through his hair. "We'll feed the discovery up through the proper channels and rush it through the approval process. This isn't just for us, there never has to be a shortage of blood again." He turned and laid a hand gently on Ava's arm. "We'll use synthetic when we give you your next round. No children need donate again for any of us."

"What does it mean if I'm purely synthetic?" Ava couldn't deny the appeal of not having to take another drop of a child's blood into her body even if it was given willingly.

"It means you're one of us love." Alistair answered for Ben. "You'll be immortal until you change over to human blood again after little Ava Junior is born. *If* you change over."

The fact that her baby was safe now settled into Ava's consciousness. *Her* future was less simple. She pondered the idea that she would be immortal like Ben and Alistair for a short time, perhaps longer should the virus make a reappearance after the baby was born and while they determined whether or not the virus had caused permanent damage. If any of that became necessary, she would not have to feel guilty for taking blood from an innocent. "That's great news." She said mildly.

Alistair stood, holding his side where his freshly healing wounds pained him. "I believe there is a nurse and glass of wine waiting for me somewhere. I have earned both." He winked, tipped his phantom fedora and exited with barely a limp.

Ava and Ben sat staring at the closed door after he'd gone. Feeling the need to move, fearing running across the residual mess of gore still in the house, Ava stood while remaining in the relative safety of the entryway. Slowly, she turned in a full circle taking in all of the damage.

"There are so many bullet holes. How do we fix all of these bullet holes?" She shook her head, incredulous at the damage.

Ben had his hand on his taped side, rising gingerly to his feet and surveying the damage for himself before coming to stand beside her. "I think we need a professional for this. He rubbed his jaw with his hand. "Patching, sanding, painting. It will take some time. I would say a week to ten days with the right crew, don't you think?"

"You have more experience with this than I do." She glanced up at him to see he was still surveying the damaged sheetrock and woodwork. "I have an apartment, someone else calls work crews." She rubbed her chin. "Although that is usually just for a clogged sink."

"Well, I assure you they will have to take extra care due to the powder residue or it will seep through the paint. We won't want to be here while it's being done." He stopped, Ava was staring at him. "What, I've had to repair several homes through the centuries. But I assure you it is much easier to repair a home than it is to move."

Rolling her eyes, Ava agreed. "Not for you it isn't. Although that's why I haven't moved even though my apartment is an EZ Bake Oven."

Ben looked around himself, running his hand through his hair. "I have had something on my mind and would like to discuss it with you."

"Okay." His formal tone put her on guard.

"We have a number of important decisions in front of us." He was watching her closely, "Please hear me out before you give your opinion." Ben took a deep breath. His nerves told Ava something big was coming down the pike. "The baby will be here before we know it."

"You don't beat around the bush, do you?" She exhaled loudly surprised by his directness.

He flashed her an uncomfortable look. "I considered myself relatively unflappable up to now but I find myself struggling at the moment."

Ava gulped nervously. "Are you sure you want to do this?"

Ben moved in close enough to touch while his hands remained at his sides. When he spoke, his nerves were gone. He was sure of his words. "I have never been more certain of anything in my life." Gathering himself, Ben looked down into her upturned face. "Ava, it would give me great pleasure if you would live here with me. I have room for all of us, the baby could have its own room."

"Ben, I would love to be here with you but what do we tell the baby as he or she gets older? How do we explain *us*? How do we explain that you don't age?" Or that she might not, she thought feeling a throbbing in her head at the threat of so many huge decisions facing her all at once.

Ben's eyes went wide and his mouth fell. "Are you telling me you're old fashioned? After all your talk of independence and modern perspectives?"

Turning her face so he couldn't see her blush, Ava admitted, "Yes, in a perfect world I am." She put her hand on her stomach, "But it isn't a perfect world is it?"

"*I'm* not ashamed to admit that I'm old fashioned and your honesty ties in with the other thing I wanted to ask you." Ben took a step back and reached for her hand, pressing against his sore ribs with his other to help him stand straight. "We have things a bit backward and I would like to remedy that." He squeezed her hand gently. "Ava I cannot imagine my life without you in it. I would be honored if you would be my wife and grow old with me."

She held her breath. "Are you saying you're ready to do that? To let yourself grow old?" His long search had ended in victory, could he so easily give up living forever?

He nodded, dark eyes damp and expressive.

Without a moment's hesitation or hiccup, Ava made the biggest decision of her life with ease. "Yes Ben, yes." She reached up to slide her hand around his neck, bringing his face to hers.

"Happy birthday Ava."

Ava was touched that he would consider his proposal his gift. “You’re early, it’s not midnight yet.”

“Then is it too early to give you your present?” His eyes held an excited glint.

“Wasn’t this my gift?”

“No, I have to say that your gift is of a more practical nature.”

Visions of washing machines danced in her head.

“I wasn’t kidding when I said I do not intend to be here when the house repairs are being done. The fumes and dust are more than irritating, they aren’t good for the baby.” He rubbed the back of her hand with his thumb. “Your mother is expecting us for dinner on Saturday but after that I have gotten approval from Elle for you to have the week off. I’m taking you on that trip I owe you.”

Her hand flew to her mouth, “Oh my God! Really Ben, Wales?”

“If you prefer not to go, that would be fine too. I know you don’t care for my making decisions for you.” Ben teased.

Playfully swatting his chest Ava teased him, “I suppose I *could* let it slide once in a while, to be a good wife.”

“See, now that wasn’t so difficult was it?” Ben leaned in and stopped her from any further arguments.

End

Acknowledgements

I would like to extend a huge and unfortunately entirely inadequate thank you to everyone who helped to make this project possible. To my family who put up with my awful hours and frequent distractions, I have to say thank you and I promise to not obsess *quite* so much on the next one. Maybe.

And to my test readers, Leslie and Dawn, Editor Sean, and the ladies at my local FedEx for their opinions and expertise.

Most of all I would like to thank everyone who buys a book regardless of the author. You let us keep doing what we love and that is truly a gift.

CPSIA information can be obtained at www.ICGtesting.com
Printed in the USA
BVOW031547231011

274264BV00001B/160/P